GIRL
WITH THE GIFTS

JOANNA
ST AMOUR

To those who read with their toes in the sand,
who dream boldly, and pay no mind to doubts and to the doubters.

I extend my heartfelt gratitude to the supporters, friends, and colleagues who offered such generous encouragement and insight when the process grew complicated. Your belief in this project means more than I can express. To my incredible husband, whose love carried me through every draft and revision. Your optimism inspires both my life and my writing.

If you are a bookstore or part of a book club interested in hosting a signing or special event, please reach out. Joanna would love to connect and plan something special together. You can contact her through her YouTube channel, *One Chapter at a Time*, or on Instagram: @joanna_st.amour.

To learn more about evobilities please visit JoannaStAmour.com and take the evobility quiz.

A Cautionary Note

Some doors were never meant to be opened. Some questions were never meant to be asked. Yet here you are. Knocking.

I didn't know if I could write this story. It isn't safe. It never was.

Within these pages you'll face shattered bones, harsh language, scenes of forbidden intimacy, and secrets worth killing for. If these make you flinch, tread carefully. But if you crave to uncover the truth, lean closer, because they don't want you asking: Could I be an uncharged Grounder?

Welcome to the Grounder world.

You've been warned,
Avi

Chapter 1

Once again, I had misjudged which Michael Orey had shown up to work today. His management style was a game of Russian roulette, one moment charming and approachable, the next cold and unpredictable. Today? Today, he was definitely the latter. And that unpredictability made me an easy target for his anger.

My damning report sat exposed on his chrome desk. Rain streaked down the large windows, distorting Vancouver's night skyline. The world beyond felt unreachable now, blurred like my future plans. Everything I'd worked for dissolved with one curious question: *Who diluted the lavender oil?*

"Avi, sweetie, listen closely. Keep your nose pointed at the beakers. Worrying about logistics is my job." Michael's tone held a warning, like the sharp crack of stepping on thin ice.

Michael labeled me a troublemaker, and just like that, the promotion I desperately needed slipped through my fingers. How could this month, this year, possibly get any worse? Last year was a disaster. But the dawn of a new decade, the second act of the millennium, had to be different, right? A clean slate. A fresh start. The universe couldn't possibly decide to double down.

Michael's gangly build, fueled by cigarettes and vintage wine, loomed over my five-foot-six frame like a praying mantis. He once said I had *that* look. The pathetic posture of someone scared of her own shadow. It wasn't hard to imagine. My brown eyes never settled on faces for too long. Loose strands from my brunette braid hid my heart-shaped face. My shoulders hunched like a shield against some unseen threat. He was right, I guess. I'd never learned to stop expecting the worst from people.

Suddenly, a searing itch ignited deep in the center of my back, like a hidden wire misfiring beneath my skin.

Oh no. Not again. Don't panic.

The sensation spread outward in an 'X,' with a strange, almost electric energy. When had the burning stress rash last appeared? My brow wrinkled.

When Fritz left.

My back arched as if possessed, desperate for relief. Sweat beaded on my brow.

If I lost control now... *Don't even think it. Just breathe.* What if I passed out from the pain? Would Michael leave me here, sprawled on the floor, drooling. No, not on his expensive rug. As long as my skin didn't blister open again, I'd be okay.

A slight furrow appeared between Michael's brows, as if my change in demeanor didn't quite register. "Our perfume's Fall Collection deadline is three weeks away. *And where* are your samples for evaluation?" He tilted his head and flicked his wrist in the air, his dramatic movements matching the loud, flamboyant pattern of his tailored shirt. "I don't know because I haven't received any. How many hours did you waste on this diluted lavender oil nonsense?"

"With all due respect, I never miss a deadline. The diluted lavender oil puts Pacific Perfume's reputation at risk." I raised my report in the air, the proof confronting him in a way I couldn't. "Is it possible a competitor tampered with our ingredients? Are other ingredients affected?"

"Ms. Voss visits this lab tomorrow to negotiate my annual bonus. So don't you dare ruin this for me." His pale, bony finger jabbed my chest. My breath hitched, the only reaction I allowed. His eyes narrowed, hungry for a chance to crush any defiance.

I knew arrogant men like him. He was a bear. And in foster care, I'd lived with predators; retreat only triggered their instincts.

He snatched the report from my hand and opened the door.

"I'll double-check your findings." And with a dismissive hand, he swept aside his jet-black bangs.

My calculations were correct. He could verify them a hundred times. Someone diluted the lavender oil. As I crossed his office's threshold, my white silk blouse clung to my hot skin, the fabric suddenly too tight, too stiff. I tugged at the black bow near my collarbone, trying to shake off the heat. "When should I expect a follow-up?"

Suddenly, he was impossibly close. The bitter scent of stale coffee scorched my ear as his voice dropped to a venomous hiss: "How do I know *you* didn't tamper with the oil to steal *my* job?" The question wrapped around my throat like a serpent, contracting until swallowing became impossible. My eyes widened with a dawning horror: *Would he set me up?*

"I *would never* hurt Ms. Voss," I stammered.

"Go home. Your shift was over an hour ago." He slammed the door in my face. The impact rattled the hinges and knocked me back a step.

Could someone please teach that jerk a lesson?

Each threat, degrading order, and slammed door slapped another layer of mortar to my facade. I became a marble sculpture depicting a woman with round eyes and a wary expression from witnessing the world's wickedness.

I walked past the perfume lab. Inside, no chemists or assistants hovered over glass vials, each one a tiny universe of fragrance. There was no plink of pipettes or rustling of papers. Like a ritual, my work became an act of worship, a sacred precision anchoring me when the outside world bore down. Staying late would just happen when I got lost in my work.

I washed down two Benadryl with a long swig from my water bottle. Would Michael take credit for my lavender findings? Of course, he would. The next quarterly email headline: *Michael Orey Saves the Company from Scandal.*

The wall clock glared eight as I dropped my white lab coat into the bin to get laundered. I grabbed my briefcase and wrapped my checkered scarf around my neck. My yellow trench coat offered a light layer of protection. Although some colors had faded from my memory, I'd never forget the sun's radiant hue.

I stepped into the elevator. The lavender oil's density reading confirmed my fears: the oil, meant to be pure, had been brazenly diluted with some cheap, inferior blend. Was it our supplier's fault, failing to deliver organic ingredients as promised? Or had Michael diluted it to save a few bucks? Pacific Perfume's reputation hung in the balance. Who else knew about the oil and did nothing? Was this office a nest of snakes?

Each blinking number on the elevator's display—five, four, three—felt like a countdown that could rewrite my career. The elevator jolted, and the doors slid open to the lobby.

"I Will Remember You" by Sarah McLachlan played overhead, as if the building were already saying goodbye to me. Dimmed lights shadowed empty couches encircling a coffee table. Peruvian cacti stood like sentinels between four windows. Advertisements for yoga and the latest juice bar cluttered the building's cork board, a jumble of distractions. *Wait, this one was important.* A thumbtack stabbed the middle of a flyer. Somona Worthington. Missing. Five-one. Brown eyes. Straight brown hair parted in the middle. Only twenty-five years old. Vulnerability slithered into my consciousness, cold and unwelcome, urging me to walk faster.

I shoved the door's rectangular push bar and stepped out onto the covered veranda.

Washington's gusty April rain carried the rich scent of fresh earth, a reprieve from burning brakes and sweat of the city.

Across the street, in the community space, the slide's ladder lost a battle with an ivy vine, and someone spray-painted a middle finger on the no dogs allowed sign.

Lifting my coat's yellow hood over my head, I descended the concrete stoop, my heels clicking against the path as it sloped left, leading beneath an archway of cherry trees, their branches heavy with blooms. Ahead in the parking lot, my old RAV4 looked just as run-down as I was.

Behind me, twigs crunched in sync with my footsteps. I whipped around, squinting to identify any shapes in the poorly lit parking lot. My stomach contorted into a knot.

Unable to see color meant I should've felt at home among the shadowed, but my imagination, like an overgrown garden where bramble bushes bit and foxglove bells whispered spells, wouldn't let me walk without agitation.

Crunch.

Every rustle and every creak tested my nerves, pushed them to their peak.

Crunch.

Loose asphalt became ankle twisting rocks. Rain filled potholes sloshed, soaking my socks.

Crunch.

Pulse pounding, I spun on my heels, ready to confront the person behind me.

A squeak.

Then a chubby raccoon toddled from underneath a boxy Kia Soul.

I exhaled. *Get it together Avi.*

My phone rang, and Quinbe's sweet tone cut through the pattering rain. "Hi, we're carpooling to Sloane's birthday party next Saturday."

I groaned. "I'm busy." The cacophony of barking at her vet clinic couldn't drown out my disinterest.

A clattering of surgical instruments erupted from the phone, making me jump. "You're going!" I imagined Quinbe in pink scrubs, her red curly hair wrangled into a messy bun, squeezing her small fists. "Stop ignoring Sloane's calls. You can't avoid her forever or blame her for Fritz leaving."

My hand tightened around my phone. The crusted wound of betrayal still wept because Sloane would never tell the truth. She sent Fritz away to break us up; I was unfit to be her daughter-in-law. No matter how sweet my tone or agreeable I acted, I never gained her approval.

"Lots of moms advise their kids to prioritize their career," Quinbe's tone wavered. "I'm stuck in the middle of you two, and I'm sick of it. You missed our last four monthly family dinners."

"Because we're not family," I blurted before my heart cautioned my head. "We can never go back to what we were."

I needed to carve out my own life.

"One day you'll realize family is more than shared DNA. Family is forged through experiences, transcending into a powerful and enduring bond. So, that's why you're going to Sloane's birthday party.

That's why you're going to smile. That's why you're going to eat some damn cake."

"Okay. Okay." Guilt cooled my temper. If Quinbe had another anxiety attack, it would be my fault. "I'll eat cake, as long as it's not carrot cake."

She huffed. "Red velvet. Are you bringing a date?" Curiosity colored her tone.

"Nope." The 'p' sound popped off my tongue like a burst balloon. Would Fritz be at the party? Would he bring a date?

"Breakups are tough, and moving on without closure is even harder, but you haven't had a fling since he left."

I laughed, though it was more out of disbelief. "Six months ago, you dragged me to Brew's Barrels for speed dating. And did I get a call back? Not a single one." I reached my RAV4 and dug through my bag for my keys.

Was she right about closure? It was human nature to crave an absolute ending. Fritz left, I got the hint, more than a hint, a slap across the cheek. A punch in the gut.

"But that means they weren't right for you," her tone softened, "I want your life to have a spark."

Quinbe had so many sparks in college, she could torch this city. "I'm taking a break—"

Crunch.

A hand grabbed a fistful of my hair, jerked me backward, then thrust me forward slamming my cheek into my RAV4's window. My phone flew from my hand, spun through the air, then hit the pavement.

A forearm pushed my shoulders against my SUV. "Hand over your wallet," demanded the stranger, his startling Gaelic accent was from a forgotten world.

"Avi?" Quinbe shouted, "Avi!"

The man's polished leather boot slammed down on my phone's screen. "Bag! Now!"

"You can have it." I flung my bag as far as I could. My keys were in the pocket but that didn't matter because my shoes twisted on the pavement, ready to run. He just needed to take the bait.

He buried his nose in my hair, inhaling deeply. "Oh yes, we'll be taking more than a wallet from you." Across the street, headlights flashed on, casting a harsh glare. A white, windowless van's engine crackled to life, like a distant avalanche rushing down a mountain. "Let's go." He seized a fistful of my hair and yanked. Pain spread across my scalp, as I stumbled back, colliding into him.

"I, I gave you my bag." This couldn't be happening. I thrashed in his grip, scouring the dark lot for help. He spun me around, grabbed my cheeks, and squeezed.

He wore a gray suit. His prominent forehead made his pale face appear stretched. With his long, dimpled chin, comb-over, and glasses, he looked more like a bookworm than a criminal. I gasped; his snubbed, rabbit resembling nose twitched faster than my racing pulse.

This was wrong. *I have a concussion?* I shook my head, but the hallucination remained the same.

He snatched a knife from his belt and thrust the blade under my chin. The point dug into my soft flesh and I froze. "You'll be a nice addition to *his* collection."

Chapter 2

y heart hammered against my rib cage. *Did Michael send him? Was he trying to silence me?* Dread crept into every muscle. My mind screamed: *Run! Hide! Fight!*

Focus. Be smart.

Trusting my gut, I hurled my fist into his eye, then delivered a kick to his balls. Like a drunk ostrich, the spindly man staggered, but he refused to release my wrist.

"Nasty bitch!" He swung out with his dagger. The blade tore through my coat, slicing deep into my forearm.

A strangled cry escaped my throat. Pain flared, but surrender wasn't an option. Tangled within his grasp, I grabbed his hair, yanked down, ramming my knee into his nose. Blood exploded, painting my pants. He slumped to the pavement, dropping his dagger.

Rough fingers locked around my trembling wrist, wrenching me from the bleeding mugger. Refusing to retreat, I swayed, cemented to the ground, like an iron bridge unwilling to bend.

His accomplice? He wasn't a giant, but he was at least a head taller than me. His eyes, dark as the storm-laden sky, held a depth that warned of quiet calculation. Rain slicked his neatly trimmed goatee, each bead clinging to the bristles that framed a mouth capable of ordering me into the van.

I swung at the accomplice's face.

Unflinching, he caught my fist inches before impacting his cheek.

"I called the police. They're on their way." His deep voice pledged more than just safety, as if he, a guardian of justice, foretold the defeat of danger. His stern yet concerned expression evoked the image of a wary Duke who had fought too many battles *and lost*. He slid between me and the mugger. "Are you okay?" His fingers glided to my elbow.

My lungs pounded so violently my lips quaked, "Behind you!"

The mugger swung a block of loose asphalt; it cracked against the back of the man's skull with a sickening thud. He staggered, then collapsed, water spraying as he hit the rain-soaked street.

I picked up the knife and planted my feet. I stood tall, wide, ready. A false sense of power radiated from me. Our glares clashed in a battle of wills.

Blood dripped down his chin. He spat in my direction, the glob landing just short of my shoes. He faked a lunge forward, but I had steel in my stance, fire in my chest, ice in my veins.

The distant wail of police sirens pierced the night, growing louder with each passing second.

He muttered a curse then bolted, splashing through puddles in his frantic escape.

Across the street the white van revved its engine. A streetlight illuminated the driver's dark curly hair and wide shoulders.

The clunky assailant yanked the sliding door open, sending a paper coffee cup and a crumpled candy wrapper tumbling to the pavement. The van lurched forward.

I squinted. Was the license plate 11Z685 or LL2GBP?

The van sprayed water onto the sidewalk as it vanished into the dark.

Damn it!

The man on the ground groaned.

I knelt and rested a hand on his shoulder. "Are you all right?"

His scalp, shaved on both sides, showcased a single braid running down his nape. Blood trickled from his injury. I leaned closer.

Blood? Blood was dark, not whatever lined his neck. Light seeped through, rendering it translucent and iridescent. Bizarre.

He patted his scalp. "Yeah. Did he hurt you?" He rested a hand on my knee. His brow furrowed into an expression of profound worry, causing my heart to clench.

"I'll live." His nearness sent an intimate ripple of excitement up my spine. My fear subsided as I gripped his hand and guided him to his feet. He swayed, then straightened to his full height.

I studied him as he studied me. He was in his early thirties. His dark wool coat, gray shirt, and jeans were casual elements transformed by the command in his posture as if they had been tailored for him.

His strange blood dripped onto his shoulder.

It couldn't be blood. It must be something else.

It glistened and swirled like oil. It was unnatural and oddly mesmerizing. No smell. I blinked.

This was all wrong.

Could my achromatopsia be getting worse? My muscles tensed. I'd worry about that later.

I unraveled my scarf, stood on my tiptoes, and applied pressure to his wound. Inviting warmth radiated from him. Admiration for this brave stranger filled me. "Thanks for helping me."

He pressed his hand against mine, increasing the compression. "I didn't do much. I'm Raiden."

Despite listening attentively, his rich, cultured accent remained a mystery. "Aviana."

"Sorry, I ruined your scarf."

"It's old. If you hadn't stepped in…" I shuddered, speaking those words aloud solidified tonight's ending could've been dramatically different. "Did you see the mugger's face?" My question wisped from my lips like a prayer. Raiden would think I was crazy if I mentioned the mugger's twitchy rabbit nose. I wiggled my fingers free, abandoning the scarf underneath his hand.

He glanced at his feet. "Just an average face. The mugger wasn't memorable. Blonde hair." He shoved the scarf into his coat pocket. From his back pocket, he retrieved a simple black beanie then slipped it on.

"Yeah. Nothing memorable."

I bent to pick up my lifeless cell phone. Splinters of glass refracted light into tiny prisms. It was beyond repair. I just stared, unable to accept it.

"You're bleeding?" He was already reaching for my arm.

As my adrenaline faded, a stinging sensation radiated from my arm, and I winced. Blood dripped from my fingertips.

He slid my jacket off my shoulders, letting the fabric fall to the ground. The wind bit into my exposed skin, but his warm hands returned, gently inspecting my injury.

"You're *not* okay, Avi." His voice was firm, steadied with care rather than force, yet that wasn't what stopped me cold.

He used my nickname.

His dark eyes and his full lips didn't stir my memory. My color blindness left me guessing at his skin tone.

With a swift motion, his hands seized my shirt sleeve, tugging hard enough to split the fabric with a jarring rip.

He balled up the torn cloth and pressed it against my wound. The pressure ignited a fresh surge of pain, forcing a gasp.

Raiden swore under his breath but didn't pull away. His gaze locked on mine as if he could infuse me with courage. "I know it hurts." His grip tightened, then he eased off. "Help will be here soon."

"Do I know you?" The question came out wrong, too accusatory, too pointed. I scrambled to recover. "I mean, have we met before?"

A grin grew across his face. "Maybe in a different lifetime."

My throat dried; he probably thought I was flirting. I gave him a closed-lip smile.

Spinning lights cast upon the trees as a police car screeched into the parking lot.

Two officers burst forth, brandishing their flashlights on the concrete. Their beams found my feet. I blocked the blinding light with my hand. When they reached us, I gave a mumbling description of the forty-something mugger man. Minutes lapsed, then spanned, as I described the white windowless van. I picked and ripped my finger's cuticle. The last of my resolve wilted when they refused to release me to my vehicle.

Their orders blurred: stitches. Ambulance. ER.

Raiden rubbed the back of his neck, and for a fleeting second a protective longing flickered in his eyes, like he might leap into the ambulance with me. I squeezed the blanket the ambulance driver had wrapped around my legs.

Raiden cleared his throat. "Put some ice on your cheek when you get home."

I opened my mouth, but my request felt too ridiculous to say: "Find me."

As the doors closed with a final clang an emptiness whipped through me. There were countless reasons why I imagined this connection: my seesawing adrenaline, the pain medication, my exhaustion. But as the ambulance drove away, he stayed frozen in place, a silent plea I somehow recognized, and a strange tingle of déjà vu struck me, as if we had already said goodbye once before.

A metal tray held Nurse Caldwell's neatly arranged instruments and used cotton balls. The white walls reflected the harsh fluorescent lights, amplifying the small room's clinical coldness. A faint scent of antiseptic and blood permeated the air.

Nurse Caldwell's dark hair was pulled back into a no-nonsense bun. Her face, lined with years of dedicated practice, showed intense concentration as she skillfully stitched. "Breathe honey, you're turning a shade of white. Inhale for three, exhale for three."

I followed her cue, breathing deep. She gently tapped my balled fist twice, and I relaxed my hand, uncoiling my fingers.

"You should be numb from the anesthetic. Do you feel any pain?"

"No, it's just." I swallowed. "As a kid I was in and out of hospitals." I didn't add physicians poked and prodded me, attesting they'd never encountered a comparable anaphylactic case. Or that years later, a naturopath at Sloane's clinic finally diagnosed the inflamed patches on my stomach and back as a stress-induced rash.

"I hate to hear that," she said gently. "Luckily, this injury won't scar." She squeezed my hand. "You're all done. Collect your things and you can checkout downstairs." She pushed the tray to the far wall, then exited.

The urge to shower and scrub the day away prickled my entire body. Heat itched my shoulders. I lifted my shirt. The two burning rings crisscrossing my body had returned. Both abrasions looped over a shoulder, then intersected at my stomach and middle back. I raked my nails across my itchy midsection.

My pride would never let me call Sloane for her handcrafted hydrocortisone cream.

I rubbed my throbbing cheek, where a lump had formed after he slammed me against my SUV. I'd been wrong about his nose. It wasn't rabbit-like. It was just a regular white-guy nose.

Nurse Caldwell popped into my room. "Your lovely aunt is here to see you."

Aunt? My brow furrowed. "I don't have—"

Sloane strode into the doorway, a wide grin taking center stage on her teardrop-shaped face. Her thick, dark hair cascaded past her shoulders in heavy waves. "Nurse Caldwell, you're a saint," she said with a slick, almost southern sweetness.

In the past, I would've traced her bohemian dress's paisley pattern with curious fingers. Savored its texture, and questioned its color palette, each touch and inquiry a quest for understanding, but today my hands stayed at my side. A braided belt cinched her lean waist. She donned faux leather sandals with wide, crisscrossing straps; soft and worn, they showed signs of age, much like their wearer. Her bracelets were a mix of handcrafted bead designs and metallic bangles.

"I can handle it from here." Her mellow tone carried a nostalgic quality that sliced deeper than the wound on my arm.

"Thanks for the cookie tray." Nurse Caldwell turned to me. "Your aunt is so thoughtful."

So, that was how she made her way in here: a bribe dressed up as kindness, concern layered on like icing. The receptionist probably grinned, maybe even took two. And just like that the rules softened.

I forced a smile as Nurse Caldwell exited the room. I slipped off the bed, grabbed my tote, and flung my coat into the trash. "What are you doing here?"

"Quinbe phoned me, clearly flustered. *First,* I brushed her off, you know how she can get, but she insisted. I contacted Nyxon, who called her buddy Patrick at the police station. He said you were taken here."

"Wow. Crime gossip travels fast."

"When your roommate is a journalist with police contacts, yeah, words buzz." Sloane rose to her toes to inspect my rash. Her floral perfume tickled my nose. "It looks like your stress rash returned. I'm happy to mix you an ointment."

I tugged my shirt to hide the rash. "It's fine. I'm fine. Really." But the words felt hollow, and despite ten *long* months of rehearsing what I'd say, the accusation caught in my throat: You could fool Quinbe and Nyxon, but I knew the truth. You funneled kids into your house to satisfy a twisted sense of superiority and reap the social accolades. You influenced, coerced, and manipulated Fritz into abandoning the life we built together.

She sighed. "I see you're still my nervous bird. I regret that we drifted apart after Fritz moved. I've always regarded you as a daughter." She tenderly grasped my forearm.

My hands clenched into fists. Anger bubbled inside me, begging for release in a stream of expletives. "First off, we didn't *drift* apart. You sent Fritz packing and then shoved me out to sea." I stormed past her and out the door. How dare she pretend to be innocent, once again skillfully masquerading as the caring mother figure. I scoffed. *Did she honestly believe I'd be happy to see her?* Perhaps she hoped I'd make a scene, act like a fool, so she could gossip to her flock of sheep.

I pushed through the double swinging doors and strode toward the elevator. Sloane's short legs struggled to keep up, her sandals thumping against the tile with each hurried step.

I rounded the corner and entered the waiting area. Across the room, sixty feet away, the elevator doors slid open and released two people.

Don't close, don't close. My pulse raced as I quickened my pace.

I slipped inside, jabbed the lobby button, then pressed the door-close button repeatedly. "Come on. Come on." Finally, the doors groaned and began to scrape along the metal tracks. I exhaled, a wave of relief washing over me. But before the metallic doors sealed me safely inside, hands caught them. Fingers so familiar mine curled into fists. They opened the doors to a smile so acquainted my lips drew into a tight line. His eyes brimmed with such deep emotion that my stomach free-fell.

I pressed my back into the far wall. *He* had me trapped.

Chapter 3

"**H**ey." A note of trepidation coated Fritz's tone. His crooked smile faded as his eyes searched mine. His nervousness manifested in a tug at his dark, unbuttoned flannel, revealing a crisp white shirt tucked into jeans that hung over his Romeo boots.

I couldn't breathe. The air felt thin and inadequate, as if every inhalation dissolved before it could reach my lungs.

He couldn't be here.

I pressed my palm against the cool elevator wall, hoping it could anchor me in the storm of panic rising within.

Sloane caught sight of Fritz standing with me in the elevator. Her caring eyes narrowed. She shook her head. Her mouth formed a silent *no* as the elevator doors closed, sealing our fate like the final clang of a coffin lid.

How long had he been in town? He hadn't bothered to call. The slight stung, slicing deep. Was it too late to retreat? I wrestled to find words, to face him, to fake a smile, because bravery, boldness, and bluffing were qualities I hadn't mastered.

The farm's earthy scent and the apple trees' sweetness no longer lingered on his skin. His lean cyclist's frame had thickened into broad swimmer's shoulders. A buzz cut replaced Fritz's wild, brown mane. His dimples still overshadowed his attempt to manifest maturity. I could lie, pretend I'd moved on since he walked away, but the truth was, every time I closed my eyes, his absence crushed me.

Fritz was the first guy to love me and the first to fracture my heart.

He sidestepped, imitating a dog about to be berated by his owner. "My mom filled me in on what happened." His tone was different, as if he lived a lifetime in the year he was gone, yet his voice still held a certain charm and honesty. "Are you okay?" His eyes shone a little brighter when I didn't respond with *fuck off*.

"Nothing I couldn't handle."

"How's work? Developing anything new?"

Furrowing my brow, I leaned away. Friendly small talk? Not a chance. "You'd know if you answered a call or email," I snapped. "Where have you been?"

He looped a thumb into his pocket. "The Cyndarian Watch dispatched me to desolate desert counties. Looking for hidden water sources. Our satellite phones rarely worked out there." His face softened and he stepped toward me. I had nowhere to run. *Maybe I should knee him in the balls, too.* "I didn't renew my contract. I'm not going back. Leaving you was the toughest decision I've ever made."

His declaration slowed time, causing the ache in my stomach to grow. He wasn't fighting fair. "You don't get to spew niceties after what you did. You asked me to marry you. The next day, before we could share the news, I watched from our bedroom window as you stepped into the backseat of a black Suburban and never came home. It hurt that you accepted the job offer. What killed me is you didn't talk to me about it. You're a coward who left a note."

He flinched, struck by my words. "It was bad timing. I didn't—"

"I'm sorry our relationship became an inconvenience for your career." The rhythm of my tapping toe echoed in the confined space, underscoring my sarcasm. I shifted uncomfortably, the hum of the machinery droning on, each second stretching into eternity.

He closed the distance between us. His eyes lingered on my Band-aid covered index finger. "You're still picking your cuticles." His knuckles brushed my arm.

I bucked from his touch and shoved my hand into my pocket. "Keep your hands off me."

His phone beeped. He pulled it from his pocket, read the message, and frowned. "Li's parked outside."

I rolled my eyes. "Just great."

"It's important that we talk, but not here."

"We should've had this conversation a year ago. How could I possibly believe any excuse or apology you give?"

"I left because I thought it would be the best *and only* way to protect you." Regret laced each syllable, hinting at a secret burden someone forced him to bear. "But I was wrong." His confession loomed like a dark cloud, poised to break over me and unleash a storm of heartache.

I crossed my arms. "Protect me from who?" The true threat lurking behind Fritz's elusive statement was probably his mother.

The elevator's bell caused Fritz to jump back, as if his nearness triggered the alarm. He backpedaled through the door. "I'll call you." He talked with a smile in his voice, like he genuinely looked forward to a future that included me in it.

Stunned, unable to form a reply, I moved robotically to the checkout counter. His words mocked me—*he'd call*. How many months had I yearned for his voice? How many times had my fingers hovered over his number before I finally deleted it? I couldn't comprehend his callousness. I cried enough. Screamed enough. He buried me in broken dreams and promises, yet I clawed to the surface. Now, I was left in a fog of confusion, it was simply unfair.

I clenched my jaw, blinking hard, refusing to let frustrated tears fall. To my surprise Quinbe, wearing scrubs with poodles on them, popped out of Nyxon's Toyota Tacoma and jogged to where Li waited for Fritz.

She leapt into Li's arms, and he playfully spun her. Quinbe's delicate frame resembled a porcelain doll compared to Li's powerful proportions. His fitted short-sleeved gray shirt outlined the contours of his toned stomach. Paired with stylish loafers and a silver watch, he effortlessly bridged the gap between casual and refined.

How did Li, varsity basketball and karate king, ever become friends with Fritz, the art-studio and welding guy? They were worlds apart.

Years ago, we would've piled into Li's electric car. Nyxon in the front, me squished between Fritz and Quinbe in the back. One of many activities I mourned.

Li's smile faltered when he glimpsed me through the window. He sat Quinbe down and dragged a hand through his thick, ebony curls, the tight coils of his afro engulfing his fingers.

I sent him a nod and he returned the gesture.

Quinbe bounced on her toes as if she hugged a celebrity. But as Fritz strode toward her, she arched her back, lifted her chin, and stomped toward the ER doors, each step a declaration of the disdain she now held for him.

I smirked. Quinbe, the peacekeeper, the girl who was quick to pout or placate so nothing would ever change, finally took my side.

Fritz met Nyxon in front of her Tacoma truck. Nyxon wrangled the brother she always wanted into a headlock to hide her excited glossed-over eyes. Even though Fritz was two inches shorter than her six-foot frame, he playfully wiggled free, laughing. Their merriment only lasted a minute before Fritz threw a hand in the ER's direction. Nyxon's lips formed a thin line.

She jabbed an accusing finger into his chest and unleashed a verbal rebuttal. Whatever she said evoked the desired effect because his shoulders softened.

Fritz was the one, but his secrecy symbolized a silo of matches. Seeing him was reliving my gray world in a blistering blaze. Smelling him was a smoke choking haze. Hearing him was crackling pop. When would the stinging stop? Shame was the tear running down my cheek. How could I be so weak? I wiped it away with my sleeve. Ashamed that I once again grieved.

Nyxon rubbed her toned forearm against the night's chill as she and Quinbe entered the ER. I could read Nyxon like a book. Whatever Nyxon and Fritz argued about still didn't sit right with her. "You both really didn't need to come."

"Nonsense. We parked your RAV4 in our driveway, and I have wine chilling in the fridge," Nyxon declared, with an air of finality. A reflection of the unwavering control she maintained over her emotions. Panic was a foreign concept to her; she dissected problems relying solely on logic and reason.

She took hold of my shoulders, her dark fingers marked by vitiligo, making them look as if they'd been dipped in white paint. She studied me, her thick eyebrows furrowed. The ends of her black, A-line haircut curled under her chin, framing her square face as she tilted her head. "Your cheek?"

Quinbe stood on her tiptoes and leaned close to inspect.

I touched the spot, and winced. "I'll need an ice pack with my glass of wine."

Twenty minutes later, with Quinbe rambling the entire way, we finally turned left into the Evergreen District. No litter. No barking dogs. No sirens.

As we pulled into Nyxon's driveway, the headlights shone through the bungalow's large living room windows. Seeing Nyxon's house hit me with the same sorrowful wave that nearly drowned me a year ago, the day I left Fritz's house, carrying not just clothes, but the hope for a second chance. But there was no second chance. No closure. No reunion. He made sure of that when he disconnected his phone. Fritz had said forever, and I believed him the way a child believes in bedtime promises.

I built my life around love, a fool constructing a castle out of straw. And when it all crumbled, I stood in the wreckage, clutching the ruins as if they were still worth my time and tutelage.

"When Fritz left, he didn't just leave Avi," Quinbe's voice rang out as we exited the truck. Nyxon strode toward the front door, ignoring her. "He left you and me too. We're *a family*, and we deserve an explanation for him disappearing."

A pang of sadness struck me: the dreaded word, family. There was tightening within my throat, as if I wanted to cry and scream all at once.

"Good night, *Quinbe*," Nyxon said flatly, not breaking stride as she ascended the front porch steps.

Quinbe spun toward me. I rubbed the back of my neck, unable to meet her exasperated gaze. Our family had crumbled, and there was no easy fix in sight.

She turned her back on me and stomped toward her cherry-red Jetta.

"Things have a way of working out," I called after her, my voice not as convincing as I'd hoped.

She didn't answer. Just sped away into the night.

Once inside, I placed my bag on the entry table. The tall, slim vase from our girls' trip to Italy waited for its seasonal dahlia from Nyxon's garden.

In the L-shaped kitchen, the ceramic chandelier with gilded arms flickered. After reading an electrical handbook, Nyxon had wired it in herself. She really could do anything.

The brass hardware on the mahogany cabinets gleamed, too ornate for my taste. I preferred black, gray, and white but it gave guests a peek into Nyxon's softer, glamorous side.

Three metal stools, their braided legs twisting like sailor's knots, stood tall near the butcher block island. Fritz had welded those stools, each one a reminder of a time before, and I was no longer allowed to touch the tainted metal.

I turned into the living room. Art Deco fan-shaped mirrors hung on either side of the brick chimney. A sweating whiskey highball sat on a coaster atop my hefty oak chest that served as our coffee table. Nyxon's book, *America's Future*, lay open beside the glass. The chapter screamed: *Heat Waves*. My eye twitched; she folded the page's corner to save her place. Use a bookmark!

A low meow rumbled from the leather chesterfield chair. Graysen wiggled her fluffy white paws, then stretched her massive black Norwegian Forest Cat body into a downward dog pose.

The gray fur around Graysen's neck resembled Queen Elizabeth's millstone collar from the sixteenth century. When I moved in, Nyxon's face held a continuous scrunch at the thought of a "smelly, shedding" cat living in her space. But now the two of them were inseparable.

My worn copy of *Because I Could Not Stop for Death: Poems by Emily Dickinson* rested on the side table beneath the lamp's warm light. The lamp's stained glass paid homage to the prettiness of peonies. Its glass flowers varied from pink to red, or so I was told.

Nyxon placed a bottle of wine on the kitchen counter. "First, follow me." She strode across groaning floorboards, then through the French doors into her office.

A white orchid with six star-shaped blooms sat on the windowsill, the night sky a background for the luminous points. Dust collected on the oak gun cabinet's glass. No chairs welcomed visitors because Nyxon brooded better on her feet. Documents cluttered her standing desk. The smell of toner hung in the air. A coffee ring stained a scribbled note. A report crumpled, then smoothed out again, probably rescued from the overflowing black circular trash bin.

The four small TVs showed 24-hour surveillance footage of the outside of our house. Nyxon was borderline unhinged when it came to personal security.

On the four-tier bookcase, a pot-bellied Laughing Buddha statue held a string of pearls. *The Elements of Journalism*, *The News Sorority*, *Fahrenheit 451*, and language dictionaries, their spines straight and stiff, posed like soldiers in front of their commanding officer. My stomach dropped. A framed photo: Quinbe, Fritz, Li, Nyxon, and me during Fritz's twenty-first birthday trip to Curaçao. The men's patterned board shorts reached their knees and flip-flops adorned their feet. Li wore a straw sun hat. A towel draped Fritz's arm. Our tropical dresses complemented those sunny days and balmy nights. We each had tucked a hibiscus flower behind our ear. Remembering the flower's sweet scent and the sea's salty spray hit me hard.

I should avoid this room. Those happy days were forever gone.

She opened her desk's side drawer and pulled out a paper bag. "I regret not giving this to you sooner." She lobbed the sack toward me. It crunched against my chest as I cradled it.

I peered inside. "Pepper spray. Hopefully I'll never have to use it. Thanks for dragging me to those self-defense classes."

"Well, you refuse to carry a gun." She tucked her cropped raven hair behind her ear. "But you did good tonight. Rule number one, never get in the attacker's car."

My attention drifted from Nyxon to the dozen missing-women posters pinned to the wall. An African American woman in her twenties with a college graduation cap, the tassel tossed to the left, smiled. Optimism brightened her eyes. Amy Allen. Photo two: a mugshot. An aged white woman. Sunken cheeks. Skin sores. In the next photo, an

Asian woman in a hard hat and high-visibility vest stood with her arms crossed in front of a construction site. She stood out, a symbol of strength and determination in a traditionally male-dominated industry.

Nyxon's perfect penmanship noted dates and the last known locations of each victim. Their stories claimed a piece of the room's energy. Printed news articles highlighted family members' accounts and clues. Their desperate pleas reverberated through time until their loved ones were found.

"What's going on?" I asked.

"Twelve women. Aged twenty-five to thirty-five. Vanished from Vancouver over the past four months. I'm reviewing their cases."

"They're all different. Ages, occupations, races. How are they connected?"

"They have…" she gave me a sideways glance, "unique genetic identifiers."

A corkscrew of uneasiness sickened my stomach. I could be on that wall.

Chapter 4

I recounted my lavender discovery to Nyxon as she paced the living room with the methodical movements of a master journalist. "I don't want to blindside Ms. Voss. *Promise me* you'll let me handle it."

She pursed her lips, but after a pause, she nodded. "But you need to show Ms. Voss your data and gauge her reaction."

The implications of sidestepping Michael's authority festered, like a thorn embedded in my foot. Michael wasn't just a senior figure, his influence ran deep and threaded through places it had no right to be. Reporting him would send shockwaves through the corporate hierarchy.

I should call in sick tomorrow. Hide away and gather my thoughts. But the Fall Collection's deadline loomed over me like a guillotine. Absence wasn't an option.

The elevator chimed softly, usually a bright note in the morning, but not today. The doors parted, revealing the sixth floor, a hub of activity and innovation. The lively buzz of colleagues collaborating on the latest perfume creation clashed with the anxiety roiling in my stomach. I smoothed down my gray blouse, trying to steady myself.

Did anyone else know?

My briefcase's strap dug into my shoulder. Despite my polished appearance, straight posture, and the purposeful click of my kitten heels, I didn't feel prepared for the day.

Rows of modern white cubicles created a hedge maze for my final destination. Glass walls encased the lab, showcasing the chemists inside, heads down with stern expressions, like master chess players in a high-stakes match. Amidst the room's vastness, I located my minimalist, photo-free cubicle.

"Avi!" Tiffany's saccharine tone ricocheted over the large space. Her wide-legged white pants swooshed as she strode toward me. Today, like most days when Ms. Voss wasn't in the office, she wore her thick blonde hair down in waves, defying the rule to keep it tied up. In a month, it wouldn't surprise me if she started chewing gum and popped big pink bubbles. A burlap belt cinched a black blouse but didn't add any curves to her twiggy shape. A white lab coat draped over her arm. Extra-large hoops adorned her ears. Her perpetual double chin gathered beneath her round, soft face. Her wide mouth, darkly painted and sharply outlined, offered no smile. "I know you almost died yesterday, but…"

She was being dramatic and uncaring, as usual.

Without warning, she slipped her arm through mine and steered me away from the cubicles.

"Michael pulled me aside," she said aghast, fluttering those ridiculously long fake lashes like she couldn't help herself.

"He told you?"

"I know everything that goes on around this place. He made it crystal clear, the Fall Collection needs your *full* attention. He's aware you're eyeing the chief evaluator role." She leaned closer to whisper, "Michael has a way of making things happen. With you stepping up, there's room for me to take over your current position. We just have to follow his lead."

Did Michael put her up to bribing me, or did she come up with this scheme on her own? Everyone knew Tiffany would claw her way to the top.

"He's looking for a team player, and I'd love to report back that he can find that in you." She released my arm.

The bitter truth was, I needed that raise. More money was my ticket out of Nyxon's house, and suddenly, my ultimate goal of owning a perfumery and bath boutique pieced itself back together, shiny and new. My dream wasn't dead. I just had to let the lavender incident go. My gut churned. Ms. Voss took a chance on me right out of university. She saw my potential. Four years later, under her wing, I owed her my loyalty.

"Humans make mistakes," Tiffany lowered her voice, "If someone in upper management ordered the wrong lavender, *or* our supplier sent us an incorrect shipment, the last thing we want to do is ruin someone's livelihood over a simple error that won't kill anyone. Does anyone else suspect the oil *might* be diluted?"

Tiffany made a valid, though not a good point. I couldn't ruin lives because of a simple, honest mistake, a mix-up, a one-time slip. "No one else knows."

Tiffany's shoulders eased, and the lines on her forehead relaxed. "You have two choices: play nice with Michael to pave the way for us or we'll both be hunting for a new job." She strode to her cubicle, three spaces over from mine.

Securing a chemist position in a different lab was impossible. Was covering up this mess more important than my integrity? My two choices created an ache in my stomach I forced down. Trusting Michael to fix this was my only option. Like he said, I needed to stay in my laboratory.

Tiffany swung her lab coat around her shoulders. "Let's get to work. I have a date with Seth tonight, so I can't stay late."

As if unfinished work had ever stopped her from skipping out early.

We walked to my cubicle, and she picked up the file folder on my desk labeled Fall Collection. I turned on my computer as she flipped to page five page and read: "We need to test the heart notes, nutmeg and sandalwood, from samples sixteen through eighty-four. What about adding cinnamon?"

It could've been an honest mistake. Repeating the phrase didn't soothe my stomach.

Tiffany's brows rose, impatiently waiting for my response.

"Tis the season for cinnamon," I said dryly. I caught the error before the next shipment moved into full development. Michael would do the ethical thing, halt distribution and inspect the orders. Everything would be fine.

"We used bergamot as our top olfactory note," she read. "You described it as light and energetic, making it an excellent counterpart to the warmer, deeper heart notes that will appear during our second trial.”

“I want to try tonka bean and patchouli for the base notes in samples one through fifteen.”

Footsteps thumped down the corridor, a steady drumbeat growing louder. Michael’s eyes were wild as he charged me with a linebacker’s ferocity.

Tiffany pushed the folder into my arms and scurried to her cubicle.

Dread calcified along my backbone as I braced for impact.

“Look busy. Ms. Voss is on her way up.” Michael carried a scent of late-night cognac and early-morning coffee. He tugged at his black blazer, then smoothed the front of his designer jeans. As always, he won the award for the most high-strung person in the room. “I read the security guard’s incident report about your mugging. The company isn’t liable when *you choose* to work late.”

My pulse raced. “I’d never—”

He raised a dismissive palm an inch from my face. Every major line on his palm bore a kink or a break. I leaned back, my brows rising. “I hope *Tiffany’s* chat with you regarding the lavender incident went well.” He raised an eyebrow, the subtle arch casting a shadow of suspicion over his face, as if daring me to challenge him.

My throat dried and I struggled to swallow. I was a butterfly caught in a spider’s web. Aware of the threat, but helpless to retreat.

Heels clicked down the long corridor, a rhythmic crescendo building with each confident stride.

Everyone stood. Chairs scraped. Fabric rustled. Heads turned. A soft, “good morning,” bounced off the white walls. Greta Voss had arrived.

Tiffany twisted her hair quickly into a messy bun.

Only Ms. Voss’s jet-black hair peeked above the five-foot-high cubicle wall as she passed.

She paused near her corner office suite. Like a queen, she surveyed her kingdom with quiet authority. Oversized black-rimmed glasses perched on her small round nose. Her geometric bob haircut and perfectly straight bangs framed her face. She wore a monochromatic dress and bold, chunky accessories.

"Good morning, Ms. Voss." As always, the impulse to curtsy hit me.

She gasped. "Ms. Neehow, I sent you an email insisting you take the week off. You experienced a traumatic incident yesterday. *Please* go home and rest." Although she spoke rapidly, a protective warmth wrapped each word. "My dear, you simply must prioritize self-care. I spoke to our building's security team. They'll be available to walk anyone to their car moving forward."

Success clung to her, just like her signature scent. A fragrance uniquely hers. She guarded its secret ingredients, withheld from all, shared with no one. Her signature scent was unapologetic, just like her personality. My keen nose detected traces of agarwood and neroli, but an elusive scent, tantalizing like freshly printed money and leather, defied my attempts to define it. Together, these elements created an olfactory symphony that exuded innovation and ambition.

How I'd love to bottle it. I stifled a sigh.

"And your cheek!" she exclaimed.

My coworkers' eyes flushed with condolences, while some flared with feminist pride.

My shoulders sagged as I patted the overly made-up area. "My new samples need strict monitoring and quality control." Ms. Voss had to choose my combination for this fall's signature scent, and Michael would absolutely hold any absences against me. If I got this promotion, in just a few years, I'd have enough saved to finally open my own boutique perfume and soap shop. Then I'd never have to answer to Michael again.

"Enough with these late nights. It's all about achieving a harmonious work-life balance." Her no-nonsense tone left no room to disagree. "Prioritize yourself dear, won't you?" She waved a hand in the air and strode to her glass-walled office, which overlooked pine trees and the rushing Columbia River.

"I couldn't agree more," Michael trilled, following Ms. Voss into her office.

I exhaled and my shoulders relaxed.

"Package for Aviana Neehow," a bored male voice called over the cubicles. Tiffany waved the mailman over, then led him to my cube.

The mailman passed me a digital notepad. After signing on the dotted line, he handed me a rectangular box wrapped in a thick white ribbon. The wrapping paper featured a horse-riding knight carrying a flag emblazoned with the word *Prorsum*. My grin waned as I traced the colorless figure.

"The wrapping paper is black. The horse and rider are silver. You're not missing anything." Tiffany tapped her toe. "So, open it."

The callous phrase "missing anything" stung. I missed things every day. My clothes rarely matched. I had to ask strangers at the grocery store which bananas were ripe. Navigating maps was a nightmare.

Tiffany yanked the small cream-colored card from under the ribbon. Batting her lashes, she fanned herself like a Southern belle. "Can I read it aloud?"

"No." I strained for the card, but Tiffany rebuffed me, raising it above her head.

"Don't be a poor sport." She tore the seal open.

"Tiffany, I—"

"Dear Aviana," she said haughtily, then glanced down at me.

Swallowing a lump in my throat, I sank into my chair. "Fine."

She smirked. "I hope this gift warms your day. If it doesn't, I know a place downtown that ferments spiced wine. Sincerely, Your Sidekick." Her nose wrinkled. "*Who's* your sidekick?"

"I'm not sure." My brow furrowed as I unlaced the ribbon. I lifted the lid and my heart rose with it. Gently, I unfolded the crackling tissue paper.

A scarf nestled inside.

My fingers glided over the soft checkered fabric, then fluffed the tasseled ends. I stared in disbelief. Who would send such a gift?

"Burberry. Black, with gray and white stripes." Tiffany pinched her fingers together, so I elevated the scarf, designing a dance floor for her waltzing digits. "Cashmere. *Very* classy."

A business card fluttered free, landing near Tiffany's shoe. She picked it up. "Raiden Graví. Private Investigator. Who's that?"

"Raiden helped me stop the mugger."

She pressed the card to her chest. "You have to call him." Then she passed it to me.

I scrutinized the simple Times New Roman font. Just his name, occupation, phone number, and address. Excitement tingled through me. My fingers rubbed the card, itching to accept his invitation but my palms grew clammy with nerves.

Should I take a chance on this stranger? What if he rejected me? "I'm…"

Getting over an ex.

Focusing on myself.

What could I possibly offer him besides a thank you?

"I'm busy right now." My mind flitted between joy and sadness, love and hurt.

Inhaling deeply, I stashed the card in my handbag next to the pepper spray.

Tiffany brought the scarf to her cheek and shut her eyes. "You can't be too busy for love *or* wealthy men. *When* you call Mugger Raiden—"

"Don't call him that," I snapped. The words flew out before I could soften them. My spine stiffened. Why did I feel the need to defend him?

She rolled her eyes. "Ask *Raiden* to run a background check on Seth." She tossed the scarf to me. "I *refuse* to date a secretly married man *again*."

Tiffany's request sparked a question of my own. Maybe Raiden could uncover who's been screwing with the lavender oil? The idea gnawed at me, like an itch on my lower back just out of reach.

He had connections I didn't.

He had tools I lacked.

He had a perspective I might never consider.

"I'm accepting Ms. Voss's offer to take the day off." My brash decision had me pushing back from my desk and rising from my chair.

"But, but the samples. I can't stay late tonight." Tiffany's palms opened in a pleading gesture. "You wouldn't believe how I met him."

"Stop right there. No." I looped the scarf around my neck.

"Avi, let me explain." Her pout paralleled a grounded teenager. "At the grocery store's self-checkout line, I bumped into this man," her soprano voice climbed an octave, *"and guess what?"*

"Spare me the guessing game." I groaned and slung my briefcase over my shoulder.

I strode toward the elevator and Tiffany trailed after me, her heels clicking across the tile in frantic little bursts. "We had the same items in our baskets! Cheetos, beer, and pickles. Isn't that wild?"

"Very wild." I faked my interest without slowing. "You're out of college. Why are you eating Cheetos?"

"When I'm thirty like you, I'll consider clean eating. Avi, it's fate. I have to go on this date."

Surprised, and mildly offended, I countered, "I'm twenty-seven."

She stomped her foot, digressing from a spoiled teenager to an emotional toddler. "You're missing the point. I know it's hard for you to understand because your calendar and bed are empty every night."

I grimaced. Her cavalier comment caught my coworkers' attention, so I questioned the nosy spectators, "Raise your hand if you're in a fairy tale relationship?" I surveyed the room. "Two out of twenty people. The odds of contracting chlamydia are one in twenty. I'll play it safe, sit on my couch, and watch crime documentaries."

Tiffany lifted her chin, leveling a look toward our listless coworkers. "Love finds a way," she stated with a conviction leaving no room for doubt. "Just because your vision is gray doesn't mean your love life has to be."

A coworker's brow rose, but no one said a word. A traitorous blush crept across my cheeks. Last month, Tiffany discovered my color blindness when I grabbed the wrong pipette, mistaking its green ring for yellow. The mistake set our project back half a day, and since then, she's taken pleasure in calling my gray world "our little joke."

Enough with the snide remarks. I wasn't going to be the punchline today. I stepped inside the elevator. "You want my job? Prove to

Michael you can handle it." I couldn't resist smiling as the doors closed on her shocked and fearful face.

Chapter 5

In Vancouver's Uptown district, where hip meets historic, I walked past Becker's Books and Bobbles. The store's cloth awning flapped, offering a dash of vintage curb appeal.

Next door, a sign on the vacant building read: "Available to lease." I cupped my hands against the glass to shield the glare and peered inside. Plastic wrapped a four-pronged farmhouse chandelier. Shelves lined the wall, destined to one day showcase elegant soaps and luxurious perfumes. I'd need a rolling ladder to stock them. The notion fluttered like a midnight moth attracted to light, brushing the edges of my awareness with hopeful anticipation.

I traversed the uneven, pansy-lined sidewalk toward Raiden's building. Across the street in Clock Tower Park, a mother, father, and daughter rested beneath a cherry blossom tree. A petal landed on the preschooler's nose and her giggle conveyed she didn't know fear. Only magic. Only unconditional love. My mom must not have found joy in my laugh. My father must not have treasured my smile. The emptiness in the pit of my belly boiled into an ache. My foot struck the sidewalk lip and I stumbled forward.

Get it together, Avi.

Minutes later, I stopped in front of the decrepit brick building with boarded-up windows. A place where dreams of success went to decay. Why would the arrow on my phone point me down this alley?

My pulse quickened. I shouldn't be doing this alone. What was I thinking? I glanced left, then right. What were the chances of being mugged and almost kidnapped twice in one week? I patted my purse, feeling the pepper spray between the folds. Last night's drama sent a chill down my spine, but I needed answers to the lavender oil case. Without a private investigator, I'd be navigating a labyrinth of lies and motives. Each turn a gamble, each forged alliance fraught with risks, each decision drawing me deeper into moral ambiguity. So, I pushed forward, fighting the instinct to turn back.

Rotting food odors assaulted my senses; I covered my nose. Beer cans clanged over potholes, caught in the breeze's throes. The temperature dropped, the three-story brick buildings blocked out the sun. My feet itched to retreat, urging me to run. No signs of life stirred behind the windows, as if this alley had become its own ghost town.

This couldn't be right. But my phone confirmed it. The sixth dented metal door on the left lacking signage. Only crooked numbers were screwed into its mundane surface.

This had to work.

I held my breath and turned the knob.

Overhead, the shopkeeper's bell chimed.

"Hello?" I became a nervous mouse, my squeak echoing through the windowless lobby. A subtle mustiness drifted through the room, reminiscent of a dusty attic. The lobby was utterly lifeless. No plants. No artwork on the brick walls. No rug on the wood floor. A secretary's desk served as gatekeeper to the frosted-glass office. I arched a brow; the desk calendar was a month behind and empty.

I ventured further into the lobby.

To my right, the conference room door was ajar. A rectangle of light shone into the room, spotlighting a black rolling chair. An empty gun shoulder holster draped over the chair, its leather straps frayed and worn. The accessory caused my gut to rebel and recited for me to reverse, but I stepped closer. "Hello?"

A journal sat on the long, grainy table, its round metal buckle glinting in the light. The buckle's tree design featured snake-like roots, while leafless branches spread wide. Etched into the trunk was a clock. Its face adorned with Nordic-like symbols in place of conventional numbers.

A floorboard creaked behind me, piercing the silence. I jolted and spun.

Raiden stood near the secretary's desk, his cellphone lowering from his ear. With a sly smile, he stowed it in his pants pocket. Stubble darkened his jawline. Loose strands of hair hung from his day-old braid that ended just above his nape. His fitted T-shirt mapped the solid terrain of his arms and shoulders. His chiseled features enhanced the contrast between intimidation and charm.

"You received my gift," his voice was breathy and deep. "I wasn't sure if you'd be working today."

"Thank you for the scarf. It's lovely." I fidgeted with a tassel.

He quickly closed the distance between us, his denim pants brushing against itself. He reached around my waist and shut the conference room door. His chest inches from mine caused goosebumps to prickle my arm. My nose hovered near his neck. He had no scent. The realization struck me hard, surfacing swiftly and startlingly, like a shark breaching the ocean's surface.

A human's scent was as unique as a fingerprint. Scents activated emotions and stirred the depths of the subconscious. He reached out and rubbed the scarf between his fingers. The casual familiarity of his fingers tracing the fabric, as though he belonged in my proximity, caught me off guard, so I stammered, "Your card said you're a private investigator."

"Oh, I see, you're here on business." Even though his tone teased, a blush bespeckled my cheeks.

"I don't know what type of private investigator you are, but I'm hoping you could help me with a work problem. I'm at a dead end and need *your* expertise."

He smirked and mulled over my request. "Let's chat. Please step into my office." He ushered me through the lobby, past the secretary desk, and into the office with the frosted windows.

Raiden hastily stuffed photos and documents into a folder, then placed it on the corner of his desk, nudging the circular paper clip container to the edge.

No picture frames. No paperweights. No books. The retro record player, sitting open on a two-tiered shelf, was the only glimpse into his personality. Records stood shoulder to shoulder, and my fingers itched to uncover his taste in music.

A chittering clink to my left caused me to jump.

It was a machine. Its cat-like eyes flickered. The machine's silver scorpion body was roughly the size of a house cat. Its stag beetle mandibles twitched in anticipation. A faint hum, a low-frequency static, coursed through its metallic components. The robot's segmented tail stood erect, writhing like a cobra ready to strike. At the tail's tip, a dagger-like stinger pointed in my direction. My muscles quivered under my calm facade.

The robot guarded a four-drawer filing cabinet. A peculiar acrid smell hung in the air around the creature, an odor like no other, that could only come from a robot on the brink of achieving artificial intelligence.

"What's that?" my voice cracked, despite my attempt to sound innocently curious and not afraid.

"I tinker with BattleBots in my free time." He signaled for me to select one of two sun-baked leather chairs. I selected the chair farthest from the machine. Raiden's eyes quizzically cruised over me, and I longed to know their color.

I confided about my work predicament, detailing Michael's increasingly suspicious behavior, all while risking Ms. Voss's impeccable reputation.

Absent-mindedly, Raiden lifted the pen to his mouth and nibbled at the end. There was a faint unevenness to his bottom lip, like it had once split open and healed without care.

What would it be like to kiss those lips?

Embarrassment heated my cheeks. *Please, please don't be turning red.*

Stay focused.

Why on earth was I harboring a secret crush on him? I could hardly believe it. Just thinking about the way he faced danger made my chest tighten. There was a rare strength in him that I'd stopped expecting from men, one that made me want to sigh and groan at the same time.

"Are there security cameras in the building?" His smooth voice held a hint of intrigue, as if he relished the cloak-and-dagger aspect of our conversation.

"Yes, in every room."

"I have to ask, do you want details on how I gather my information? Sometimes it's best not to know." His words carried a note of warning.

My fingers were ripping at my cuticles, so I quickly shoved them beneath my thighs.

The bell above the door clanged. Raiden's jaw tensed, a deep crease forming between his brows as he stood. Startled, I did the same and faced the doorway.

A short, plump woman burst in, panting as if she'd been fleeing shadowy pursuers. Tiny, stitched roses adorned the edge of her black hood. A thick belt cinched her trench coat around her waist, and Velcro straps secured her ill-fitting shoes to her wide feet. Her plain, stiff dress resembled a 1920s nurse's uniform. She lowered her hood, revealing waves of blonde curls that framed her face. One eye was light, the other dark, probably blue and brown, but both reflected a childlike panic. "Mr. Graví? Mr. Graví!" Her round cheeks trembled; her voice thin and wavering, like someone accustomed to being overlooked.

Raiden's expression didn't relax as he put out a hand to me. "Wait here." He strode into the lobby. "Marthane. I…" He shut the office door.

On cue, the BattleBot marched in place and snapped its silver jaws. I leapt away, bumping into the desk. The paper clip container tipped over, spilling the silver looping wires to the floor, an inch from the line containing the BattleBot. Hairs on my neck prickled.

It was a machine. It couldn't, wouldn't, hurt me.

"He knows! He knows!" Marthane screamed.

"Keep your voice down. What does he know?"

"I'm giving you information!"

"Do you have somewhere to hide?" he asked.

"No." A sob choked her throat.

A long pause. "My friend Bashiri can get you to Madras, Oregon and put you on a ship to send you home."

Ship? Motorized boats weren't allowed on the Deschutes River.

"Don't go back to his house. Don't call anyone. *Just go*," Raiden ordered.

A surge of empathy caught me. Was she fleeing from an abusive husband? I recognized the tremor in her voice. Guardians whose moods could turn on a dime, tempers igniting over any perceived slight shaped my childhood. But the sheer helplessness, the bleak edge of destitution in her voice was a different kind of monster altogether.

"Go to this address. Bashiri can give you cash. Thanks to your information, I'll be able to cripple his network. Then he won't have time to look for you. Follow me." Their footsteps led them to the conference room.

The BattleBot stomped. Its pupils enlarged, fully filling the eye sockets.

Squatting slowly, I shoveled paper clips into my palm, then rose.

I funneled the paper clips into their container and my eyes wandered to the folder. The corner of a photograph peeked out, revealing two legs striking a sultry pose, one leg kicked back at the knee, exposing the 'LV' label on the sole of her high heel. The shoe's beaded straps draped like a chandelier around her ankle. Chills swept down my spine. I recognized those shoes. Holding my breath, I pulled the picture from the folder and gasped.

A floorboard creaked behind me. I whirled. Pulse pounding.

Raiden stood in the doorway, a twitchiness creasing the corners of his eyes. My fingers flexed, wanting the pepper spray in my purse. The air thickened, suffocating in its intensity.

His eyes darkened. He knew exactly what I'd seen.

It was pointless to deny it, so I held up the candid photo of Quinbe and me laughing. Quinbe leaned on me with one foot in the air. Her head tilted back, red curls tumbling down her spine like silk. My braided hair draped over one shoulder. Quinbe's New Year's Eve sequin romper outshone my black strapless knee-length dress. I tossed the photo on his desk. Every muscle in my body coiled tight, ready to bolt. "Why do you have pictures of me from before we met?"

Chapter 6

Raiden's voice caught before words formed, then he drew a breath he didn't seem to need. "It's not what you think. I'm not a private investigator. I work for the… a government."

"Like the FBI?"

"More covert. More international."

"The CIA?"

He ran a hand through his hair. "I didn't want to involve you in this problem, unless I had to."

He didn't answer my question.

I retreated into the corner. Was he a savior or stalker?

He strode to the filing cabinet, sidestepped the BattleBot, opened the top drawer, and pulled out a tablet. The screen brightened, casting a faint glow across his fingers. He swiped left again and again, soft swooshes breaking the silence, until he stopped on an item and turned the screen toward me. A man stared into the camera with compassionate resolve, reminiscent of a benevolent general surveying his troops. His oval face and soft jawline were at odds with his thin lips and black silky hair, as if his Caucasian and Asian heritage vied for dominance. "This is your father. Uzziah Markosyan."

My body went rigid. Our similarities didn't blare. Narrow nose and dark hair, it ended there. I fought the impulse to ask Raiden about Uzziah's eye color. He wore a high collar military suit with gleaming buttons down the middle. Stitched upon his coat was a circular patch featuring an hourglass, filled not with sand, but crystals. A numbness washed over me and my mouth dried. I could pass him on the street without a second glance.

"Uzziah stole the ancient Tiara of Tuskia from a collector's vault. Uzziah is a ruthless thief. Five people were killed during the robbery. He left an accomplice to suffer and die." Raiden's eyes darkened. "That accomplice told me Uzziah is searching for you. I found you first. I have sixty days to return the tiara to its rightful owner and ensure Uzziah faces the full force of the law."

He inched closer to me.

"I need your help tempting Uzziah to come out of hiding." His hushed request carried the intimacy of two people sharing secrets in a dimly lit alley. "We have to stop him before more innocent people get caught in his crossfire."

My lips parted, but no sound came. The grudge I harbored over the years tightened its hold, leaving a throbbing loneliness. What did I expect from parents who abandoned eight-year-old me at a bus stop? Left me like litter. A disposable inconvenience. Fury boiled within me, melting away any hope of a civil reunion. My jaw clenched, pressure built until I feared my teeth would crack.

"*You* were using me as bait." The sickening revelation transformed into barbed wire and twined around my heart. "*You* didn't bump into me on the street." The wire constricted.

With defiance etched across my face, I unfettered the scarf from my neck and flung it at him.

He caught it. His chin dropped as he thumbed the fabric, treating the scarf as more than a manipulation.

"Does my mugging have something to do with my—" the word *father* stuck to the roof of my mouth, "Uzziah?"

"I'm not sure. The mugger wasn't one of Uzziah's known associates." Setting the scarf on the desk, he offered me the tablet like an olive branch. His eyes locked on mine and refused to break our stare, it wasn't a dare, the corners of his eyes softened with care.

My hand fought with my mind; I didn't want to take the tablet.

I wanted to run out that door.

I wanted to call Nyxon.

But for years I yearned for this information. Could I trust what he offered?

It wouldn't hurt to peek. "Drop it on the desk and back up."

He pushed the tablet across the smooth wood. Its screen reflected the overhead lights as it came to a stop.

My fingernails tapped along his desk as I approached. Was I ready for what lay within?

Slowly I scrolled, a cold sweat breaking out across my forehead. A photocopied picture of my driver's license. Then in bold font the words, *Patient Records,* blared. "How did you get my medical history?"

"My hacker friend owed me a favor. Life must be hard with achromatopsia."

I gritted my teeth. The first of many diagnoses dogging me to maturity. Would he ignore the trauma beneath? Did his heart have that type of capacity? Oppositional defiance, reactive attachment, anxiety. Was I forgetting some? Did he unearth each and every one? When the white coats weren't labeling me, the kids took their jest. No matter how hard I tried, I couldn't shake the epithets slapped upon my chest. "I was eight years old when my world turned gray. Don't even think about asking me what color something is."

His hands rose in sincere surrender. "I won't. Promise. I'm sure that gets annoying."

As a teen, my colorblindness fueled a bitterness that consumed me, exposing itself in the form of fits of envy and self-pity. I could never truly experience the world around me. Life was a constant reminder of my limitations and it frustrated me to no end. I shifted from foot to foot. I needed to steer the conversation in a different direction. "If you have all of this, what do you need me for?"

"I wanted to contact your foster parents to see if Uzziah reached out to them." He wrestled a pen and notepad from a drawer. "Can we start at the beginning?" He clicked his retractable pen and sat on the desk's edge.

A wave of incredulity hit me. Was I really going to lay my shameful past bare? My past truths pressed heavily upon me, its ugliness a burden I'd long concealed. The BattleBot's hum grew louder in my ears. If I confided in Raiden, it meant I agreed to assist him. But if Uzziah found out I assisted Raiden? Uzziah's wrath made my pulse thump.

If I didn't partner with Raiden, could I live with the consequences of my silence? Also, this was my first solid lead on my family, a true glimpse into their existence, the first clue to unraveling the puzzle of my life and I couldn't ignore the call to action. I had to pursue it, no matter where this mysterious path might lead. "I entered the system at age eight." Remembering my trials and tribulations soured my stomach, but I gulped down the rot. "There was Amy and Brad Wellington. She got pregnant, and I no longer fit into their picture-perfect family. So, my caseworker dropped me off at Trista's house, which reeked of moldy cheese. I don't remember her last name, but if she's still alive, she'd be useless. She had the IQ of a household sponge." He chuckled generously at my attempt to joke about my less-than-idyllic childhood. A drop of blood dribbled from my thumb. I had picked my cuticles raw. I stuffed my hands in my pockets and held in a grimace. "After running away from Trista's because of her creepy son." His eyebrows shot up, concern flickering in his eyes. As he shifted closer, his soft gaze deepened into protectiveness.

I cleared my throat. "I was sent to the Larkson's, but when they divorced, I got the boot." Periodically, the past escaped from my eyes and trickled down my cheeks, but not today. I wouldn't allow it. "I ran away from four group homes. At sixteen, I landed with Sloane Patel and Quinbe. But I'd prefer you *not* bring them into this. If Sloane had information about my parents, she would've told me."

"Quinbe, the red-haired girl in the picture."

My body stiffened. I despised that he'd secretly photographed Quinbe. His nonchalant demeanor made a mockery of my frustration. "Quinbe came to live with Sloane at ten. She views me as an older sister."

"Is that why she was adopted and you weren't?"

The question stung, but I straightened. "It was pointless, I was too old. Quinbe's obsession with adoption was only topped by her habit of rescuing stray animals."

He studied me, then nodded—understanding the delicate thread that ties friendship and family together. "The exclusive Six Stones Auction House is hosting a private event at Fort Vancouver Wednesday night. If I'm able to get on the guest-list, I want you to come with me. They cater to collectors of the paranormal or mystical arts. Their auctions offer a curated selection of cursed objects and forbidden texts."

I scoffed, a reflexive response to the sheer absurdity of what the rich will spend money on.

Raiden smirked. "So, you're a nonbeliever?"

The way he conveyed it, with clandestine assurance, made me feel like a foolish skeptic. So, I answered with a question of my own, curiosity rising. "Does that make *you* a believer?"

"There's more to this world than meets the eye. Why are certain relics hidden away, *secured*? Those relics hold more than just stories. They are keys that unlock forces beyond our comprehension."

My eyes widened as Raiden's words sank in, leaving me feeling electrified, like I'd just glimpsed a power beyond human reach. Forces we couldn't comprehend? What kind of power was so dangerous, it had to be hidden? A thrill threaded through me, the unmistakable feeling of crossing into uncharted territory, into a wild adventure.

"Uzziah's top lieutenant, Sellow, will be bidding on Napoleon Bonaparte's en bataille hat and Anne Boleyn's iconic 'B' necklace." He leaned toward me and I held my ground. "I've pored over your file, but I still can't figure out why Uzziah searches for you now. Is there anything, any small detail, that connects you to your childhood?"

A black impenetrable wall, constructed by my subconscious, blocked my painful past. It was an insurmountable task to recall details from my youth. Yet, against all odds, one memory glowed vividly, like a radiant sunrise breaking through stormy clouds. "The necklace." My voice sounded far away as if this was all a dream, nightmare really. Raiden leaned in, with a look begging me to continue. "I was found wearing a necklace. I had it appraised. The expert chalked it up to worthless costume jewelry." I pulled out my phone and swiped through an old photo album.

Found it. The only link to my mysterious ancestry. A pendant-shaped cross, adorned with three blue stones. Within the blue stones, black flakes swirled, like a galaxy trapped in celestial sapphire. The necklace's filigree design imitated ornate wings on both sides of the center cross.

Raiden's brow furrowed as he bit his lower lip. "I'll be damned. The blue-black stones are fertorium. They're very rare *and* expensive. Actually, that description doesn't do the element justice. I've never seen it manipulated into jewelry. A mom-and-pop jeweler wouldn't have the knowledge to identify it."

"Why would the person who dumped me at the bus stop leave it with me?" My mother or Uzziah must have stolen it.

My toes began to tap. Raiden's gaze dropped to my face, then lifted back to my face. He angled his body toward me and leaned in, inviting me into his calm, confident presence.

"I'll find Uzziah faster if we work together, and then you can ask him. Help me ensure he doesn't hurt anyone else." Desperation laced his tone. "And in exchange, I'll find out who is tampering with the lavender oil."

My skin prickled. How could I turn him down? I inhaled slowly and swallowed. What's the worst that could happen? "Just promise to keep Sloane and Quinbe out of this." Shame burned my cheeks imagining Sloane gossiping to Fritz about my father's criminal past. She already thought so little of me, this news would cement her opinion of the "type of stock" I was bred from.

"I won't involve them," Raiden vowed, his voice like steel. "I'd like to see the necklace. Can I come over Saturday?"

I rummaged through my mental calendar. Nyxon would be at a teachers' picket line, protesting low pay and overcrowded classrooms. "Yes, but you'll have to come between eight and ten in the morning, because Nyxon and Quinbe planned a weekend getaway for us at the beach."

"That will work."

"What about my mother? Is her last name Neehow?"

"She doesn't appear in any of my reports." A thin veneer of unease coated his voice. His eyes shifted to the filing cabinet, betraying the lie woven into his words. "Then again, neither did you until a month ago."

A single nerve ignited, and like a string of firecrackers, a foreboding feeling flared through me. Was he deliberately keeping her from me? Was she hiding from Uzziah? My feet itched to pace. Was she dead? A stab of anguish clenched my chest. My mother. A person who was always just away, now seemed ghost-like.

"Once we capture Uzziah, you can ask him." He cleared his throat. "I'm entrusting you with this confidential information. If this gets out, there will be irreversible consequences."

Excluding Quinbe and Nyxon made me jittery, but keeping them safe mattered most. Once we had answers, I'd use our findings to track down my mom, and the good news would drown out any questions about my father's whereabouts. I nodded, reassuring myself, but Raiden took the gesture as if I agreed with him.

"You'll need my cell phone number." He motioned for me to pass him my phone. My throat dried as I pulled the new device I'd bought this morning from my purse. His fingers grazed mine as he took it.

He tapped buttons. "Call day or night." He clicked off my phone and held it near his body, forcing me to step out of my comfortable bubble into his. I accepted his challenge, and we stood toe to toe, but he didn't let go of my phone. We were close enough for his body heat to thaw the frost around my soul. "Go home, act like everything is normal. Do you have a gun?"

My eyes widened. "No. Do you think he'd hurt me?"

"He's capable of anything to get what he wants." Raiden walked to his desk, his warmth giving way to a coolness that tickled my skin. He opened the top drawer and grasped the barrel of a black pistol, then extended it to me.

My hands rose, palms up in protest. "I've never loaded or fired a gun."

"It's time to learn."

I stood in front of the full-length mirror rimmed with pearlized shells. I glossed my lips in a rosy sheen, sprayed my wrists with my bold signature scent, then unclasped the top two buttons of the bandeau-style bodice of my chiffon dress.

Flapping the weightless material at my sides, self-consciousness reflected in my eyes. "Aviana Markosyan. Markosyan." The name clunked off my tongue like a foreign word.

Was I in over my head? What other choice did I have? Raiden held the only lead on Uzziah, and most importantly, I must safeguard Ms. Voss's reputation.

Graysen's fur skimmed my leg as she sauntered by, her tail giving a slow, swish, pure feline indifference.

The doorbell's chime rang out. Graysen led the charge toward the entryway, and my pulse raced at her pace.

I opened the door to Raiden's smiling face. The sides of his scalp were freshly shaven. His slicked-back hair gave him a sophisticated yet rugged appearance. His Dri-Fit shirt clung to his stomach, hinting at lean strength, while his chino shorts revealed taut runner's calves. Raiden's clean-cut goatee had returned. I stood there, caught off guard by the duality between his polished appearance and the smoldering confidence he carried. It awakened a quiet ache, where curiosity brushed against heat.

"Thank you." I accepted it, but the lid popped off as I adjusted my grip. Hot droplets splattered onto my hand and his shoe.

I hissed and hurried to the kitchen island, setting the coffee down then shaking off the sting. "Sorry about your shoes. I'll grab a cloth."

"Are you okay?" His focus snapped to my hand. "Forget the shoes. Do you need ice?"

"I'm fine." I turned away, sidestepping to grab a dish cloth.

Cloth in hand, I bent to wipe the splatter, only for him to reach at the same time. Our heads knocked together with a dull thunk.

Graysen leapt from the couch, a flurry of fur, sprinted toward Raiden. Though her tufted ears and gray mane gave her a whimsical look, she zeroed in on him with a lethal grace. She raised one paw to strike. I dropped the rag and, with a swift motion, swept her into my arms, rescuing Raiden from the impending onslaught. Even in my embrace, she hissed and spat in his direction.

"What's gotten into you?" I bounced her in my arms like a mother comforting a baby throwing a tantrum.

"Cats usually like me." He reached out a hand for Graysen to sniff.

She lashed out again, but Raiden jerked away just in time, to my relief.

"I'll put her in my room." She twisted against my hold, a writhing knot of fur and claws accidentally grazing across my arm. A hiss burst from her, I flinched, my grip loosening just enough for her to kick off me, launching herself through the air, landing with a thud, then scrambling onto the chesterfield's armrest. Graysen tucked her paws under her body into the grumpy loaf position and emitted a low growl.

I shook out my stinging arm. "What's wrong with you?"

He took my arm and examined the tender, raised lines. "They're red. Pretty angry-looking."

Raiden's touch caused my heart to skip in a way I couldn't quite explain. I took a deep breath, trying to steady myself.

"I'm okay. Cats can be finicky," I offered.

"That's the truth." He gazed past me, his focus drawn to something over my shoulder. I turned, following his line of sight.

His eyes roamed over the missing women posters and the map dotted with red pins denoting last known locations. "That's quite a wall." His tone was a mix of awe and admiration.

"That's Nyxon's office. She's a journalist." My explanation came out matter-of-fact.

Amusement and mischief flickered in his eyes. "And a podcaster."

"*Right*, you did your research."

He sipped his coffee. "A friend of mine hacked into Pacific Perfume's security cameras." His eyes were serious, making it clear that the confidential information he was about to reveal demanded caution.

Chapter 7

My jaw dropped. "Hacking the security cameras is…" Illegal. Impressive. Brilliant. I swallowed. "What did you see?"

"A tall, thin man—"

"Michael. It has to be Michael."

He raised an eyebrow, ordering me to be objective. "At 6:00 a.m., *a tall, thin man* enters your lab with a duffel bag. He selects half-filled bottles, places them in the bag, and moves them into the storage room. There are *no cameras* in the storage room."

I seethed. "I knew Michael was guilty!"

"Wait a minute. There's a woman. Her coat's hood obscures her face as she returns the duffel bag to your lab and places the bottles on the shelf. The only distinguishing feature was a gold laurel wreath bracelet around her wrist, studded with small rubies." From his pocket, Raiden placed a small, matchbook-sized camera into my hand. "I need you to hide the camera in the storage room."

My throat dried as I stared at the small square. "Don't we have enough evidence?"

"It's not evidence because it was illegally obtained. We don't know what he's filling the bottles with and who his accomplice is. If you can't do this, our investigation is at a dead end."

My fingers curled around the white cube. "I can plant it on Monday." I doubted Tiffany was his accomplice because she was never on time for work, let alone arrived early.

He relaxed. "I was able to bribe the Auction house's guest coordinator, and she added us to the guest list. I had her use the name Aviana Markosyan. Is that okay?"

His question hung in the air, then cannonballed into me. Markosyan. The name my father never wished for me to wear. It was a stranger's name. My knees felt like Jell-O as I considered the implications of presenting myself to the world with that name. I wanted to blurt, *no*—but another part knew the auction was a golden opportunity.

Could I act like an experienced bidder? Looking clueless filled me with dread, but a small part of me craved the adrenaline rush it would trigger.

Raiden stepped closer, the intensity in his gaze daring me to close the final inches between us, as if this movement would seal my commitment to his mission. "With you as a distraction, I can detain Uzziah's captain, Sellow." The cunning way his eyes flickered to my lips made it impossible for me to focus on his words. His hand grazed down my arm, lingering a heartbeat too long at my wrist before falling away, sending goosebumps racing across my skin. "I'll keep you safe."

My methodical breaths were distinct, like a ticking clock counting down the seconds until I accepted his request. There existed no alternative path to uncovering Uzziah's whereabouts and attaining the answers I sought. He searched my expression, and I hoped he saw bravery. "Yes," I uttered, but as the word floated between us, I silently beseeched the heavens for guidance.

"Can I see your necklace?"

"Follow me."

In my bedroom, we passed my desk, cluttered with vials, pipettes, and trial fragrances.

We strode to my whitewashed wooden dresser, where delicate perfume bottles were neatly arranged atop it; a curated collection of Pacific scents alongside my own carefully crafted creations.

In the bottom drawer, like a dog who buried a bone, I stashed the pistol next to a few treasures. I touched the gun's cool steel. I had plunged into an exotic environment of espionage; I was absolutely in over my head. Was Uzziah brazen enough to assault or kidnap me in a public place? Doubt it. But in the end, only Uzziah knew the truth about my family. What if I had a sister? I'd always wanted a sibling. What if she couldn't see color? This could be a blessing. I wouldn't be alone. My feelings cycloned. Identifying my genealogy wouldn't change my future, merely put a lid on my past and help me understand my true identity.

I pushed the gun aside and my gaze landed on the metal origami manatee Fritz molded for me after our spring break trip to Florida. I threw most of the silly origami creatures in the garbage after he left. Quinbe swore if I threw this one away she'd rescue it and place it next to the German Shepard keepsake he had molded her. But secretly, nostalgia resisted sending this one to live in some landfill. Gloom gurgled in my belly. Everything changed when Fritz left.

An opera-length silver chain glinted. A cross-shaped pendant embedded with three blue stones was the sole object connecting me to my shadowed heritage. Within the blue stones, black flakes swirled like a sinister snow globe. The necklace's filigree pattern looped into outstretched wings. As a child, wearing it brought me comfort, a sliver of false faith for my parents' reemergence. After years of waiting, their hazy faces became gray, hooded ghosts slinking through my thoughts, haunting me. I relinquished the pendant into Raiden's palm, and my optimism went with it.

He admired it, then snapped a quick picture. "Wear this necklace to the auction." A subtle demand rippled beneath his tone.

Raiden placed the necklace in my palm, then directed his attention to the line of perfume bottles atop my dresser. His fingers brushed along the row of perfumes before he carefully selected a circular one. "Did you create this?" His tone told of intrigue as he uncapped it with a soft twist, then sniffed.

"Yes. *Pacific Paradise*. 2025 Spring Collection."

He lifted an eyebrow. "But it's not your favorite."

I tilted my head slightly. "What makes you think that?" He was correct, but it was *this* scent that caught Ms. Voss's discerning eye. She crowned my fragrance the defining note of the collection: the first time my scent was chosen.

A slow, knowing smile curved across his mouth. "It's too sweet, too fun. You're stronger. I bet you keep that part of yourself hidden at work. Am I wrong?"

It was his job to see beyond the surface of a person. But did I want him to notice all the pieces I kept carefully tucked away? It left me exposed in the most thrilling way.

I drew a slow breath, torn between the loyalty I owed my job and what I could admit. "When you work for a company, you don't get the freedom… you make what sells."

He took my wrist, his thumb brushing the delicate skin, then inhaled. His nostrils flared and his eyes closed, as if he were lost in my scent, savoring a pleasure only he could appreciate. His warm breath ignited a tingling sensation that spread like wildfire, making me acutely aware of every nerve ending. "Now, this is you. Your own creation."

Suddenly, a loud clunk interrupted the moment, and I whipped around.

A glaring Graysen sat stiffly on my desk, emitting a low, drawn-out grumble, a warning she was watching.

Always watching.

Her paw rose slowly into the air, and with a swoosh, she knocked another perfume bottle from the desk to the floor.

She did that on purpose!

My front door rattled. I wrapped the necklace in the cloth and shut the drawer.

A metallic chink sounded, and the deadbolt unlocked.

A giggling Quinbe walked through. When she laughed, men cocked their heads in her direction. Her velvety siren song exuded vitality and zest, and that was what Raiden did, his eyes brightened as he turned to look.

Great. Just great.

I swallowed my annoyance and inclined my head toward the living room, a cue for him to follow.

Quinbe dropped her key into her black clutch, the faux leather contrasting stylishly with her wrap sundress. The delicate lace of her ballet flats spiraled around her slender ankles like ribbons adorning a Maypole, adding a touch of ethereal charm to her pearl complexion. Quinbe slid her sunglasses onto her head, revealing doe-like eyes that perfectly matched the soft roundness of her face. "Hey girl hey." She pulled a small suitcase behind her. Delighted shock rippled across her features as she looked from me to Raiden. "Sorry, I'm early. Am I interrupting?"

I quickly recounted how Raiden and I met, condensing the chaos into small digestible parts. Quinbe's brows lifted as she listened. I finished my story with the diluted lavender oil mystery, deliberately skipping the part about my thieving father roaming the streets.

"*You're* an everyday hero." Her eyes shone with admiration.

"Hardly a hero." Raiden chuckled, and joy lit his features. "Just in the right place at the right time."

My fingers flexed. Was my rapid pulse from envy or protectiveness of Quinbe? Did I wish to receive his attention instead of her? The steely line of his jaw was impossible to ignore, yet an aberrant aura of danger hung around him.

The front door swung open, and I jumped. Nyxon, typing furiously, strode toward her room. "The teachers' picket line was enlightening. The district's offering a mere 2% raise. Insufferable bastards."

"Meoooow!" Graysen screeched. "Mewrue!"

Nyxon looked up, taking us all in.

Graysen crowed complaints until Nyxon picked her up. Graysen nuzzled Nyxon's neck, as though she shared a secret.

I huffed. I fed the big beast, and what did I get in return? Not much. I straightened and said, "This is my friend Raiden. He stopped by to say hi."

Nyxon always carried herself with a sense of alertness, her mind primed for swift assessments, and today was no exception. "Men who drop by without an invitation wave red flags for future stalking behaviors." Graysen purred contentedly under Nyxon's smooth strokes, seemingly enjoying Nyxon's reproach of Raiden.

I softened my tone to balance Nyxon's bluntness, "She's joking."

She squared her shoulders to her towering six-foot height. *Oh no.* She was going to correct me. Please, for the love of everything, do not scare Raiden away.

Nyxon was like Graysen slow to trust, slower to let anyone in.

Poised with the quiet authority of a woman from India, she commanded attention as she began her monologue, "There are over seven-million stalking victims annually. I don't joke about safety or crime stats." Nyxon's dark eyes bore into Raiden, he tensed under her scrutiny, swallowing hard. "Does your friend Raiden have a last name?"

"Graví," I volunteered.

Raiden checked his classic black watch. "I need to get going. Nice meeting everyone."

Quinbe expressed a heartfelt goodbye and implored him to visit soon. Nyxon just strode with Graysen into her room to pack for our beach trip.

I walked Raiden to the door.

"I'll text you the Auction's details. 7 p.m. Wednesday." He stepped toward the front door, and I followed. "The event is semi-formal."

"I'll dust off a dress and meet you there."

"I can't wait." A mischief glint shone in his eyes, and a playful smirk tugged at his lips.

I shut the door, pressed my spine against it, and sighed. Crushing on him was an awful idea. He probably had a badass, leather jacket wearing girlfriend. Despite everything, a restless flutter moved through me, like a dove against the bars of a rusty cage.

"You didn't mention Raiden was *adorably handsome*," Quinbe teased.

"It was dark," I mumbled, "and raining." Before she could interrogate me further I took control of the conversation, "What color is your dress?"

"This old thing." She strummed the elastic spaghetti strap, and it snapped against her skin. "It's forest green."

I imagined her: eyes and dress the color of clovers, locks and lips the color of currants, and skin and shoes the color of cotton.

Quinbe draped her thick curls over one shoulder, letting them fall below her small breasts.

Red must be an alluring color because men always fidgeted with her springy spirals. With an intimidating stare and a modern A-line haircut, I'd never seen a man stroke Nyxon's strands.

"That yellow dress looks great on you. Yellow is definitely your color."

"I'll take your word for it."

Quinbe drummed her manicured nails on her cup.

I bet the nail color was pink. She always celebrated spring with pink.

Quinbe's grin grew, copying a cat that had enjoyed too much catnip. "Are you two *sleeping* together?"

I scurried to the kitchen and grabbed my latte. "No."

"I walk in and you two are leaving your room looking flustered."

Nyxon dropped a duffel bag by the front door. "He's not her type."

Nyxon was right. I'm attracted to good-guys you invite to Sunday BBQs. Snuggle, eat buttery popcorn, and watch movies with. Raiden appeared carefree. On the weekends, he probably rock climbed, then partied at the club. I was a stickler for the rules, he broke them. And if his bare office was any indication of his ability to commit to someone, he didn't dream of planting roots anytime soon.

"Gray didn't like him," Nyxon added.

Quinbe opened the fridge and selected the OJ bottle. "The brainiac Nyxon takes dating advice from a cat?"

I smirked. "What does Raiden look like? You know, his colors?"

"He has brown eyes, brown skin, black hair, *capisce*," Nyxon deadpanned.

Quinbe shook her head and crooned, "He doesn't have brown eyes. Raiden has these amazing hazel eyes. Like honey and whiskey. Trusting, sincere eyes." She paused, tilting her head in contemplation. "You know? When he saw me, I swear he looked relieved to see me. Like he knew me."

I swallowed a lump in my throat. Because he's been watching us from the shadows.

"*And* his complexion isn't brown, it's olive. Maybe he's Italian and African. But Nyxon got his hair color correct."

I frowned. The color olive escaped my memory.

"I say leap off your couch and ask him on a date." Quinbe raised her glass to me.

My coworker Tiffany's statement fluttered in my chest: "I'm sure love will find a way."

Nyxon chuckled. "Did Quinbe put *whiskey* in your coffee? Because you *must* be drunk."

I sipped the latte Raiden bought me. It was perfect. Vanilla matcha latte with oat milk. Exactly what I would've ordered.

✦

Wednesday, 6:00 p.m., and Fritz still hadn't contacted me.

I stood in front of my full-length mirror and twisted my fertorium necklace around my finger.

No text.

I tugged the hem of my black knee-length dress.

No email.

Why was I surprised? Ghosting someone was Fritz's modus operandi. A deflated feeling pulled on my shoulders; he wasn't into me and we'd never be friends. At least going with Raiden to the auction tonight will fill my time.

Just then my phone buzzed with a text from an unknown number:

Avi, I can't stop thinking about you. I was such an idiot. Can we have dinner at my place tonight at 7? I promise to tell you the truth, to tell you everything. Yours, Fritz.

My heart stumbled in its rhythm as cold shock coursed through me. I read the text again.

The phone wobbled in my trembling grip, slipping, I snatched it just before it teetered free.

If I went to Fritz's tonight, he'd be waiting on the front porch of his white farmhouse. His eyes a little watery as he took my hand, our fingers fitting together like they always had. Then we would recline on the porch swing, gazing out over the apple orchard and rows of grapevines. He once dreamed of filling the red barn with apple crates and wine barrels, running his own farm stand, until his mother's ambition got in the way.

Nostalgia lifted me like helium, weightless, untethered from the past and future.

But I caught my reflection in the mirror and my smile faded. The sleek dress I bought on Monday, a day brimming with excitement, was now a cruel reminder of my commitment to Raiden. The onyx sequins lining the neckline and pooling at the hem had lost their luster, dulled by guilt.

But Raiden came this far without me, if I go to that auction, I'd be an alien in Raiden's world of elegance and artifice. I'd just get in his way.

I blinked, taken aback by my quick willingness to accept Fritz's invitation and tear up my prearranged plans. An inner yearning tugged at me, whimpering I couldn't miss this opportunity to reconnect with Fritz. After Fritz left, every day was a battle between wanting to forget him and still hoping he'd return. I focused on everything but him, throwing myself into work. I had days, then weeks, when I didn't think of him. Yet, like today, memories of his caressing fingers, the softness of his lips, the weight of his body against mine, sent a tingling flush across my cheeks.

But Raiden's past plea cut through the haze: "I need your help." And I owed Ms. Voss everything. I couldn't let Michael and the mystery woman ruin her company.

But could I really let the chance to reconnect with Fritz pass me by?

Chapter 8

Moments ago, warm thoughts of Fritz, his smile and laughter, flooded my mind. Fritz promised we'd locate my parents together. But each vow he gave was a grain of sand tumbling into the bottom of an hourglass, leaving only emptiness behind. I needed to understand why my parents left and confront harsh truths without Fritz's guidance. This auction symbolized the first falling domino. Sellow's capture would lead to Uzziah's arrest, providing me with clues to find my mother. Was her last name Neehow?

My fingers hovered over a rejection text to Fritz, but a rewarding feeling of spite, a bitterness I was unfamiliar with, escaped my lips as a chuckle. I'd leave Fritz wondering if I'd show. I'd leave him wondering where I was. I'd leave him wondering why I hadn't called. Just like he did to me.

The cab driver whisked me from the concrete jungle across the Confluence Land Bridge, transporting me to a landscape where past centuries converged. This thirty-three-acre historic site boasted barracks, battle stations, and an officer's row of grand, white, columned houses with wraparound porches and balconies.

My heels struck the pavement, creating a confident cadence. I embodied this facade, even though anxiety and doubt threatened to slow my stride. I fiddled with my sleek, low ponytail that cloaked one shoulder. Massive hydrangeas pom-pommed in greeting, their sweet scent wisped around me. A communal garden offered a glimpse into Vancouver's rich agriculture history. Buzzing bumble bees bounced from lemon balm, bearberry, and borage. Beans began their lattice climb. Corn sprouted in uniformed rows.

From behind, a high flirtatious whistle roused my attention.

A dry male voice said, "Well, well. Where you goin' all dressed up?"

I recognized that impassive tone, and as I turned around, I braced for the cut that always followed.

Li's cinder-block shoulders shadowed me. His black complexion gleamed halo-like against the backdrop of the sun. But I knew better, he was no angel. He circled me, his steps were casual, rock star-like, projecting a power that came from an innate sense of self-assurance. His figure-hugging button-up shirt, leather jacket, and slim-fit pants screamed sex. His air of authority was further underlined by his icy eyes that kissed at the corners. If men and women didn't swoon over him, they'd challenge his visual caress with envy, and lose. But there was no attraction, no love between us. After Fritz left, he vanished, too. I thought we were friends, but I was merely Fritz's accessory.

"A friend invited me to a jewelry auction at Fort Vancouver."

"You're lookin' pretty polished for someone about to stomp through the dirt. Lemme guess. This is one of those times you're, like, hopin' it's a date, but he's already put you firmly in the friend zone?" His voice dripped with that signature arrogance he always saved for me.

"No." My body shrank in on itself and I squeezed my black handbag. "It's a semi-formal event." Li scanned the streets, half listening. "What are you doing here?" I straightened my shoulders, but my question caught in my throat.

"Drinks, dinner, the usual."

His voice was so monotone, why did he prolong our interaction? "I'm running late. I have to go." But for some odd reason my feet didn't move, as if I waited for him to excuse me.

"See you around." The side of his mouth twisted into a smirk. "By the way, one of your diamond earring studs is blue, and the other is purple."

Damn. I scrambled to remove the stones as Li strutted away. My eyes watered. Feeling exposed, I tugged strands of hair from my ponytail to cover my naked ears. A rush of vulnerability, a deep helplessness, welled within me for not seeing colors like everyone else.

How humiliating, showing up to a jewelry auction with no jewelry! Hopefully, Raiden wouldn't notice, but a hollowness in my chest grew with each slow step.

I pulled out my phone and texted Raiden: I'm here.

Before I could put my phone away, it buzzed with his reply: That purse doesn't look big enough to hold a gun.

I spun, looking left then right, but he was nowhere in sight. I texted a reply: Why would I need a gun when I have you and pepper spray to keep the bad guys away?

Suddenly, the crowd parted and he walked through. His gaze moved with unnerving thoroughness over my body, sending a maddening shiver down my spine, as I prayed for his approval. Every second dragged until his lips curved into a smoldering smile, and like striking a match his stare blazed. He had never looked at me this way, more possessive than playful.

His tailored black blazer fit snugly to his body. His rolled up sleeves revealed thick forearms. I'm sure if I could see color he'd be worth his weight in old Italian gold. His pants match the blazer's cuffs, a color I couldn't identify. His slicked-back hair gave his sharp jawbone even more eye-catching depth, and I imagined the stubble scratching my inner thigh. My throat tensed. He was cool and scorching all at once. Suddenly, my little black dress belonged at an eighth-grade dance, not here. Not next to him.

He stepped closer. Tonight, his cologne was unmistakable. Rich and spicy. A warning to women that a rendezvous with him would be a night to remember.

"You look beautiful," his voice was smooth. He reached out, his knuckles brushed my breastbone as he prudently placed the pendant in his palm. The cross-shaped pendant embedded with three fertorium stones filled the space of his hand. Within the stones, black flakes swirled on a sea of blue, like ash from a forest fire whipping across a lake. The necklace's filigree pattern appeared delicate compared to his calloused palm. "When you walk into that auction no one will be able to take their eyes off you."

A lightness undulated in my abdomen, and I forced my fidgeting fingers to still as he led the way forward.

Flowering quince trees, smelling like a cross between apple and pear, lined the cobblestone path. In the town square, couples linked hands, and friends leaned into each other, as they waited in line, ten deep for a chance to taste old-world meats.

Many visitors were ready for a picnic, carrying a blanket, a basket, and a raffia-tied bottle of wine. The clinking of glasses and scraping of cutlery mixed with fiddle players' melody from the bandstand.

"The auction is inside the fort." He pointed into the distance where the wildflowers ended and a dry treeless plain began.

Fort Vancouver's wooden walls cast an intimidating shadow over the market. Within the three-story bastion tower, two suit-wearing guards with binoculars scoured their surroundings. The massive wooden doors were swung open, but a velvet rope restricted admission. Signage promoted *VIP Auction* passage only.

A skinny, snobby, clipboard-toting woman with a pointy nose and a heavily hairsprayed bun motioned with two manicured fingernails to the Polynesian bouncer. He was a gray-suited mountain of a man, with long dark hair loosely tied at his nape. He unclipped the rope, allowing a stoic Asian couple, dressed to the nines, to pass. Opulent treasures weighed down her wrists. Her collarbone was a sea of pearls.

Raiden pressed a hand to my lower back. "We have two hours before the auction starts. Let's survey the grounds and visit the vendors to see if anyone inquires about your necklace."

Reenactors in 1840s attire whittled wood, tanned hides, and hammered horseshoes amid the scent of woodsmoke. Women wore bonnets and patterned dresses with bell-shaped skirts. The fabric swished as they promenaded, their excited chatter mingled with birdsong. Together Raiden and I discovered tales of conflict and community. During a grand reenactment, Ilchee, a tribal princess, declined a commander's courtship. Her stunning beaded dress mesmerized the audience. But via my eyes, gray colors left me yearning for more.

"Raiden, um." I bit my lip and immediately wished I could rewind five seconds. "Never mind."

"What's wrong?"

His eyes searched mine as my gaze flicked between the reenactment and his face. "Could you describe their costumes? The colors."

The creases on his forehead relaxed. He pulled me into a side embrace to whisper, "Her copper bracelets represent wealth and power. Blue beads line the hem of her dress and collar. Red and black beads ornate her moccasins. She was a woman who rowed her own canoe."

Raiden clasped my hand. A jolt raced past my wrist and up my arm, twisting and stopping at my elbow, not daring to travel further.

He ushered me to the idyllic Traders Row. Canvas tents cracked above merchants. Walking sticks carved with ivy vines leaned against woven baskets. My stomach rumbled at the sight of golden fry bread and jars filled with jam. He pointed to a clay water pitcher and cup set. "This artist favors ocean colors. Navy at the bottom and greens towards the top. Oh, and over here." He pulled me toward a rack of dresses. "These are like a sunset. Reds and oranges." He turned to a spinning rack of embroidered bags. "The beaded roses are yellow and the tulips are pink."

I covered a chuckle with my hand. Via his vibrant narrative, I grew to enjoy his quick wit and realized his charm went beyond his coy grin. He had an air of mystery about him, causing my curiosity to swell with each passing glance. Getting to know him wouldn't be terrible.

Each time a vendor solicited my attention, my nerves spiked, only to settle again when their focus stayed on selling their arts and crafts, not what weighed heavy around my neck.

Under the shade of the bandstand, an all-male quartet, composed of a fiddle player, a trumpeter, and a drummer, produced a swing-dancing beat.

I froze.

Li sat on a picnic bench smirking. Peacocking, with his elbows resting atop the table. And he wasn't alone.

Nyxon sat across from him. Her sleek A-line haircut and dark, cat-shaped eyes warned others not to get too close. She paired a black crop top featuring a chain link halter neck with high waisted black capris that showed off toned calves. With crossed legs, her black ankle boot bounced to the beat. She floated me a flirty wave as Li jumped off the table and disappeared into the crowd.

My eyebrows rose as I half-heartedly returned the gesture. She shouldn't be here. I glanced at Raiden. He was bargaining with a vendor over a pocketknife. Nyxon wasn't a history buff or Saturday market kind of girl; she'd rather drink whiskey and play poker at Alejandro's Cigar Lounge.

My phone buzzed with a text from her: If I knew you were going out with Raiden, I would've given you the results from his background check beforehand.

Annoyance threatened to smudge Raiden's and my outing like an oil spill.

I shoved my phone into my purse. When it beeped again, I ignored it.

Raiden appeared by my side. "Ready to go inside the fort?"

"We better, Nyxon's here. I'm afraid she'll race over and ask questions." I rubbed my arm to fight the chill from a breeze. Raiden stepped in front of me and slipped off his blazer. He wrapped it around my shoulders. His hands tugged the collar shut, then lingered near my throat. With his face so close, my eyes darted to his lips. As if sensing my gaze, his hand brushed softly against my cheek.

"Hey, you two," Nyxon shouted as she bounded toward us. Raiden jerked his hand away.

"Hi," we said in unison, our matching nervous tones betraying our true feelings.

Nyxon raised an eyebrow. "Join us for a drink at our table." From under her shirt, Nyxon produced a Rue belt-wallet. She pulled out a fifty-dollar bill, then planted it onto Raiden's chest. "Be a dear, go stand with Li in the beer line and give him this. First round on me."

Raiden's eye twitched as he took the bill and crinkled it into his palm.

My brow furrowed. "We don't have time. The auction starts soon." I plucked the bill from Raiden's hand then extended it to her between two fingers.

She didn't reach for the money. "Aha, so that's why you look gorgeous."

Heat warmed my cheeks. My fingers curled around the bill as my hand dropped.

"You're leaving us poor peasants for the opulence of the fort," she teased. "Those events never start on time. And if they do, you have to sit through the customary introductions and acknowledgements of the donors. Come on, one drink."

My gaze shifted between Raiden and the growing beer line.

Would Li relay to Fritz I was out tonight? A quiet anticipation stirred within me as I imagined Fritz's shocked reaction. I hope jealousy punches Fritz in the gut. Nyxon would say I was being petty, Quinbe would cheer me on.

Raiden caught the flicker of indecision in my eyes, and with an easy smile, said, "I'll go help Li. But, drinks are on me."

"Handsome and generous. So to find a man in this city a woman has to fight off a mugger."

I bit back a laugh.

Nyxon linked arms with me. "Dark beer for me. Pale ale for Avi."

Raiden eyed me for confirmation and I nodded.

As Raiden walked toward the beer tent, Nyxon leaned into my ear and whispered, "Nice necklace. *Be careful,* wearing a piece like that in public could attract the wrong kind of attention."

I protectively closed my fingers around the pendant. The hair on my nape prickled. Did she know? Definitely not, impossible.

She steered me left, into a booth with a spinning rack of glass earrings.

"We need to talk about Raiden," Nyxon said sternly.

I slipped from her grip with a huff and spun the jewelry rack, wishing Raiden was here to describe their colors. "You have one minute."

"The background check didn't find anything."

"Good. Then he meets your standards."

"No, I mean. He's never gotten a speeding ticket, a jury summons, nothing. In fact, four months ago, he applied for a driver's license for the first time ever." Nyxon held an inquisitive stare, taking in every detail of my reaction.

"I think he worked overseas before moving here." I kept my expression neutral despite the sweat glistening on my brow. She was a bloodhound on the hunt for secrets, and she knew I guarded a prize worth uncovering. *Should I come clean? She'd demand to be involved.* I pride myself on honesty, but I wouldn't divulge information that could invite trouble to her door.

I gulped. *Act casual.*

I strode to the next stall and Nyxon followed.

"The address on his driver's license is his office building. He sublets the space from someone named Bashiri Nova. *And* Raiden has no social media accounts, no college transcripts, zippo."

"Wow, Nyxon, you outdid yourself. Do you interrogate the men you go out with?"

"Yes. So, what did you learn on your date?"

"It's *not* a date. We're just hanging out. We chatted about his travels abroad. We both love croissants." I tilted my head. "*Wait.* Why are *you* here?"

She rubbed her neck. "I'm here because of Allison."

My brow furrowed.

From her back pocket she unfolded a missing person flier. Allison Tangland. Blonde wavy hair. Bright green eyes. Thirty-years-old. "Allison was last seen at the Woodlandia Tulip Festival. Dancing to *that band's* set." She pointed at the musicians strumming and pounding away. "A witness saw three men stuffing Allison into a box truck that looks eerily similar to the band's truck for transporting their instruments."

I spun to observe the portly, perspiring fifty-year-old men, their faces glistening under the setting sun.

"I plan to ask the band a few questions after their set."

I took Nyxon's hand. "The last thing I want is for you to waste your time worrying about me. You have more important things to do." Nyxon read this truth in the way my eyes shone and how my brow softened.

We strolled in silence to the next booth. Allison's disappearance was a stark reminder of how fragile life was, how quickly joy could turn to despair, and how missing someone could leave us feeling powerless.

A woman slowly stood from a rickety wooden stool, her eyes gleaming with a grandmother's kindness. Wrinkles lined her face like creases in old parchment. Her black, cotton dress skimmed cracked leather loafers. Nyxon slid the flyer into her pocket. The woman offered Nyxon a leather bracelet to admire. I seized the moment to slink inside the tent, grateful to avoid more of Nyxon's inquisition.

Inside, a nostalgic aroma of life and earth, like roses and sun-tea, engulfed me. Dresses hung from racks and fluttered from the canopy's rafters.

Suddenly, a rustling from behind. As I turned, a black-gloved hand clamped over my mouth. My nostrils flared. Shock hit me like an earthquake, jarring and jolting, shaking me to my core. A man's chest slammed into my back. An arm wrapped around me, lifted me off my feet, and dragged me past a rack of clothing. I thrashed, swinging my shoulders in a feeble attempt to knock dresses to the ground, but I was yanked out the rear of the tent in under twenty-seconds.

To my right and left, rows of plastic crates, stacked six-feet-high shielded us from view. Ahead lay the vendor's parking lot, filled with cargo vans and box trucks. He dropped me on my feet and I stomped hard on his shoe. He grunted. My teeth sank into the gloved fingers, but the leather held firm, impervious to my bite. I shook my head like a pit bull, a growl rising in my throat. Adrenaline rattled my entire body.

His vice-like grip around my arms pinned my hands to my sides, cutting off circulation and sending pain and tingling across every nerve.

Another assailant emerged from behind a stack of plastic crates. His gaunt cheeks and pale skin gave him a sickly look. His long, rounded chin had a central dimple that gave him a warlock-like air. A gelled comb-over exaggerated his high forehead. He pulled down his KN95 mask.

I gasped.

His snubbed, rabbit resembling nose twitched faster than my racing heart. This was wrong. This couldn't be real. But the hallucination remained.

I slipped one arm free and reached above my head to scratch the man holding me. My fingers found hair and a hat. I yanked, but there was no tension. Instead, a black wig, with a black baseball hat flew through the air and landed in the dirt.

The rabbit-nosed assailant grabbed my throat, the man behind me removed his hand from my mouth, but before I could scream, the mugger shoved a stained, white rag into my mouth, stuffing my cheeks, muffling my cry.

I gagged and shook my head, trying to dislodge the filthy cloth. I moved it with my tongue and grit crunched between my teeth, vomit threatened to choke my airway. My attacker looped a rope over my head and bridled the rag between my lips. The coarse rope grated against the corners of my mouth, creating a sandpaper-like hiss of friction, a rawness that sliced my skin. The thick rope reeked of fish and hints of diesel. My molars sank deep into the frayed fibers. A tang of brine assaulted my taste buds and a foul stew of scents that solely sprung from sailing the sea.

I kicked my legs into the body behind me. A zip-tie click-clicked, the hard plastic constricting, digging into my wrists as they secured my arms behind my back. Desperate tears blurred my vision as I wailed into the rag and squirmed like a wild animal.

The man squeezed my throat. "Nice work, Ellis."

Ellis unlocked his vice grip around my body and fetched his toupee and hat.

The man lifted me onto my tiptoes. My nose flared for air.

The wig wearing lackey restored his toupee upon his shiny cue ball head, then crossed his arms. When he turned to us, I blinked. Ellis was not a he but a she.

A strange bright puppy-like excitement lit her eyes, as she waited for praise from her master following a job well done.

A numbness ran down my spine.

No eyebrows, no lashes, no hair covered her body. Her upturned nose was too small and narrow for her round face. She uncrossed her arms, and my eyes widened. Her forearms were unusually long, with fingers that dangled down to her knees. While her wide-reaching arms gave her a distinctive silhouette, they lacked the muscular bulk of a bodybuilder, creating a spider-like dexterity.

His nose and her hands caused my world to tilt just enough to distort my reality, revealing the disturbing undercurrent of the supernatural, the freakish, the unbelievable.

Chapter 9

The man pushed his rabbit nose into my hair then dragged his wet lips down my neck, leaving a slug-like slime trail. I thrashed, but he squeezed my neck tighter. I wheezed for any wisp of air.

"Oh, yes," he panted into my ear, his hot breath dripped off my skin like inescapable humidity, "the Doctor will enjoy you."

Over his shoulder, a box truck crept down the service entrance.

If I could get their attention!

The box truck parked fifty yards away. Two men, medium height and build, dressed in black shirts and jeans, jumped out, their black combat boots thumped the ground. Their keen eyes surveyed the area and spotted me. Pure joy exploded through me, and the rag muffled a triumphant laugh.

The man gave no hint of alarm, his twitching nose maintaining its rhythm.

My gloating tasted bitter on my tongue.

The two men by the truck placed black logo-less baseball caps on their shaved heads. My attacker raised his hand, then gave them a beckoning wave. They mechanically hoisted an eight-foot-long rolled-up rug with frayed edges from the truck's floor onto their shoulders. Dark stains splattered the carpet's cream-colored underside. How many victims had they wrapped within the carpet? The victims' skin scraped against its thick fibers, their lungs compressed, barely able to breathe. An intense terror, a claustrophobic anxiety squeezed me from all sides.

The band's loud drumming beat in my ears.

Think! Think!

The men carrying the rug were only fifty yards away. What would Nyxon do? I couldn't throw elbows. Couldn't sink my teeth into him. He dodged my kick. Suddenly, it came to me, like a light bulb bursting its glass: my last resort. My knees buckled, and I hit the ground, rolling onto my back, becoming dead weight.

They stared, dumbstruck. I lifted my heels and kicked the air. I'd maximize my weight and land a heel strike to someone's chin.

The man's face twisted into a loathing expression. "Dumb bitch." He grabbed my right ankle, his grip bruising skin.

I pulled my knees in and drove my heel into his stomach. The impact knocked the breath out of him. Staggering backward, he folded in on himself and planted his hands on his knees.

Ellis rushed to him and rested her hand on his shoulder, which he batted away.

A torrent of triumph charred all thoughts of raising my inner white flag. I did it! Nyxon's fiercely, proud smile blazed in my imagination, solidifying a boldness within me, so I twisted left, slamming my feet into a stack of plastic crates. The top box fell and cracked on the ground. I kicked another stack and two more toppled over.

The old woman angrily croaked, "What's going on back there?"

Ellis sneered and spread her fingers wide, poised to lunge at me.

"Hey asshole," Nyxon said, low and cutting. She sat her beer on the ground at the end of the row of tents, yards away from me. She pulled a switchblade from her boot and flipped it open with a click.

I kicked one more box, and when it hit the ground, the bang was like the firing of a starting gun for a track meet. Nyxon sprinted toward us.

The men carrying the rug abruptly switched direction and retreated. The earth seemed to quake under Nyxon's long, powerful stride.

The box truck sped off, leaving the man and Ellis behind. They scrambled down the line of tents, chasing after it. Bolting into the crowd, knocking over anyone in their way. Nyxon closed the distance between us, but she didn't slow, instead she high-jumped over me.

"Really, Nyxon! Are you serious?" The cloth muffled my tirade of complaints. I pounded my heels on the ground and lashed out at the earth beneath me.

"Raiden, help Avi!" Nyxon ordered from over her shoulder.

Raiden turned the corner, a beer in each hand. His eyes widened when he spotted me in the dirt. On impulse, his hands opened, the plastic beer cup hit the ground, the brew splashed skyward like a bubbling volcano.

My body didn't relax until he knelt beside me. He whipped out his new pocketknife. The shiny blade furiously sawed the rope near my ear. The rope fell away and he ripped the rag from my mouth. I spit, then gasped for air as the first hint of rain hit my cheek.

He cut the zip ties with quick movements. I shook out my hands. Dark abrasions ringed my wrists.

Raiden cupped my cheeks. "Are you okay? What happened?"

I leaned into his chest and the beating of his heart quickened. "The mugger! He *didn't* have a normal nose!"

He wiped away the droplet, guilt flickering across his face. "I, I."

"He was after me," I choked on my words. "He didn't glance at the necklace."

"I'm getting you out of here." He prepared to scoop me up, but just before his arms could close around me, I twisted and wriggled free.

"I'm not broken." My dress was torn at the knee. My ponytail, once sleek, had twisted into a tangled mess. Dirt streaked Raiden's jacket. My legs were caked in grime, but they could carry me.

I slipped off my heels, opting for barefoot stability. Passersby would assume I was just another tipsy girl.

He gripped my arm and guided me to my feet. I swayed slightly, but he steadied me. His fingers intertwined into mine becoming a physical anchor in the chaos.

He led me through the crowds, across streets, never letting go until he opened his Dodge Charger's door and I slid inside.

I leaned against the car's window, a feeble barrier against the pandemonium trailing us. My legs throbbed with an insistent itch to keep running.

"Where are we going?" I stammered.

Sweat beaded Raiden's brow as he gripped the steering wheel. "To my office. But I'm parking a few blocks away in case someone follows us. I have sensitive files inside my office that I need to safeguard." He flipped the wipers on high to erase the rain, but their fast tempo was too much for the small drops and the blades screeched across the windshield. "We'll call Nyxon from there." He hit the gas, lurching us forward.

I tugged my seat belt to loosen its choke hold.

At each stoplight Raiden checked the rearview mirror. I held my breath every time a car followed us for more than a block.

My knee bounced. He placed a hand on it. His touch brought a welcome calm, but his eyes warned the respite was fleeting.

When we reached the last stoplight, Raiden checked both directions before speeding through the red light.

I clenched the leather seat.

He skidded into the parking garage. Cars and SUVs filled the spaces. We circled and circled, passing concrete pillars until we swerved into a spot.

Not built for cloak-and-dagger games, I stayed stone still. What I'd just seen? His nose. Her arms. It wasn't right. Not even close.

Raiden stepped out and circled to my side, opening the door with quiet care. He gently squeezed my shoulders, sensing my hesitation. I clutched my shoes and angled my knees toward him.

His hand traveled down my arm as he kneeled, taking my shoes from me. Then those same strong fingers found my foot. They were surprisingly gentle, tracing slow, circles into the aching sole, then working skillfully over my arch. The warmth of his touch spread through me and my pulse slowed.

His massage crept upward, wiping away any traces of dirt. Every nerve in my body stirred, awakened. His hands lingered at my calf, expertly kneading, melting away all traces of tension.

He took my other shoe and presented it near my toes for me to step into.

I dipped my toes into my shoe.

He pressed his thumb against a small cut on my ankle. His hands glided up my calf. His touch was the cure for all my stress and worries. When his hand reached my knee, and continued to glide up my thigh, a sensation akin to a wildfire coursed through me, setting ablaze every fiber. His fingers paused at the top of my inner thigh, a place no man had touched in a very, very *long* time. My breath quickened.

Tires squealed. My eyes widened. Raiden grabbed my hand and drew me up into his body. "Those stairs lead to the street." His breath brushed my ear. "Ready?"

I straightened myself. "Yes."

Fingers laced with mine, he led me cautiously as if letting go would break the bond between us. The buzzing fluorescent lights flickered, casting our reaper-like shadows across the walls. Car exhaust saturated the air.

His gaze retraced our path. I followed his line of sight, scanning the parking garage with renewed vigilance. Caution coiled within me.

We descended the stairs, breath coming in shallow pants.

At the landing, Raiden stepped in front of me. Our eyes locked, fear mirroring fear. He plucked a twig from my tangled hair. Then his thumb wiped a smudge from my cheek, causing my heart to stutter.

"Go left toward my building. I'll follow a block behind and watch for anyone tailing you. Okay?"

I wanted to say, *"No. Stay by my side,"* but my words caught in my throat, trapped between terror and humiliating cowardice, so instead, I simply nodded. Instantly, the ache of regret filled me. I'd be walking the dark street alone. My knees shook, it'd be easy to crumble into Raiden's chest and beg him to keep me safe.

A breeze coaxed Raiden to move. He stepped out, scanned the area, then gestured for me to proceed.

On any other day, I could ignore the rain, but tonight I cursed the clouds. No birds sang. No brave umbrella toting tourists. No bar lines. The closed bike shop and empty thrift store created a ghost town tableau. The crisp wind nipped my skin. A thousand thoughts cycloned through me, but the rain drowned out all but one: I liked Raiden's hands on me.

I turned right, two blocks to go. The whipping wind was a breeze compared to the thunderstorm churning inside me. I flexed my fingers, wishing to hold Raiden's hand. Did Nyxon catch the mugger? My heels splashed into a puddle and the cheerful sound they made earlier tonight belonged to a stranger.

I veered left, plunging into Raiden's alley, step after step echoing off the brick walls. A hand landed on my shoulder. I jumped.

"All clear." His hand moved to my lower back, and I exhaled as he ushered me through the front door. But the bell didn't ring, it lay crushed in the middle of the floor.

The office door behind the secretary's desk swung open. The calendar's pages flapped with the created breeze. I clutched Raiden's arm as he pulled me close. His BattleBot charged us.

Raiden put out a hand as if halting a rabid Rottweiler. "Access code: zero, one, fourteen, eight-two. Stand down." The BattleBot emitted a whiny *beep bop* before the lights abruptly shut off.

I stood frozen, wide-eyed. He rubbed my back.

A short man peeked into the doorway. His dark, tapered hair was gelled backward. The tops of his ears folded over ever so slightly.

Raiden's shoulders relaxed. "Shit, Bashiri. What's going on?"

"Sellow was h-here!" Bashiri said meekly.

Fear resurfaced inside me, and I gripped Raiden's hand.

"Did-d what you t-taught. Activated b-bot." His voice cracked, "Marthane." Bashiri glared up at Raiden with round, close-set eyes. He dressed too rich and pretty for his twenty-something age. His tailored button-up shirt fit his stout five-foot-two frame snugly. A sweater draped over his shoulders and his sleeves were rolled up to mid-forearm. His silver belt buckle gleamed against his cream-colored pants, as if he had just left social hour at the country club. He side-eyed me, then grumbled at Raiden, "You shouldn't be *pulling* on th-that string."

"We'll talk *privately later*. We need to leave *now*. They'll be back." Raiden's fingers squeezed mine.

Bashiri grabbed Raiden's arm with short, chubby fingers, pulling us apart. "It can't wait-t." A small bead of perspiration ran down Bashiri's broad forehead. "They t-took boxes. They left behind…" He raised a fist to his lips.

Raiden's jaw clenched, a fortress against the onslaught of torrential thoughts. His eyes darted between Bashiri and me, hunting to find the right choice. "Avi, can I have a minute?"

I wanted to tell Raiden no, to stay with me, but the words lodged in my throat. They were stuck between what I wanted and what I knew were pathetic, childish anxieties. I was in his office, surrounded by safety and familiarity, yet the bell on the floor gave me pause.

I forced the sour, false words out, "It's fine." But it wasn't fine. Fear gnawed at me like a festering wound. I longed to be held close and protected, but at the same time, I hated my own weakness. With Raiden walking away, the chill from the rain seeped into my bones.

Bashiri snorted, not liking that Raiden had asked for my permission. He turned on his heels and trailed Raiden into his office. "I didn't know Sellow would take things this f-far. I'm an I.T. guy, not a s-spy. Neither of us can outwit her. Or outrun her m-minions—"

Raiden shut the door. The frosted window's glass silhouetted him as he sat behind his desk, and Bashiri paced in front of it.

I slipped out of Raiden's damp coat and slung it over the reception chair. The calendar wasn't empty anymore. Written in today's box: *Date with Avi.*

A flutter of giddy delight stole through me before I could stop it. He had called it a date. A date! My first instinct was to call Quinbe at once, to share the delicious news, but a prickle of lingering unease checked me, tugging me back to my senses. No. Nyxon first. Without question.

I unzipped my purse, pulled out my phone, and furiously texted Nyxon my location. Seconds turned into minutes. Why didn't she respond? A vine of vigilance knotted in my stomach. With each passing minute, a thorn of worry germinated, increasing my discomfort.

My knuckles whitened as I clutched the phone like a lifeline. My palms sweated as I texted again: Are you okay?

I tapped the phone against my leg. What if she was hurt? My phone slipped from my hand and clattered to the ground. Shit!

I squatted to pick it up but froze. Like a bread trail, dozens of small dark droplets led to the conference room. My forehead furrowed as I rubbed the damp droplet between my fingers, then brought them to my nose. A shudder coursed through me.

Metallic. Blood.

My lips pursed, and I stole a worried glance toward Raiden's office. Heated voices clashed beyond the walls. Were they fighting about what hid behind the conference room door? Should I pursue the blood trail or stay put? Haven't I risked enough for one day? Torn between courage and caution, indecision rooted me to the spot. What would Nyxon do?

Chapter 10

Nyxon would barge into that office and expect me at her heels. The thought earned a curse; I could never be as brave as her. But…

I had placed the camera in the storage room.

I had gone to the auction with Raiden.

I had fought off my attacker.

Suddenly, a surge of confidence filled me, nudging curiosity to win out over any faux pas of entering his personal space or fear.

I walked to the threshold and forced my trembling fingers to slowly twist the handle. Hinges groaned as I entered the rectangular room. My steps echoed off the chipped, century-old brick walls.

Three black rolling chairs were eerily arranged around the long, grainy table: one at the head, two on either side, as if poised for a gathering of villains. Four recessed lights spotlighted a stack of folders jumbled amid pens and legal pads scattered across the table. The trail of blood ended at a cardboard box on the floor near the far end of the table. As I stepped farther into the room, my fingertips brushed across the table's cold surface. The same journal sat on the table, adorned with a circular metal buckle. My fingers recoiled, as if possessed by an independent mind. I had already invaded his privacy by entering this room, opening the journal, reading his private thoughts, would be taking it too far.

Instead, I selected a folder labeled, *Contacts*. Inside was a photo of a dark-skinned teenage boy who stared blankly into the camera. His Afro couldn't hide his tufted ears stretching to a point at the top of his head, more cat-like than human, similar to Africa's desert caracal. A note written in cursive read: *Evobility: Catalyst. Informant states Uzziah hasn't been seen in two months.* Curiosity and disbelief churned within me because my eyes refused to blend the bizarre and unbelievable.

I flipped the page. A bald, pale man smiled menacingly into the camera, displaying needle-like fangs. *Evobility: Probedarth. Informant states the missing fertorium necklace is the key to winning the war against the human virus.*

My necklace? What did evobility mean? Curing sick humans? Or were humans the virus?

Next page. *Evobility: Servalina.* Her greasy blonde hair framed her gaunt face and sunken eyes. Both palms were directed towards the camera. Under her wrists, razor-sharp hawkbill blades sprouted, like dewclaws. These extra curved appendages allowed a swift, clean cut. *Released. Opportunity for confidential informant.*

What did this mean? Wonder and wariness wrenched me in opposite directions. *Did he interview people from a traveling circus?*

Next page. A fifty-something woman with an expression of bored annoyance, wore a spaghetti-strap tank top. An excessive amount of gel slicked her short, dark hair back, as though she'd sprung from the ocean. Across her breastbone and around her neck, tentacle tattoos marred her fair skin, possessing a realism beyond mere illusion. *Evobility: Quadia. Refused to cooperate. Liability. Terminated.* The clinical terms sent a shiver down my spine. Terminated. Just like that. This woman, stripped of all humanity and reduced to a liability. These unnerving images couldn't possibly be genuine, but the memory of my attacker's rabbit, snubbed nose hit me hard.

What had Raiden dragged me into?

Shaking my head, I pushed the strange snapshots aside and flipped through a different stack of folders. Nestled inside a large envelope was a subfolder labeled *Targets*. I swallowed and tilted my head ever so slightly, straining to catch any approaching footsteps. Only the oxygen rushing through my nose rustled the silence. I flipped open the *Targets* folder. A candid photo of a young woman walking down the Clark College's cherry tree-lined campus. Her smile shone bright, like how she thought her future was. Black hair. Dark eyes. Amy Allen from Nyxon's missing persons wall.

Why did he have this?

I turned the page and drew in a stuttered gasp. The hairs on my neck stood. A picture of Nyxon, sitting at a bistro table outside the quaint *Latte Da Cafe* across from my work. Various circular paper lanterns hung from the oak tree's limbs above her head. She wore jeans and her favorite white leather jacket. Her dark, A-line-styled hair curled under her chin. She blew on her steaming mug. *The Arts and Sciences of Habits* book rested in her lap.

Why did he have a picture of her? Had partnering with me been a ruse designed to learn about Nyxon's investigation into the missing women? A revelation dawned and a surprising suspicion staggered on the tip of my tongue. What if he was the villain? My mind spiraled, Nyxon cautioned me and I hadn't listened.

"You shouldn't be in here." Raiden's words fell like icicles, cold and cutting.

I jumped back, my heart leaping into my throat.

He stood in the doorway, his body blocked the light from the lobby, casting a shadow upon the table.

I was trapped and at his mercy.

Raiden's posture stiffened as he inventoried the forbidden folders, his head swiveling back and forth. Suddenly, he froze. His eyes narrowed on the journal. His palpable frustration filled the room making it difficult to breathe.

I gulped and tossed the folder onto the table. The documents splashed across the desk like blood spatter from a crime scene. Gruesome photos of the dead or missing, pages of scribbled notes, and dozens of crime reports. "What is this?" I spat. Tension replaced timidity.

"My job," the brevity in his curt tone revealed the peril I had just put myself in.

He prowled into the room and shut the door. I retreated to the other end of the table, like a deer bolting to the far side of a clearing at the sight of a wolf. I stammered, "You don't work for the government."

"I do, just not yours."

His cryptic words slapped me across the cheek. I was so wrong about him, and now it was too late. How hadn't I seen his malicious intentions?

An electric charge scourged my back like a sparking high-voltage cable. A gasp escaped me as I gripped the table's edge. My stress rash returned with a vengeance. The burning rings crisscrossed my body until they completed their hellish loops.

"What's wrong?" the fury fell from his voice. His face softened as he strode toward me.

I shuffled away, increasing the distance between us, stumbling backward, my heel kicking the cardboard box and flipping it over. The lid flapped open and a clear plastic bag rolled and collided with the wall. Through the fogged film, a mouth gaped. Light hair stuck to her bloody chin. Her milky eyes: one light, the other dark gawked at me. A metallic rot wafted into the air.

A head! Marthane's head! The cloaked woman from the other night.

Raiden raised both hands. "Avi, stop and listen."

"Stay away from me." The words erupted in a flawed plea rather than a demand, leaving a bitter sting in my throat. I should be stronger.

As Raiden slowly moved closer, the energy in the room turned suffocating, like the air itself was pressing down on me, forcing my body to shrink in on itself until I cowered. If I stayed, frozen in fear, what would he do to me? My feet felt like lead, and my lungs tightened as panic set in. I scanned for any objects to use as a means of defense.

But the immediate area was barren.

He was now close enough to lunge for me if he wanted to.

Pulse pounding, I dashed around the table, thrust open the conference room door, it hit the brick wall with a bang, and I sprinted for my only exit. His footsteps were sledgehammers behind me. I didn't waste time looking back.

I jerked open the front door, but Raiden slammed it shut. My fists banged against the metal. "Help! Help!"

He grabbed my wrists and pinned them to the door, high above my head. He leaned in. I flattened my warm cheek against the cold door. His breath was hot on my neck.

"I would never hurt you," he murmured with such tenderness and sincerity that my whole body tensed.

I shook my head, I knew better.

He was a master manipulator, and I fell for it. Every smile, every touch, every kind word blinded me from seeing his true colors. There was nothing he could say or do to make me believe him now. "I don't know you, but I know people don't keep *bloody heads* in their office!"

He whipped me around. We were nose to nose, our breath intertwined. He released his iron grip, and my hands fell to my sides, but his palms pressed the door near my ears, boxing me in.

He arched an eyebrow. "Please don't knee me."

The temptation had struck me.

My rash scorched hotter, and I winced.

He pulled my dress strap down my shoulder. A friction burn welted my skin. Raiden traced the loop with his finger, down to my breastbone. The tingle of his touch battled the broiling bands.

"Let me go." The words tasted like ash on my tongue. With every inhale and exhale, the rash's constriction worsened. Sweat built on my forehead. "My body has a stress reaction. I need a hospital."

"You can't go to a hospital, and you can't hide from what's coming." Helplessness and finality weighed down his tone.

My fingers frantically foraged the inside of my purse. "Hide from this!" I snatched my pepper spray and blasted his eyes. The streaming liquid permeated the space between us. The acidity stung my nostrils.

Raiden howled and covered his face, unfettering me from his blockade.

I careened into the narrow alley, coughing violently while hurtling forward to the boulevard. Cold rain streaked my face, blurring my vision as I desperately wiped it away.

Raiden's steps crunched behind me. "Avi!"

I navigated around a tire. *I can make it!*

Twenty yards, ten yards, five. Wheezing, I rounded the corner. "Help. Help?" No one. Not a soul.

Raiden's footfalls grew louder, sending a jolt of panic through me. I scrambled across the street, splashed through potholes, then leapt onto the sidewalk. The uneven pavers morphed into a labyrinth of opposition. My ankle twisted. I skidded across concrete. Tears rushed down my cheeks.

A hand clamped my shoulder. I screamed!

"Avi, are you alright? Nyxon sent me." Fritz's voice held an underlying grit I didn't recognize, like a boy thrust into manhood, forced to face far more than he should.

Rain dripped from the brim of Fritz's weathered baseball cap. He shouldn't be here!

"Who are you running from?"

"He—he killed a woman!" With a trembling finger, I turned and pointed behind me.

"He who?"

No one was there.

A plastic bottle rolled across the alley, propelled by a gust of wind. I whipped my head around, searching for Raiden. Fritz's hand cupped my cheeks, a tentative attempt to calm my frenzied movements, but I recoiled—an instinctive rejection, a clear protest, a defiant declaration that the bitterness between us was still very much alive.

Fritz's composure cracked: a twitch in his jaw and the tightening of his mouth exposed the vulnerability beneath.

How could I possibly explain the bizarre pictures? Questions intertwined with fear's inky tendrils, but one inquiry surfaced: Am I putting Fritz in jeopardy? My heartbeat pounded like a war drum. His breath caught as he inspected my scrapes and bruises.

I grimaced as my searing rash blazed, becoming a brutal bear hug, squeezing the oxygen from my lungs.

What was happening to me?

It was the rash! It wasn't just burning now, it was alive, writhing beneath my skin. I cried out, my body seizing with pain.

From his coat pocket he produced a mini alcohol-like bottle, and gave it a hard shake, mixing its oil and pulpy contents. I recognized the liquid as one of Sloane's naturopath concoctions. As he moved the coat opened and a black handgun, strapped to his belt, reflected the fierceness in his wide eyes.

Why did he know to bring these things?

"Drink this."

I chugged it in two gulps.

Fritz slipped his arms under my legs, scooped me against his chest, and lifted me off the wet concrete.

"I've got you." Fritz's voice resonated as a steady beat, a metronome of strength and calm.

I relaxed into Fritz's arms, but when I looked up, the terror in his eyes had faded and was replaced by a glimmer of guilt.

Before I could ask why, the darkness dragged me deeper into the void of unconsciousness. As it swallowed me completely, Fritz's whisper slipped through the blackness: "Only I know how to save you."

Chapter 11

A fuzzy paw prodded my nose. Wet sandpaper scratched my forehead. The hiss of steam. Drip. Drip. A hazelnut aroma. I squinted against the light spilling from the kitchen, stabbing straight through my pounding headache, evoking images of my hellish encounter. My mind split between sobbing or blubbering hysteria.

Oh god. I covered my mouth. Raiden was the bad guy.

He knows where I live. He knows who my friends are.

I put them in jeopardy.

Dread, once a dollop in the pit of my diaphragm, distended into a malignant disc. I hoped to locate my mother before telling my friends about Raiden and Uzziah. Her return would've been a joyful distraction from questions about my father. But it was too late for happy endings.

I had to tell them the truth: Raiden kidnaps women, and he was aware that Nyxon, like an inescapable tornado brewing on the horizon, was closing in on him.

Graysen jumped off the couch's armrest and sashayed toward the kitchen, her tail flicking once, twice before squatting in front of Li's feet.

Why was Graysen here? What time was it? Ten o'clock at night?

Why was I at Li's house on his couch? The L-shaped sectional *(tan, I think. It had been a year since my last visit)* bore deep indentations that made the hard surface beneath impossible to ignore.

His living room had the ambiance of a party that never quite ended. The stale stench of beer wafted from the corner where a giant pyramid of Bud Light cans were stacked precariously atop a sticky ping-pong table. Across from me, two TVs hung side by side. One broadcast highlighted Portland Thorns' blowout win in last night's soccer match, while the other displayed the Call of Duty video game home screen. Fingerprints smudged the glass coffee table: a poltergeist reminder of past parties. In the greasy Little Caesars box, hardened pizza crusts crowded a glass pipe, its polka dot-patterned bowl cradled blackened buds. Li, the frat-boy who refused to grow up.

On the floor by my feet, Sloane's black duffel bag with a silver diamond-shaped logo featuring a backwards seven at its center was open. This bag stayed hidden beneath her bed, brought out only during my stress rash episodes.

Someone had stuck extra-wide bandages to my knees. My muscles ached. My fingers were swollen sausages. The rings still chafed. I patted my chest. My necklace was safe.

The kitchen cabinets creaked as I peeked over the armrest. Sloane moved about, her khaki skirt rustling while her metallic bracelets clinked against the coffee mugs in her hands. Her thick brown hair was braided. A deep frown dominated her teardrop-shaped face, a mirror image of the stern woman in Grant Wood's masterpiece, *American Gothic*.

The ordinary kitchen was a mess. Dishes were stacked in the sink. Magnets affixed Li's swim schedule to the stainless-steel fridge. Under the schedule was a photo of Li and his swim pals, cheering and waving their rainbow flags above their heads at the Portland Timbers soccer game.

Li and Fritz sat around the eight-player poker table that doubled as a dining table. Li lounged in a black folding chair, one leg casually kicked out, while his dark coat draped over the back of the seat. His WSU gray T-shirt clung to his biceps, while his black athletic pants hung loose at his hips.

"Son, it's a bad idea to involve yourself in this mess. You should've stayed home," Sloane's whip-lashing tone flayed the line between motherly love and possessiveness. "You need to leave before Avi wakes up."

"Sloane's right. You just returned," Li's words didn't capture the depth of his worry, yet everyone could hear the underlying sadness beneath his gruffness.

"Nyxon called *me* because she trusted me to find Avi and keep her safe," Fritz's statement gushed from his mouth, a river of conviction.

Bruising marbled his right eye. His bottom lip puckered from a split that would take days to heal. Fritz's fatigued, pale skin painted a picture of a man who hadn't slept. He stuffed his hands into his Carhartt jeans pockets. His wrinkled white shirt added to his disarray.

What happened to him? I gripped the couch's edge as panic filled my mind with horrific possibilities. Li, of course, was the opposite. Cool and calm. Not a single scratch marred him. He exuded an effortless charm, embodying the best of his Black and Asian heritage.

Graysen rubbed against Li's leg, then meowed. Her usual doleful eyes were wide and alert, as if conveying urgent news.

"Go home," Li's order had a sense of finality, like a door slamming shut. "You being here will confuse Avi."

Fritz waved him off. "I'm the only one who knows how to help her. I hoped my suspicions were wrong but on Cynder, the inmates assigned to the clam fields displayed similar ringed rashes. It's an abraylix. *Not* a disease, *not* an allergic reaction."

Sloane stepped between Fritz and Li. "Son, we've all had a long night, you need to go—"

"No." Fritz stood. "Cyndarian surgeons implanted an electric wire-like bondage called an abraylix under the prisoners' skin to prevent them from using their evobility. It's a form of restraint, torture, punishment. Abraylixes are composed of titan-hydrogen fibers. The surgeon uses a magnet to feed the titan-hydrogen wire into the body, over the shoulder, then around the torso. Lastly, they're screwed together to complete the loop. When Grounders use their evobility, they excrete a hormone called libidopa. The abraylix's titan-hydrogen fibers react negatively to the libidopa. The libidopa ignites a chemical ionization, burning and constricting, until the Grounder deactivates their evobility." He exhaled as if he were a prosecutor in court who just won his case.

Our planet? Cynder? Grounders?

I must've hit my head when I fell; it was the only logical explanation. But he used the same word I read in Raiden's files. *Evobility.*

Li massaged his jaw. "So, an abraylix is an anaconda on fire?"

Fritz sighed. "I suppose. Imagine wearing two Scottish sashes, one on each shoulder, looping to the opposite hip, they bisect to make an 'X' on your stomach and spine. Avi has *two* abraylixes because she has *two* evobilities. She must've subconsciously tried to use her VidaLumin evobility to determine Raiden's true intentions. The other abraylix blocks access to her Slyfen evobility. Like a slinky, an abraylix expands as the person ages, but there are limits to their stretchability."

I was trapped in a nightmarish hallucination because the terrifying reality unfolding before me couldn't be real.

I rubbed the area near my belly button, where the markings intersected. Could there really be foreign wires buried beneath my skin? No! The doctor diagnosed it as a stress rash! Suddenly, a faint resistance in my abdomen made me doubt my own sanity.

"An abraylix's protective coating doesn't last forever. It gradually disintegrates, causing the ends to snap, and leak toxic materials into the bloodstream. Every twenty years, a surgeon must undertake the delicate task of replacing the abraylix." Simmering resentment glazed his eyes. "Avi will die in twelve months if we don't remove them, but you knew this didn't you *mother*?" His accusation matched that of a detective laying out damning evidence.

The word *die* slammed into me like a runaway freight train, my whole body rattling with the force. Fritz must be wrong.

Sloane's gaze darted to Li, hoping for an ally, but found none. Her lips quivered, searching for a defense. When her words never formed, her eyes became slits, morphing her face into a mask of malice.

My body trembled. What had she done? How could she? She couldn't because this wasn't real!

"Does Nyxon know?" Fritz demanded.

"No," her voice was resolute.

"You have to cut them out," Fritz's order sliced through the charged atmosphere.

"I'm not equipped to safely remove them." Vexation coated Sloane's clipped tone. But when Fritz's glare didn't soften, her tone mellowed, "Like a bomb, there is a constant current flowing through the wires, if the wiring gets cut—"

"Boom, baby." Li extended a fist then his hand burst open as if he held a firecracker.

Fritz popped Li's shoulder with his knuckles. "We have one option. Sneak her to Cynder so a Cyndarian surgeon can remove them."

"Wait just a minute," Sloane fumed. "If Avi goes there, she may never return to earth. We'll be fired, separated, and punished. Sent to who knows where." A sharp intake of breath punctuated her rambling, the sound of a heart beating too fast.

My eyes widened. What they discussed was out of this world. The reasonable explanation: Sloane had given me medicine from her bag, causing hallucinations, some type of adverse reaction. I side-eyed the marijuana pipe and wrinkled my nose. Who knew what kind of drugs I could've encountered on this couch?

Graysen meowed again. This time, Li glanced down. His eyes tracked Graysen, who trotted to the couch I was lying on.

"She's awake and eavesdropping." Li's inflection oozed disdain, each syllable sliding off his tongue like sludge.

Sloane rushed over as I rose to a sitting position. She scooted onto the couch and grabbed my shoulders. Her dainty digits were probes, prodding my sore muscles. "You gave us quite a scare. What do you remember?"

"Why am I not at a hospital?" My question felt oppressive because my gut knew the next words to leave her lips would be a lie.

"I'm a naturopath, honey, I'd know if you needed a hospital." Her tone was too soft, too sweet.

The hairs on the back of my neck rose. "Why is Graysen here?"

"There's a gas leak at your house." Sloane placed the back of her hand on my forehead, but I batted it away, and she frowned. She haughtily turned and dug into her medical bag with a loud clunk and clank. "You'll have to stay here. Nyxon will be here later tonight."

I took a gamble. "I know you're lying." My voice shook, but my bold move paid off because guilt from their misdeeds shone in their eyes and etched lines across their brows. "Raiden murdered a woman. We need to call the police!"

"No," they said in unison, startlingly loud. I shrank back, as if volume alone could bruise.

Sloane patted my thigh. "You are just a perfume chemist. Don't worry about Raiden and the murdered woman, it will cause your rash to flare." She produced a small bottle with the similar oily liquid from before. With a shake, she mixed its pulpy contents, causing bubbles to rise to the surface. "Sip this. You'll feel better."

"I won't drink any more of your concoctions." I stood. The thick bandages on my knees felt superglued to my skin, tugging painfully at the tender flesh beneath. Taking a deep breath, I ripped them off and flung them onto the coffee table. Raised, inflamed scabs marred my tender skin. "Why did the drink Fritz gave me earlier cause me to pass out? It had never done that before. Did you change the formula? Knock me out on purpose?"

"Avi, give us a chance to explain." Fritz tripped mid-step as he rushed to reach me.

But I extended my palm, stopping his frantic approach. "Stop!"

Li rose, his chair scraping against the floor. Goosebumps prickled my arms. He shuffled left, blocking the hallway that led to the front door. Would they let me leave? Would they chase me? Would Quinbe believe my wild story? Whose side was Nyxon on?

"Avi deserves to know the truth. We're all sick of juggling double lives." Fritz pleaded with Li and Sloane. "The abraylixes *will* poison her."

"Fritz, shush!" Sloane scolded.

Poison. The word caused fear to boil in my gut, begging to fume, fizz, foam from my lips as a scream. I never thought about death, now it saturated the room.

"Fritz, if you interfere, the Queen won't hesitate to toss you back into that hellhole." Li's eyes challenged Fritz to disagree. "Avi, knowing the truth won't repair your relationship."

"I know it won't fix us," Fritz said through clenched teeth.

"Hellhole? Queen? What is going on?" They ignored me. "I want to call Nyxon." My feeble demand mimicked a criminal's desperate plea for their one phone call. Frustration threatened to spill tears from my eyes. "Be honest with me or I'm leaving."

Li huffed and stepped in front of me, blocking my path. "Go ahead and try." He stood like a brick wall. His hulking frame cast an ominous shadow over me. He crossed his arms, veins pulsed, sending ripples of exasperation through the air, a reminder of his physical dominance.

"Michael will wonder why I missed work," I stammered.

"Nyxon already hacked your email and sent Michael a message explaining you had a dental emergency," Li countered.

Nyxon, my best friend, worked against me. Horror and hurt surged, like molten lava, burning me to the core. How could she betray me?

Li exhaled. "Let's wipe her memory again. Start over. It'll be easier."

My brow wrinkled. "Wipe?" I faltered, stunned by the words I couldn't utter.

"I've already hired a Mind Niche. She'll be here tomorrow." A glint of mischief sparked in Sloane's gaze as she turned to me, my pulse quickened as her smile grew wide and wicked. "It's a brutal procedure, but you'll survive it, you *always* do. This would be your seventh session. We're not perfect, we've had a few slip ups. If you want, we can erase you and Fritz's relationship. This could be a clean slate for both of you."

Her callous suggestion swept a numbness over me. I couldn't muster the courage to face Fritz. Did he regret proposing to me? Doubt and insecurities squeezed my throat, suffocating me. Would he validate his mother's suggestion?

I slowly peered beneath heavy eyelids. To my relief, Fritz's contorted expression matched my own, shock warped with disgust.

"Sounds like a fine idea to me." Li playfully patted my shoulder, but I batted his hand away.

"No one touches me." I seethed. A familiar undercurrent of restraint kept my full fury in check.

"Enough. You're scaring her." Fritz's hand rose as if halting traffic. "How many more times will we have to call a Mind Niche in her lifetime? It's not feasible." This time when Fritz crossed the room to stand between me and Li, I didn't argue. "Avi ought to know the risks. It's for her own protection."

"No, no, no." Li's head bobbed from shoulder to shoulder as he spoke.

Sloane folded her arms over her chest, her eyes backlit with resentment.

My brain hollered to hurry for the hills, but my heels heeded my heart and stayed glued. "Start talking." My boisterous tone splintered, confessing I actually felt like a powerless prisoner.

Fritz gestured to the group. "We. You. Nyxon. Aren't human. We're Grounders from Cynder. We use electrons—"

"Stop it!" My gut pitched. "That isn't true."

"Pft. We're going to regret this." Li left his blockade. His eyebrow rose, daring me to make a break for it. He plopped onto his crappy couch and stretched his arms wide, resting them atop the back.

Fritz's finger tapped a nervous beat on his thigh, as if he second guessed his commitment to his truth. But he shook the thought aside and continued, "Our bodies possess a genetic link with planets, allowing us to harness abilities from the planet's constituents of matter. This ability is called an evobility."

"Constituents of what? Evo-bil-ity?" Every answer was a clue meant to assist me in navigating this labyrinth which was now my life. Where the walls shifted in perpetual flux. But my insatiable curiosity propelled me forward, urging me to unravel the mysteries concealed within.

"Our DNA mutated with Cynder's chemical elements and developed adaptations enabling us to survive on our dry, dangerous planet," Fritz spoke with a measured slowness, "Children inherit one or two evobilities from their parents. Each evobility has a name. For example, Bmine expels an odor that burns its enemy's eyes and blinds them for a few days, and Silsonics produce and direct sound waves through sand to drive off bloodthirsty, lobster-sized creatures called rabicks. We charge our evobilities through physical contact with the

Earth, like walking barefoot on grass or sand. This connection allows the body to sync with the Earth's natural electrical charge."

This couldn't be true.

These people molded my world. Fritz and Li were there during high school. I met Nyxon in college, and she stayed awake all hours tutoring me so I could pass my exams.

The tulle veil of false security they had draped over me for so many years snagged on the hooks of truth Fritz daringly dangled.

"Everyone, take a seat." Sloane's order resembled an irritated teacher. "I'll brew some tea." She smoothed her skirt as she sailed to the stove.

"I'm not sitting or guzzling anything you give me." No matter how parched I was. I brought my hands up to my head. This couldn't possibly be real. "I'm in a coma at the hospital. Maybe a car hit me when I crossed the street." No. My memory was a bit hazy, but I could swear Fritz had been there.

"Mind Niche," Li muttered. Sloane's sigh swirled with the steam from the kettle.

Fritz rubbed his palms together. "How about I show you."

Chapter 12

He strode to the kitchen and pulled an eight-inch chef's knife from its wooden block. He laid the blade between his palms. Centimeter by centimeter, the knife wilted in his hands, becoming silver putty. The wooden hilt plummeted to the floor. His fingers smoothed the tapered, beveled edge.

The disbelief on my face failed to express the sheer impossibility of what I witnessed. Melting metal and sulfur, like fireworks on a summer night, mixed with the air evoking a unique nostalgia that instantly transported me back to the metal origami animals he had lovingly crafted.

"You owe me a new knife," Li deadpanned.

Fritz paid him no mind as he slid next to me. "Put out your hand." I balked at his closeness, but he took my hand and placed the mollified metal disc in my palm.

"Oh. Wow. It's slick as ice. I thought it would burn."

His pointer finger sliced the metal. I braced for the shrill screech of nails against a chalkboard, instead came a low popping and searing hiss. Fritz blew on the metal, his eyes blazed with elation, inviting me into his mysterious world and my fear faded away.

"I'm an I-forge." He eased his hands away, leaving an engraving on the disc.

My heart broke all over again. It was our mark. A reminder of us.

After all the emotions this man had put me through, he still remembered. How could someone inflict so much damage while still being wonderfully thoughtful? In a university history class, we'd been tasked to create a family crest. Our mark is two interlocking mountain peaks and a crescent moon inside a radiant rising sun between the lofty summits. I brought the disc to my breastbone. It symbolized: day or night you'll never climb mountains alone. His endearing gesture, an atone, a future touchstone, was the first patch of many needed to repair what he had broken.

"Li, are you…" My calculated speech confirmed that a part of me still didn't grasp my question. "An I-forge?"

He scoffed. "Look at me." He lifted his shirt, unveiling washboard abs. "I can do more than pattern a paperweight. I'm a Jagwar."

"And the trouble with Jagwars?" Fritz asked rhetorically. "They grow into full-sized gladiators, but their brains stay stuck in golden retriever puppy mode."

Unbothered, Li slid a hand through his ebony curls. "I'm your security, *darlin'*. Strong. Quick healin'. The whole package." He slowly ran a hand through his ebony curls.

The sliver of hope that he valued our friendship, dissolved. It was never a friendship. He was simply doing his job. I cleared my throat to disguise my disappointment. "What is Nyxon?"

The kettle whistled and Sloane poured the tea into a cup. "She's a Frigellen." Sloane strode toward me, her hand outstretched, ready to exchange the treasure Fritz created for the white mug. Her fingers curled in a "give it to me" motion.

I fought an impulse to twist away. Internally, I screamed at Fritz to explain his thoughtful gift, but on the outside, I had to remain composed and unflustered. So, I handed the metal object to Sloane.

She scrutinized the design, and as if touched by an artist wielding a dark palette, a paint brush swept across Sloane's features, each eye twitch and frown line appearing as sinister strokes. She shoved the warm mug into my chest; it sloshed against the rim.

The tea's lemony, soothing fragrance promised relaxation, but I didn't dare drink it. She rested her hand on my shoulder, then forcefully guided me to the couch and I reluctantly sat.

With a determined stride, she collected the knife's wooden hilt. Once inside the kitchen, her foot pressed the trashcan's lever, the lid sprang open with a clatter. She dropped the hilt and Fritz's object carelessly inside; it clunked against the can's metal bottom.

My eyes fixated on the trashcan, my muscles itched to burst into action, to launch myself, spilling my steaming tea in a glorious arc, all to rescue my precious belonging. But I stayed rooted to the spot. Did she remember how much the symbol meant to me? No, she couldn't. But contempt curled the corners of her mouth.

"Nyxon can learn things ten times faster than any Grounder or human," Fritz proudly shared, "She can also link to other Grounders to pass on her wisdom."

"Wisdom?" Li slapped his knee. "What has she been researching? Passing on these days? She's holding out on us."

Fritz's crooked grin grew. "Because you're only interested in learning karate or the Kama Sutra."

Li winked at me. "True."

My indignation showed in a dramatic eye roll.

Graysen leapt onto the coffee table, then pawed the air. "Thrilled to be, what humans say? Out of closet." Her regal, haughty accent was a cross between an apathetic duchess and a yowl.

Li shook his head. "No, that's not it at all."

I jerked back. "You're *talking to me!*"

Graysen shrugged. "Learning still. But we schedule meeting. You switched to *generic* cat litter."

My jaw dropped. It was impossible, yet here Graysen was, spouting out fragmented and unfinished sentences. "How did this happen?" The last twenty minutes tested my worldly perception.

"Nyxon," everyone deadpanned.

Li added, "She needed a challenge. And was bored when it was her turn to follow you around."

Graysen lifted her chin. "Told Nyxon a brown-haired bozo Raiden snooped. He has no scent, I no like that."

"No scent?" Li's brows pinched together.

Fritz crossed his arms and tapped his foot against the floorboards. I rubbed my palms against my thighs, as if trying to ground myself, while Sloane stared at Graysen, eyes wide, her usual poise cracked by confusion.

"Wait a minute, so at the Fort Vancouver auction, Li and Nyxon were spying on me?"

"That's my job, sweetheart. Looked like you were havin' a good time on your *date* and might finally get some ass. *Too bad* Nyxon cock blocked you." Li smirked.

Heat rushed to my cheeks.

Fritz cleared his throat. "Nyxon called me after losing the mugger in the crowd. She sent me your location."

My eyes darted from Graysen to Fritz. My ears buzzed with an alarm that refused to die. What did I get myself into? "Where is Nyxon?"

"She's at Fritz's house interrogating Raiden." Sloane's voice was cold, like a machine calculating probabilities and solutions. "As of right now Raiden is tied to a chair and will only speak to you. But she'll break him soon."

Could Nyxon really be hurting him? It was too outrageous to process. She followed the rules, upheld the law. I couldn't fathom her torturing anyone.

"You'll stay here until we can figure out what's going on." Li pointed to the rolling suitcase on the floor. "Sloane packed you a bag."

Like my childhood, I'd returned to living out of a suitcase.

Like my childhood, I was at the mercy of others' generosity.

Like my childhood, anxiety was the bogeyman beneath my borrowed bed.

"Once we get the information I'll dispose of Raiden," Li stated.

"Dispose?" My voice pitched high, on the verge of shrill.

Li waggled his brow. "What's wrong? Do you have feelings for this loser?"

"No. Of course not. But are you going to ki—" I couldn't finish without choking.

Li let out a cynical huff. "I didn't plan to *kill* him. Fritz and I will haul him to Madras, Oregon for detainment by the Cyndarian Watch, then they'll ship him back to Cynder."

"A Cyndarian jail?"

Li nodded smugly. "The sooner you talk to him, the sooner we can bounce. We should roll up there right now. Ready to grow a backbone and confront Raiden?"

I was finished living as the outlander. "I'll talk to him. It's important." After years of living in limbo, my gut trundled, sounding an alarm because Raiden's admission would frame the foundation of my future.

"Bring your suitcase. You can stay with me. My house is remote and has better security." Fritz stated as if my opinion didn't matter.

Yesterday, returning to Fritz's place had the makings of a romantic reunion. Now, resentment tore through me. It was a bitterness born when your soulmate ends everything with a note and nothing more.

When he vanished our relationship became transactional: I was welcome to live on the farm until the end of the year. Like an intruder, I traipsed through his home. Like a trespasser, his fields I roamed. I watched dust collect on his counter. I smelled a mustiness on the drapes. I heard crows feast on his grapes. Time and weather took their toll on his tractor. The apple trees' branches buckled from unpicked produce. He disappeared in spring, and by summer I left my key on the table. I didn't belong there.

My untouched tea trembled in my hand, I couldn't sleep under Fritz's roof without cuddling beside him.

"Better security? I don't think so. You just have more guns, because I'm superior with my fists. Care to tell Avi what happened to your pretty face?" Li jested.

My brows rose. Fritz spoke through clenched teeth, "After bringing you here, my mom stabilized you. Me and Nyxon returned to where I found you. Raiden refused to come with us willingly."

Li snorted. "Oh, and Avi, great job with the pepper spray. *Classic move*."

"Thanks," I muttered, all edge, no warmth.

Fritz's forehead creased. "Avi, where do you want to stay?"

Sloane's mouth opened, then snapped shut, determined to debate with confidence and eloquence, if I agreed to stay at her son's house.

"Um, Li's house."

Fritz pressed his lips together and exhaled through his nose. "Graysen favors my place." He stroked Graysen's back.

The mere idea of stepping into his house caused every muscle in my body to stiffen like a sailor's grip on a storm-tossed mast. Graysen, ever perceptive, swatted his hand away. "Nature? Eat me everything wants. Hawks. Coyotes. *Fleas*." She braided between my legs and I scratched her spine.

Fritz leaned toward Graysen. "I hung a new bird feeder." Graysen's head whipped around. Fritz lowered his voice as if to share a secret, A Steller's Jay visited the feeder yesterday.

Her gaze ping-ponged between me and Fritz, a fierce tug of allegiance warring within her eyes. With a defiant chin tilt, she declared, "No, no, no."

A comforting warmth bloomed within me. Graysen was a faithful friend, even if she was a spy.

"What about Quinbe?" I asked.

Li laughed. "No way she's one of us."

My brow furrowed. "She's smart. Talented. She could be."

Sloane's countenance softened. "She's uniquely astute."

"So, Li is your mom really from Japan? Nyxon's parents from India?"

Li scoffed. "No way would our families mix with a human. Cyndarians consider humans trash."

Typical Li acting superior. "What is my evo-bil-ity?" I stretched out the word.

Graysen's ears twisted and she lifted her head into the air, fully alert. "Listen. Hear that?"

Instantly the atmosphere in the room shifted. No smiles. No words. No movement.

Graysen dropped from the coffee table and trotted to the poker table. She sank her claws into the sleeve of Li's leather coat and brought it to her twitching nose.

Li scrambled to his coat. "Whoa whoa." He snatched the coat from her. "This is custom made." He wrinkled his nose as he inspected the sleeve.

Graysen's back arched, her gray fur stood at attention. "Wrong. Something there."

We all exchanged puzzled glances.

Li checked one pocket. Nothing.

He slowly inserted a hand into the other. His eyes widened. He pulled out a titanium beetle. Surprised, he flung it to the floor.

A halo of lights on the machine's back blinked. Sleek black wings ejected from the upper part of its body, resembling helicopter blades. A compartment detached from its underbelly as if it was about to launch mini warheads.

"Take cover!" Fritz tackled me to the floor.

Sloane scrambled behind the couch. The militant beetle lifted into the air; its buzzing wings created a high-pitched whir as it hovered. Li darted into the kitchen and pressed his back against the fridge, surprisingly his countenance was a mix of astonishment and excitement.

The beetle fluttered, hovering in place. Fritz squeezed me tighter. His lips were near my ear. "The beetle is attracted to movement. Its darts cause paralysis."

The beetle closed in, its wings slicing through the air with a hiss.

Graysen, a blur of sleek fur, jumped onto the couch's armrest with the grace of a practiced acrobat. Her tail flicked like a whip for balance as she crouched, eyes glinting. Then, coiling her body, she sprang into the air, twisting mid-flight, claws extended—*wham!* She struck the beetle. The strange machine spun wildly, as if caught in a tornado, before crashing into the beer-can pyramid. The cans toppled with an aluminum clatter, like cymbals smashing together.

Li charged the beetle, cans crunching underfoot. His fist slammed down on the beetle with a loud crunch. Metal collapsed as its legs buckled and fell from its caved-in body. A sad, melancholic beeping faded, then its lights dimmed out.

Sloane gasped. "We have to leave. *Now!*"

Chapter 13

Fritz pulled me through Li's front door, his grip like a vise, into the eerie dusk. I stumbled, struggling to match his swift stride. His gaze cut across the yard and street, searching for threats I couldn't see.

Graysen scouted ahead, bounding back and forth along the concrete path.

A cornhole board and two stacks of bean bags rested in the unmowed lawn, surrounded by cheap plastic chairs. Laughter mixing with the sizzle of burgers on the grill had always filled this yard; I had a sinking sensation that those days were over. Fritz was intent on protecting me, but from whom? From what? I wanted answers.

Fritz's jaw clenched as his chest heaved. His contagious desperation chilled me to the core. I had never seen him so scared before. A thick silence followed us, punctuated only by the click of Fritz's key fob unlocking his black 4-door Jeep truck.

"What was the beetle thing?" I demanded.

"It's a tracker." Fritz's fingers increased their pressure around mine.

Li scooped Graysen into his arms. Graysen snapped, "Be careful, you brute."

Li slid into the backseat. "Apologies, my lady, we're in a rush."

Sloane stepped up and into the front seat.

Fritz grabbed the Jeep's door handle for me, but I placed my hand on the frame and kept it shut. I needed to confront a truth that could shatter the very foundation of who I was, everything I thought I knew, tainting the memories I once held dear. "You and I…" My throat dried. "When we dated, was it real, or were you just doing your job, playing your part?" My shoulders shrank as I braced for his answer, like waiting for a slap I couldn't dodge.

"How can you ask me that?"

"Because I don't know what's real anymore." I held back tears.

He gripped my hips. I jumped, but it didn't discourage him from pulling me near. "Of course, it was real. I didn't choose to leave. Every day, I—"

"What's the holdup?" Li shouted. "We gotta bail."

Fritz stepped back. Words glossed his lips, but he shook them into the wind, opened his door, and slid behind the wheel.

I climbed in and wedged my elbow against the window, propping my head on my hand.

Fritz maneuvered out of Li's college neighborhood, past homes with porch couches and WSU flags in the windows. He floored it on the freeway. Graysen nuzzled my elbow and I snuggled her, soothing us both. I clutched my pendant necklace. It once brought me hope and I needed that right now.

They argued about who could've and would've put the tracker in Li's coat. Sloane and Fritz blamed Li for associating with the "wrong Cyndarian crowd." Li didn't deny this fact, but defended himself with, "There's a lot of strange shit happening right now." Their argument spun into a tornado. Piece by piece, my everyday existence lifted off the ground, defied gravity, shredded apart, and strewed into the sky.

I couldn't bear the bickering and blaming. My fingers itched to untangle the knot of my life. Li and Sloane's previous threat of a Mind Niche buzzed in my ears. What would be worse: living unaware in the comfortable shade or confronting the truth at a perilous price paid? Or navigating this world, uncertain but seen, somewhere betwixt the known and the in-between?

I stifled my submissive tendencies. "Stop arguing! Sloane, call off the Mind Niche. I don't want my memories wiped."

"Avi, dear, you don't understand the risks involved." Sloane folded her hands in her lap like a patient teacher explaining basic math. "I only want the best for you and Fritz. But if you keep your memories, *we* both know that puts him in danger."

"Nyxon said the Grounder with the rabbit-nose is a Limier. Erasing Avi's memory would leave her an open target. He has her scent and *won't* stop hunting *her*," Fritz warned. "Nyxon would agree with me that Avi should keep her memories."

The room stilled as everyone speculated which path Nyxon would choose. Dread drilled into my bones—a flashback of the Limier's hot breath on my neck. This hunter was relentless, his pursuit of me unstoppable. Could my motley crew of friends protect me? Or was it time to learn how to protect myself?

Sloane narrowed her eyes on me. "It's not up to you. It's not up to any of us. Those are our orders if you discover your heritage. Given to us by Princess Hydraxia. Your mother."

"That's the first time I've heard my mother's name." I gritted my teeth to hold in a sob. "You know who my mother is?"

Fritz squeezed the steering wheel. "We wanted to tell you, but we took an oath to stay silent."

Li shrugged. "To be honest, I didn't really care."

"The fear and anxiety that people will abandon me stems from being discarded like trash by my parents. And you all let me stew in my misery."

Li rubbed his neck and avoided my glare, copying the other con artists.

"Tell me about her. *And* my father." My inflection was forceful.

Sloane cast a loaded glance at Li in the side mirror. It was met by a thick, dense disdain. Without a word and as if passing a ball, he shot a glance at Fritz, who shook his head in response.

Sloane's gaze softened. "Your father, Prince Uzziah, and mother, Princess Hydraxia, were a beautiful match. After a decade of war, their love was a rare harmony. A symbol of peace and hope in the wake of darkness. But the costs of the Great Evo-Liberation War—food shortages, orphaned children, environmental ruin—slowly cracked the foundation of their reign."

I struggled to believe the news. I dreamed of a life beyond my circumstances, one where their absence didn't echo through birthdays and holidays. But now, with this new knowledge, a lightness undulated in my chest. Where would this truth lead me?

She gazed out the window. "Cynder wasn't always a dry planet. When the rain dwindled, your great-great-grandmother foresaw the crisis. Before our lakes and rivers dried, she engineered the aqueducts and the water creation stations we rely on today, and all the water rights associated with these vital systems. Uzziah preached that access to clean water was a birthright. He proposed legislation making the privatization of water illegal, preferring a public trust that manages the water supply, essentially destroying your grandmother's dynastic fortune. She demanded Uzziah cease his political activities. But he ignored her and paid the ultimate price. The Queen secretly ordered his death. My husband, Fritz's dad, was his executioner."

"That's not true," I blurted. Everyone whipped their heads to me. "Raiden said Uzziah is alive. In Vancouver, searching for me."

Fritz's jaw dropped. Sloane stiffened.

Li's eyes widened. "Uzziah *is* dead."

Sloane's fingers trembled as she raked them through her hair.

Fritz tilted his chin. "Mother, is Avi's dad alive?"

She pursed her lips. "There are rumors."

"Come on. Could this day get any worse?" Li's frustration hung in the air like a storm about to break, buzzing with unspoken secrets, life-altering decisions, and hidden dangers.

Amid the swirling turmoil, I stood on the brink of understanding, piecing together the shards of truth strewn before me. I must unravel this knot of deception. Every second counted in my desperate quest for answers. "But how did I, *we,* get here? On earth?" I still had trouble believing my own question.

"I jumped at the chance for Fritz and me to start fresh on Earth. After you bounced from foster home to foster home, I offered to adopt you, but your mother forbade it. You're still royalty, and Fritz and I will always be the help. Then she sent Li to watch over you."

"I did *not* volunteer. I was voluntold," Li added.

"I assumed," I quipped.

Her words made me question who I really was. Would this change my friendship with Nyxon? I glanced at Fritz. His solemn expression suggested he feared I'd now see him as a servant. Was this why Li and Sloane hated us dating?

"Princess Hydraxia didn't understand the trauma of abandonment. When I updated her about your life, her response was always clipped with jealousy. I can't imagine the anguish she still endures for sending you away," Sloane said. "When she finally allowed me to welcome you into my home, you were too jaded, hardened by life's cruelties. Lastly, she sent Nyxon to offer companionship. Even from afar, your mother cared."

Always cared for me? I yearned to believe but the abraylixes scorched a different narrative. "What kind of mother wipes her daughter's memories then dumps her on the sidewalk *alone*?"

"You were never alone," Fritz mumbled.

"Do *not* judge your mother. Keeping you safe was her sole objective." A shadow descended upon her face, like a Hannya mask slipping into place. "Mothers will do whatever it takes to protect their children, even if their actions seem barbaric." Her intonation was as important as her words, emphasizing the righteousness and fierce devotion inherent in a mother's love for her child. Fritz and I locked eyes in the rearview mirror, both of us wondering if she was talking about me or him.

We exited the freeway. Li twisted in his chair to ensure no one pursued us.

We passed a weathered two-pump gas station, its white paint flaking with age. It was a marker that we'd entered Fritz's rural territory, where deer outnumbered people. Miles of generational farms competed for land with wineries bought by outsiders. It was a quiet reminder of a changing landscape and a fading way of life.

"Is my mother's last name Neehow?" I leaned forward.

Li laughed. Fritz's lips pressed into a thin line.

Sloane rubbed her temple. "Neehow means *mouse* on Cynder."

I sank back into the seat. "Why would you give me that last name?"

"Behind us," Fritz tried to control the concern in his voice, but his eyes flicked to the side mirror and his foot pushed on the gas pedal. "Avi, duck down." I hesitated, but Fritz's eyes widened, so I obeyed.

Graysen's ears perked up, and an annoyed hiss split through her teeth.

Li grabbed the oh shit handle. "Chill, bro. We have that death curve ahead, we don't wanna fly off the road into that nasty slough." To the right, aquatic plants snaked their way across the stagnant expanse. The murky slough stretched languidly. To my left, mossy pines lined the weaving road.

Two black Lincoln Navigators devoured the space between us.

Inside the Jeep, we waited for the worst possible thing to happen. Any minute now, they would force us to pull over.

As the two SUVs roared past, the four of us sat frozen. Sloane gazed fixedly on the road ahead. Despite her outward composure, I could sense the undercurrent of terror that ran through her. The SUVs' tinted windows thwarted anyone's attempt to spy the occupants inside. Fritz's knuckles turned white around the steering wheel, his mind racing with what the SUVs might signify.

"Man, did you see the rims on those SUVs? Must be the bachelorette wine tours." Li checked his watch. "I know a guy at the Rusty Grape. Take a left at the next stop sign. We could all use a glass of merlot."

"Not now, Li," Fritz muttered.

As the SUVs pulled further and further ahead, disappearing around a bend in the road, a collective sigh of relief rippled through the truck. But even as we exhaled, I couldn't shake the feeling that this wouldn't be the last time we had to flee. This was the beginning of a chain of events beyond our control.

I moved to the edge of my seat. "Why can't I meet Uzziah?" Everyone flinched at his name.

Sloane's throat throbbed. "Even whispering his name could land us in the boiling clam fields."

"He was on the wrong side of history," Fritz stated.

It wasn't fair. What would it be like to face Uzziah, to ask about my childhood, about my mother?

Sweat slicked my palms. In twenty minutes, we'd be safe. In twenty minutes, I'd face Raiden. In twenty minutes, I'd get answers. My future wasn't just bound by these abraylixes, but by forces beyond my control. "If I didn't have these abraylixes, what two evobilities would I have?"

Li scoffed. "You'd be a greedy Slyfen. Absorbin', *stealin'* other Grounders' evobility. All Slyfens are the same, selfish to the core."

I locked eyes with Fritz in the rearview mirror, my pulse quickening as I silently begged him to object or clarify. But he stayed silent.

Fritz sped around the 'S' curve, forcing my body to lean left, then right. "I'd never—"

"Spike strips!" Li grabbed Graysen.

A boom reverberated through the Jeep. A repeated flapping of punctured tires hitting the pavement.

The Jeep careened into the opposite lane and plowed against the guardrail, creating an ear-piercing grinding of metal on metal. Sparks pattered my window. We sailed back over the double line and off the road down the twenty-foot embankment. Graysen's eyes widened, and her claws sunk into Li's jeans. Li curled into a ball around her. My body lurched as the Jeep cartwheeled, hood over trunk. My seat belt dug into my shoulder and abdomen as I was thrown forward, the horrifying sound of shattering glass filling my ears. The airbags deployed like gunshots. A splash of dark, grimy slough slammed against the windows as we came to an abrupt halt. A loud whoosh of water surged into the cabin, rising to my ankles like a flood forcing its way through a breach in a dam. We had seconds to act!

Chapter 14

We were stuck in the slough. The Jeep's front end dipped beneath the surface. It was sinking fast.

Inch by inch the rear tires lifted toward the sky, tilting the cabin at a stomach-roiling angle. The seatbelt's straps dug into my shoulder and abdomen, a tender bruise already forming beneath the pressure. Pain engulfed my neck, as if my head were too heavy for my shoulders to bear.

Graysen's claws pierced the upholstery. Her body pressed flat against the seat, trying to keep herself grounded. Her gaze darted between me and Li, poised to spring but unsure how to escape this sinking, mud-bound trap.

My pulse thundered as I fumbled with the seatbelt, fingers trembling. Once freed, I threw my shoulder into the door, but it was jammed and wouldn't budge. Shit, shit. "Fritz, the door!"

Blood wept from Fritz's nose and dribbled onto the airbag. A moan fell from his lips.

Sloane punched at her airbag, a bruise swelling on her cheek. "Son!"

Li's arm hung awkwardly and limp at his side, his shoulder visibly out of place. The angle grossly distorted the natural curve where bone should've met socket.

A subtle grimace crossed his face, and his eyes darkened as he gripped the wrist of his limp arm. Then, with a calm, almost detached focus, he twisted his arm outward, braced his shoulder against the door, and gave it a hard, forceful shove. A wet pop followed by a brief hiss as the joint snapped back into place.

My jaw went slack and Graysen's ears flattened against her head.

Li rolled his shoulder, testing his range, as if he hadn't just reset it with a move that would've brought anyone else to their knees.

Li touched a lump on his forehead from where his head hit the front seat, and before my very eyes, the swelling decreased then disappeared. I blinked, convinced my eyes were playing tricks on me. It couldn't be. People don't heal like that, but Jagwars do.

"Sloane, I'll get you both out. Avi, follow me," Li ordered. He lifted the car's center console and pulled out a pistol and tucked it in his waistband. He twisted toward his door and delivered a powerful kick. The impact thundered through the space as the door flew open, shaking the walls and sending shockwaves through me.

"Avi, move!" Li's words held enough force to make the bravest hearts quake.

I leapt into action, adrenaline spiking as I clambered over the seat, shattered glass from the back window digging into my palms.

I plunged into the foul water, sinking under the surface. The world above became muffled, a distant, murky blur.

I kicked. The thick, mucky water clung to me like tar, slowing my every move.

My arms flailed wildly. My lungs screamed for air. But gravity's long fingers wrapped around my ankles and dragged me deeper into its oblivion.

The dim moonlight above seemed miles away. Desperation powered every stroke. Graysen was still in the Jeep, and I couldn't let her drown. With a final heave, I broke through the surface. Gasping, I bobbed in a stew of filth. A slimy film coated the surface, each ripple carrying the stench of decay.

Graysen's panicked but relieved meows matched my own inhalations.

Sloane's window was broken. She was nowhere in sight.

Li moved around the hood toward Fritz, who was slumped unconscious in the front seat, blood streaking from his nose. The water rising past his stomach.

Graysen's eyes locked on mine. Her hind legs tensed, her body coiled to leap in my direction. As I treaded water, I opened my arms and beckoned with my fingers for her to jump.

The moment she hit the water, her instinct took over, paws churning in frantic paddling. Her splashing and thrashing became a beacon for any onlookers. I held her near my neck, and she clawed onto my shoulder. Flinching, I sucked in a ragged breath.

Like an ark, I steered us through the foul sludge and fallen branches. Mosquitoes buzzed relentlessly near my ears, their high-pitched whine a maddening reminder of how exposed we were. I whipped my head from side to side, instantly regretting the movement as a throbbing ache flared in my neck. The pain intensified with each frantic kick and paddle of my arms, a cruel echo of the whiplash I hadn't fully felt until now. Then came the sound, a bolt-breaking crunch of metal being ripped apart by a giant. I jolted, Graysen's claws digging deeper into my shoulder, and I stifled a cry.

Li, his presence a harbinger of havoc, flung Fritz's door aside with a force that sent it splashing through the water. It bobbed like a helpless witness to tonight's tumultuous events. The current lapped at Li's chin as he hauled Fritz's limp body through the waterlogged terrain, a determined resolve etched upon Li's furrowed brow, a testament to their unwavering bond.

My feet finally hit the mucky bottom. The ground beneath me came alive, a thick, unforgiving thing that sucked at my heels, threatening to swallow me whole.

Once the water was shallow enough for Graysen to stand, I released her.

I scoured the marsh for Sloane. We shouldn't have split up. This decision pressed on my chest like an asthma attack tightening its hold.

Graysen hissed, "Stay low."

I checked my pockets. No phone. Crap!

The mud squeezed between my toes, letting out a sickening *squelch*. The sound seemed deafening in the silence. I tried to lift my feet carefully, but the swamp was determined to betray me.

Five-foot-tall cattails stood like soldiers, their pale rectangular heads a stark contrast against the evening sky. As I crouched past, their musky scent wafted like cough-causing smog, yet I held the itchy feeling inside my throat and sealed my lips shut. One careless cough could give away my location. I uprooted weeds, while trying to heave myself over a decayed log.

I started up the twenty-foot berm that led to the road, slipping and sliding. When I lost my balance for the third time, I gave up on staying upright and resorted to an army crawl. My fingers dug into the damp soil; the whites of my nails darkened as the earth pressed into their beds.

The slam of SUV doors fractured the night, followed by the pounding of combat boots crunching over twigs.

I crested the hill, the narrow, winding road stretched out before me, framed by towering pine trees. Two black SUVs straddled the white line. A woman pulled her jacket's zipper up to the standing collar, the buttons on her cuffs gleaming like tiny, polished stars.

Three people circled her. I squinted; I had used the term *people* too quickly.

Identical islander twins stood side by side, comet-like streaks appeared and vanished across their irises. With a balance of power and poise, their crane-like bodies moved with quiet precision. Jet-black braids lashed against their tailbones. One, coltish and lively, wore a poncho edged in silver fringe that swayed over her form-fitting shorts and grazed the tops of her thigh-high black boots. Her sister, by contrast, wore an onyx bodysuit. A marvel of scales that armored her with otherworldly elegance. The suit snaked down her small breasts, flowed over her shoulders, and extended along her arms, ending in jagged cuffs that caught the faintest glint of light.

Not human.

A man, under five-feet tall, shuffled forward like an eager vulture, his pickle-like nose dominated his face. A puffy gray vest hung over his tucked-in white t-shirt, while a roll of fat oozed over his too tight belt. His worn jeans clung to his stocky legs. His muscular arms strained against the sleeves, veins bulging.

Not human.

Lastly, at the helm of this alien entourage, stood the woman in the button coat. An ebony-and-ivory striped baton on her hip. Her long, hawkish nose and short light hair, spiked meticulously in every direction, crafted an image of someone demanding respect. Every inch of her curvy frame radiated self-assurance, leaving a lasting impression on anyone bold enough to meet her gaze. I couldn't pinpoint why her presence scabied my skin, but employing a combination of logic and intuition, I concluded she wasn't human.

Her eyes, cold and calculating, scanned the surroundings as if assessing her next move in battle. "Polon, scan for body heat signatures."

The short Grounder with the long nose walked to the edge of the berm, raising his palms at the Jeep. My breath caught in my throat. He had no thumbs, just four chubby fingers on each hand. His nail beds flickered with light, like synapses firing in the brain. He waved them slowly, his hands moving like a puppeteer commanding his marionette, and I fought the urge to bolt.

The hawk-nosed woman turned to the twins. "Okya. Comb their vehicle."

"On it." The woman in the black scaled bodysuit dashed over the berm, a blur in the moonlight, slipping between trees and over roots as if the forest itself obeyed her.

Her poncho-wearing twin shifted anxiously from foot to foot as the shadows swallowed her sister.

"Olliope, stage the vehicles in case nosey drivers pass by." Sellow's command bore a frosty detachment, signaling a woman who deemed this mission beneath her.

Olliope flipped on the SUVs' hazard lights, then popped both hoods, revealing the engines. She located the jumper cables and draped the cables from one SUV to the other, imitating car trouble.

Polon whirled in our direction, his fingers flashing against the dark sky. I ducked low, becoming one with the crud.

Thump… thump… louder and louder his footsteps beat in my ears.

Every nerve screamed that if I moved or even breathed he'd hear me. It was too late to run. He was going to find us. How could I be stealthy with my heart banging against my ribs? I have to keep Graysen safe. Naive escape plans ricocheted against my skull, unable to land on a concrete plan, driving me to white-knuckle a thick branch. Graysen squirmed into my side.

Polon's boot tip hung over the edge, a tiny pebble tumbled down and past my nose. The stench of his cigarette billowed toward us like a Reaper looking for its next victim.

"I found the traitor!" Okya crooned like someone who had marched through countless battlefields and emerged victorious, again and again.

Polon lowered his flashing hands and stepped back from the embankment to join the others.

My pulse raced. Who did they find? Should I take Graysen and run into the woods? But it was my fault we were here!

I cautiously inched above the overgrowth to spy.

Sloane, stuck in Okya's headlock, kicked wildly and scratched at Okya's neck and arm. Sloane's five-foot frame was no match for Okya's biceps which rippled with the force of a steel cable.

Olliope danced around them like an acolyte ready to begin the sacrificial ritual.

Sellow confidently strode in front of the SUVs' headlights, her breathing steady and sure.

Polon copied his captain, mimicking a mountain lion's measured prowl.

Okya flung Sloane in front of Sellow, Sloane's chin coming close to colliding with Sellow's polished boot.

The SUVs' headlights morphed into interrogation spotlights.

"Long time no see, Sloane. Did you think hiding could save you?" Sellow stood tall, a condescending curve crossing her face. "Polon, cuff her."

Sloane rose to her knees, shoulders squared despite the mud clinging to her skin. "Hello, Sellow." She then tipped her chin toward each individual. "Okya. Olliope. Polon." She rolled their names on her tongue, as if speaking them was a chore.

Polon yanked Sloane's hands behind her back and locked them into place.

"Well, this is awfully dramatic for you, *Sellow*. I could expect this from Okya and Olliope. Does Uzziah really have you out chasing commoners now?" Sloane goaded.

Sellow crossed her arms and widened her stance as she studied Sloane, allowing a nervous energy to fill the space between them.

Polon squatted in front of Sloane—eye to eye—in a tense standoff. Sloane met his challenging glare with a defiant gaze. From his back pocket, Polon pulled a cigarette from his pack, lit it with a flick of his lighter, took a slow drag, then exhaled, sending perfect smoke rings curling into Sloane's face.

She closed her eyes, but her fierce features remained fortified.

Polon coiled a handful of Sloane's raven hair around his fingers. "When the queen sent your pitbull husband to hunt us…" Polon's voice had a shrill, nasal twang, as if he was a pre-teen bully threatening his victim. "You kept quiet." He drilled the cigarette into Sloane's cheek. The white paper accordioned in on itself. She squirmed, but he held the back of her head firm. "Coward." He twisted the cigarette until her flesh extinguished the coal.

Her breaths turned shallow and rapid, tears slipping down her cheeks as soft whimpers broke past her lips.

Sellow shoved Polon aside and seized Sloane's cheeks, her fingers digging into soft flesh. "Where's Aviana Markosyan?"

Chapter 15

A surge of adrenaline, like a wild river, flooded me. Sloane was about to give me up. There was nowhere to go, nowhere to hide, nowhere to turn but back into the slough. I pulled Graysen close, her tail twitched, but she didn't protest.

Sloane glared at Sellow. "Avi is already gone. On a plane to Georgia. Leave her be."

I blinked, struggling to make sense of Sloane's lie. The same woman who'd coldly kept Fritz and me apart, now lied for me. Me.

I searched Sloane's face, half-expecting to catch some hidden agenda, some sign that this was another one of her tricks. But all I saw was a fierce determination. Her loyalty was baffling. Why would she put herself in harm's way for me?

Graysen's ears swiveled—one flicking forward, the other backward—as if trying to decipher Sloane's protective behavior.

"Avi?" Sellow scoffed, the sound full of ugly disdain. "Her name is Aviana Markosyan, and King Uzziah wants her by his side when he returns to Cynder. Those are my orders."

Her mercenaries grew increasingly impatient; Polon cracked his knuckles, the popping mimicking a ticking bomb. Olliope and Okya slinked in a circle around their prisoner.

How much longer would they wait before they took drastic action? If Sloane told them the truth, they'd drag me away, then she could escape with Fritz and Li.

"You're just as stubborn and foolish as your husband." Sellow sneered.

Sloane's stony expression wavered, a hairline fracture splintering across her composure.

Sellow seized Sloane's moment of weakness, leaning in, her eyes glittering with cruelty. "Uzziah stole the traitor's evobility. Then I crushed his skull with my boot. He died like the pathetic traitor he was."

A guttural wail ripped from Sloane's throat as she doubled over. Her eyes were filled with a sorrow that went beyond tears, beyond words. Anyone who met her gaze would feel that depth of pain, as if looking into a mirror of their own worst memories. "You're a monster," her voice broke. She wrenched against the bindings. "He was the love of my life. You were jealous because you could never have Uz—"

Sellow's knee rocketed upward into Sloane's chin, the cracking of teeth was like a branch breaking underfoot. Sloane's head whipped back violently. She crumpled to the ground, her cheek hitting the dirt with a sickening thud.

Oh my God, did Sellow break her jaw? My hands trembled. I needed to do something! Anything! But my body betrayed me, frozen as if Sellow had struck me instead.

This couldn't be happening. My mind scrambled for logic, but the crunch of bone and the lifeless way Sloane fell shattered any denial.

Sellow's large and imposing figure dominated the space above Sloane. "You're on the wrong side of history. Cyndarians will cheer Uzziah and me as Cynder's saviors when we liberate them from under the Queen's boot." Her voice became a rallying cry. She opened her arms to her legion. "They'll revere the warriors who bring lifesaving resources to our starving brothers and sisters. Their hope, their future. Y*our* destiny, *your* legacy. Begins here. Begins now."

A branch snapped. All heads turned toward the timbers.

My heart dropped like a lead weight in my chest. One careless mistake revealed Li and Fritz's position. Would Li bravely, but naively fight for their freedom? Fritz surely couldn't. Was he even conscious?

Sellow's hand moved to the ebony-and-ivory striped baton fastened to her hip. Her fingers tapped against the metal as if it were a piano and this was her solo performance.

She unclipped the baton. With a bullwhip-like motion, the baton's joints clicked into place, replicating a blind man's cane. She thumbed a lever, and a broad, curved blade unfolded at the tip. A reaping hook. Its chipped edge glinted like broken teeth, hinting at a long and violent history.

She circled Sloane, dragging the blade against the pavement with a screech. Her strut was unnervingly placid, as if she were on stage, not about to unleash torture. "Where's your son, Sloane?" Her taunting tone trilled with an ominous edge, and I shuddered.

"Graysen," I murmured, "hide in the woods."

Graysen dropped back on her hindquarters. Her doe-eyes widened, her whiskers twitched. Unsure whether to agree or argue, her front paws rose in a praying position, crossed over each other, then repeated the gesture.

"I can't help Sloane while worrying about you," I pleaded.

She lowered her head and obeyed, albeit reluctantly, to my relief.

Polon waved his palm at the tree line. "I'm sensing body heat, east of that willow tree."

Sellow instructed, "Olliope. Okya. Capture the voyeurs."

It was now or never. I dropped the branch and scrambled over the berm. "Stop!" I raised my hands.

Olliope shifted into a fighter's stance. Okya prowled protectively in front of Sellow.

Summoning courage felt like striking a match in a storm. Still, I spoke. "I'm Aviana. What do you want?" My voice quivered like a leaf in that wind.

I didn't think Sellow's posture could become any straighter, but it did. "Our mission is to bring you to your father. Your Cynder heritage was stolen from you, he plans to rectify that. It's time you took your rightful place beside him."

Sellow's claim beckoned me forth, yet every nerve in my body bristled with warning against placing my trust in her.

The prospect of meeting Uzziah felt like staring across a black chasm because one false move could send me plummeting into consequences I wasn't ready for. Should I take the risk and meet Uzziah tonight? The answer eluded me, torn between longing for a connection and fear of the unknown.

In my core one thing blazed unmistakably clear: Sellow and her merry band of fanatical zealots threatened Sloane, Fritz, and Li's safety.

"No one needs to get hurt. I can meet Uzziah tomorrow at 6 p.m. at the pier downtown."

To my relief, Sloane forced herself upright. Swaying slightly, she shook her head at me.

Sellow stepped beside Okya. "What did I say to make you think this is a negotiation?" Sellow's evil tone was the opposite of her elated eyes. She plucked a shiny five-inch scale from Okya's sable suit.

Olliope giggled, her eyes burning with fervor, her laugh high-pitched and manic as she flapped the hem of her poncho.

With a swift, sudden motion, Sellow plunged the scale into Sloane's stomach, the impact was as jarring and explosive as a lightning strike.

My hands flew to my mouth, stifling a scream.

The metal sank deep, eliciting an agonizing cry from Sloane. Again and again, Sellow stabbed, her grin widening with each merciless thrust. Blood spurted in dark arcs, splattering the ground and staining Sellow's arm. Sloane's shriek rose in a horrific crescendo.

Li burst from behind an evergreen, gun raised, he emptied the chamber on Sellow, each shot a booming bang echoing through the night. Birds screeched and took flight.

Shock coursed through my veins. I scrunched into a protective ball while covering my ears.

In an instant, Sellow's pupils splintered into a dozen diamond patterns. She cut the air with her staff, deflecting bullet after bullet and whizzing them back at Li. He dove behind a rock.

"Okya, we'll take care of the big boy." Sellow flipped her reaping hook like a conductor's baton. "Polon and Olliope, seize Aviana!"

Polon rushed me, wearing a joker's smile. Fritz exploded from the bushes. A three-pointed sai in each hand, the word Jeep visible on the middle prong. Fritz slung a gleaming sai through the air with a lethal precision I didn't know he possessed, and it found its mark, burrowing deep into Polon's shoulder.

Polon roared, a mix of pain and pugnacity. He yanked the steel from his flesh. A dark stain rapidly expanded as the blood flowed freely. He charged Fritz like a bull.

I screamed, "Fritz, run!"

Fritz barrel-rolled to the left. As he twisted away, he extended his foot, landing a solid kick to Polon's jaw. Polon staggered, then dropped to one knee, battling against the brutal, disorienting blow. Blood trickled from the corner of his mouth.

Fritz's fingers heated the metal with a focused intensity until it melded into a glowing cord. He leapt onto Polon, flipping him over and hogtying his arms and legs behind his back with the manipulated metal. Polon struggled, but his strength was no match for Fritz's bindings. Though he was at Fritz's mercy, his angry gaze never wavered.

I bolted toward Sloane, my arms pumping, every instinct screaming for me to reach her before it was too late. But in my periphery, I saw it. The embodiment of beautiful destruction, Olliope, moving quickly toward me. Her poncho billowed out around her, spreading like bat wings.

Fritz's skilled hands melted and reshaped his last sai into a deadly throwing star. With a sidearm motion, he released the weapon, aiming for Olliope. The throwing star sliced through the air, shaving her braid in half. A high-pitched shriek erupted from her as she skidded to a halt. With a forceful stomp, her foot struck the earth, which seemed to fracture beneath her ferocity. In the depths of her eyes, rage flickered like an uncontrollable flame. Her hesitation was a gift, giving me just enough seconds to reach Sloane's side.

My hands pressed against the warm slickness of her wounds. "I'm getting you out of here," I vowed, but beneath my trembling fingers, blood flowed relentlessly.

"Save Fritz," Sloane spoke with a choked sob, the sound of her heart breaking in her throat. "You must protect him."

Olliope spun toward me. Her poncho rose above her waist, and her heel connected with my jaw. I sprawled backward. She leapt onto my chest. Her delicate, cupid-shaped mouth brushed mine as swampy smoke billowed past her lips. The vapor, smelling of moldy cheese, stole my oxygen.

My lungs burned. I coughed.

She laughed; it was a chilling sound of a predator toying with its prey. Then she bombarded my face with another toxic zephyr. I sealed my lips and shook my head, but the nebula hovered at the tip of my nose, waiting patiently for me to inhale.

A cat's yowl skewered the night. Graysen sprang from a thicket, her tousled fur a black silhouette, as she landed on the ground, claws clicking against the rocks. With feral eyes, Graysen snarled, then lunged onto Olliope's back. She sank her fangs deep into Olliope's neck. One paw raked down Olliope's beautiful face, leaving beastly bands of blood in their wake.

Olliope cried out. I pushed past Olliope's fumes and bit her forearm. She jerked her arm violently, but my jaw stayed locked.

Sellow tore Graysen from Olliope's back and flung her skyward. Graysen yowled mid-spin, claws slashing the air before crashing into the thicket with a harsh snap, vanishing beneath the branches.

"Graysen!" I screamed.

A faint whimper replied, thin and pained.

Olliope slammed her forehead into mine. Stars burst behind my eyes. Sellow pressed her boot to my forehead, forcing my skull into the earth, but I turned my head, tears streaming down my face. With both hands, I gripped her boot. *We're going to lose. We're all going to die.*

Sellow seethed. "Fritz, you're not quick enough to save Sloane and Aviana."

Li hurled Okya into the SUV's windshield. The ear-piercing shatter signaled no one was ready to surrender. Li fired two shots at Sellow. She sent one flying at Fritz. It sliced across his brow, and blood streamed into his eye. But Sellow missed the last bullet, it punched into her thigh, and blood rained down on my face. Staggering backward, she limped toward the SUV.

Okya sprinted across the SUV's hood like a furious black panther, each step landing with a clang that dented the metal.

Li jogged my way, but Okya vaulted onto his back. He flipped her over his shoulder and she landed on her feet. She leapt onto his chest, bear-hugging him with her legs. She blew a gray nebula from her lips. Lightning bolts flashed within the rumbling smog. It spun hurricane-like and slammed into Li's eyes. His face contorted as he struggled with the alienish cloud.

Okya sprang off Li in a back handspring, a satisfied smirk on her face.

Sloane coughed, blood splattering her chin. Suddenly, this woman who had always loomed large in my life looked fragile. Resignation and surrender, an emotional collapse, melted her features. The corners of her mouth dropped, and her body sagged as if drained of all strength. How could I save her?

All around me, chaos and confusion reigned, with indistinct shouts and shrieks and blurs of black-and-white motion. Sloane's eyelids fluttered open and close, weak and desperate, like the last flickers of a dying flame. I was powerless to help her. If only I possessed an evobility that could make a real impact. Heal Sloane or fight for us! A foreign energy surged inside me. Could it be my Slyfen evobility craving to be used? The abraylix singed my skin, demanding my composure, but achieving an ounce of serenity in the midst of the deafening discord was impossible. A sense of finality fueled more fear like an avalanche of horror, threatening to bury me.

Within a blink of the eye, a blazing light radiated from my skin. Its brilliance reached out like a sunbeam to every corner of the marsh. My evobilities wrenched on the abraylixes demanding to be set free. My scream speared the night, an eerie war cry that rattled the ground.

Shielding her eyes, Olliope flung herself away, scrambling behind the SUV.

Voltage hurtled through me like thunder in rapid succession. My spine whipped in and out of the fetal position, my body was no longer under my control as it slammed my skull into the earth. Each collision sent shockwaves through me. The abraylix squeezed, but my evobility fought back, pushing the abraylix to its limits! Like a rubber band stretched beyond its breaking point, the abraylix snapped. My light didn't just return; it slammed back into my chest like a white-hot fist, bringing with it a searing scent of ozone and dust.

Fritz unclipped a push dagger from his ankle, then pressed it to Polon's jugular. "Avi, don't move. You broke an abraylix."

"Fritz!" Li waved his hands out in front of himself.

Okya unbuckled her belt and lassoed it around Li's throat, constricting like an unforgiving iron collar. She kicked the back of his legs, and he dropped to his knees. Blood ran from the corners of his eyes. His pupils, once green, were now gray. She tugged a shining obsidian scale from the wrist of her bodysuit and ran it threateningly down Li's cheek, then whispered into Li's ear. His chin dropped, the muscles in his neck contracted. His shoulders rolled left, then right, a gesture of defeat and despair.

Fritz's eyes narrowed on a panting Sellow. Blood snaked down her thigh and dripped to the ground. "*Go now*, leave one of your SUV. I must get Avi and my mom to a hospital." Fritz's tone wasn't commanding or pleading; it was the sound of a tactician issuing a calculated demand. The boy I grew up with, the farmer who cultivated respect for nature, and the man I loved were all obliterated tonight, and I felt sick wondering what might remain of him.

Sloane coughed. Breaths coming in shallow, uneven gasps, each one weaker than the last. Her skin, once warm and vibrant, had turned ashen.

I had to save her. Stop the bleeding. I tested my strength. A needling stinging barraged my nerves and I slumped back to the ground. I was powerless.

Sellow regarded the opera seria unfurling around her. Gritting her teeth, she clamped down on her wound, desperate to staunch the crimson tide. She spoke through gritted teeth, "Carry the princess to the SUV. We're leaving."

"You're not taking her," Fritz snarled as he shoved the knife against Polon's throat. A thin rivulet of blood trickled down his neck.

"She'll come to us willingly, sooner or later." Polon's voice was low. "Once she knows what's at stake, once she learns you're a coward. She'll leave you behind."

The words hit their mark; Fritz gritted his teeth. "You don't know a damn thing about her. And you sure as hell don't know me."

"You're outnumbered. I'll trade you a vehicle for the girl," Sellow spat back.

My brittle voice broke the stalemate like cracking ice. "Fritz… let me go."

The plea was a dagger to his resolve. Fritz's gaze flickered to Sellow, then back to me as his fingers flexed for just an instant.

Olliope stomped over to a limping Sellow. "We're duty-bound to execute the traitors."

Sellow glanced at Li and studied his blind predicament. "I see one traitor who's as good as dead, a pitiful princess, and two foolish kids." Her condescension seemed to slap Li and Fritz across the face. Then, without warning, Sellow wrangled Olliope by the collar. "Assist Polon." She shoved Olliope toward Polon. "Okya, pick up the princess. We're leaving."

Okya peeled her belt from Li's throat and looped it around her waist.

Fritz shoved Polon aside, then ran to Sloane, dropped to his knees and cradled her head. Her cough was wet and labored. Sorrow bore down on his hunched shoulders. He turned to me, the vulnerability in his eyes mirrored the profound anguish in my heart. "Avi, I'll never stop searching for you."

Tonight, there were no goodbyes. I was gone, and so was the life I once knew.

Chapter 16

Metallic memories slammed into my mind. Musky medicine muddled my mouth. I groaned.

A frog croaked. A woodpecker rapidly drummed.

No honking. No motorcycles. No planes hummed.

I wasn't in the city.

Weight shifted at the foot of my bed.

I squinted. Sunlight reflected off a man's receding hairline. Clean shaven. Sunken brown eyes. Brown? Brown! "Br—" My tongue didn't believe my eyes.

The room radiated luxury, wrapped in gold and silver damask wallpaper. Each pigment, distinct and bold, formed a symphony of forgotten shades. My jaw dropped as I beheld the full spectrum of life's beauty. Tears streaked my cheeks. This unexpected miracle went beyond anything I ever imagined.

In one corner of the room, pink perfume bottles sat upon a make-up desk, adorned with bulb lights and a white plush stool. Even the color white, so familiar and plain, now shimmered with a newfound brilliance, standing proudly alongside its newly awakened kin. Each hue breathed life into my ordinary world, transforming it into a wondrous and magical place, as if an enchantment had been lifted. This couldn't be. The open window's drapes flapped. "Those curtains. What color are they?"

Amusement coated the man's throaty chuckle. "The drapes are indigo." Each crisply enunciated word had an air of sophistication.

"Indigo. Indigo." The curtains made the room feel alive with vibrant, botanical energy. I sniffled. "Indigo is beautiful."

"I finally found you, daughter," he said softly with an almost disbelieving tone. His eyes glistened with the enduring power of love and the unbreakable bond between father and daughter.

I covered my mouth to stifle a gasp. His blue collared shirt and onyx slacks accentuated his tan complexion, confirming he gifted me my golden undertones.

In the photograph Raiden showed me, Uzziah's face had been fuller, radiating health. But now, the hollowness of his cheeks and the lines creasing his eyes told a different story: one of struggle, whispering that his journey was far from glamorous despite his current living conditions.

Yet here he sat, my father. His voice trembled with emotion when he uttered a simple yet profound word, "Daughter". He was a missing piece of my identity. A wave of wholeness drifted over me as I offered him a tentative smile, seeking to bridge the chasm of lost years with a simple gesture. I should say, I love you. I miss you. Where have you been? But shock still clung to me, like the smell of smoke after a fire had finally been smothered. And my questions carried a harshness I wasn't sure he deserved, so I blurted, "Why can I see color?"

"The abraylix prevented you from accessing your VidaLumin evobility you inherited from your mother. As an unexpected consequence, it restricted your ability to see spectral composition of visible light. Your VidaLumin evobility shows you a person's true nature. Their desires, ambitions, and fears, each one on display for you. Study their colors and shapes. Your evobility is your only defense in a world built on deception. Power doesn't come from strength, it comes from knowing who to control, and who to destroy."

Who could I trust? A foreboding flurry frothed in my gut as I foraged for familiarity in my father's face. His voice rang with memories of rocking me in his arms. His smile held a spark of teaching me my first words. His eyes gleamed like a proud father witnessing his daughter's first step. He conveyed emotional cues of recognition, but to me he was a stranger.

I was left with a vexing question: was I a prisoner or guest? I wasn't handcuffed to the bed. Yet I was alone, kidnapped. "What happened to my friends? Where am I?" The words rasped from my dry throat. I sounded weak, helpless, like a dog still wagging its tail for the hand that struck it.

"You're safe. As for your mother's staffers, who lied to you your entire life…." Uzziah shrugged, as though he had no cares in the world. "More importantly we need to discuss your remaining abraylix. That form of cruel punishment is used for prisoners, not princesses. The timing and audacity of it all points to one person, and one person only: your grandmother."

Had she always been as cruel as Uzziah claimed? Or did war and the fear it brought change her?

"The second abraylix is blocking the evobility *I passed down* to you. You and I are Slyfens. We can steal evobilities from other Grounders." The word steal slid off his tongue with ease, as trivial as sneaking a cookie from the cookie jar. "I'm able to hold two or three evobilities at a time, depending on how much energy they require."

A lump built in my throat. I could *never* steal someone's evobility.

"Once the evobility dies inside me, I steal another. This is how you turn on your Slyfen power." He used his left hand to tap his pulse point on his right hand. Deceptively delicate, black barbed nettles sprouted from his right hand's fingertips. "These stingers momentarily paralyze our victim, giving us time to steal their evobility." A cuff snapped into place around his wrist, made from bone, long stripped of life, reclaimed by some dark force. I recoiled. This evobility wasn't a gift. It was a curse.

"Grounders assume stealing an evobility is easy, that you simply take and wield. But to summon your Slyfen, you must find that part of you that craves more, demands more, the part that's done being shit on by the world. Find the rage buried beneath your ribs. The kind that doesn't scream but swears vengeance. When your Slyfen reaches out and takes hold of a foreign evobility, it's like trying to catch a flame. Don't fight the burn. Let it remake you. Burn through what you were, so greatness can rise from the remains. It's a painful rebirth. You'll think, *I could never do this again.* But you will." His eyes burned with a fury that had been forged, not sparked. Using his left hand, he tapped the pulse point on his neck twice and the cuff splintered and popped, the smell of burned flesh wafted between us, then the cuff crumbled to ash, leaving only a red ring around his wrist. "Some Slyfens don't survive the becoming. They lose control, and fiery rage consumes them. That's the price. Only what doesn't die in the fire gets to wield its heat. I can teach you how to welcome the pain." His words sounded rehearsed, not because they'd been practiced, but because they'd been earned. "Your remaining abraylix is dangerously embedded. Our nurse couldn't extract it. You need an experienced surgeon. There's a Grounder doctor renowned for his unconventional methods. But he can be… overzealous, risking lives for science." He looked away, as if reluctant to utter the next sentence. "I'll summon Doctor Monrowvia today and assess his willingness to cooperate under my terms."

The joy of color battled against the terror of witnessing what I just saw. My fingers closed around the unfamiliar, deep-red sweater dress. Surprise flickered through me. They'd dressed me. The square neckline framed my many bruises and scrapes. The hem stopped just above my knee, it would've been a cozy choice, but against the crisp white sheets, I stood out like a bloodstain on the bed. My clothes had been laundered and were neatly folded upon the stool, with my necklace coiled on top. As I stared at the necklace, a surge of confidence swirled within me. Steadying my nerves, I asked, "Where am I?" This time I spoke as if we were equals.

"The Bridge of the Gods."

Near the small town of Cascade Locks. I'd traversed the bridge to hike the trailhead. Escape was possible. Running was inconceivable, but if I had to, I'd hobble the twenty miles to civilization. "How long was I asleep?"

"You were in a medically induced coma for five days."

"Five days! My friends will be worried sick. My job! I have to go home."

"Your Vancouver life is over. As your father—"

"You missed my entire childhood, every milestone. You can't claim that title." The words flew from my mouth, each one a pointed accusation, cutting the air like a knife.

"I would've been there for every moment, but there's a bounty on my head. Once I made alliances and fortified my forces, I searched for you." He rested a hand on my shoulder; I winced. "Relax. Our nurse worked tirelessly to remove the broken abraylix. Toxins seeped into your veins, but Cynder medicine counteracted their effects before reaching your heart. You have an incision near your spine. Be mindful not to rip the stitches. Also, breaking an abraylix," his head pendulated back and forth, "dissolved the collagen and fat in your face. We did what we could with Cynder creams. You're lucky Sellow brought you here as quickly as she did."

"Lucky? Your goons attacked my friends. Hurt Sloane and Li!" My nails prodded my palms. Was Graysen safe?

Uzziah raised a hand to calm me. "Apologies for my so-called goons," he drawled, his voice silken and cold. "They tend to be, shall we say, overzealous. But be careful who you assume the villain of this story is. We're all trying to survive. As for Sloane, she got what she deserved. We had to send a message. No more sitting on the sidelines. A Grounder must choose, are they our ally or enemy. So, if your so-called friends don't fall in line they'll share her fate."

"You don't sound like the kind man Sloane described." Trepidation and disappointment dripped from each syllable.

"To survive what's coming, you'll have to adapt. Just like the rest of us." His voice carried the weariness of someone who'd endured heart-wrenching changes. Beneath his commanding exterior, there was a flicker, a hint of a man still grappling with the uncomfortable truth of who he had become. "Tomorrow, we'll walk the garden barefoot to charge your evobility. If I don't teach you how to control it, the consequences are deadly."

My chest tightened. I was leaving tonight, even if that meant escaping.

Clopping steps announced a Grounder's approach long before he reached the door.

My eyes widened, I didn't know they stitched suits that big. The strength of his body was clear, even under the slate fabric of his clothes. His legs rivaled tree trunks. His well-defined trap muscles bulged around his neck. The man's full, jet-black beard curled around his ebony square face. His flawless skin hid his age, while his dark eyes burned with blind loyalty. A wide nose and pronounced brow enhanced his powerful presence. "Sir. Call." He extended a cell phone to Uzziah.

I resisted the urge to lunge for it, my fingers squeezed the comforter.

"And the twins brought you a gift." His deep humble voice was like a rumble from a dormant volcano, as if he was a descendant of Hephaestus.

Uzziah stood, much thinner and shorter, but commanding in his own right. "Aviana, meet Boron Fimm. Whatever you need he's your man."

"*I need* to go home," I stated. Boron glanced from me to Uzziah.

"Aviana, all you have to do is look in the mirror to know you're unwell." In the intricate dance of power and persuasion, he held all the cards and knew it.

I had bigger issues than my appearance, but my aching body jonesed for another hit of Cynder's medicine. "Dinner tonight. Then I'm leaving."

"Wonderful." Uzziah kissed my forehead, and I flinched. He either didn't notice or didn't care.

"*I also need* a phone. Now."

"Yes, yes. I'll have one delivered," he casually confirmed as he strode toward the door.

I swung my feet off the bed, and they sank into the soft cream carpet.

"Where are you going?" Uzziah's question had mild heat behind it.

"The bathroom," I deadpanned.

Boron stepped to my side and extended his arm.

"I don't need…" My words wavered as a spasm shot up my spine like an electrical current, radiating outward in dizzying waves. A grimace twisted my face as I reconsidered my protest.

"I'd be happy to assist you, Princess." Boron's gentle tone accompanied a sheepish smile.

I begrudgingly took his arm, and he assisted me as if I was a fragile senior citizen.

Once in the bathroom, my jaw dropped. "What the hell?" My reflection in the mirror must be lying.

Chapter 17

"**M**y neck is an accordion. I have saggy jowls!" Boron's thick lips twitched with suppressed laughter as his eyes crinkled at the corners. "Our nurse, she's *real* talented. She made these creams here, usin' the best Cynder ingredients." He pointed toward two jars, one labeled day, the other night. "Don't you go panickin'."

My complexion had a greenish-gray tint. Forged near my eyes, chasmal wrinkles stretched to my hairline, as if crows squabbled across my face.

Bracing the counter, I hung my head.

Don't freak out until you know for sure your face won't heal.

Don't freak out.

I counted the passing seconds as my pulse slowed.

I had to focus on what was most important: finding a phone and scouting the property.

Staring at my bare feet, I wiggled my toes, then straightened my shoulders. "Boron, can you please take me outside. I want to charge my VidaLumin evobility."

Boron's expression softened as he gave me his arm.

Once outside my room, we walked through arches framing the hall. On a slim table, fresh-cut white and pink roses perfumed the space.

We passed an office with glass French doors. A large map was pinned onto the wall. Stacks of documents sat atop a stately mahogany desk awaiting scrutiny. A galvanized steel chest, stretching almost six feet, sat beneath the bay window. I paused.

Boron followed my gaze. "That's a map of Cynder." Then he tugged my arm, guiding me toward a corridor, away from the kitchen and living room.

Boron opened the sliding glass door, and the friction murmured its clandestine melody. Cobblestones formed the veranda's foundation.

Polon, the stocky, short man with pinched eyes and a long, thick nose, sat lazily on the rock steps. His bare feet firmly planted in the grass. He sneered at me, then rotated his shoulder with a wince.

A half-smile curved my lips. Fritz's sai had left its mark. Good. I tilted my head in Polon's direction. "What's his evobility?"

"He's a Palmthermic. Polon's palms contain sensitive receptors that detect the infrared radiation emitted by warm-blooded creatures. On Cynder, this adaptation to sense body heat is crucial for hunting prey or avoiding predators."

A Rapunzel tower defined the house's stone exterior. Two guards stood on the property's east and west side, eroding the storybook home's charm. One guard was definitely a Jagwar. He was blockish, like Li and Boron. But the other three were either too thin, too tall, or too short.

Boron slipped off his shoes. We stepped off the patio and onto the grass, my toes curled into the cool blades. The heaviness weighing on me inside the house melted away with each step. The wind hinted of pinecones. The setting sun's rays battled against the tree's dense canopy. A chittering chipmunk clutched an acorn to its chest, then darted toward the circular garden.

My shoulders tensed as I peeked at the blue sky. "How do I know if my evobility is charging?"

"Tranquility sweeps over you. Imagine having worked a fifty-hour week and can finally rest. Your mind clears. We laid you in the grass yesterday, hoping to spur your evobility from its slumber."

Slumber was an understatement; I had been bound and burned.

As we approached the circular garden, I followed Boron's instructions, though my thoughts swirled like storm clouds.

I sighed exasperatedly. "It's not working."

He tenderly patted my forearm. "Be mindful of your surroundings' sounds and smells." He shepherded me into the garden. Lining our path, clusters of vibrant rhododendrons burst forth with bold pink and purple blossoms. Ferns carpeted the garden's shaded corners. Elegant honeysuckle towered above. Their yellow and white petals were soft as watercolor strokes, releasing a jasmine-vanilla scent that lingered in the cool air. Lavender sprigs stood tall next to pink peonies. Hundreds of blossoms blended into an intoxicating scent that made me yearn for my laboratory at Pacific Perfumes. What would become of me now?

A chubby, fuzzy caterpillar scooted across the cobblestone path. "What color is this?" I bent down and pointed to the pigment next to its black stripe.

"Orange. It's a woolly bear caterpillar."

As I rose, Boron's soul slowly billowed into focus, with a gray brilliance. "I can see it! I can see your soul."

His face brightened as he took my hand. "What do you see?"

An uplifting lightness swept over me, and the magnitude of this newfound power left me in awe. "A gray fog surrounds you. A white light appeared and disappeared, like a lighthouse." I was no longer an outsider; I had stepped into their magical and extraordinary realm. "What does it mean?"

"Well, a lighthouse symbolizes guidance, safety, and hope, serving as a beacon in the darkness, guiding ships to shore. But it's your evobility, it's for you to decide."

A soft warmth spread through me; I didn't need to fear him.

Where was my soul? I flipped my hand front to back, searching for a flicker, for anything. Nothing. An ache bloomed beneath my ribs. It was cruel, crueler than any bruise or broken bone, to see a stranger's aura yet never glimpse the truth inside myself.

I pressed my palm to my chest, willing it to appear, as if my own heart might whisper its shape back to me. What color would I be? What secrets would I finally know? Or was I just damaged goods? Broken beyond repair. Too far gone to have anything left worth seeing.

What would Fritz's soul look like? Would it be quiet and steady, or flicker wildly when he laughed? Raiden's? Would his soul betray the secrets he hid behind his sly grin? Maybe one day I'd know. For now, the world's colors would have to be enough.

Ahead, a creeping passion vine had overtaken its trellis. Its bizarre purple whiskers belonged in my new reality. All colors were beautiful. How could anyone have a favorite?

Rosebuds peeked with color, petals fell, vines withered; the cycle of life and death was on full display.

Death.

Was Sloane? Graysen? Li?

Behind us a sliding glass door screeched open.

Uzziah stood on the stone patio, enwreathed by the cascading branches of weeping Japanese maples, his pose reminiscent of an eagle guarding its nest. His soul glimmered with a dazzling display of pixels, a mosaic of ever-shifting colors. Emerald flickered into fiery red, only to spiral into a wave of deep purple and orange. Each pixel pulsed with motion, undulating up and down and side to side. His hypnotic kaleidoscope of color had no discernible pattern, only the mesmerizing madness of constant transformation. "Boron, your assistance is needed." Although Uzziah's shout carried easily across the grass, the words were calm, almost bored, as Uzziah turned and disappeared into the house.

Boron led me to the patio. "Miss, can you walk on your own?"

"Yes, I feel better."

He pointed to the right side of the large house. "That's the door we came through. Walk down the hall and take your first right to find your room."

"Will you bring me a phone?"

"I'm sure Uzziah has placed one in your room."

Hope ignited in my chest. I fisted the hem of my dress and raced toward the door as fast as my body would allow. I flung it open. The hallway with the flowers stretched out before me.

"We had a *deal*," a man nasally bellowed, his voice carrying like a foghorn down the hall.

I froze mid-step.

"You steal the keys. I build the infantry. I'm holding up my end of the bargain, you're not!" the same man accused.

I should continue to my room. Stay invisible. But what if this conversation was important? I shifted on the balls of my feet. The phone would still be in my room even if I took longer to get there. I swallowed hard. What would Nyxon do? Fritz would tell me to run, but

I was tired of running away. But I needed that phone. What should I do?

Chapter 18

Being brave begins with a single step. I sucked in a shaky breath and slipped down the hall.

The kitchen gleamed ahead. A large white island made the space feel small. Red apples piled in a ceramic bowl matched the crimson pots swaying above an eight-burner gas stove.

I crouched low, heart hammering, and peeked around the island's edge.

The open floor plan featured a spacious living room with floor-to-ceiling windows. Two cream colored leather couches flanked a glass coffee table. Between them, a voguish woman sat with her ankles crossed in a Gothic wingback chair. Her professionally painted, blue fingernails, adorned with white tips, were folded in her lap. Her royal blue stilettos matched her lipstick, a color that perfectly complemented her supple sable skin. Diamonds sparkled from her ears. The neckline of her white suit plunged past her delicate breasts, framed in a sweep of white feathers. Her regal expression revealed a cunningness as lethal as her beauty. I ceased breathing, as if the sound would entice this predator into action. She wasn't human. Anyone, from any galaxy, could sense this queen of cruelty.

Behind her stood a young man whose black complexion carried silver undertones. His round face suggested he was about twenty-one years old, and his honey irises darted around the room, absorbing everything with guarded curiosity. He hooked his thumbs into his belt, tilted his pelvis forward, and puffed out his gangly chest.

Uzziah paced the living room in front of a peculiar man who seemed out of place in his surroundings. The man stood at five-foot-four, and his unbuttoned plum-colored suit jacket revealed a bulging belly that strained against the gray suspenders struggling to support his black trousers. His skin had a sickly, white-green hue. His heavy-lidded, bulging, green eyes made him resemble a bullfrog that had somehow stumbled into human form.

"Doctor Monrowvia, patience is imperative if this partnership is to endure. I found a Slyfen capable of wearing the Tiara of Tuskia. But convincing her will require finesse. She has an abraylix that must be removed immediately. This is a delicate situation, and you're infamous for your risk-taking and insensitivity toward your patients." Uzziah's condescending cadence seemed to be the natural inflection of his voice.

The doctor waddled into Uzziah's path, forcing him to halt. Uzziah wrinkled his nose, his gaze dropping disdainfully. "My *research subjects* are none of your concern. Vana hired *me* to produce results." He pointed at the woman sitting on the couch. "The longer the bitch queen retains her position, the more Cyndarian citizens sink into complacency. To overthrow the usurper, we need the Slyfen to wear the Tiara and join our side. This is the prophecy the ChronoCoil Architect foretold, is it not?"

Instead of a swift rebuttal, a collective murmur oozed around the room.

"Drive the girl to my lab, I'll rip out the abraylix. No problem. Then I'll *persuade* her to wear the Tiara within an hour." Sweat trickled down Doctor Monrowvia's temple. "We are running out of time."

Uzziah exploded forward like a ferocious beast, his face twisted into a snarl, shocking the room into silence. Uzziah seized the Doctor's collar and drove him into the cream wall with a resounding thud. Uzziah's fingertips sprouted with the paralyzing black nettles.

Monrowvia flapped his flabby arms. "Not my Attercopi evobility. You can't have it, Slyfen."

Uzziah shook him. The Doctor's jowls jiggled and pink rushed to his cheeks. "Pillaging your evo would be a waste."

He swung the Doctor away from the wall and released him into the center of the living room. The Doctor stumbled, his weight throwing him off balance. His rotund body teetered on the edge of a fall, but just before his chin could crack against the tile, two spare arms shot out, slapping the floor with a smack of skin on stone.

My jaw dropped. This level of violence and these strange beings were my new reality and the thought sank in my gut like curdled milk.

"The Amarmet council will hear about this," Monrowvia blubbered.

"Shout it from the rooftop for all I care." Uzziah's neck muscles bulged.

The woman rose. "Enough." She didn't raise her voice, but a chiding laced her inflection.

The Doctor wobbled to his feet, his four hands fussing with the gray suspenders. He tucked two arms back into the folds of his purple jacket, the fabric curling around him like the wings of some dark insect. A strange symbol emblazoned upon his jacket: a staff flanked by horned bat wings. Atop the staff, rested an eye with an onyx orb as its pupil. I recoiled, as if gazing upon it would stain my very soul.

The woman promenaded around the men, chin high, hands clasped at her waist. "*I* own the council so updating them is *unnecessary*. We need this Slyfen girl to advance our plan, so Uzziah will focus on convincing her to wear the tiara. Doctor Monrowvia, you're correct about running out of time, but you need to pause your research with the Tiara of Tuskia until Uzziah and I can come to an agreement about how to best use the Slyfen girl. I'll—"

"Pause? I can't pause!" His voice turned shrill. "Not when the Tiara of Tuskia is the only object facilitating my efforts to unravel our genetic code for creating the perfect Grounder soldier."

The young man stepped toward Monrowvia and crossed his arms, disliking that Vana had been interrupted.

Vana's expression didn't falter, only her lips pursed as seconds ticked. "Doctor Monrowvia, I'll take your request into careful consideration." Her measured and controlled tone gave nothing away. "I handpicked you both for good reasons. Squabbling amongst ourselves won't help us return home." Her authoritative statement was like a judge hammering a gavel to settle a verdict. This was a woman who planned and plotted. The men's faces eased, scarlet signs of anger and embarrassment dissolved. They knew who was rooted at the top of this precarious pyramid.

Uzziah nodded solemnly at Doctor Monrowvia, and the doctor copied the gesture.

The woman motioned to the young man. "Yttrium, see the doctor out."

Yttrium escorted him to the door and discreetly whispered final instructions.

Danger lingered at every corner, and I didn't trust the Doctor to operate on me. I had to escape, but I could be anywhere on this mountain. I was lost and trapped.

Then, like a flash of lightning, an idea hit me: the office. Maybe a letter would have an address. There could be information in there that Nyxon would deem useful, leverage that could protect all of us from Uzziah and the Doctor. But if Uzziah caught me… the consequences… my heart skipped a beat.

Going back to my room and playing the good houseguest was exactly what the old me would do. Smile, stay quiet, pretend I belonged. But I wasn't a guest here. My estranged father had dragged me into this house against my will, and every polite step I took felt like a lie I couldn't swallow.

Hunched, I scampered across the hall toward the French doors. Every nerve in me buzzed with the need to know, to pry into their secrets.

I turned the handle and slipped inside. My pulse pounded louder than any footsteps that could come my way. I had minutes, at best.

Thumbtacks pierced the quail-patterned wallpaper, securing the map of Cynder to the wall. Four spheres, each the size of a baseball, were arranged in a diamond formation. The Shimmer Domes!

Desert as far as the eye can see. Towering gold mountains. Small pyramidal towns. Deep canyons skirted and separated the spheres. A double line linked all four spheres. Roads? Bridges? Red thumbtacks punctuated three clusters of pyramidal structures, and a single Shimmer Dome labeled Wrangler. I took a shaky breath and pushed down the dread coiling in my gut. I had to work fast. I pushed papers. Read receipts. Deciphered documents. I stepped back, papers in hand, and my heel kicked the steel chest by the window.

A *thud, thud* from the steel chest.

What the? I sprang away from the sound.

Thud. Something inside the chest demanded its freedom. *Thud.* The chest's three square nickel buckles rattled.

My breath caught. I snuck in here for an address, for facts—forget the chest. But what if a woman from Nyxon's wall was inside? Someone could be in danger.

My fingers moved of their own accord, hovering over the buckles, trembling as they found their place. I flipped the buckles and they snapped, mimicking mousetraps. I glanced over my shoulder and listened. No heels clicked. No footsteps shuffled.

I strained to lift the massive lid and gasped.

This stunning unveiling was bigger than any confession Uzziah could've given, hit harder than a baseball bat to the gut, because the secret inside changed everything I surmised about the evils of the world.

Chapter 19

A woman lay crumpled inside the chest. Her broad shoulders, wedged against the walls, were turned inward by the cramped confines. Frost glistened on her lashes.

How long had she been in there? Each breath I took dragged the bitter cold into my lungs, as if freezing me from the inside out.

Handcuffs shackled her wrists together. Hulking chain-mail gloves encased each finger. Gray duct tape bound her ankles, knees, and elbows together against her body, as if this was a harrowing prelude to her impending mummification.

My trembling fingers hovered over the tape around her elbows. "Hold on. Oh God, hold on," I whispered.

Hoarse oxygen raced from her nostrils, matching the quick rise and fall of her chest. Curly brunette roots encroached on her brassy dye job. A black, quarter-size mole on her right cheek contrasted with her brown skin. She squirmed and squealed like a feral ferret, the temperature around me dropping with every frantic movement as my breath puffed out in tiny clouds. Her turquoise irises shone unnaturally bright. I leaned in.

Tiny snowflakes dissolved then reappeared within her pupil.

She was a Grounder. A Grounder from Nyxon's wall? I raised a finger to my lips. "Shh. I'm here to help." I didn't dare rip the tape from her mouth, fearing she'd scream.

I rushed to the desk, fumbling for anything sharp, her squeals rising behind me. "It's okay," I whispered over my shoulder, my voice shaking as much as my hands.

I grabbed a letter opener, then hovered over her bound form. With fevered motions, I serrated the tape on her ankles, each cut dragging, as I prayed we wouldn't be caught. Fear and adrenaline coursed through my veins as I worked to free her knees.

When the last strip of tape fell from her elbows, I grasped her shoulder to pull the duct tape from her mouth. Suddenly tawny, red beady-eyed locusts poofed from her body, and swarmed my face.

I flung onto my back and wildly swiped at… nothing.

Their innumerable bodies blocked out the light but there was no wisping of wings beating the air.

No legs prickled on my skin.

It wasn't real… it *was not* real. What the fuck?

Her muzzled cries escalated to a feverish frequency. She sat up, stiff as a board, and her locust plague increased their frenzied flight.

"Oh, shit." I scooted backward, colliding with the desk. Her desperate expression pivoted to perplexity.

My VidaLumin evobility? I turned it on somehow! And her soul was made of bugs.

She stretched out her cuffs and rattled them at me.

"I don't have the key," I stammered.

Tears welled in her eyes; the duct tape prevented a sob from exposing us.

"If you promise not to scream, I'll remove the tape from your mouth. Nod, if you agree."

She nodded, and her head didn't stop bobbing until I crept closer and reached for the frayed edge of the grimy tape.

With a swift tug, the adhesive tore away, leaving a red mark on her skin and producing a ripping noise as if the fabric of my reality was torn with it.

Her muffled cries turned into gasps of relief. A shudder coursed through her, rattling her metal bindings, disbelief at her newfound freedom evident in her eyes.

"What's your name?" I whispered.

"M-Maria." Her Latin accent quivered. "The key. Top right drawer."

I crawled to the drawer and rifled through. Pushing aside batteries, a lighter, and pens. I lifted a keychain with a dozen silver keys.

"Hurry," she pleaded.

My jittery hands fumbled with the keys. Each click of metal against metal rang like a death knell. Sweat beaded on my forehead as I frantically tried key after key in rapid succession.

"What did it look like?"

"I don't know," she wailed.

From outside, car doors slammed. We froze. Two engines roared to life.

"Boron, bring Aviana to me. It's time." Uzziah's voice boomed from the living room.

Time for what? Could I sneak her to my room? Boots battered the hall floor.

"I have to go. Someone's coming."

She shook her head vigorously and the locusts poofed toward the ceiling. "Don't leave me," she begged.

"If I stay, we're both caught. I'll come back tonight. I won't lock the lid in case something," I gulped, "happens to me." I glanced at the bay window, scanning the frame for a way out. No latch. The damn thing didn't open.

She whimpered but didn't protest as I flattened her into the chest. I tucked the letter opener and the keys under her shaking palms, the chain-mail around her trembling fingers produced an eerie one two beat as I shut the lid.

Exhaling through clenched teeth, I ran. Every step, though light and noiseless, pulled at the stitches along my back. My wound throbbed, but I didn't stop.

My breath came in short gasps as I burst into my bedroom and quietly shut the door behind me.

I scanned the room. No phone. Fear bubbled into anger.

Boron knocked, then said through the door. "Your father would like to meet with you."

I flung the bedroom door wide open. "I didn't receive a cellphone."

A charged pause lingered between us.

He folded his hands in front of him. "We had an unexpected guest. Please follow me." He stepped aside, gesturing toward the corridor. "You can ask him yourself about a phone."

It was clear I'd never be given a phone, so tonight I'd have to steal one.

My stomach was a rain barrel in a monsoon, bubbling over with questions, condemnation, and repugn. I meandered at a cautious pace, even though I had waited years for this commune.

In the living room, Uzziah stood with his back to me, facing the elegant woman in the white suit and the young man from earlier. They held wine glasses, each with varying amounts of red wine. The young man's dark skin glowed with a tipsy warmth as he sipped.

Uzziah turned and smiled. "Daughter, meet Vana and her son, Yttrium." His hand swept toward them.

I forced a tight smile at the stoic pair. Vana's amused gaze swept over me from head to toe. Barefoot and disheveled, I squared my shoulders and faced her immaculate self. Her stilettos and lipstick were perfectly matched. White feathers draped the suit's plunging neckline.

Her soul came into focus. A murky-green liquid surrounded her, as if she were a swan gliding atop a pond. Slate shark fins dove and breached around her, predatory creatures on a marshy merry-go-round. If her green soul had a scent, it would attract flies. My hands grew clammy, a bead of sweat formed on my forehead, as if she'd brought Louisiana's heat and humidity into the room.

Yttrium's umber soul hung off his narrow shoulders and fluttered like a cape in a current of air. Hockey puck-sized milky blobs bobbed on its surface.

Weird.

A server approached me with a glass of red wine on a tray. I waved it away, so she placed it on the coffee table.

Uzziah navigated around the coffee table, took me into a side hug and dragged me over to chat with the group.

"How are you feeling after your garden walk? Nature can do wonders for the soul," he mused.

Small talk? As if he were a doting father, and I were a kid home from soccer practice. I could cling to my wallflower ways, play along with this merry make-believe reunion, but my petals had wilted after Marthane's head rolled out of a box, after blood gushed from Fritz's forehead, and after I found a woman in a chest. Tough questions had to be asked.

"How does stealing the Tiara of Tuskia help you?" I demanded.

Vana went rigid, and Yttrium recoiled, a look of contempt on his face as if I'd just stepped on his new Nike shoes.

Uzziah blinked. "Steal is a harsh word." He chuckled and Vana copied the sound. "The Tiara of Tuskia rightfully belongs to you. It's your birthright."

Approaching heel clicks caught Uzziah's attention. Sellow limped into the living room. Her sleeveless pencil dress was a dark purple, almost black in the right light. A white zipper originated beneath her armpit, jetted across her abdomen, and veered south over her left hip. Despite her pearl earrings and delicate makeup, she was still intimidating. Her arms were formidable, honed like weapons. A salute to women who preferred weight lifting over cardio.

My father grinned like a foolish teenage boy. A subtle blush kissed Sellow's cheeks.

My nose wrinkled and I didn't hide my frown.

Suddenly, Sellow's soul flashed into existence. I inhaled and stumbled back. Yttrium's brow furrowed, his lips pressing into a thin line, clearly unimpressed and confused by my theatrics.

Rising like an ancient kraken, four thick tentacles extended from Sellow's back. Their rounded tips were bent and slumped like weary wrists. Her soul could be a creature from the Mariana Trench.

Her moment in the spotlight was short-lived. Vana walked beside Uzziah and rested a hand on his bicep. His gaze shifted to her, and Sellow's smile faltered. Vana gestured to the cream-colored couches like a grand hostess. "Everyone sit."

Servers in white moved silently through the room, setting napkins, appetizer plates, and two bottles of Merlot on the table.

"Yttrium, sit next to Aviana on the couch," Uzziah offered.

The corner of Yttrium's mouth twitched, then he glanced at his mother.

"Aviana's face normally doesn't look *so*... wrinkly," Uzziah added. I frowned at both men.

Vana pressed her hand between Yttrium's shoulder blades, so he wordlessly moved as Uzziah instructed. His mother stationed herself in the plush wingback chair next to him. Sellow settled beside Uzziah on the couch, across from me.

Boron's heavy steps announced his return. Grinning, he motioned for two assistants to set down the appetizer trays. "Garlic Butter Shrimp Skewers. Next to the fresh sourdough bread from Macfarlane's Bakery, is my creamy fontina cheese spread with diced pink lady apples, spinach, and homemade Dijon mustard dusted with tarragon."

Uzziah took the serrated bread knife and sawed at the loaf. "Boron is a master in the kitchen."

Boron beamed as the others mumbled their agreement.

"You know, it's so important to have hobbies that bring joy into your life," Uzziah said, spreading the mixture over the slice, plating it, and passing it to me. The room stilled as everyone anticipated my first bite. Boron leaned slightly forward.

I crunched into the sweet apple chunks and flavors bloomed. Since I was on display, I deliberately paused, letting the moment stretch before offering a thoughtful, "Mmmmm."

The others congratulated Boron as if he'd just won *Food Network's Chopped* competition. Pressing a hand to his chest, he humbly dipped his chin.

He turned to leave, but Uzziah beckoned him back. "Join us."

A server quickly approached Boron with a glass of red wine.

Boron waved the glass away. "Please enjoy without me." He strode to the front door, where an attentive Jagwar was posted, and took his place beside him, hands clasped behind his back.

As the pungent parmesan aroma enticed everyone to fill their plates, I took the opportunity to steer the conversation toward their past and future plans. I had to understand their alliances, so they couldn't manipulate me. "How do you two know each other?" I asked Vana.

"We have a common enemy." Vana twisted the stem of her wine glass between her fingers.

Uzziah and Vana's shared smile floated across the glass table as if sent to kiss its intended's lips.

"Your grandmother," Uzziah said coldly.

"Even if I strangled her with my own hands, an ache in my soul would remain for everything she stole from us." Vana's velvety voice raised goosebumps on my skin. "My son grew into a man without his father's guidance. My parents never embraced their grandson. A terrible reckoning roars her way."

Few things were as formidable as a woman who had been blighted, battered, betrayed, and yet had rebuilt herself from the ashes, refusing to remain broken.

Uzziah added, "Your grandmother's water dynasty wields too much power and has strangled Grounders for far too long. With her demise, the floodgates will open and quench our citizens' thirst."

The way Uzziah and Vana spoke, with an air of familiarity and shared history, made me feel like an outsider peering into a private world I wasn't meant to be a part of. It was all too much, too sudden, and I couldn't quiet my inner voice that warned my role in this story was shifting in ways I couldn't control. Where was my mother in all this? Whose side was she on? I picked at my cuticles as I mustered the courage to ask, "Can you tell me about my mother?"

"Hydraxia." He swirled the wine in his glass, watching it catch the light and leave thin, glimmering trails along the rim, like a map of loss and longing. "She meant everything to me." Each word felt heavy, lodged somewhere between confession and ache, and he sank deeper into the curve of the glass.

Sellow rustled in her seat, then patted her lips with a napkin. Vana began a side conversation with Yttrium, not threatened or interested in our history. But I rehearsed my mother's name—Hydraxia, Hydraxia—like a sad record, and my stomach sickened.

"We met as kids during the Great Evo-Liberation War. Your grandmother promoted my father to serve as her star general. For years, your mother and I suffered and scraped by. Your grandmother preached and promised social reform. So, the Grays rallied to our aid. They were essential in overthrowing the greedy Amarmet."

Yttrium's nostrils flared and his face twisted into a snarl. Vana patted his hand and cooed into his ear.

Uzziah continued, oblivious or not caring that his statement upset Yttrium. "When she won the war the world was suddenly at our fingertips. We never forgot how Grays risked their lives by hiding us from our enemies, expecting nothing in exchange, and your grandmother *gave them nothing.* Once your grandmother sat high upon her throne, she forgot about the backs she stepped on to get there. Hydraxia and I sought to revolutionize Cynder. We planned to educate the poor. Solve generational inequalities. She was a born leader, a skilled negotiator. I, her champion, and she mine."

My parents weren't just survivors, they were visionaries. Dreamers who believed they could change their world.

"Who—what is a Gray?" Curiosity tinged my voice.

"When a Grounder is born without an evobility or has it stolen by a Slyfen," Uzziah said, his tone more formal then friendly, "their skin and hair turn gray." He pours red wine into an empty wine glass and pushes it in my direction. "Parents usually leave the child outside the Shimmer Dome, where they become food for the blood-sucking, lobster-like sand rabicks."

"That's awful." His story triggered my own fears and memories of abandonment, and my fingers itched to reach for the wine.

"It's for our own safety," Yttrium stammered. "With no moon, the Grays turn savage during the nineteen hours of night. The entire Shimmer Dome goes on lockdown." His mother rested a gentle, reassuring hand on his.

His shoulders relaxed, just enough for him to jab a shrimp with his fork and slide it off the skewer. He brought the shrimp up to eye level, inspected it, and his face soured into the perfect little pout. His manicured nails and tailored shirt gift-wrapped an image of a posh existence, but there was a tired gloom under his inexperienced eyes. "What is this?"

"Seafood, dear. Uzzi and I asked Boron to create a special feast to celebrate Aviana's homecoming," Vana said smoothly.

She had a nickname for Uzziah, interesting. Sellow stiffened, and Vana chuckled into her wine glass.

Yttrium shoved the shrimp into his cheek. His face contorted as he chewed. "I'd rather eat a rabick," he murmured, then spit it back onto his plate. "Boron, cook me chicken nuggets."

Boron stepped toward the kitchen, but Vana's palm shot up. "Boron, no." He heeded her decree. Her brow furrowed. "Yttrium, you *will* eat the food in front of you or go without." Like a child, Yttrium pushed his plate to the table's center and crossed his arms.

The silence stretched just long enough to feel awkward before Uzziah blurted, too cheerfully, "Aviana, you haven't tasted your merlot. It's a local vineyard." He snapped repeatedly. "Sellow, what's the vineyard we love?" His tone brought an artificial lightness to the room.

Sellow purred, "Viento. In Hood River." Then side-eyed Vana.

I rolled my eyes. I wasn't in the mood for fake pleasantries or female posturing. "Why did you ship me to Earth?"

"I didn't. I was outside the Shimmer Dome, traveling to a symposium on sustainable crop production when raiders hired by your grandmother attacked me and my entourage. Boron's wife was killed."

Boron hung his head. "She was family to all of us. Her laugh, I fear one day I'll forget the sound."

A sorrowful shadow crossed Uzziah's face as he raised a glass. "To Clementeen. A sister to all." Everyone but Yttrium raised their glass then sipped.

Uzziah cleared his throat. "A broadcast claimed that a faction of Grays, known as Red TaKa, synchronized our assassinations. They demanded an aqueduct be built for those outside the Shimmer Dome, threatening to hunt down aristocrats until construction began. I discovered the broadcast was a lie. The queen ordered *Sloane's* husband to execute me. Believing you were murdered by Red TaKa broke me. Only Boron and Sellow's unwavering faith kept me alive." He met their steadfast eyes; a silent acknowledgment passed between them. It was a simple gesture, yet it spoke volumes, conveying solidarity, respect, and a mutual recognition of the past and what was at stake in their future. "Four years ago, I discovered you were alive. On Earth. I believe Hydraxia sent you far from your grandmother for your own safety. Your grandmother's no fool. Without us in the way, her beloved Hydraxia could remarry someone *more pliable*. And blaming Red TaKa gave her the leverage to steal their lands and expand the Shimmer Domes from three to four. But I have an evobility that will protect you when we return to Cynder. The Dracophelia." The word Dracophelia curled through the air like a serpent. "The Dracophelia awakens the mind to limitless possibilities in battle. Offensive strikes and defensive maneuvers flow from you like a grandmaster moving across a chessboard. There's a ritual to liberate the Dracophelia from the Tiara of Tuskia. Once I teach you how to control the Dracophelia you'll be free from fear."

He planted a seed of a future for us, but this was a date I intended to reschedule, a class I intended to skip, a moment I planned to rewrite. I looked between Sellow and Vana. "Why don't one of you wear the tiara?"

Vana volunteered, "A female Grounder's heritage must contain at least twenty percent Slyfen origins. Or else their blood vessels will hemorrhage. *Death* imminent."

Cracking glass reverberated through the hallway like clashing cymbals. Everyone jumped.

Boron sprung to attention and barked orders into the radio while running toward the commotion.

Vana sat her wine glass down with a loud clink. Then she scraped her long blue and white nails together, sparking like a friction wheel of a lighter. Electric energy bubbled outward, engulfing herself and her son.

Sellow stood defensively near Uzziah. Her soul's tentacles fanned around him, fully alert.

My friends found me!

"Sir. Please, go to the panic room." Sellow put a hand on his shoulder.

"Is that really necessary?" Uzziah deadpanned.

Hesitantly, I raised a shrimp skewer and poked Vana's blue, lightning-charged dome. It zapped me; a shock twitched to my elbow, my hand involuntarily opened, and the skewer fell to the floor. "Your blue nail color isn't paint."

"It's a force field, dear." Her tone dripped with condescension, as if I were a naive child.

Discussion over their next move spiraled out of control, drowning out Sellow's pleading to relocate. Their questions collided with the chatter on a guard's radio.

Protectiveness pulsed through my veins; I couldn't risk my friends getting hurt. I swiped the serrated bread knife from the appetizer tray and tucked it into my cloth napkin.

I turned away from everyone and faked a cough into the napkin, sliding the knife down the front of my dress and wedging it beneath my bra, where it stayed flush against my skin.

I sat the napkin on the table. It was now or never.

I shot to my feet and bolted toward the source of the commotion.

My aching muscles begged me to slow, but if I stopped, my friend's blood would be on my hands.

Chapter 20

As I approached the office, a thrumming energy coursed through me, keeping me on edge and vigilant, ready for anything. I skidded to a halt in the open-door frame, my mind scrambling to make sense of what I was witnessing.

Boron knelt over the empty steel chest, his thick fingers squeezing the side, glass shards scattered across the floor.

I was mistaken in my friends' devotion. Tonight brought no solace, no rescue.

Sellow grabbed my forearm, her fingers digging in as she yanked me against her chest. "Where are *you* going?" Boron slammed the lid shut. "A bird broke the window. Dinner is over. Princess, go to your room."

No feathers. No bird. No blood. Just curtains flapping from the breeze. Uzziah, Vana, and Yttrium clattered around the corner.

I wrenched my arm away from Sellow. "I'm leaving."

"Leaving?" Yttrium chirped.

"I guess you didn't know they kidnapped me," I spat.

Sellow jutted her chin. "You couldn't walk. We *escorted* you here to meet your father, our king. *You're welcome.*"

"I couldn't walk because your merry band of murderers ran us off the road."

"She can't go," Yttrium declared, his harsh tone directed at Uzziah. "You said we need her to return home. I can't waste any more time on this planet."

Vana shook her head, her demeanor poised yet condescending. "An astounding exhibition of ineptitude, Sellow. As always, you rushed headlong into action. First, you let Raiden get away, now we learn you put Uzziah's daughter in harm's way."

Sellow's cheeks flushed. "*Raiden* escaped because *your* nurse, Marthane, tipped him off."

Vana ignored Sellow and strode beside Uzziah, linking arms with him. "Uzzi, I've always maintained that your reunion required my delicate approach. An invitation extended with grace." Sighing, she turned to me. "But here we are. Aviana, Earth isn't safe for you *anymore*. Instead of running from your father and your future, you ought to thank him for preparing you for the war to come… *mine did not*." Vana's tone dripped with forced warmth, "Stay the night. In the morning, you can get to know your future stepbrother better. With you here, our family is now complete." Her lips curved into a wry smile, aware of how her declaration stung the ones left outside her inner circle.

My jaw slackened. Sellow's eyes bulged.

Vana's grin bared all her teeth. "We're officially announcing our engagement when a few loose ends are *severed*."

"*We are* your family, and we need you at our side when we return to Cynder." Uzziah nodded at Sellow, who swiftly seized my arm again. "We leave in thirty days."

The word "*no*" scraped against my raw throat as I struggled and twisted to break free, but her iron grip held firm. Without warning, she dragged me down the hall toward my room, my feet tripping over themselves in protest.

Uzziah followed a few steps behind us. "The doctor has the equipment needed to remove the final abraylix—"

"I'm not going anywhere with you!" I didn't care how badly I needed his doctor's expertise.

"Sir, we'll need to sedate her," Sellow stated, a smile tugging at the corner of her mouth.

My pulse spiked, a jolt of panic surging through me as I struggled against Sellow. "Wait. No."

Sellow shoved me into my room.

Uzziah stood in the doorway. "Aviana, no one will *ever* love you more than I do." Somberly, he shut the door, the subtle snick of the lock resounded through the space.

I hurled the perfume bottles at the door; they shattered on the carpet. Their glass shards became gravestones in a cemetery. The longing that drove me to find my parents, now held me captive and powerless, a cruel cage of irony.

By some miracle, I hoped the woman from the chest had fled this mountain. A shiver rattled my spine; I'd be following in her footsteps at sundown.

Tonight, I'd need hiking shoes.

I opened the closet and my heart sank like a stone.

Elegant dresses and ironed pants dangled from hangers. Rows of shoes stood in perfect alignment, creating a magazine-quality display. This closet was outfitted for a woman who planned to make this place her home. The fine garments served as a deceptive bribe, masking Uzziah's true intentions: he never planned on letting me go.

I paced from wall to wall, the sun's slow descent my only measure of time.

A tap-tap on my windowpane jolted me from my angry contemplation. I whirled.

Yttrium pushed on the window. But the newly drilled screws in the window frame prevented my window from opening more than three inches.

My brows pinched together, but I walked over and slid the pane the allowed three inches of latitude. "What do you want?" My tone was brittle with blame, even though he wasn't the one who trapped me in this room.

"*Do you* have a plan to escape?" Amusement laced his tone, as if he already knew the answer would be no and he enjoyed taunting me. "*Because I do*."

"Why would you help me?"

"Uzziah needs to focus on finding the keys. *You're* a distraction."

"But you need me to go to Cynder."

"Uzziah believes this. Mother doesn't. *She says* we'll carve our own way," he said with unwavering confidence.

What other choice did I have? A grueling minute lapsed. "If I shatter the window, the Jagwar outside my door will storm in."

"I'm a Fluora."

"What's that?"

"Move away from the window, and I'll show you," he sassed and slid the window back down.

I scrambled to the foot of my bed.

The roof of his mouth unhinged, revealing a hidden chamber. A hose-like tube extended an inch past his teeth. Yellow-green snot rocketed from the tube and splattered against the window. I reeled back.

The slimy, sizzling goo burned and smoked a golf ball-sized hole through the glass. Freedom smelled acidic and slightly sour. Overwhelmed, I fought off exhausted tears of joy.

As he spewed more venom, I dashed to the closet and grabbed a pair of black tie-up ankle boots. I sat on my bed, slipped them on, the hem of my red dress brushing my knees as I bent forward to tie the laces.

Inch by inch, I subtly slid my hand under my pillow, grabbed the knife, and wedged the cold metal into my boot.

Minutes grinded like hours. "Can you stand on the stool and squeeze through?" he whispered. The acid made a perfect hole in the windowpane.

I carried the stool to the window. "I can fit. But wait, I have to grab something." Racing back to my dresser, I grabbed my fertorium necklace and linked it around my neck.

With a deep breath, I stepped through the warm opening. Yttrium gripped my leg to steady me and whispered, "Once you've made it down the hill I'll come back and smash the window, so they don't suspect that I helped you."

The glass tinkled softly as I passed, and Yttrium's firm hold kept me balanced.

My feet thumped on solid ground. The cool air enveloped me, carrying a crisp scent that felt alive and liberating.

"This way. I have a car waiting."

Scampering over the grass, I followed Yttrium through a labyrinth of trees then down the winding driveway, every nerve alert to the inevitable rumble of engines racing to retrieve me. My heavy breathing competed with a hooting owl. As we hurried across the rickety covered bridge, the roar of a rushing stream muffled the thud of our footsteps against the wooden planks. I glanced over my shoulder, half-expecting the Headless Horseman to burst from the fog atop his sable stallion, his ax raised high, ready to give chase.

We turned left and the main road stretched before me. In the distance, red taillights became a beacon of hope. Even the dark forest seemed relieved, leaning away from the road, allowing the moon to cast a silvery celestial path toward our escape.

I panted. "Thank you."

A twisted, cocky sneer crept across Yttrium's face.

A sinking sensation sickened my stomach and I slowed.

"Move it," Yttrium demanded.

A lanky, blonde-haired man stepped out of a windowless white van. His rabbit nose twitched in a steady rhythm.

"No. No. Not him."

Yttrium gripped my forearm forcefully, enough to leave a bruise. "Don't make this more difficult than it needs to be."

My exhausted legs wobbled. The urge to wail in despair and crumple to the ground overwhelmed me.

"We can't wait for you and your father to kiss and make up. Mother said this is the way." Yttrium pushed me toward the van.

My feet skidded across the loose gravel, sending stones scattering. Each step was a battle against defeat. Every pause met with a shove from behind.

"Keep moving! When Uzziah wakes up tomorrow, we'll simply say you escaped. The doctor will remove the abraylix and insert the Dracophelia. Mother will recite the ancient incantation to control your mind, reducing you to the status of a dog, as befits your bloodline." Yttrium's eyes were alight with dreams of conquest and power, a future as bright as the moon. "Then Mother will reign Cynder, as she was destined to, and I'll sit by her side. *Prince* Yttrium Amarmet."

In a surge of desperation, I veered left, sprinting for the looming woods. Yttrium closed in behind me. I reached out, the branches scraped my fingertips, so close yet not close enough. His hand buried into my hair, he yanked my head backward. The force slammed me into him. I lashed out with my elbows, frantic and wild, but he swatted them aside with infuriating ease.

His arm clamped around my throat in a chokehold. "You can walk, or I can drag your unconscious body to that van. Your choice."

Seconds stretched into eternity as I thrashed for air. My lungs burned, my vision blurred, and tears spilled down my cheeks as the last of my oxygen slipped away.

"Aviana?" he growled. I tapped on his forearm. He flung me back onto the road, leaving me sprawled on the ground, the taste of dust and defeat bitter on my tongue.

I curled into a ball, my fingers silently searching for the hilt of my hidden knife. The cold steel against my palm reminded me to be victimized or be vicious.

With a grunt, Yttrium yanked me to my feet. "Damn, you're heavy."

Like a viper, I drove the blade into his forearm: once, twice, three strikes. Blood spurted in wild arcs, warm and slick on my knuckles. I didn't hesitate, didn't falter, each strike was swift.

"Bitch!"

I expected him to fight for the knife, but instead he shoved me with such velocity I tumbled backward down the embankment. The bloody hilt slipped from my grip, as I rolled and rolled, crashing through a thorny thicket, until I slammed against a log.

Holding my breath, I didn't dare make a sound.

Yttrium paused at the embankment's edge. He brought his injured arm into his chest and put pressure on the wounds. "Aviana!" His rage hit me like a shot.

The roof of Yttrium's mouth distended. A glob of acid whizzed past my ear, searing the tree trunk to my left. It hissed and crackled, burning through the trunk, leaving a smoky trail in its wake.

"Come back." Yttrium inspected his arm, his face surprisingly calm. "There's bears." Slapping his neck, he wrinkled his nose. "And mosquitoes. I *hate* nature."

Should I return to him or take my chances in the forest? The dark wood's gnarled branches reached out like skeletal fingers.

"If you hide, we'll destroy everyone who gets in our way. We *will* find you. So come out *now*!"

A chill raced down my spine. I'd already put everyone in danger. Was Sloane alive? Graysen injured? Guilt and fear filled my veins. Please, please let them be safe. My past choices and failures clung to me like a second skin. What awful things would me and my friends face if I got off this mountain tonight? Dread drilled deep into my bones because a fate far worse awaited me if I returned to Yttrium.

"Mother will be very angry." Yttrium sniffled. "Wolfram, use your nose to hunt."

I held my breath and dashed into the forest. Leaves and twigs crunched under my boots, like a trail of gun fire. Branches whipped my face. Snarls of thistles tore through fabric and flesh alike, leaving fiery trails of pain with every desperate movement.

Ebbing waves grew louder in front of me. My muscles burned. Behind me, Wolfram charged like a bull, storming through the undergrowth.

"I love a good chase, but you're a weak, pathetic woman. I can smell your fear from here." Wolfram's raspy shout sliced through the thicket.

I burst through the forest, the trees opening to the cold, raging river.

My only chance lay in its rushing current. I plunged in, the icy water biting my legs as I waded hip-deep and surrendered to the flow. I clamped my jaw shut because a scream of dire disappointment clawed at my throat, threatening to shred the night sky.

The river swept me downstream, granting me a precious head start, but I was on borrowed time. I had twenty-nine days to master my evobility. Twenty-nine days to warn my mother before Uzziah invaded. Twenty-nine days to defend my friends because I wouldn't be running away again.

Chapter 21

I crouched, lifting the potted lavender to retrieve Nyxon's hide-a-key tucked beneath. With a quick twist of the lock, I stepped inside.

The rich scent of chocolate filled the air, a welcome reprieve from my horrific night.

Quinbe appeared, wire whisk in hand, batter dripping onto the floor with each step. "Avi!" She flung the whisk into the sink with a clatter. She ran toward me, her red ringlets bouncing wildly. She skidded to a halt, and her curls kept flying forward as her eyes widened, taking in my disheveled state. "*Oh*! Is it okay to hug you? You look… fragile." Her soul, a sunset of oranges and purple, fanned her frame like a frill-neck lizard.

"Yeah. I'm healing." I closed the distance between us, and she embraced me as if I was a hummingbird in her palm. Even with color highlighting my world, my life would be mundane without her.

Quinbe plucked a few twigs from my matted hair. My arms and legs ached. Every muscle screamed with the memory of the river's rocky shore and the forest floor's tangled roots. I smelled like a rutting elk—damp, earthy, tangy with sweat. I just wanted to shower and sleep in my *own* bed.

"Nyxon, *Graysen,* and Li told me everything." Quinbe gulped, as if swallowing her own doubts. "They're with Raiden, following up on leads to find you." Her voice was steady, but her eyes betrayed the turmoil beneath the surface.

"Raiden?" His name was bitter on my tongue, a spike of anger ripping through me. "How could Nyxon and Li trust him? He brought trouble to our door." My hands flexed at my sides.

Quinbe shifted, tucking a loose strand of hair behind her ear, the vivid red catching the light. The simple movement drew my attention, and I reached out, entwining a silky strand around my finger. "Red hair is lovely." I spoke softly, almost distantly, trying to distract myself from Raiden.

Quinbe's hand flew to her hair, fingers brushing through the strands. "You can see color? How?"

I recounted my escape and how I'd hitchhiked home, fabricating a story for the truck driver who picked me up: I swerved to avoid a deer, sending my car into a ditch.

My breath locked in my throat. "Sloane, is she?"

Quinbe's eyes, usually full of tender mischief, dulled as my question sank in. Time slowed, trapping her in the truth she dreaded speaking. Tears pooled, trembling on the brink before finally falling, carving wet paths down her cheeks.

She wiped them away, but they only came faster, each tear carrying the grief unique to a girl who had lost her mother. Her small frame shook, and a faint whimper escaped her lips.

"No, no! Sloane couldn't." I rocked as regret crashed within me like a tide against the shore.

Sloane didn't deserve death.

Now, she'll never see Fritz at the altar on his wedding day or feel the warmth of her grandchildren's embrace.

The power of moments, I then understood, were weak threads weaving our lives together. The small, seemingly insignificant moments, like the way her laughter filled a room, and the vast, defining ones, like her final words, spoken with concern solely for her son. *Save Fritz.*

If I could turn back the clock, I'd change everything about that day, that month!

As we clung to each other, the urge to scream intensified, our tears soaking into each other's shoulders. Our collective anguish opened a floodgate of memories. Each one a vivid echo of Sloane's warmth and kindness, now lost to us. Sloane once painted her white house's shutters black, so I knew the hallmarks of her home. A fleeting gesture to an angry teen, but it was the only ebony item in my past gray world that coaxed a smile. The impact of Sloane's passing, the enormity of her absence would forever alter our reality.

Quinbe released me, her body going rigid. "I didn't know what to do, so I baked. Fritz won't talk. Li got black-out drunk. Nyxon's stone-cold. She threw herself into finding you. They buried her under the big oak tree behind Fritz's house. Li dug a hole. *A hole!*" Every emotion and injustice she had bottled up erupted like a shaken soda can, uncontainable and overwhelming. "Sloane had so many friends. Nyxon emailed them, explaining it was a family emergency, then flipped her natural path store sign to CLOSED. I still can't believe it. The only sane person was Raiden, but I guess he's not a person. They aren't, you aren't..." She said more to herself than to me. "Raiden promised he'd get you back. He took us to a few of his informants' houses, demanding information. You should've seen him, he was so intense. Brave." A sad sigh passed between her lips, honoring Raiden's courage while mourning its cause.

"You have so many bruises." She dabbed her eyes with her yellow sleeve, then nervously rambled, "I reminded Nyxon to email Michael so you wouldn't get in trouble for missing work. You're working really hard for that promotion."

"Quinbe," I interjected delicately, anticipating her reaction to my next sentence.

"And once things settle down, we can go back to normal." She tilted her head expectantly.

"Quinbe, we can't go back to normal," I whispered.

She blinked, her chest stopped pumping. The silence stretched as the impact of my words hung above us like an axe poised to fall.

Quinbe's shoulders rounded. "So what? All you *Grounders* are going to fly off to Cynder and leave me behind?" Her tone revealed the hurt and betrayal beneath her brave facade.

"Of course not. I'll *never* leave you. But things will change. Change can be good."

Quinbe's brow furrowed as she searched my eyes for confirmation of my promise.

I gently squeezed her arm and her face softened. "I appreciate everything you've done. Even if the others don't say it, they appreciate you too. You're the glue that keeps us together."

The complexities of death and change were treacherous to navigate. For Quinbe, life was a tumultuous sea, and Sloane's ever-vigilant presence was a lighthouse, casting a warm glow of safety upon her, guiding her back toward hope and love.

She sniffled. "I need to call everyone and tell them—" She looked me up and down. "You're home. And you need to shower, then rest."

I closed my eyes, but Sloane's desperate face and haunting plea refused to fade. Her death was my fault and that fact pressed down on me with relentless blame.

Stuck in a bleak, dreamless sleep, the creak of my door jolted me upright. I was home. I was safe. I was… Fritz stood in the doorway. The living room light spilled over his shoulders. The wound across his brow had hardened but still stark against his pale skin. Exhaustion etched every line of his face, the swelling around his blackened eye merging with the deep shadows beneath it. His complexion held a sickly pallor that made my chest ache. Where was the glowing boy I'd grown up with? The earthy, steadfast man I'd once loved?

I would never let the color fade from his face again.

"I'm so sorry," I whispered, guilt coating my words.

My evobility flickered like a faulty television, blinking on and off in an erratic pattern, giving me small glimpses of his gold-and-silver soul.

He tried to speak, to force out a feeling, anything past the lump formed in his throat, but no sound came. Instead, he nodded, a gesture so small it almost broke him, because behind that nod was a tidal wave of misery and fury threatening to drown him.

I threw off my blankets and moved to him. Without a word, I pulled his hand into mine and guided him to sit on my bed. I held him, he closed his eyes and sank into me.

"I don't know what to say," I admitted. My words felt small, inadequate, but they were all I had. "I wish I could take away your pain."

Minutes passed before he finally replied, his voice hollow. "She's gone. And nothing will ever make it okay."

"I'm here. I'm not leaving you," I promised.

"Why do you care after everything? After the lies. After she tried to keep us apart."

"Because everything she did, she did it out of love for you." And because I knew the ache of losing a loved one becomes a constant companion, riding along with you through the motions of daily life. Then, without warning, it flares, triggered by the simplest reminders: a familiar scent in the air, a song she used to hum, or her favorite flower in bloom.

"I can't imagine my life without you in it." Suddenly his soul appeared. Two metallic arches rose above his shoulders like wings, then cascaded downward to brush against his heels. His glowing form left me breathless, as if I gazed upon a fallen angel, witnessing someone divine, someone not meant for this world.

"Avi!" The spell broke with Raiden's shout from outside my room.

We pulled away from each other and rose from the bed. Fritz cleared his throat. A flush crept up my neck, my heart pounded from our closeness, and I prayed Fritz didn't notice.

"Nyxon, I need to talk to her. Avi!"

I hurried to the door.

Chapter 22

"I texted you that Avi was home as a courtesy, not as an invitation to come over," Nyxon deadpanned.

"Where did you find her?" Raiden asked.

"She escaped," Nyxon stated, and I swore pride rang in her voice.

I inched open my bedroom door. Nyxon stood like a sentinel, fists on her hips, her body becoming a wall of defiance, blocking Raiden from moving forward. Her sable leather jacket hugged her six-foot frame, accentuating her imposing presence.

Raiden stood his ground, but a subtle rigidity in his stance betrayed his silent acknowledgment of the power dynamic between them.

My eyes lingered on his skin, a warm blend of bronze and earthy tones. So that was what the color olive looks like. This observation lingered in my mind longer than it should have.

Nyxon lifted an eyebrow in my direction. I nodded so she moved aside to let him pass.

Raiden strode to my door, then softly pushed on it, but I planted my foot, wedging the door from opening further. Raiden's hazel eyes were an unfamiliar color, warm and layered like the forest in autumn.

He wore slate pants and a charcoal T-shirt. Stubble shadowed his iron jaw, but a golf ball-sized bruise peeked through.

"How did the pepper spray taste?" I asked.

His frown creased into a teasing half-smile. "It stung. A lot. That wasn't very nice."

"You wouldn't let me leave."

"You wouldn't let me explain."

Suddenly, his soul appeared, and scarlet flames pushed into my room. At its core, midnight-blue sparkled and spun like a galaxy. I took a step back, and Raiden flinched.

"I'm not your enemy."

I opened the door an extra inch. "How the hell did a…" My throat dried. "*Head* end up in your office?"

His gaze dropped to his shoes, and he rubbed the back of his neck. "Marthane understood the dangers and rewards when I recruited her. Her son works the Clam Mudflats on Cynder. I offered to bring him to earth. He could start a new life. All she had to do was report back to me if there were any signs of Uzziah. I sent Bashiri to her house when she never showed up in Madras, Oregon for extraction. The box you knocked over was on her doorstep. Sellow followed Bashiri back to my office. I wish you hadn't seen…" He stiffened. When he finally spoke again, his voice was taut, as if struggling with every syllable. "Your grandmother hired me. Kill order for Doctor Monrowvia. He is a threat to every human on this planet and every Grounder on Cynder. Avi, this is why I work alone. I never wanted any of this to happen."

"Death found me when you entered my life. Now you pretend to give a damn about the consequences. You got Marthane killed. Sloane…" I couldn't finish the sentence. Saying her name with anger felt wrong. "I wish I'd never met you. You and your fake concern can leave."

Raiden's soul slowed its flame-whipping motion, then sagged off his rounded shoulders. He reached into his pocket and pulled out the white camera I had hid in Pacific Perfume's storage room and dropped it into my hand. "You were right about Michael. But we still don't know who his accomplice is, but this shows them filling the bottles with cheap, non-organic ingredients."

I squeezed the small cube in my palm. "There's no 'we' anymore." I swung the door shut, only for Fritz to catch it with his hand, his fingers locking onto the wood.

"This isn't Raiden's fault. Blame rests with *your father* and Sellow. Get dressed. We need to discuss next steps." Fritz walked out of my room without a backward glance.

I stood there, stunned. The atmosphere in my room cooled with Fritz's abrupt shift in demeanor and departure.

I turned away, pressing my spine against the wall, wishing I could rewind to the minutes before Raiden shouted my name. I sighed, defeated.

Raiden's soul drifted toward me, tentative and slow.

I wasn't someone who crushed souls. I drummed the back of my fist against the wall, compassion bubbling up. "Tell me, Raiden, why the queen? How do you know you're on the right side of this fight?"

"Sometimes there isn't a right side. Sometimes you choose the side that'll hurt less. Sometimes you choose the path that'll hurt more because you found someone worth risking it all for." He spoke with soft sincerity, each word carefully curated, as if revealing a deep truth. One that could make anyone feel chosen, cherished.

He gently curled a loose strand of hair behind my ear. "I truly want to help you."

His touch conveyed vulnerability, tempting me to lower my defenses. Despite the pull, I wouldn't relinquish control to him. A newfound priority fueled my resolve: keeping my friends safe. I wouldn't allow his objectives, his job, or his hidden agenda to come before that. Because I'd be damned if I let Raiden inadvertently lead a furious Yttrium, Sellow, or Uzziah to my friends.

Raiden continued, "If returning to a normal life is what you prefer, I can—"

"I don't want normal." My words surged forth, bearing a determination that surprised even me. "I want this last abraylix off. I want to *feel* free, to *reclaim* my evobility."

He met my declaration with a mischievous glint in his eye, suggesting he hoped for that response, as if he had waited patiently for this moment, eager for my acceptance of his extraterrestrial reality.

Nyxon's pacing in the living room felt like a ticking clock, every footfall vibrating through the floorboards. "Raiden, your time is up."

Raiden's gaze held a desperate plea to disobey Nyxon and allow him to stay.

My throat tightened. The truth was: he had information we needed. "Raiden stays," I shouted, then shut the door before anyone could protest.

I limped to the closet. My clothes would never clash again. Shopping with Quinbe would never feel like an obligation. I picked orange yoga pants and a charcoal off-the-shoulder shirt.

I rolled my tangled hair into a messy bun. What was in store for me? My future formed a sickening lump in my gut. Could I still open my own shop? Would they make me move from Vancouver? Would I even get a say, a vote? Questions piled like a Jenga tower, ready to fall. Which friend would pull the piece that toppled the life I built?

I shuffled into the living room. Raiden had an elbow on the fireplace's mantle, giving everyone a wide berth. Quinbe sat cross-legged on the couch with Graysen in her lap. Graysen's azure and graphite pebbled soul cemented to her anatomy like armor.

Li and Fritz grumbled in the kitchen. For the first time, I saw Li as he truly was—a masterpiece. His black skin, rich and smooth like polished obsidian. His eyes that narrowed toward both the inner and outer corners held a depth I'd never noticed.

Nyxon leapt from the couch with a blanket. Her observant brown eyes gleamed with urgency. Her bronze skin intertwined with the pale streaks of vitiligo along her fingers as she wrapped the blanket around me. Leaning in, she whispered, "Fritz is on edge. He seeks revenge, but he's no match for Uzziah. Don't divulge Uzziah's whereabouts."

Sloane's final plea, save Fritz, squeezed my heart. Fritz intended to confront Sloane's tragedy head-on, seeking closure in a perilous pursuit that might leave him dead. My lips quivered. I must lie to protect him.

"Now that we're all here, we can begin. Avi, where did they take you?" Fritz's stern expression bore into me. Raiden's attention piqued. Li's eyes darted to Nyxon, then back to me. They must share the same plan to keep Fritz safe.

"I—I don't know."

The vulnerability Fritz showed in my room vanished, replaced by a thirst for vengeance. "What did the house look like? Which highway did you take to get back to Vancouver?"

"A red brick house. When I escaped it was dark, I ran out the back into the woods and never saw the house number." My palms dampened. "I came from the coast."

The corner of Raiden's mouth twitched. I could be honest with Raiden tomorrow. But would I feel guilty if he was injured? Does Raiden deserve someone on his defensive line? If Fritz couldn't confront Uzziah, why could Raiden?

Fritz broadened his stance. "I find it odd that Uzziah would treat his daughter like a prisoner."

Sweat pricked my skin, betraying me. Stay strong. He must be kept safe at all costs. "For the first few days I was in a coma." My mind raced for my next line. My fidgeting fingers ravaged my cuticles.

"Stop harassing her," Quinbe scolded.

"Her brain is probably foggy. Give her a few days." Li surprisingly came to my defense.

Fritz huffed, then turned his glare to Raiden. "You claim to have information that will help us find Sellow and Uzziah. Prove it."

Chapter 23

Raiden pulled a sleek black laptop from his briefcase and placed it on the table. "To find Sellow and Uzziah we first have to track down the Tiara of Tuskia."

I slid onto the chair next to him. The others gathered around, the tension in the room thickening by the second.

"This is Cynder's version of a laptop," Raiden explained to me and Quinbe. "It's called a filament." He snapped his fingers, and the device hummed to life. He pressed the screen flat, and four tan folders hovered above. Tapping the QHC file, he opened it with a whoosh. Digital documents arched upward. Only Quinbe and I looked impressed.

He skimmed, then selected an image labeled *First Tiara Sighting.* "This is the Queen wearing the Tiara of Tuskia."

I gulped. Weeks ago, my lineage was barren. Now I stared at my grandmother. She wore a tan, zip-up uniform similar to an air-force flight-suit. She was short and solid, built like an oak tree—rooted and unshakable. Time and turmoil had etched rings beneath her eyes, each wrinkle a tally of battles won. A circlet of quills sat atop her head. Their brown bases faded into bone-white tips that jutted in all directions.

"This tiara is more than a symbol. It serves as a conduit, linking the Dracophelia to its host. If Avi summons it, the Dracophelia will amplify any evobility she possesses."

"That sounds fun." Quinbe's eyes lit up, the first spark since my return.

Raiden frowned. "Avi doesn't know the first thing about commanding a lethal, volatile evobility." He tipped his head at me, his expression like a disappointed father's, ensuring I knew he was serious. "You'd lose control. Your blood would boil, your organs would rupture." Quinbe and I exchanged a tense glance. "Years ago, Slyfens would steal evobilities, hex an object to contain them, and set them aside for later use, to trade, or simply as a trophy. The Queen outlawed the practice because the hex could fail and the evobility would possess the object. They call it diabolical infestation."

Quinbe stammered, "Dia—bolical what?"

Raiden continued, "Without a Grounder to regulate the evobility, it turns aggressive, hysterical, desperate. Humans encounter these objects and mistake them for a demonic possession."

My eyes narrowed on Raiden. "So, this demon tiara wasn't stolen from a collector in Italy?"

Raiden rubbed his neck, sheepishly. "A Grounder stole it from the Queen's treasury."

I slowly shook my head and crossed my arms, a declaration of disdain and disgust.

Li arched an eyebrow, a hint of amusement in his gaze. "*Wow. Of course you swallowed that lie.*"

Embarrassment flushed my cheeks. Li's jab had spotlighted just how naive and gullible I was.

"It was stolen. That's the truth." Gratitude for Raiden's interference was like a balm on my warm skin. "The Queen commissioned me to retrieve it. The tiara's quills come from a pack predator called a riptor. Imagine an ostrich with porcupine quills and a Komodo dragon's head. During the Great Evo-Liberation War, Mercer Markosyan, Uzziah's father, traded it to the Queen in exchange for Uzziah's marriage contract with Hydraxia."

I shifted in my seat. "So, it wasn't a fairy-tale romance like Uzziah described." I should've known.

Nyxon tilted her head. "With the right ingredients, love can grow anywhere."

"Where did you find that quote?" I joked.

"On a Dove chocolate wrapper last Valentine's Day."

"I agree with the chocolate wrapper," Raiden teased.

Fritz's guarded gaze fixed on Raiden. "Continue."

Raiden flicked his wrist, swiping the photo aside, and selected another. A man in his fifties, his long brown hair matted to his cheeks from blood loss due to the slash across his throat. His caterpillar eyebrows arched in a painful final expression. Burned into his forehead were two letters: AA.

"Raiden!" I looked away.

"Sorry." He swiped it aside. "I discovered Meskel's corpse near the Bridge of the Gods five months ago. He had stolen the Tiara of Tuskia from the queen's vault for Uzziah. But Meskel learned the Tiara's true worth and planned to double cross Uzziah, sell it at an auction instead."

Nyxon leaned back. "*AA* is a warning from the Amarmet Alliance. I thought the queen eliminated them?"

"Well, cockroaches never die." Li frowned.

"What is the Amarmet Alliance?" I stammered.

"Families who opposed your grandmother during the war." Nyxon's tone was clinical, almost as if she discussed a case study. "When she declared victory over the king, Stracid Amarmet, they went underground. Becoming a terrorist resistance."

"The Amarmet Alliance gaslights and spreads fake news in order to divide its citizens to regain power," Fritz added, his fingers flexing as if he could shred the very name from our conversation.

Raiden brought up another photo: a chubby, balding, fifty-year-old man walked across an airfield. "Doctor Monrowvia. He's sadistic. He was arrested for trying to mix evobilities to create a Super-Grounder soldier for Amarmet. Wolfram broke him out of a prison camp two years ago."

"I saw Monrowvia at Uzziah's house. They argued about the Tiara."

"Their partnership is an unpinned grenade." Raiden's knee brushed mine under the table, then stayed.

I didn't pull away. The touch was subtle, but not accidental. I could easily dismiss our closeness or turn away. Yet I let the connection linger. It sent a humming sensation beneath my skin, warm and alive, reassuring me I could handle whatever news came next.

"For them, Uzziah is another usurper. When Uzziah's no longer useful, they'll kill him." Raiden stated flatly, as if he spoke about a rabid dog and not someone from my bloodline.

"Uzziah called Monrowvia an Attercopi. He had four arms. Why would a Grounder need that?"

"His extra two hands and feet are sticky so he can climb quickly. It's an escape adaptation," Raiden explained.

My nose wrinkled.

"*Ouch.*" Raiden jerked his leg away. We glanced under the table. Graysen's claws hooked his pants, her grin Cheshire-wide. Evidently, *someone* took issue with Raiden's closeness.

I told them about Wolfram. Then the ice-woman who broke free from the chest. They believed she could be another face on Nyxon's wall. Every woman on that wall was a Grounder—gifted, but doomed. I racked my mind to call her by name, but it was lost in the flood of the river and the shadow of the mountain, erased by my meeting with Uzziah, and by Vana and Yttrium's attempt to hand me over to Doctor Monrowvia. The terror stole it from me, leaving only the hollow ache of not knowing.

I ended with: "Monrowvia knows how to remove my last abraylix." Every sound seemed to vanish at once, as though the room had drawn a breath and held it.

"The most important thing now is to find that doctor," Fritz cut in, his words piercing the tense air.

A rush of conflicting emotions swirled within me. Here he was, my ex-fiancé, his voice filled with fervor, urging everyone to save my life. Was it duty or affection for me?

With a mixture of apprehension and gratitude, I nodded.

"You need to hide at my house until Uzziah leaves for Cynder," Fritz added.

Raiden's knee began to bounce under the table.

"I'm not hiding while women vanish," I stated.

Nyxon crossed her arms. Her brilliant mind worked overtime, trying to devise a better solution, but the longer she thought, the more frustrated she became. "First, we infiltrate the Amarmet Alliance to locate Wolfram and the doctor. We'll dismantle the Amarmet Alliance's organization, taking out key players like pawns on a chessboard. Starting with the low-level operatives and working our way up. As we progress, we'll uncover the truth about the missing Grounder women and make sure the culprits face justice. Since Cynder laws hold no sway on Earth, we'll be the ones to balance the scales."

Balancing the scales. I clung to that.

"Once we locate the doctor, why would he help me?" I despised my defeated tone, knowing we were in dire need of any small win.

"You possess *someone* he wants." Raiden's throat constricted. "The Doctor wants a pint of my blood. We'll do a trade."

I stared at my hands. He offered a piece of himself to save me. Gratitude and guilt churned in my gut. Each one battled for dominance. How could he be so calm? "What would the Doctor do with your blood?"

Raiden closed the filament softly. "He'll push the limits of Grounder biology. And we'll have to live with the fallout."

A shiver ran down my spine. What horrific thing would unfold because of the trade? How could I accept this sacrifice knowing what it might cost? I met his eyes, searching for any sign of hesitation or doubt. Only a steely determination lit his hazel eyes. "Thank you." The words felt pitifully inadequate. I wanted to say more, to make him understand the depth of my appreciation, but the words lodged in my throat, choked by our suffocating situation.

"The Cyndarian Watch knows of a few Amarmet members that were banished to Earth. We should start there. And someone must go to Cynder and alert Princess Hydraxia. It's best if Fritz stays here." Nyxon shared a knowing look with Li. "And we *omit* Avi's kidnapping from our report."

"Leave my name off too," Raiden said firmly. "Princess Hydraxia doesn't know I'm here, and the queen and I have our own way to communicate."

My eyes narrowed on him, but Nyxon nodded. What was he hiding? We were playing this exhausting game of tug-of-war with truth and lie.

Li smirked. "Yeah, yeah. It's me who's goin'."

"But Li is Avi's security," Quinbe objected.

Nyxon chuckled. "Want to explain, Li?"

"The best offense—fighting, which is totally me—is the last resort. Nyxon's all about strategy and defense, like, she's the coach."

"I'll arrange for Li to catch a ride with the Cyndarian Watch operating from Madras, Oregon." Nyxon spoke casually, as if organizing a simple carpool. "Avi will need knowledge transfers and to learn how to protect herself."

I blinked. "How do you transfer knowledge? Does it hurt?"

She rocked on her heels. "How about I show you?"

Chapter 24

Nyxon placed her fingers atop the inside of my wrists. Her vitiligo spread up her arms like spilled bleach, stripping her tanned skin's color and staining her elbows. Her hands withered and warped, as if cursed by a witch's wrath, each finger transforming into a corpse-like relic.

"Nyxon, you're freezing." I squirmed.

"Shhh. Let it sink in," she said softly.

A tingling sensation skittered up my arm, imitating an infantry of icy ants marching to war. My face contorted.

"Stay still," Li advised.

Easy for him to say. The parasitic horde continued to climb. My fingers curled and uncoiled in a wicca chant. My neurons integrated with the frigid ants. Then suddenly, like bombs splashing into the Pacific, Nyxon's powers of enlightenment obscured my vision. Gray nebulas churned in a swirl of cosmic storms, like the universe was painting another world into being. I felt weightless. Seconds stretched into minutes as I existed between two dimensions. I was nowhere and everywhere, a wraith in the void.

Li chuckled. "The fogged pupils are my favorite part of the transfer process."

The mist parted like Broadway curtains pulling back. A grayscale film whirred. The speed increased, and the whirring grew louder, like the rush of wind through a narrow tunnel. Images blurred and blended, a rapid montage of words and numbers. My pulse raced, trying to keep pace with the torrent of information overwhelming my senses. Just when I thought I couldn't endure any more—*snap! Tick, tick, tick.* Like the snapping of an ancient film projector reaching its limit.

Nyxon released me, and the fog dissipated. I blinked, my vision slowly readjusting to the normal world around me, but nothing would truly be normal again.

"That was…" Mind-bending. Disturbing. Spellbinding. "Cool."

"Not exactly an orgasm." Nyxon's eyes shone with an inner glow she rarely let shine.

"What knowledge did you transfer to me?"

"Tune into your thoughts," Nyxon guided. "Feel the pressure in your skull and a faint tapping. Focus on it."

I swallowed hard, as if Nyxon's directions had turned to stone in my throat.

Nyxon continued, "When the knowledge reveals itself, it will seep into you as a sensation, like the first touch of snow. The knowledge will be memories that feel as real as your own."

I tilted my head. "The same person voices Yoda and Miss Piggy. *Really, Nyxon*? That's what you gave me?"

Amusement burst amongst the group. Nyxon smirked. "Keep rummaging."

My brain buzzed with new knowledge, concepts, and memories that weren't my own, yet felt as familiar as my own heartbeat. "Peanuts are an ingredient in dynamite."

Li smirked. "Nyxon loves her bombs."

"I understand the poetry of chaos," she said, a hint of sass in her voice.

"Salut, comment allez-vous? I can speak French!"

"I gave you a few elementary translations. Je vais bien, merci."

"Pourquoi tu n'as rien enseigné à ces idiots?"

She laughed lightly, making the others exchange glances. "I currently speak six languages, but if we don't use the knowledge regularly, we'll forget it. I'm not a Rekall."

"What's a Rekall?" I asked.

"They remember everything but grasp complex studies at a snail's pace. My evobility has limits too. I cannot build upon the ideas or concepts I attain. I can only pass on what I learn from others. My evobility is an unwanted recessive gene. My mother blames my father's side, and my father blames my mother's."

"I think it's amazing." My compliment came freely because it was true. Even without her evobility, Nyxon was remarkable.

"I want a knowledge transfer," Quinbe demanded. "I refuse to just stand by on the sidelines. Teach me how to fight."

"You need to stay far away." I shook my head.

"I won't be left behind." Quinbe glared at me.

"Sorry, Quinbe, but a human's brain neural tissue isn't built like a Grounder's. Your protective layer is too thin for a transfer. Your brain would sizzle like a fork in a microwave," Nyxon said.

Quinbe jerked back, eyes wide. Relief hit me. She would reconsider now. She would go back to her normal existence, to her safe routine.

Nyxon raised her hand. "Everyone in Avi's inner circle must be prepared to protect themselves. We can't predict what extremes Uzziah will take to find you. I can teach you how to handle a gun and some self-defense moves."

Quinbe clapped and bounced lightly on her toes, pleased with the compromise.

My stomach twisted. "Just be careful, Quinbe." A helplessness bled into my voice.

Raiden rose from the table. "On Monday, when Avi goes to work—"

"No way. *You're not* using Avi as bait," Fritz snapped, his voice steely.

"It's the best way to catch Wolfram," Raiden countered. "Wolfram will lead us to Doctor Monrowvia."

"Raiden's right. I understand the risks. Giving up my work means losing a part of me. Creating fragrances is my passion, and I refuse to let fear steal that from me." I stood firm as Fritz turned his back to me and paced. Nyxon and Raiden exchanged glances.

Quinbe spoke up, "She shouldn't have to walk away from the one thing that makes her feel alive and free."

Human, I wanted to add. "What if we increase security measures?"

Li added, "It's a secure building, so the Limier can't get inside without causing a scene."

"The three of us can take rotating shifts escorting Avi to work and scoping out the area," Raiden volunteered.

"Raiden's hidden camera proved Michael isn't working alone. Right now, Ms. Voss needs me, *us,* more than ever." I shifted my gaze to Raiden, and he nodded.

Holding onto a bit of my humanity meant Quinbe secured her spot in my life as well.

Journal Entry One:

Where do I begin? Here's a history lesson you won't find in an Earth textbook. Cyndarians see Earthlings as rebels. Cyndarians colonized Earth 65 million years ago. Nyxon said, "It's not as crazy as it sounds. Sharks have existed for over 200 million years. Cockroaches, 150 million." After decades of forced labor, the Earth colonies rebelled, demanding independence. In response, Cynder's king and council voted for swift punishment: bombing the thirty colonies, erasing them and the dinosaurs from existence or so they thought.

On Cynder, Grounder evobilities are vital for survival. Giant birds snatch you off the ground. Plants see you as food. Will I ever go to Cynder?

On Earth, Grounders stopped teaching their children to connect with the planet. They preferred parking lots to fields and cars to walking. If parents didn't charge their evobility, there would be none left to pass on. How many people are walking around with an uncharged evobility?

Cyndarians are divided into two subgroups, Grounders or Grays. Grounders believe humans don't turn feral or Gray because Earth has a moon, unlike Cynder. The moon's pull calibrates our circadian and hormonal rhythms, especially those tied to aggression and impulse control.

Li's soul: a myriad of brightly colored stars that twirl slowly, and bounce up and down, creating a mesmerizing wave-like display. When it showed itself, I had to bite my lip to hold in a laugh, he fuckin' looked like Rainbow Brite.

Nyxon's soul begins at her feet, widening like a triangle. Her soul's yellow and black stripes were reminiscent of a honeybee wasp. The smooth stripes buzzed with a swarm's relentless energy.

My soul: A veil of sapphire and silver tinsel trailed behind me, long and luminous as it skimmed the ground. I spun like a bride admiring her wedding dress. My soul didn't look broken. My soul didn't look incomplete.

VidaLumin: my mom and I. What I'd give to meet another VidaLumin who could teach me how to decipher everyone's soul colors and shapes.

Slyfen: an evobility I could never use. Steals evobilities.

Nitro Snap: The Grounder imprisoned at Uzziah's house. Has snowflake pupils. They chill nitrogen, argon, and oxygen, allowing them to freeze air. "Snapping their fingers sparks a chain reaction. If her ice hooks you, it's a horrible way to die," per Li.

Bmine: Grounder woman, Okya, sprayed a blinding cloud from her mouth into Li's eyes. Effects: temporary blindness; dry, itchy eyes. Duration: several days for most, one day for a Jagwar.

Arsinna: Grounder woman, Olliope, blew a death cloud from her mouth into my lungs. Effects: choking, respiratory distress. Cloud is lethal, meant to suffocate victims.

Last night, Li left for Cynder, his parting words stung like a slap to my face: "Don't get Fritz killed." I'd risk anything to keep Fritz safe.

I asked Nyxon if she'd included Raiden's interference in her report to my mother, and she shot back, "Fuck yes." She also included a pre-approval letter for a million-dollar bounty for Sellow, Okya, Olliope, and Polon. The bounty did nothing to temper Fritz's anger. I don't know how to reach him before the rage consumes him or how to stop him from choosing vengeance over himself.

<u>*Journal Entry Two:*</u>

Inside Fritz's red barn, the reason for his boxing ring and why he and Li spent hours here became clear: it was their job to stay in shape and keep their minds sharp. Climbing molds dotted the back wall, and Nyxon scaled them effortlessly to the loft while I struggled to keep up. We rotated through the rower, dumbbells, and squat rack. Quinbe was the least coordinated, but she had plenty of moxie. When rain kept us off the deer trails, we sweated on the treadmill.

Along the left wall sat a fridge, two computers, and a printer. Folding tables overflowed with pens, neon highlighters, and Post-its. The wall matched Nyxon's missing person displays from her office: photos, notes, and interview summaries. Only half the women's families even knew about their Grounder heritage.

We took extra precautions for my safety: a tracker on my phone and watch, check-ins every hour, a switchblade strapped to my ankle, and pepper spray in my purse. Nyxon constantly reminded me, "If anything happens, you run. Get away."

At the lab, I threw myself into my creations. Tiffany could barely keep up as I rattled off ideas. "Tiff, we're starting with a base of vetiver." Leaning in, I measured the essence. "It's earthy, strong, and it lingers." This time, I wasn't just making perfume, I was crafting a statement of defiance.

She typed notes furiously. "Got it. Next?"

"Add jasmine and rose absolute. The jasmine represents grace and beauty under pressure, while the rose adds an element of timeless strength. It's classic but powerful."

As the delicate floral notes mixed with the smoky base, a surge of determination filled my veins. "For the top notes, let's go bold. Pink pepper. The pepper brings a spicy, invigorating kick. It's a reminder that even in the darkest, most difficult days, one can find light and energy."

Tiffany grinned, catching my enthusiasm. "This will be amazing."

The complex and layered scent evolved with every breath. I held the finished bottle up to the light, the amber liquid gleamed.

"What are you going to call it?" Tiffany's voice carried an undercurrent of awe, as though naming it would seal its importance.

"Indomitable," I whispered. This was my answer to Uzziah. To Michael. To any man that would slam a door in my face. It was a blend of eccentricity and unyielding spirit. An embodiment of resilience. I'd captured more than just a pretty scent. I had captured my resolve.

⁘

<u>*Journal Entry Three:*</u>

Fritz's home had always felt safe. Solid. Like I believed he was. No matter what he was doing, when my car crunched gravel, he greeted me on the front porch, rocking gently on the wooden swing, his eyes lighting up like nothing in the world mattered but my arrival. But today, we pulled up and he wasn't there. Or yesterday. Or the day before. He'd been gone a lot lately, and it worried me. When I asked questions, he just grunted, walked away, or picked a fight (demanding I tell him Uzziah's whereabouts). So I retreated, creating more distance between us, scared my words might give him the hint he needed. Maybe this was what Li meant by keeping Fritz safe?

Lavender oil update: Tiffany promised to help track down the woman with the gold cuff, practically buzzing with eagerness. She was a social butterfly. She'd find the culprit faster than I could. It had to be an office assistant working outside the lab. Someone close enough to daily operations to manipulate things without suspicion.

I sighed and tapped my pen against the page. Could I really trust her? I shook off the thought. Tiffany, for all her flakiness, was harmless. Besides, jewelry wasn't allowed in the lab. That simple rule had been drilled into us from day one.

I turned the page. My scribbling became a way to get my roiling thoughts down and bring me peace, but I paused before my pen traced R-a-i-d-e-n.

Raiden: It's been a week since I last saw him. He should've given me a ride to work, but Nyxon covered for him. Twice. He's on Earth for a job, nothing more, but we were supposed to work together. Was that <u>really</u> all I cared about? Honestly, I developed a crush on him. I'm drawn to him in a way I can't explain. It doesn't make sense. Maybe it's his mysterious nature or bravery. I want to deny it, but just thinking about him makes my heart race. I'm a fool. He plans to leave the planet!

I dropped the pizza boxes on Fritz's dining room table and Nyxon, Fritz, and Quinbe pulled out chairs and gathered round.

Nyxon opened a tan folder and pushed a mugshot of a thirty-year-old man in my direction. "This is Argon Jintide Loomis." Peeking through a wiry hickory beard, thin lips scowled. "The night of your mugging, a Moon Dime Cafe coffee cup with the initials AJ fell from the van. Argon lives within two miles of the cafe. A barista recognized his photo, though she couldn't confirm his visit the day of your mugging. Credit card records didn't show his name, suggesting he may have paid in cash or had someone else purchase his drink. Additionally, his house is within three miles of where street cameras last spotted the van before it entered the residential neighborhood. In the realm of journalism, Argon's proximity to both the café and the van marks a pivotal nexus. Argon wasn't your main attacker. It was Wolfram, the Limier, but Argon could've been the driver. Do you recognize him?"

Chapter 25

Fritz's dining room felt like a stage set for a high-stakes thriller, where my revelation could tip the scales of fate and unravel this mystery.

I scrutinized Argon's pale face. "The driver had big, curly hair and broad shoulders. I saw his arm on the wheel, deeply tanned, the wrong skin tone entirely. It wasn't Argon."

The energy in the room sank. "Don't worry. Argon's affiliations with the Amarmet Alliance may lead to Wolfram." Nyxon added, "The Cyndarian Watch has monitored Argon for eight months. Every last Wednesday of the month, he drives to a warehouse, picks up a van loaded with supplies, and then heads to, guess where?"

"The Bridge of the Gods," I blurted, and the chill of regret hit me instantly. I'd made a colossal mistake. Fritz's head snapped toward me, suspicion hard as steel in his stare.

The pizza lost its garlic scent. The steam curled into the ceiling, mocking me with its emptiness. I had to think fast. "Because that's where Raiden found the man's body with the AA burned."

The charged silence stretched unbearably, every second brimming with the weight of my blunder as I braced for his response.

Fritz's jaw flexed. "You sound awfully confident about that *guess*."

"Good deduction, Avi," Nyxon interjected. "Argon rendezvouses with a fertorium shuttle headed to Cynder and loads it up with supplies."

"What's in the van? Weapons?" I asked, trying to keep the conversation going.

"No. Cyndarians' weapons are far superior to human weaponry." Fritz's fingers tapped impatiently against his crossed arms. He knew I was holding back on Uzziah's location. "Uzziah needs money to fund an army. My guess, they're taking a mix of valuables to auction. Precious stones, wine, nuts, *chocolate*."

Quinbe joked, "Chocolate *is* a priceless commodity."

Nyxon smirked. "Absolutely. Cynder doesn't have plants that guzzle water."

I flipped through Argon's extensive rap sheet. Drug distribution. Battery of a prostitute. Violating the restraining order his ex-wife, Maria, had against him. I cringed at the last gut-wrenching offense; he threw her kitten in the microwave. I couldn't read any further and shoved the folder to Quinbe.

Quinbe ripped a yellow Post-it note from the folder. "Evobility: Trigrandar. What's that?"

"He has a third eye socket on the back of his skull. He's able to insert eyeballs into the extra socket, allowing him to see an attack from behind," Nyxon said.

Fritz's nose wrinkled. "He takes eyeballs from humans or Grounders and implants them into his extra socket. Eventually, the stolen eye withers away, leaving him in constant need of a replacement."

Quinbe's complexion paled. I recoiled. "Gross," we said in unison.

Nyxon pressed her palms against the table. "At noon, Argon stumbles to the corner store for beer and cigarettes. The real action starts at three, with visitors coming and going until 2 a.m. But on the last Saturday of each month, he drives to the Bridge of the Gods' airfield. Tomorrow night, once he leaves, Fritz and I will sneak inside his house to plant listening devices and search his place." She dug into her bag and retrieved two quarter-sized metallic spiral-cone shells. She pressed a blue button located at the shell's base; a snail head emerged from its protective home. Four antennae extended outward, featuring human-like ears and human-like eyes at their tips. Quinbe and I exchanged a bewildered look. "These machines are attracted to sound, and record audio and video. But they're sensitive to light and vibrations. So, they're *very* good at hiding. Inside each shell is a receiver so I can download their data while parked outside his house." The snails sucked their heads and tails into their shells, and Nyxon returned them to her bag. "Quinbe and Avi will surveil from the car. If anyone comes to his door before we're out, text us. If we don't respond in thirty seconds, honk twice."

Quinbe bounced in her chair, and her curls sprung in unison. "A real-life stake out!"

Nyxon side-eyed Fritz. "I suppose…"

Quinbe mumbled, "I'll bring snacks and binoculars."

Fritz leaned her way. "We have binoculars, and you know Nyxon doesn't allow eating in her truck."

Journal Entry Four:

At the gun range, I ignore my sweaty palms. I ignore the body-jolting recoil and the ear-splitting bang. I ignore the vexing comparisons between my misses and Nyxon's perfect-circle grouping. So, I practice. Shame and doubt, with their wolfpack-like speed and razor-sharp teeth, hunt the minuscule part of me that believes I can do this.

When I'm not holding a gun or wearing boxing gloves, I focus on soaking up Earth's energy to charge my evobility. Even Quinbe joins us, cloud-gazing in the field in her red lace bra and thong, while Nyxon and I relax in our black hipsters and sports bras. Our laughter soars to the summer leaves. With my bare skin against the earth and no weapons strapped to my body, therapeutic serenity immerses me. In our field, I learn to control my evobility: On. Off. Dim. Repeat. The longer I keep my evobility on, the more I have to ground myself to Earth. When I use my evobility, my pulse quickens, not like the pounding rush of a spin class, but there is a subtle difference.

Nyxon explained that mastering eye-hand coordination takes longer to develop than transferring knowledge of language or math. This is because coordination requires the brain and body to build a complex connection between sensory input and physical response. Unlike language or math, which rely primarily on abstract reasoning, coordination needs muscle memory.

Inside the barn, two white fans whirred, but they failed to alleviate the setting sun's stifling heat within the boxing ring. I wiped sweat from my brow.

"Tired?" Fritz's yellow boxing glove flew for my cheek, but I dodged it.

From her laptop, Nyxon didn't look up. "She has twenty more minutes in that ring. I can't transfer stamina to someone."

"I'm not tired. Nyxon, can you transfer judo throws to me?" I bounced away from Fritz.

"Give me forty-eight hours to stabilize my blood-sugar levels. You drained me yesterday." She picked up her spoon and dunked it into the jar of peanut butter. "Don't doubt yourself. You've been training hard." She pulled the spoon from the jar then stuffed the glob of peanut butter in her mouth.

"Can you transfer confidence or bravery?" Quinbe asked.

"I can't adjust emotional intelligence. I can teach you the importance of being brave, but I can't make you *feel* it."

Quinbe continued, "Could you convince someone they love me?"

Nyxon cocked her head right then left. "Yes. But an ethical Frigellen would never do that."

"Everyone has a price." She winked at Nyxon.

Nyxon shook her head. "Trust me, a *love adjustment* never ends well."

The monotone female voice of Fritz's security camera announced, "Motion at the front gate."

My gloves dropped to my side, thudding against my thighs. All eyes shot to the barn door. Heart pounding, my grip tightened inside my boxing gloves.

From the treadmill, Quinbe teased, "Did someone order more pizza?"

"I could use a slice of anchovy and cheese," Graysen drawled from a chair.

But deliveries were not allowed here. Nyxon's orders.

Fritz exited the ring then lifted the boxing rope for me to duck under. I did, then stood near the punching bag.

A car door slammed. Footfalls. Finally, a long shadow crept up to the barn.

Raiden.

Shouldering his black briefcase, he swaggered into the room. "Mind if I join?" he asked no one in particular.

I scoffed. His collared midnight-plum shirt hugged his biceps and cuffed at his elbows, revealing brawny forearms. He wasn't dressed to play.

Quinbe swooned, calling from the treadmill, "We don't mind one bit."

"What are you doing here?" Nyxon's voice carried a warning of repercussion if he didn't provide an adequate answer. We had all agreed that we would only meet Raiden at Nyxon's house.

Fritz tucked the sparring gloves under his arm. "*I* invited him. Raiden has a lead on Polon, so we're surveilling him to see if he shows up at his favorite restaurant tonight." He paused, his gaze locking on me. "Unless you've suddenly remembered useful information?"

I faced the boxing bag to avoid his stare.

"We leave for Argon's house in an hour," Nyxon stated.

"You don't need me for that." Fritz grabbed a towel off the rope and dabbed his temple.

Nyxon and Fritz bickered over the change of plans, allowing Raiden to drop his bag on the table and slink toward me.

Could we trust Raiden? Why did a small part of me yearn to? The more people, I mean Grounders' allies, we had, the better our chances of locating the Doctor and Wolfram. But at what cost?

He braced my boxing bag, and I curiously fixated on his soul. A swirling bluish, galactic hole with red flickering tips.

I sassed, "Where have you been?"

"Did you miss me?"

I punched the bag. "*No.*" His soul sprang forward to inspect my blue glove, but I recoiled.

He whispered, "Why are you blushing?"

"I've been working out." I threw an uppercut at the bag. He was here because he had a job to do. Nothing more. Again, his soul leapt to cocoon my hand and the vortex at his soul's center increased its dizzying rotation.

"This bag won't give you an authentic experience." He selected a pair of purple boxing gloves. "Try to hit me."

"I don't want to hurt you."

"Ha! I'd love to see you try." He trotted toward the boxing ring and lifted the rope for me.

I'd show him. A sheen of sweat highlighted my arms as I lifted the rope for myself.

As I met him in the middle, the air buzzed with anticipation.

Our eyes locked in a challenge. He threw the first punch, a heavy thump as it met my guard. My punches followed, a steady stream of jabs and crosses that would've earned Nyxon's approval. In contrast to my snappy strikes, Raiden's punches were primal. His jabs, though not as swift as mine, had an impact that demanded respect, shocking me and vibrating my entire body. He wasn't holding back.

Our bodies dove and bobbed. The thump of gloves meeting their targets, the cadence of footwork, and the occasional grunt or exhale created the music and choreography of combat. But our antics didn't amuse Nyxon. Quinbe wiggled the ring's red ropes and cheered me on. Fritz gave our bout a few side-eye glances.

"Are you even trying?" I lured him into breaking a sweat while I fought to steady my climbing pulse. He took the bait and threw an impulsive punch that I dodged. I returned one of my own to his abdomen. I fought the urge to shake out my hand. It felt like I'd punched a brick wall.

He swung his leg low, connecting with my calf and sending a painful jolt through my legs. I stumbled back, fighting to regain balance and control. But the momentum proved too much. I toppled in an ungraceful descent, crashing onto the canvas.

Raiden leapt on top of me, his muscular thighs squeezing around me. His eyes burned and a wild excitement surged through my chest, like a horse breaking into a run.

Our chemistry transformed, crackling with an unexpected flirtation. A gasp from Quinbe left me blushing and flustered. Good thing there wasn't an evobility for mind reading because my thoughts had gone entirely off script. What would've happened if the others weren't here? Wanting him was reckless.

Fritz's expression turned stern. "All right, you two. Raiden, let's go." He pulled on a gray T-shirt that hugged his broad shoulders and thicker waist. He'd put on weight since coming home, and it only made him more himself. He crossed to the barn door and waited outside.

Raiden, still catching his breath, removed his gloves. "Looks like I won this round."

"Stalemate. We were interrupted," I shot back, refusing to concede defeat.

"I'd be happy to take you to the floor and straddle you another time." His words were a secret promise, meant for my ears alone, their intimate tone creating a conspiratorial connection that triggered a tingling wave across my skin.

Caught between the exhilaration of flirtation and clueless about how to respond, I pulled off a glove and swung it at him, the leather landing against his hip with a thud. "Get off of me."

His playful banter was a distraction, nothing more, and I didn't have time for that. I had to tread carefully. I was acutely aware of Raiden's dangerous magnetism, capable of luring a woman into his grasp and drowning her in a whirlpool of passion. My gut warned me that indulging in this dalliance could only lead to an empty encounter. Sharing Raiden's bed for a night would leave nothing but a hollow aftermath. And then he'd be hard to forget, setting a challenging standard that other men would struggle to match. Despite knowing the inevitable outcome, I couldn't resist the temptation of just one more word, one more interaction, one more foolish flirtation.

Smirking, Raiden rolled away, but the lingering tension hinted at more heated moments to come.

Nyxon advanced to the ring and, with a sigh, lifted the rope for me; her disappointed expression not escaping my notice. "Have I taught you nothing? When you had an opening, you should've struck him in the solar plexus."

"Struck him where?" I lumbered from the ring and landed hard on the floor.

"She means the penis," Graysen drawled.

"*Nooo.* Avi, remind me to add human anatomy to your knowledge transfers." Nyxon tossed me a water bottle. "He's taller than you. Your first instinct should've been to get him to the ground, then pound."

Quinbe fanned herself. "Oh, Nyxon, now you're speaking my language."

Nyxon flung one of my gloves at her.

I couldn't help but steal a glance toward the exit. When Raiden met Fritz, they shared an easy camaraderie that ignited a spark of discomfort within me. How long had Fritz been meeting with Raiden behind our backs? There was a time when I knew everything about Fritz. A strange paranoia gnawed at me about letting him go alone. Well, he wasn't exactly alone. He had Raiden. But Raiden wasn't one of us. Raiden's loyalties lay elsewhere, not with Fritz's safety. I shoved my water bottle into Nyxon's arms and took off after him.

Once outside, the gravel crunched beneath my feet, each step mimicking the urgency thrumming through me. "Fritz, we should stick together tonight!"

Fritz slammed his truck's tailgate shut and walked to the driver's side door. "I'm sick of playing Nyxon's spy games. You could've told me where Uzziah took you, but instead you cowered behind Li and Nyxon."

My thoughts scattered like startled birds. I fumbled for any words that might make him stay. "At Uzziah's house there was a map of Cynder. There were red pins stuck in teepees and a circle. It looked important. If you found me a map I could, maybe—"

"*Maybe*, you should..." His thumb lingered on his new Jeep truck's handle, as if remembering his old Jeep still crumbled and half-submerged in the deep, cold slough.

A sadness consumed me. That was the last trip we shared.

When Sloane's light went out.

When my world warped.

When Fritz lost his way.

"Start telling me the truth." His eyes darkened. "Bridge of the Gods?" His question wasn't just accusing; it was emotionally raw.

I grabbed his arm. "I'm trying to protect you."

He yanked his arm free, his eyes blazing. "*Your mother* sent me to hell, and I came back. You have no idea what I can handle." His words hit me like a slap. Before I could form a reply, he stepped into his Jeep and slammed the door.

We surveilled Argon's small, yellow square house. Two large windows, framed by peeling white trim, peered out like inebriated eyes. The windows' dingy plastic blinds, hung in a state of disarray; several white slats were missing. Weeds sprouted through cracks in the carport's concrete. The chain-link gate swung with the breeze. But nothing could distract me from Fritz's accusation about my mother. What had she done to him?

"How much trouble could they possibly get into?" Quinbe sighed.

"A lot." The binoculars stayed fixed to Nyxon's face.

"Argon should've left four hours ago," I said impatiently. "What if he doesn't leave?"

"We'll return next month," Nyxon said dryly.

"We don't have thirty days to sit and wait." I shifted in my seat. "I'll knock on his door, and see if he'll invite me in, sell me some drugs, then I'll plant the listening devices."

Nyxon remained inscrutable. "A person's character is measured by the choices they make while waiting."

I rolled my eyes. "In the file, it said he has an acquaintance named Jasmine. I'll say she sent me. If it doesn't work, he'll just turn me away."

Nyxon stuffed the binoculars into her bag. "I'll do it, since you're discounting my wise words."

"You scream law-abiding nosy neighbor," Quinbe blurted.

Nyxon examined her reflection in the rearview mirror. "True."

"*He'd* let me in," Quinbe said, her voice brimming with confidence and self-satisfaction.

But we quickly met her with a chorus of strong, resolute "*no*"s.

Nyxon pursed her lips. "While Avi distracts him, I'll pick the back lock and plant the second listening shell."

Quinbe grabbed my hand, her eyes lighting up as she squeezed it. "Let's go, girls!"

Stepping onto the pavement, the world appeared to narrow into the confined space of the dimly lit street.

Nyxon's determined eyes glinted, so I stood straighter, feeling empowered by her. With her pointer finger, she motioned for me to turn around. Confused, I obeyed.

She grabbed the sides of my loose black Eras concert t-shirt and with nimble fingers she tied the sides together into a knot, the fabric shifted, baring my belly button. A prick of vulnerability crept across my skin.

"Quinbe will call in ten minutes. If you don't answer, *I'm charging in*." Nyxon placed a listening device in my hand.

"Give me twenty minutes. I can do this."

She frowned and reluctantly said, "Fine. Be safe. Don't take any chances."

"I will." I've trained nonstop, I can do it.

I stalked toward the house. Each step carried both caution and conviction. In the night's stillness, the world seemed to hold its breath.

I pushed the rusted gate. It creaked like the anguished wail of a wraith. One porch light was burnt out. An intricate spiderweb glowed in the other.

They were counting on me. I tapped the side of my jeans. I got this.

The TV blared WWE wrestling. The doorbell emitted a feeble, gritty buzz, as if its once vibrant tone weathered and bore scars of countless pushes. I instantly regretted pressing it. No floorboards creaked. No shadows shifted behind the curtains. If this didn't work, at least I could say I tried. But that would mean failing in front of my friends. What would they think?

I raised my hand to pound on the faded cream door, but it swung open.

Argon Loomis lazily pointed his beer bottle at me. "Who-o-o are you?"

I wasn't sure where the beard ended and scraggly hair began. His flaxen toenails and hairy feet were more mutant than human. His crimson soul hiccupped on his bony shoulders. I lurched back. Thick milky maggots wiggled to the surface then sank.

He raised one thick eyebrow. I regained my composure and flipped my hair. "Hi, I'm Amber. My friend Jasmine said *you* could hook me up." I displayed my fifty-dollar bill.

He coldly assessed the cash before fixating on me. "What pretty eyes you have." His voice was a slick mix of predatory intent and weariness, like an aging wolf past its prime, fangs long gone.

I swallowed hard.

In a startling display of agility and swiftness, he grabbed my wrist and pulled me uncomfortably close to his protruding beer belly stomach. My pulse pitched into a panicked pace. I struggled against his grasp. His breath reeked of cigarettes and cheeseburgers. I underestimated him!

"Jasmine owes me two-hundred bucks-s-s." He raked a dirty fingernail from the corner of my eye to my jaw.

I should move. I should strike. I should grab his wrist and bend it backward. But my limbs were leaden and locked.

"Are you gonna pay her debt?" His question dripped with disturbing condescension that would repulse every human being.

"If-if you give me a day I can come up with the money." He flung my wrist away and I shuffled back a step.

"Tell her, she don't get to deal in dollars anymore."

"What does that mean?" My voice climbed an octave. *Get it together, don't show fear.*

"She'll kno-o-ow." He slurred and thrust the door closed, but I planted my boot inside, and the door whacked it. "And what the hell do you think you're doin'?"

His blatant disregard fueled a fire that boiled in my core. Resentment blended with the resolve of a warrior.

No more slammed doors.

I wasn't inferior. Not anymore.

Chapter 26

My nails dug into my palms. No more slammed doors. "I know you're a Grounder."

The pressure of the door against my foot lessened, inch by inch Argon opened it halfway to peer out. "So what?"

"You're committing crimes on Earth."

"Crimes? Is that what the Cyndarian Watch is calling it?" He jabbed me in the chest with a filthy finger. "I'm a Cyndarian citizen and have every right to use my evobility."

I snatched his wrist so fast his eyes bulged from their sockets. I flung his wrist aside and kicked the door open, sending it crashing against the wall.

No one was ever going to touch me without my permission again.

He stumbled back, blundering into the hall, dropping his bottle. It clinked and spilled across the linoleum floor.

I crossed the doorway's threshold. "I'm here to *balance* the scales." Adrenaline pumped through me. Bowing down to this man, retreating, was what the old Avi would've done.

"Get the hell out of my house!" He charged me. I kicked. My boot collided with his soft beer belly, and it felt like kneading bread dough. He doubled over and slumped against the hallway wall.

I took another step forward; a storm was building behind my eyes. One way or another, this motherfucker would cooperate.

Gasping, he retreated, ricocheting like a pinball down the hall, then careened through the kitchen and into a rear room.

He wasn't so tough.

I plucked the steel shell from my pocket. The peeling linoleum guided me to stained carpet. The mingling of stale beer and cigarettes burned my eyes. I wiggled my nose, as if that could chase away the stench.

A ripped leather chair sat directly in front of a thirty-inch TV. Surrounded by beer bottles and a bag of BBQ chips, it was a throne fit for a king who wallowed in a cesspool of moral depravity.

Flies ushered me down the hallway and into the kitchen. Four black garbage bags blocked the wooden back door. Day-old mac and cheese with hot dogs sat on the stove, cemented in a pot. An orange tabby hunched over a crumpled fast-food box on the kitchen table. It gnawed on a half-eaten chicken nugget. Its fur hung in matted clumps, streaked with grime. One ragged ear twitched at my approach, but the cat didn't bother to lift its head.

Cupboard doors were absent or left open, revealing empty dusty shelves, and a few cans of Vienna sausages and chili.

"Mr. Argon Loomis? I just want to talk." My voice carried a confident slight, sing-song tone.

The pump of a shotgun echoed from the rear room, and my smirk vanished. Fear devoured the courage I'd foolishly toyed with. If I ran for the door, he'd shoot me in the back.

I snatched a beer bottle off the counter and wedged myself behind the room's door and wall. My heart thudded so violently I was sure he could hear it. I had to hide long enough to sneak out the back door when he walked into the living room.

A single barrel shotgun inched from the bedroom.

I forced my breathing to slow. One wrong move, one twitch of my hand, and the barrel would find me before I could even think to react.

Suddenly, the faintest of tinkering came from the back door. To my horror the handle twisted with the gentlest of turns.

Oh no—Nyxon. The barrel pivoted toward the sound. If Nyxon opened that door, Argon had a clear shot. Sweat slicked my palms. Nyxon's safety depended on my next choice.

Without wasting another second, I shattered the bottle across Argon's cheek. The gun barrel veered wildly in my direction. I stabbed his trigger hand with the serrated bottle and grabbed the barrel with my other hand, forcing it upward. *Boom!* The popcorn ceiling exploded, coating us like snow. Blinking debris from my eyes, I spat chalky drywall dust from my mouth. He whirled the gun barrel, striking my chin. Blood sprayed my shirt. I stumbled back, colliding with the stove.

Nyxon crashed through the rear door, tripped over the garbage bags, and into the wall. Argon swung his gun at her.

I seized the mac and cheese pot and smashed it into his temple. His eyes rolled back, then he nose-dived to the floor with a thud. The gun clattered by my feet. My ringing ears couldn't drown out my heavy panting. I collapsed into a chair and rested my trembling legs. "Mr. Loomis, it *hasn't* been a pleasure to meet you."

Nyxon scowled and kicked the gun aside. "You deviated from the plan."

"I improvised." The truth was I'd been naïve, letting pride guide my steps.

She grabbed a paper towel, tore off two sheets, folded them, and handed them to me. "Improvising equals injuries."

Quinbe burst in from the hallway. "What the hell happened?"

"I *improvised*. Now, these listening devices are useless. Only an idiot wouldn't be cautious."

Nyxon pulled out her shiny shell and beckoned for me to give her mine. I dropped the shell into her palm. "We need to hurry. Avi, check Argon for a phone."

"I'm sorry. I messed up. I wish—"

Nyxon didn't miss a beat. "Avi, Clementine Paddle once said, 'Never grow a wishbone where your backbone ought to be.'"

Quinbe followed Nyxon into the living room and said, "Well, he's a few beers short of a six-pack. What do we have to lose?"

"Was that a joke?" Nyxon asked, a smile in her voice.

I crouched over Argon's body and patted his pockets for a phone. No luck. I was here… I had to peek. A pungent stench of decay clung to Argon's hair. My fingers brushed the strands aside; an unpleasant stickiness transferred to my skin. One milky-green eye, oozing pus at the corners, stared blankly to the left.

Nausea hit me, and I recoiled. "Disgusting." I rushed to the sink and flipped on the faucet. Water cascaded over my hands. I reached for the soap. Only dish soap in sight. I scrubbed my hands vigorously, trying to cleanse away not just the physical grime but the mental image.

I investigated the bedroom. A poster of a woman wearing a plaid school-girl skirt, bent over a desk, served as a headboard for the spent mattress on the '80s shag carpet. Dingy, caseless pillows were scattered atop a lumpy brown comforter, but still no phone. An ashtray, packed beyond capacity, created a fire hazard. Soda cans and shotgun shells littered the floor. Like breadcrumbs, I followed the shotgun shells to a gun cabinet. The wooden cabinet stood tall in the corner of the room. Two glass panels, like sinister eyes, seemed to relish the debauchery that unfolded within the room.

My pulse quickened as I opened the glass doors.

Argon had a cadaverous collection.

I gasped, unable to tear my eyes away from the haunting jars that lined the two shelves.

Within the jars, a slimy, snot-like substance quivered with vitality, more a living slither than inert goo, as if it hungered for the observer's ocular orbs. Bubbles rose from the bottom and popped at the surface. I teetered backward, crushing a soda can under my foot. It clamped around my shoe, and I flapped my arms wildly to hold my balance.

"Gotcha." Quinbe caught me. "You challenged a grown man with a shotgun, but a tin can tripped you up?"

I steadied myself. "*Eyes*! Jars and jars full of them." I pointed.

She peeked into the cabinet. Her expression twisted with revulsion. "Where does he get them all?"

I stepped beside her. "At the front door he implied that when people don't pay their debts, this is their only option." I selected a jar and threw it at the far wall. The glass shattered, and the eyeball splatted, seeping into the carpet.

Quinbe raised a jar. "For some odd reason, I thought the eyeball would bounce." She hurled her jar at the wall too.

Nyxon appeared in the doorframe, flustered. "What's going on?" She covered her nose.

"We're getting rid of Argon's memorabilia." I tossed a jar at Nyxon. She caught it one-handed and examined the contents. She frowned before tossing it back. "I found his phone on the armchair. Grab those two rifles out of the case. He *definitely* shouldn't have those. We vacate in three minutes."

We destroyed the remaining ten jars with mild bravado, then met Nyxon in the kitchen. "We need to leave him a warning. A message so clear he'll never steal eyes again," I said.

"Hitting him in the head with a pot wasn't enough of a message?" Nyxon's voice had a razzing quality to it, as she prodded Argon with her boot.

Quinbe chuckled. "Smooth move, Avi."

I grasped the wobbly drawer's worn handle, and with a determined tug, the drawer ground open. Dust particles puffed into the air as I sifted through AA batteries, a spatula, and ketchup packets. A pen. No paper. The woman in the poster leered from the bedroom wall. "That'll do."

Marching onto his thin mattress, I tore the poster from the wall.

Nyxon waved the phone above Argon's face. The screen brightened and unlocked. She lobbed it to Quinbe. "Change the setting so it can't lock."

I swept the nuggets off the table and wrote a note of demands:
Mr. Loomis,

That escalated quickly. This is your only warning. Stay away from your ex-wife. Stop harming humans and animals. The eye of the Cyndarian Watch is upon you.

Nyxon's lips curled into a wry grin. "Nice pun. But Grounders like him never change."

I wasn't praying for a Christmas miracle, just to give humanity some peace.

Nyxon grabbed a plastic grocery bag. Then selected a dirty steak knife from the sink and positioned it between the two joints of Argon's thumb.

I jerked back. "What are you doing?"

"The Cyndarian Watch tracks Grounders that dabble in a life of crime. They'd prefer humans didn't discover us. So, when a Grounder gets out of line, they deal with it. They requested I collect his fingerprint and a blood sample if it was possible. *Well*, you made it possible."

"*Oh.*" My expression crinkled.

She jutted her chin at Quinbe. "Stomp on the knife."

Quinbe didn't hesitate. I held my breath, as her Timberland sole crashed down on the silver blade. A squish. A crack. Blood splattered onto Quinbe's boot and pooled on the laminate floor.

Bile threatened to climb my windpipe.

Argon moaned.

Nyxon dropped the thumb into the bag, then purloined Argon's shotgun off the floor. "That's our cue to vacate this shit hole."

As we moved past the living room, Nyxon scooped up the scrawny orange cat. "You're coming with us too."

The cat hissed, a thin, raspy sound. It twisted, tail flicking, but it was too weak to put up a real fight.

Once the doors to Nyxon's truck slammed shut, our voices rose higher with each retelling of our triumph. The taste of sweet victory coated our lips and mingled with the electric joy pulsing in the air.

Quinbe's phone rang. We barely noticed at first, too caught up in the moment to care. But then she answered, and the color drained from her face. "Fritz has been shot!"

Chapter 27

Nyxon snapped into military mode. We were in and out of Quinbe's vet clinic with lifesaving supplies in under ten minutes.

Now, we stood on Fritz's porch. A cold sweat dampened the back of my neck. Quinbe's face stayed ghost-pale.

The turn of events didn't seem real. All I could do was stare down the driveway, afraid that if I spoke, I'd cry.

Quinbe clutched the overfilled duffel bag. "Fritz should go to the hospital. I'm a resident veterinarian, not a human surgeon."

"Doctors ask questions," Nyxon snapped, nostrils flaring. "You're going to have to be whatever we need tonight."

"Fritz could die," Quinbe wailed.

A wave of nausea rolled through me. Fritz was out there bleeding and suffering.

"When he gets here, we move fast. No delays. No second-guessing yourself." Nyxon stated.

I swallowed hard. "Quinbe, you've got this. You've saved lives before." Fritz couldn't die. Not like this. Not when there was still so much left unsaid between us. And Sloane, I'd promised her.

Suddenly, a beam of headlights speared through the darkness. No one moved. No one spoke. My lungs strained for breath.

The Jeep truck veered wildly, skidding across the uneven terrain as loose gravel spat up like shrapnel against the undercarriage.

Time seemed to stretch unbearably thin, each second dragging like the pull of a tide. The truck loomed closer, its hulking form swallowing the distance with a deafening roar. My heartbeat pounded in my ears, each pulse a thunderclap.

"Brakes!" I screamed, lunging for Quinbe, my fingers digging into her sleeve as I yanked her back. Tires screeched and the truck bucked like a beast straining against its leash, as it barreled forward, unstoppable. I had a vision of porch boards splintering and flying through the air.

With a jarring shudder, the truck ground to a halt.

Inches separated us from disaster.

Raiden stumbled out of the driver's seat. His shirt was torn from shoulder to stomach as though shredded by a tiger. Blood soaked his torso. "Help me!" Raiden threw open the rear door.

Fritz slumped against the window. His wounded leg lay across the seat. Bare chested, he used his shirt to compress his upper thigh.

Nyxon and Raiden lifted a moaning Fritz. His breath came in shallow gasps as he clutched Raiden's arm, his bloodied fingers leaving red streaks. His head lolled to the side as incoherent words spilled from his lips, a mixture of pleas and protests as they rushed him inside.

I trailed behind. Tears streamed down my face. Memories of Sloane, helpless and dying, blurred the present with the past.

"Put him on the dining room table," Quinbe ordered.

He was pale. My fingers shook as they interlocked with his cold hands. "Dammit, Fritz. I can't lose you."

Quinbe reached into her bag, retrieved a pair of scissors, and snipped down Fritz's pant leg. Blood wept from the bullet wound and dripped to the floor. But she transitioned like this was her millionth surgery.

I squeezed his hand. He finally looked at me, really looked at me, and I berated myself for not being as composed and calm as Nyxon.

"I'm sorry," he whispered, as a glassiness coated his eyes.

I hunted for words, but only a simple, aching plea emerged: "Stay with me." Hoping it might anchor him to this world, hold back the inevitable.

Quinbe tossed Nyxon a cord. "Apply this tourniquet two inches above the wound."

Fritz coughed as he struggled to sit up, swaying unsteadily. "Avi, in the barn there's a fridge. Bottom shelf. Indigo duffel bag. You'll find pints of my mom's—" The room fell quiet. Fritz's body slumped, his head dropping heavily onto the table. His mortality, accentuated by the haunting loss of his mother, etched a brutal expression across his features. His gaze ascended to the ceiling, as if he communed with Sloane's ghost.

Was he seeking guidance, reassurance, or some form of endorsement for his actions? I wasn't sure.

Nyxon placed a hand on his shoulder. "I'll get you a pain pill. Our brand, not that lousy Earth crap."

He turned his head slowly, his gaze analyzing her with an expression that teetered between confusion and disbelief, as though he'd forgotten she was there.

Nyxon grabbed my arm. I jumped. "Sloane's," she hesitated, then took a shaky breath. "Her blood can't heal the wound or fix an artery. But it would give Fritz the energy he needs and clear any infection."

"S-Sloane…" I stuttered, a cold shock seeping into my bones.

"Go now, run!" She shoved me toward the door.

I stumbled outside, the screen door clattering shut behind me.

Raiden sat on the porch swing. His head hung between his legs, but his hand pressed against his chest. I didn't have a minute to waste badgering Raiden about his recklessness. My task pressed down on me, each minute was vital. I could confront him tomorrow. Tonight, there was too much at stake.

My feet pounded against the earth as if I were running from Sloane's accusing stare, one that said I had failed her and she expected nothing less.

I reached the barn door; its hinges screamed as I flung it open.

The fridge! Back corner of the barn.

Inside, the indigo duffel bag with the inverted seven glared at me like an accusation; I was supposed to protect Fritz.

My hand hovered over the bag. This was all that remained of her, and her son needed it, needed her. It was twisted. I grabbed the bag, hauled it into my arms, and sprinted back toward the house, every step heavy with regret. I should have done more to protect him!

Panting, I staggered into the dining room and dropped the bag at Nyxon's feet.

She delved into it, rustling and clinking, and tossed nonessential items to the floor with a flick of her wrist. "Fritz, you're as white as a ghost. How much blood did you lose?"

"A lot. We got Polon. The Palmthermic who burned my mother with a cigarette," he said through gritted teeth,

I rested my hand on his chest, acutely monitoring its rise and fall. "We'll talk about that later," my voice cracked. If Fritz died… an aching breath ignited a wave of regret. An undertow of complacency had swept into our friendship. I'd taken him for granted, never thanking him for all he did to prepare me. Now, staring down at the fragility of life, I wish I could turn back time, to appreciate every shared smile and every ordinary day we had together.

Quinbe instructed, "Avi, switch spots with me and keep pressure on the wound. When the blood soaks through the gauze, don't remove the gauze. Put more on top. Once the blood flow stalls, I'll suture it. I want to unfasten the tourniquet in fifteen minutes."

I did as instructed. Fritz closed his eyes. The sight of him, wounded and vulnerable, sent tendrils of dread snaking around my wrist and made my hands tremble.

Quinbe rummaged through her bag and pulled out a needle, thread, and a pair of gloves. She snapped her gloves against her wrist and slung a pair to Nyxon.

"The… blood." I gulped. "Has slowed." The floor was a sea of red. Soaking into seams as if the old house was trying to drink it in.

"Nyxon, sanitize the area," Quinbe ordered.

Quinbe and Nyxon worked. Hyper-focused. Quinbe's perfect stitches silenced the wound so that it no longer gaped like a mouth screaming for help. They cleaned and stitched the exit hole. From the living room, eleven bongs resounded from the grandfather clock, signaling another hour had passed.

Quinbe selected tubing. "He's ready for Sloane's blood transfusion."

The worst was over. At least, that was what I told myself.

The room was a battlefield: bloody rags heaped in a corner and an antiseptic smell cut through the coppery stench. I picked up rag after rag. Each rag felt like a piece of him, slipping through my fingers.

Why was I cleaning? I needed a task, an action that didn't involve looking at the man I loved so broken, so still. His blood soaking into my hands, my clothes, my hair, made it all too real, a vivid reminder of how close I'd come to losing him.

He'd pulled through, but for how long? What if the stitches gave out? I squeezed my eyes shut, but it was no use. The moments were burned into my mind: Quinbe's steady hands working frantically, the way she barked orders, the groan that escaped Fritz's lips when the needle pierced his skin.

I shuffled through the screen door. The night air was cool against my damp skin. My hands gripped the blood-soaked rags like they were the only thing tethering me to reality.

Raiden sat on the porch steps, still clutching his chest. I sidestepped him without a word and strode to the trash can. I dumped the rags inside, and my adrenaline dropped with them. The worst was over, I repeated, clinging to the words like a lifeline. But deep down, I knew it wasn't. Not for me. Not for him. Not for our future.

I returned to the porch, my hand lingering on the edge of the screen door. Why did this happen? Raiden knew and I'm betting it was his fault. Fritz, pale and bloodied, flashed before me, and my resolve hardened.

I turned, cornering Raiden before I could second-guess myself. "What happened?" My voice was low but firm.

He shifted, his gaze slid away, but then he exhaled, his breath carrying more than air. It was a confession full of guilt. His shoulders slumped, the tension leaking from his frame like a deflated balloon, but to my frustration, his jaw remained locked, a fortress guarding the truth.

I waited, letting my long pause press on him. His hand raked through his hair, fingers trembling just enough to betray him. "It wasn't supposed to go down like that," he finally muttered, voice taut as a pulled wire.

"What wasn't?" I stepped closer. The light from the porch lamp caught the shadows under his eyes, hollow and bruised like a man who hadn't slept in days.

His gaze fell to the ground. "In exchange for cash, my informant, a Servalina, told me Polon had made dinner reservations for them at the Garlic Steak. After dinner, we tailed him and the Servalina to her house. When we charged in, Fritz didn't stick to the plan. Interrogate him, then leave. Polon told us Doctor Monrowvia planned to kidnap a female Jagwar. The Doctor believes blending a Jagwar and Slyfen evobility would enhance the female's control over the Dracophelia, since Jagwars healed quickly. Fritz got what he wanted, then killed Polon. Did Polon deserve to pay for his crimes? Yes. But my informant, the Servalina, saw everything. And Servalinas hold grudges. She shot Fritz. I knocked the gun from her hand, but she sliced my chest with her retractable dewclaw. Luckily, she missed my throat." He flinched and tried to rotate his shoulder. "She was hysterical. I didn't know she was in love with Polon. I gave her my word that Polon wouldn't be harmed, that I was only trying to find the tiara and the doctor." A twinge of guilt laced his words. "I knocked her unconscious and dragged Fritz away before the police showed."

A split-second decision, a gunshot fired, a claw slicing through flesh, each action set a spiraling nightmare into motion.

"It isn't a question of if, but when and how the Servalina will claim her justice. And now Monrowvia knows we plan to warn and save the Jagwar from him."

Time wasn't on our side, and the stakes were higher than ever.

I squinted at his ripped shirt, expecting to see the crimson hue of blood. But to my surprise, his blood wasn't red, but translucent. It shimmered and shifted, as if it had a life of its own. It blended and changed depending on its surroundings, much like a chameleon, seamlessly adapting to whatever it touched. I couldn't tear my eyes away from the mesmerizing sight. I reached out, curious to feel its texture, but before my fingers made contact, Raiden caught my wrist.

"The red blood on your shirt belongs to Fritz. The night Wolfram tried to kidnap me outside my work, the officer couldn't see your blood, so he didn't administer medical aid. I could see your blood when I was colorblind because I focused on the movement, not the color. Does your blood have anything to do with your evobility?"

Chapter 28

Raiden sat frozen. His life, a story he refused to read aloud. "Tell me about your blood," I demanded.

The corners of his soul dimmed like a dying ember clinging to its last bit of warmth. "Please don't tell the others what you saw."

"What are you hiding?" My frustration mounted. "Does your blood have a connection to your evobility? Why don't you trust me—us?" I corrected myself.

He stood and took a step back, then another, toward his car. "When Grounders learn about my evobility, they treat me like a weapon. And the repercussions? Disastrous. Someone *always* pays the price… with blood. Every. Single. Time." His resolve hardened, as if we'd argued about this before. "But there are some Grounders I can't refuse."

"Who? Your employer, the queen?" I accused. He stared, as if he saw through me. A small part of me surmised I got it wrong.

His biceps flexed as his weight shifted, his wary stance mimicking a puma poised to bolt at the slightest sign of danger.

I've lost him, he's going to leave and I'll never learn the truth.

Pain and pity gripped me as I pictured him slipping away into the night, consumed by whatever demons drove him from help, from safety, from me. "Wait." I raised my hands in a placating gesture to pause his retreat. "Let's compromise. If you don't want them to see—" I waved a hand over his ripped shirt, the fabric barely holding together. "Let me clean you up. Give me a chance," I pleaded, willing my words to loosen the tight lines of his shoulders.

His gaze turned to the dark forest, searching for answers in the labyrinth of crooked branches, their jagged silhouettes shifting like restless spirits in the moonlight.

Finally, he gave a small nod.

Without wasting another minute, I flung open the screen door and rushed into the kitchen.

This felt like a test. If I connected with Raiden on a deeper level, he wouldn't allow Fritz to follow him into risky situations. And if I uncovered his blood secret, we could link it to an evobility. These weren't isolated problems; they were threads in the same web, tugging at the edges of everything I was trying to protect and build.

Nyxon's proud voice rang in my ears, commending me for a job well done. But the praise triggered a familiar, inept ache because I lacked Nyxon's clever tongue that could easily untangle any lie. I lacked Quinbe's round, empathetic eyes that could soften even the hardest hearts. I had little experience coaxing men into conversations, and that truth clung to me like a stubborn stain.

I opened the freezer. Raiden needed ice for his black eye. Of course, the ice cubes had frozen into a big block. A bag of frozen peas would suffice. I collected a cloth and first-aid kit.

He needed a fresh shirt. I stared at the looming staircase leading to Fritz's room. I hadn't dared climb the flight since he returned. But Raiden was counting on me.

I moved to the stairs and placed my items on the step. I steeled myself and slowly climbed, each creak echoing down the narrow corridor. Memories floated toward me: Fritz and our laughter, soft and haunting, slipped under his door like a ghost.

I paused at the top, flexed my fingers, then gripped the doorknob.

Inside his room, *nothing* had changed.

A white quilt lay neatly tucked across his king-size bed. Two navy square throw pillows were propped in the bay window. On his dresser, dust had collected on a framed photo of us at Cannon Beach, our smiles frozen in time, and vanilla ice cream dripped from our cones. My fingers tingled with opposing impulses: one demanded I throw the photo in the trash can, the other yearned to brush off the powdery particles and hold it to my breastbone.

Why would he still have this? This snapshot felt like an alternate reality. When we dated, did his soul pull away? Had my own desires consumed me so completely that I overlooked the warning signs? Fading affection. Staying out late. His focus turning to the glow of a phone screen. If those signs were there, I had missed them. But now his soul made it painfully clear and screamed a truth I couldn't ignore: staying by my side was his duty.

I strode to his small reach-in closet, and snatched the first item I saw, a blue T-shirt with the NFL Cowboys logo on the left corner.

Clutching it, I fled down the stairs before more memories could snare me.

Nyxon's brow knit at the sight of my full arms.

Please don't follow me. Please… don't… follow.

I scurried outside, the screen door slamming behind me.

At first, Raiden's eyes widened with worry and he leaned away. Then recognition softened his features.

I placed the bag of frozen peas and first-aid kit next to him on the porch steps. "First, let's lift your shirt."

His knee bounced. "If you leave the supplies, I can do this on my own."

"I'm helping." I sat beside him. I squeezed the cloth because if I didn't, I would've placed my hand on his knee. And what if he pulled away? I'd look like a fool.

He closed his eyes and took a deep breath before exhaling.

I took that as a sign, so I timidly tugged the translucent, blood-soaked shirt above his head, and prepared for the blood's metallic smell to hit my senses, but nothing. Strange.

Then I saw them and gasped. Scars crisscrossed his back, thick and thin, long and short, each one a ballad of survival, trauma, and violence.

I pressed the cloth against the oozing wound on his chest muscle. "What happened?" I asked delicately.

"How much time do we have?" The scars weren't just marks; they were memories, each one speaking its own painful truth in a language only survivors could understand.

"We don't have to talk about it." My fingers mapped a thick scar on his shoulder, two raised lines forming 'LL'. Its roughness sent a shiver through me.

"I earned that scar at age eleven. A Cynder's City Level Enforcer caught me jumping economic class levels. They branded me with a heated blade. Their twisted way of teaching me a lesson I'd never forget: I'm a low-level Grounder. I learned the hard way that if you can't beat them, you join them." He pointed to a star pattern near the left side of his abdomen. "At twenty-eight, I tried arresting a Grounder for smuggling water from a resource container. He shattered a bottle and stabbed me with it."

I flinched. He endured so much, it made me want to pull him close, shield him from his past pain, and be the safe haven he needed.

He tossed the bag of frozen peas in his palm. "What's this for?"

"There's swelling around your right eye. The bag of peas will act like an ice pack." I lifted the rag slowly, just enough to see the wound. "You need stitches."

"Okay, doc. If you say so." Instead of pressing the bag against his face, he dropped it and rested his hand on my knee. His thumb stroked the inside of my leg.

My breath caught. I didn't move. I was stunned. His gesture shouldn't matter, but for some odd reason it did, more than it should.

"You helping me feels like a gift I didn't earn. I know I'm the outsider. Now they think I'm the troublemaker."

Sadness struck me. I hated the way *outsider* sounded. So forlorn and isolating. You were on the outside looking in, no one extending a hand. I knew how deeply labels could cut. The fear and frustration that fueled me when the Jeep skidded into the driveway dissipated. "Fritz was on edge, searching for a fight. Luckily, you were there tonight. Can you put this shirt on? In case someone comes outside. I'll hold the cloth against your wound."

As a team, we fumbled to slide the blue shirt over his head while I held the rag firm. His breath hitched with each movement. His fingers, stiff with pain, gripped the hem, and tugged it down.

"It's a little snug. But I appreciate it," he joked gently, as the shirt clung to his biceps and stopped short at his waist.

His hand slipped under the shirt, resting atop mine. His touch was tender; his fingers traced the ridges of my knuckles. His breath brushed my skin, and the tension turned electric. Did he sense the subtle shift in the air, the quiet intimacy thrumming around us?

No, he couldn't. But his mouth parted slightly, as if to agree, but no words came.

Vulnerability pulsed in his silence like a candle flickering in the dark, torn between the urge to burn brighter and the fear of being extinguished. I tried again, with a softer insistence, "Why is your blood translucent?" His jaw tightened, betraying the war between the trust he wanted to give me and the fear he couldn't shake. I slowly shimmied my hand free, but I swear, for an instant, his fingers tightened as if he was reluctant to let me go. "We can talk about something else, even the weather, but I'm genuinely interested in getting to know the Grounder who started me on this journey." I took the bag of peas and pressed the cold bag against his cheek.

"It's a defense adaptation. When my blood mixes with a large amount of nitrogen and oxygen, it turns translucent and odorless so predators, or my enemies, can't track me. Employers value someone who doesn't leave traces of themselves behind."

"Thank you for trusting me. Now, you need stitches. I can stitch you discreetly in the barn where no one will see." The truth rang in my voice. "I just need to go inside and grab supplies."

He scratched the back of his neck while he mulled over his options.

Finally, his hand stilled, as if accepting the fact that this was, indeed, the best course of action.

I rose, held my breath, and reached out a hand.

Ridiculous. That was how I looked. How could he place faith in someone as inexperienced as me?

To my surprise and relief, Raiden took my hand and stood.

"I'll be right back," I promised.

I entered the stoic living room. Fritz still lay on the dining table.

I patted Fritz's cold hand. "How are you?" Would his leg fully heal? What emotional damage had been done?

His glossy dilated pupils roamed over my face. "You—you be-eaut-t-tiful." The crooked line that gave his smile its unique charm was hardly visible.

I chuckled, even though dread still pressed heavily upon me. "A true Casanova," I teased, then turned to Nyxon. "Raiden has a cut on his chest." Urgency crept into my voice. "I know you're busy, but can I *please* get a knowledge transfer about how to stitch Raiden's wound? And a Cynder pain pill?"

Nyxon crossed her arms, becoming a fortress of frustration. "He deserves to be in pain."

The air crackled with friction, like the atmosphere before a tornado.

"Stop it, Nyxon," I snapped, my flaring temper surprising everyone in the room.

Nyxon raised an eyebrow, her expression a mix of amusement and disdain. "Pain is a teacher that offers a valuable lesson."

I wasn't in the mood for a lecture, and I had no idea how to grow Nyxon, The Robot, a heart.

Chapter 29

Quinbe's head swiveled between us as she listened to our argument, her eyes creasing at the corners with concern. Finally, she sighed. "Stitching someone is more complicated than you think Avi, even with a knowledge transfer." Pursing her lips, she dug into her medical duffel bag and pulled out a white, hammer-like device. "A medical staple gun will be easier."

She dropped it into my hands. Black words on the sleek handle read: *Vet1000 Precision.* "I don't know how to use this."

"Point. Shoot. Simple," Nyxon stated.

"Sound advice," I said sarcastically. "But what about pain relief? It's late, hasn't Raiden suffered enough?"

Nyxon tapped her foot and glanced at the grandfather clock, its gold pendulum swinging steadily in wide arcs.

"Fritz getting shot isn't *entirely* Raiden's fault," I countered.

Nyxon's narrow gaze flashed to Fritz. He shrank, his shoulders curling inward. If he could sneak into the kitchen to hide, I bet he would have.

Quinbe considered my plea, her veterinarian's heart swelling with empathy. "Come on, *Nyxon.*"

Nyxon groaned, spun on her heels, and strode to the couch. She dropped onto the cushions, propped her boots on the coffee table, and just as angry heat surged into my cheeks, she pointed at the black duffel bag.

"The side pocket. Purple bottle." Her tone was flat. "Take two white capsules. One now, one in the morning. There's a glass spray bottle. Use the silvery-blue mist on any cuts. It sanitizes and speeds up regeneration."

"He'll really appreciate this." I breathed, relief loosening my shoulders as I turned away.

As I pushed through the front door, Raiden stepped off the porch, heading toward his car. "Raiden?"

"I can take care of this scratch at my hotel," he mumbled without turning around. His one hand still tucked inside his shirt to hold the rag against his chest.

"Wait." Confusion evident in my tone as I strode after him.

He didn't pause; instead, he moved faster, his silhouette outlined by the harsh glow of the moon.

"Raiden." I begged. My breath came out in quick, visible puffs as I closed the distance between us.

Out of habit I reached out, curling my fingers around his forearm. I pulled him to me, but he winced and broke my grip. My stomach twisted as if I shared his pain. "Sorry, but it's not a scratch. A Band-Aid isn't going to fix your problem. So, stop being stubborn."

His nostrils flared. "I heard everything from outside. Nyxon is right, I deserve to be in pain."

"Nyxon is wrong. I see the parts of you no one else does, I see your soul. You don't have to hide your pain from me." My fingers brushed his, and he looked down at them, then back toward the house, his expression a heartbreaking mix of longing and yearning.

"You should be at Fritz's side. He wants you there. That's where you belong." Raiden's voice dropped, low and strained, as if he longed to take the suggestion back.

"I can help both of you." A lump formed in my throat. I would never pick Raiden over Fritz, but tonight I had the space and capacity to be here for both. The chance to do right by them. "Go to the barn," I ordered, trying to mimic Nyxon's steely authority.

He studied my face, his eyes softened, and his lips curved in humorous affection. I had no idea what he sought: understanding, forgiveness, compassion. Still, I hoped he'd found peace with me.

We moved toward the barn, but a haunting loneliness clung to the way he walked. An owl screeched. An omen of trouble brewed. My eyes fought tricks and subterfuge. This was our safe place, our refuge. Although the coyotes whooped, I reminded myself there was nothing to fear. No one could hurt us here.

The barn door creaked as I pushed it open. A single lamp near the table illuminated the space.

Raiden sat on the table and propped his feet on a metal chair.

My lips parted to offer a glimmer of comfort, but the words felt fake and frail, like tying a ribbon around a broken bone. Instead, I created a mask of confidence. It wasn't for me; it was for him. An offering of strength in a storm he was never meant to weather alone.

He saw through my mask, of course, his posture eased just enough to show he appreciated my attempt to be calm for him.

The staple gun caught his attention and he arched an eyebrow. "Have you used that before?"

"Yes."

"Liar."

"Point. Shoot. Simple."

He lifted his shirt, pulling it high against his collarbone and revealing the hard, sculpted lines of his stomach. The rise and fall of his chest quickened.

As he slowly peeled the rag away from his injury, his muscles flexed. A translucent stream of blood traced the contours of his pectoral. The sight was strangely intimate; I saw a part of him he never allowed others to witness.

Without thinking, I lunged forward, grabbing the rag and landing between his legs, quickly pressing the rag back to the wound. Our closeness brought goosebumps to my arms. His thighs tightened ever so slightly against my hips, sending a ripple of heat through me. An image of his hands gripping my hips and pulling me closer flooded my thoughts. Every inch of my body responded to his nearness, as if the space between us had vanished.

I slowly lowered the rag and aligned the staple gun with the top of his wound. It hovered there as guilt held me back, I didn't want to cause him more pain.

He noticed my hesitation. His hand closed over mine, guiding the staple gun to his skin. Our breaths synchronized like the ebb and flow of a tide. The staple gun became a shared burden; it symbolized the repairs, both physical and emotional, we had to make. My throat dried, he nodded, and I pulled the trigger. A loud, quick snap echoed in the barn, followed by a muffled grunt and the smallest flinch from Raiden.

His soul reacted instantly. A vivid pulse that shrank inward, folding in on itself like a wounded dog retreating from a blow.

This personal, intimate reaction caused remorse to thrum through my veins, so I quickly deactivated my evobility.

"Fritz is a nice guy. I'm happy for you both." Raiden's words slipped out like a sad sigh, distant and heavy.

I released another staple from the gun. "What are you talking about?" Fritz and our history were buried under layers of mistakes.

"I thought you and him were together?" he asked, as I fired staple number three.

This should have been a cut-and-dry yes or no, but I hesitated. A month ago, our relationship was a chapter long closed, a book gathering dust on a shelf. Since Fritz's return, work and training have ruled my life. Romance? It was an afterthought, eclipsed by the constant thrum of impending peril.

Raiden leaned in, his eyes flickered, eager to reveal a confession and gauge my reaction. "You're all he talks about. Your happiness, your safety, it's his top priority."

His unexpected warm words clashed with my cold reality: Fritz had lied to me and his soul pulled away.

Deep, deep down, a small part of me longed to believe Raiden, that Fritz truly cared. I fought to suppress the small smile tugging at the corners of my mouth. The idea that I mattered that much to him was too dangerous, too vulnerable to entertain. "If my happiness was his main concern, then he wouldn't have run off without me tonight." My words were laced with all the doubts I tried to bury. "And finding out he befriended me because it was *part of his job* really put a damper on anything romantic."

Raiden's lips pressed into a thin line as he studied me.

He didn't believe me, and his pity-filled pause pushed me to fill the silence. "It's complicated."

"That's how you know its love. I don't mean that love is pain, but it endures. Life is the long winter; love is the promise of thaw. Through barren fields and frost, through trembling buds and blooms, love remains the hidden root beneath it all. That's why when a love like that reveals itself, you must have the courage to claim it."

I couldn't let myself fall into that loop of hope and heartbreak. "Even with him back, it doesn't feel right. And trying to fix it now? It's bad timing."

"What if it's never good timing?"

"Then it's not meant to be, I guess."

The staple gun's staccato clicks faded into the background, losing their jarring harshness from when we began. We were no longer adversaries or mere acquaintances, but confidants to each other's painful past.

I took a step back. The staples gleamed under the lights. I'd massacred his well-defined chest. My sympathy swelled, realizing that if it scarred, it would blend in with his biography.

I dropped the white pills into his palm. "Pain relief. One capsule now, one in the morning. You're welcome." I tried to sound casual. He swallowed one right away. I shook the spray bottle. "This is a disinfectant. It'll speed up the healing process." I twisted off the lid and sprayed his wound. An oily blue mist, resembling cooking spray, bubbled on contact.

Raiden sucked in a breath through clenched teeth. "Sorry for ruining your night."

How do I respond? They scared me half to death, but perhaps in his life, he'd known little comfort. I didn't have much to offer, but I could give compassion freely, so I patted his hand. "Don't let it happen again."

His eyes held a deep regret, a remorse that spoke louder than words ever could.

"Now, hold this sterile pad, and I'll tape it in place."

Once I finished, I took a step back and he inspected my handiwork. "Looks like a six-year-old wrapped a Christmas present," he teased.

"I'm sure lots of ladies would enjoy you under their tree."

He leaned in. "And what about you?"

"Wouldn't you like to know?" I turned away, desperately hiding my flushing cheeks.

Hastily, I shoved the medical supplies into the kit and zipped it shut. "Fritz has a guest bedroom. You should sleep there."

"I don't want to impose more than I already have." He shifted uncomfortably, glancing at his bandage.

"What if your cut opens?" I touched his arm, a rigidity coiled in his muscle, but I refused to shy away. "Fritz won't mind. The drive into town is over thirty minutes, and it's already late. Spending the night would be the sensible thing to do."

He looked outside, where the wind howled through the trees. His attempt to maintain a stoic demeanor wavered, revealing the wear and tear of a resilience frayed at the edges. "I could use a comfortable bed."

"Come on," I urged, my voice carrying a soft insistence.

Suddenly, he reached out, clasping my hand in both of his. "You have a kind soul." A faint flex of his fingers sent a spark straight to my chest. I did what anyone would've done, well, at least Quinbe would've done. When he let go, the ghost of his touch left a heat I wasn't ready to relinquish.

As we walked to the house there was a change in Raiden's posture, a resolve that hadn't been there before. Perhaps our encounter in the barn laid the groundwork for a friendship. A partnership, at the very least. Forged out of necessity. I could almost feel the thread of trust forming, stretching between us. He could be more than an obstacle or a stranger. I could be more than a pawn or plaything. Alliances could be more than convenience; they could be survival.

Inside the house, the night's chill clung to our clothes. Raiden paused. An eerie oppressiveness hung in the air, as if Death sat on the living room couch, disappointed by the lack of a victim.

I grabbed Raiden's hand and dragged him through the kitchen toward the back bedrooms.

I flicked on the light, and a soft glow filtered through the pendant's frosted glass covering. The queen-size bed, with its quilted coverlet and mahogany headboard, lent the room a rustic charm. The nightstand bore a faint tea-stained ring. The old house's original pink rose-vine wallpaper, which I normally despised, brought a peaceful end to tonight's chaos.

Gratitude gleamed in Raiden's eyes. "I honestly don't know what I would've done tonight without you." He brushed a stray lock of hair behind my ear, his thumb caressing my cheek. I couldn't resist leaning into his touch. Hope, allegiance, and longing surged through me, tangled beyond understanding.

His hand found my waist. "How can I repay you?"

"Ahem." Nyxon cleared her throat and planted a hand on her hip.

Raiden jerked his hand away.

I scooted back.

"He's staying?" She shot a pointed look at us, daring either of us to confirm it.

Her suspicion and condescension pricked my skin. Raiden didn't move a muscle, and the urge to protect him built inside me, like the rumble of a volcano before it erupted. I couldn't give in to her judgment. Not now. Not when things were already so complicated.

"He's tired and hurt. It's one in the morning. It's the polite thing to do," I said, my tone thick with justification, making it impossible for her to argue without looking like a complete ass. I brushed past her, adding, "I'm taking a shower, then crashing in the other guest room. Good night."

But as I strode to the bathroom, I could feel Nyxon's gaze burning into my back.

At 8 a.m., my grumbling stomach demanded food. Donning Fritz's Washington University purple T-shirt and black cotton shorts, I padded into the kitchen.

Pancakes would work. Blueberries, check. I sliced an apple. As I whisked together pancake ingredients, Raiden's blood secret nagged at me. His blood was strange, but did that make his evobility dangerous? If I told Nyxon, what if he found out? How angry could he get? Why risk making him our enemy? Raiden had been clear; his ability was a vulnerability.

The batter sizzled as it hit the hot griddle. I flipped a pancake. It flopped unevenly, creating a mess that mirrored my thoughts. If I kept quiet, what was the worst that could happen? I'd be betraying my friends.

"Hello?" Nyxon snatched an apple wedge. "You're burning the pancakes."

"Shit." I lowered the stovetop temperature.

Nyxon leaned against the counter, her gaze probing. "You and Raiden spent a lot of time together last night." She bit into an apple slice with a crunch. "Learn anything interesting?"

Chapter 30

My loyalties lay with Nyxon and Fritz.

Betraying Raiden felt wrong. But there was so much at stake.

I glanced over her shoulder, then whispered, "I have a clue to Raiden's evobility." This confession was a stone thrown into still water; its ripples spreading outward, carrying consequences and regrets I couldn't foresee. "His blood isn't red. It's colorless and mirrors whatever it touches. It glistens slightly."

Nyxon's gaze sharpened as her mind raced through the vast archive of her memory. "I have no recorded data or prior exposure to an evobility exhibiting those characteristics. It could be a protected evobility. When Stracid Amarmet ruled, he authorized his Slyfen priests to seize any evobility deemed a threat to national security, driving the most powerful evobilities to near extinction. Grounders forfeited their evobility or were executed. There were close to five thousand unique evobilities before the purging. Now, less than two thousand remain."

My forehead creased. "Why didn't anyone stop him?"

"His Slyfen priests swept through the poor and uneducated. Grounders no one cared enough to protect. Amarmet said it was for their own good. They were too unpredictable, too different, he claimed, to be trusted. The middle and upper-class agreed. *Then* Amarmet targeted the middle class, claiming it would bring national stability. The upper class agreed. But when he came for the rich, their gated communities couldn't protect them, and that's what sparked the Great Evo-Liberty War. The war your grandmother won." She bit into her apple. "The queen's first bold move was annulling the law requiring evobilities to be registered and forfeited. Her ruling marked the start of acceptance and preservation, creating a society where the diversity of evobilities could flourish without fear of persecution or coercion."

"Is your evobility protected?"

She huffed. "No. The upper class finds my evobility tedious. Li's and Fritz's evobilities are useful but too common to be valuable." She paused, listening to the echo of footsteps down the hall, then whispered, "I'll drive to Madras, Oregon. The Cyndarian Watch's database could hold the key to uncovering Raiden's secrets."

Raiden turned the corner, still wearing the same clothes from the day before. "I smell sugar and butter."

Nyxon returned his greeting by crunching on her apple.

"Pancakes," I deadpanned.

"Last night's outcome could've been much worse. After breakfast we need to talk about our… *partnership*." Partnership slid off Nyxon's tongue reluctantly.

I couldn't shake the nagging fear: Fritz wouldn't stop until Sellow, all of them, were dead. Sloane's last words wove around my neck and tightened like a noose: *save Fritz.*

Raiden's eyes searched mine, seeking forgiveness or perhaps a trace of the connection we shared last night.

I cleared my throat to alleviate the tightness in my chest. "Nyxon, can we go home? Graysen is probably wondering where we are."

There was only one way to protect my friends. Surrender to Uzziah.

But would he make me wear the Tiara of Tuskia? Would he read the incantation to control me? Would he do whatever it took to win his throne?

Yes.

⋅✦⋅

Journal Entry Five:

> *As the week unfolded, Raiden seamlessly wove in and out of the barn. His comings and goings caused Quinbe to burst into a flurry of delightful activity, each visit leaving its imprint on the space's ambiance. While I was bench pressing, Raiden offered a spot. A thrill ran through me as he positioned himself behind me, guiding*

Fritz hobbled into the barn on his crutches with a rolled tube-like paper tucked under his arm. "You mentioned seeing a map. Nyxon had this hidden in her closet."

I hopped up off the rower and tightened my ponytail.

Fritz unrolled the map and pinned it to the barn wall. As he smoothed out the corners, a handful of photographs slipped free and scattered at my feet. I bent to gather them.

Succulents the size of cars, blazing neon under two desert suns. Groves of strange trees, their trunks braided gray and black like rope turned into stone.

Fritz tapped a finger on the photo. "These trees don't grow leaves. Instead, they sprout clusters of pods filled with water that the locals outside the Shimmer and wildlife rely on."

His hand drifted lower, to a thorny clump at the tree's base. "That's a numbtum. Looks like a tumbleweed, but those thorns can rip through most fabrics. Their toxin paralyzes on contact. Once you're down, *it feeds.* Draining blood and fat until there's nothing left but a husk."

He took the photos and turned toward the map. "Do you see anything familiar?"

I traced my finger over the faded lines. Fritz's throat tightened as I pointed to a cluster of four perfect circles, each no bigger than a baseball, arranged in a diamond. "The Shimmer Domes?"

He gave a short nod.

I ran through the pin placements I'd seen back at Uzziah's. "And these small pyramids. What are they?"

"Slums outside the Shimmer. Their houses, made from clay, are teepee-shaped so the sand blows around them."

"Are these lakes?" I ask, pointing to the dozens of teal pools scattered across the map like a surreal oasis.

"Definitely, not a lake. Those geysers shoot sulfuric acid at nearly 300 degrees. The steam burns your eyes. The water singes your skin. With a pH over twelve, it's basically bleach. Only chlorina clams and anacondents survive there. Workers in specialized suits wade through the mudflats to harvest pearls from the clams. They use a pry bar-like tool to open the clam's mouth, while the other cuts out the pearl. The fertorium pearls power everything. Shimmer Domes, homes, vehicles, weapons. You sweat in that suit all day. One break for food and the bathroom. Miss it and you go hungry. You piss in your suit. It's brutal. Twenty-foot anacondents lurk below, with barracuda jaws and bodies like tree trunks." He held out his hands to show the size.

A chill slipped down my spine.

"And if a shell slices your suit, the acid floods in. Your flesh is gone in minutes. When your mother found out about us, she exiled me to those mudflats. I watched Grounders burn or vanish beneath the water." A flicker of darkness crossed his eyes, his thoughts pulling him inward, dragging his whole expression with it.

I took Fritz's hand, anchoring us together, a physical plea to pull him back from his nightmare. How could my mother, *any* mother have done that? I would never let him face such a fate again. "If I had known." A wave of powerlessness washed over me. What could I have done?

He averted his gaze. "She wanted to teach me to follow the rules."

His truth granted the closure I hadn't realized I'd craved. Every lie had been rectified, every truth unveiled, as if the canyon of deceit that cracked between us filled. I longed for nothing more than to take away his past pain, not out of obligation or pity but from a place deep within me that still cared for him. Despite the changed titles, from lovers to friends, my affection for him remained unaltered.

"You were worth breaking the rules for. You still are." He slipped his arm around me, pulling me into the hard contours of his chest. The suddenness of his embrace left no room for resistance, and the world around us faded, leaving only the cadence of our shared heartbeat.

Our breaths blended. His mouth tenderly met mine, reviving a long-lost tango, creating a volatile dance of desire and an unapologetic declaration of defiance. I missed this for a year, and it was just as sweet as I remembered. Our bodies fit together in a way that unraveled me, dissolving the angry walls I had built. Nothing remained but the ache of longing for him.

His soul sparked and jerked away, its reaction zapping me back to reality. What was I doing? This was why Fritz was sent to hell! Pushing him away, breathless, I stepped back.

"I thought…" His angelic soul blinked like a dying lightbulb.

Tears stung my eyes. "Your soul is terrified of me. It shrinks away or—" my voice quivered, "reacts violently when we touch." Each word wounded the softest parts of me.

The color drained from his face and his shoulders sagged. "It's not your fault."

"I thought we were happy before." An ache grew in my gut as I imagined the possibility that our years together were a lie: built upon a false sense of security, driven by convenience, or shrouded in a veil of contentment.

"We were. I was." He grabbed my hand and his soul simmered. I swear it hissed like a cat.

"But your soul must've sent a signal to stay away from me. Or that," I couldn't believe what I was about to say, "we're not right for each other."

"Loving you was as instinctive as breathing. Every part of me recognized you as the one I couldn't live without, and losing you never changed that truth. The clam mudflats broke me. I need time to relearn who I was, so don't take it personally when my soul reacts negatively toward you." His gaze locked onto mine, searching for any sign that I understood his plea. Patience was his request, and in response, I tightened my grip on his hand, and the stiffness in his shoulders faded away.

"How did my mom find out about us?"

"I don't know. Nyxon, my mom, and Li tried to dissuade me from getting involved with you. But they'd never turn me over to your mother. Li incessantly ambushed me with blind dates, but you were the only one who clicked."

We did click, but that was then. Before. Before I had to stand on my own. Before I had to pack my things and move out of his house. Before I had to learn to be a 'me' instead of a 'we'. Before Raiden, no, I couldn't factor him into my life. What if Fritz and I were just falling into comfortable old habits? Or what if this was our second chance at happiness? My head and heart seesawed, each vying for my attention, eager to steer me toward either commitment or cold feet.

The barn's door rattled open.

We stepped away from each other, just as Raiden and Graysen walked through, catching the last remnants of my interaction with Fritz.

"Good morning." Raiden's tone was as cold as the void between stars.

"When the cat is away, the people will play." Graysen looked unimpressed with Fritz and I's closeness.

"Mice. Not people," I corrected her.

"Same scurry, different feet," Graysen countered.

Nyxon and Quinbe walked through the doors. Nyxon waved a tan folder in the air. "Come sit. We've got a solid lead on the female Jagwar."

I pulled a chair out next to Quinbe. Fritz's kiss still tingled on my lips, and a flutter of desire stirred within me. With him, life was easily manageable. My dreams and goals were in reach. Could he be that steady place again?

Fritz's crooked smile had lit up his face.

But Raiden's demeanor changed, a seriousness fell over him.

Was our kiss a mistake?

Fritz was my forever. And now, after all this time, that kiss brought back everything. The warmth, the safety, the unresolved feelings. *What should I do next? Would my choice put Fritz in more danger than he already was in?* I sighed, trying to focus on the task at hand, but my thoughts kept circling back to that kiss.

"The female Jagwar's name is Mizumi. She bartends at Dosalas. Her shift starts at 9:00 p.m. tomorrow, but the manager won't give me her contact info." Nyxon shrugged. "Good on him for safeguarding her privacy. Fritz is coming with me to pick up Li tomorrow in Madras, Oregon. We want to search the database for the twins and Sellow. Whatever information the Cyndarian Watch has on them could be useful to find the tiara and the doctor." Nyxon side-eyed me. I know the truth. They planned to search the database for Raiden's evobility. "So, Raiden, can you go to the bar tomorrow?"

"He's still injured," I interjected. "Quinbe and I will go. We have no choice but to act, any hesitation could mean the difference between life and death."

Quinbe nodded but the others stayed silent.

"Nyxon and Li can go on Sunday," Fritz offered.

"The bar isn't open on Sunday," Nyxon deadpanned.

"And what if one day is one day too late and the Limier tracks her down?" I warned.

"Then Avi and I will go pick up Li, and Nyxon and Raiden can warn the Jagwar," Fritz countered.

Nyxon raised a brow. "The Cyndarian Watch doesn't know Avi exists. You can't roll up to their base and ask for a guest pass."

Fritz steamed.

"Me, Avi, and Quinbe can go," Raiden stated. "Yes, I'm injured, but as long as you don't ask me to do any push-ups, I'll be fine."

Nyxon sighed, her expression tightening. She knew I wouldn't like what she was about to say. "We need to decide… do we warn Mizumi or let the Limier grab her and hope they lead us to the Doctor?"

Arguing erupted between us all. Nyxon and Fritz stood firm on team *Wait and Watch*. Quinbe and I were already on our feet: *Warn Her Now*. Raiden ping-ponged between us, caught in the current.

"We can have two goals. Remove the abraylix and protect Grounder women. I have time to remove the last abraylix, Mizumi doesn't," I said firmly.

"Fine. But remember, we don't know how Mizumi feels about the Amarmet Alliance or the Queen. If she asks, you work for the Cyndarian Watch."

"And Avi, grab a handgun from my safe and put it in your purse," Fritz stated with no compromise.

"I'm graduating from pepper spray?" I met Raiden's eyes, humor passing between us.

"Yes. The combination is zero-nine-two-seven." Fritz scribbled the numbers on a Post-it note. "Remember what I taught you. Only use the gun if it's an emergency. Guns draw unwanted attention."

"*And* you'll need a disguise." Nyxon smirked.

Chapter 31

Raiden waited in front of the restaurant, his hands tucked into the pockets of his dark jeans, as I stepped out of the taxi.

"You went with a blue-eyed blonde. Bold move." Raiden's lips curved into a flirtatious smirk.

That smirk should've come with a warning label. It wasn't fair how easily he could pull my thoughts away from the mission and onto him. His dark eyes glinted as if he knew exactly what he was doing to me.

"I didn't think you could handle two redheads tonight," I shot back and adjusted my fake reading glasses, perched delicately on the bridge of my nose.

Raiden's maroon button-up shirt stretched taut over his broad shoulders, each motion pulling the fabric tighter against his frame.

A low whistle escaped from him. "And those knee-high boots with that dress, I'm not sure what to compliment first."

"A wise man would do both."

He took my black and white scarf and rubbed it between his fingers. "Since you can see color, I'll have to buy you a different shade."

"You're very generous. We'll have to go out on the town more often, so I can wear it." Warmth bloomed at the base of my neck, spreading upward. Did I just try to flirt with him? I tugged the hem of my navy-blue tank dress as he opened the door to the Latin kitchen and tequila mixology lounge, allowing *Bon Jovi's Livin' on a Prayer* to skip into the fresh air.

Across the bar, at a corner bistro table, Quinbe waved eagerly, her magenta strappy heels tapping nervously against the barstool footrest. The tiny pearls dotting her high-neck sable babydoll dress gleamed with each restless shift.

We threaded through the vibrant crowd, the murmur of lively conversations buzzing around us. Vancouver's nightlife had become a distant memory. My routine was reduced to work, train, and sleep. The outside world appeared only in passing, caught through a car window.

His hand grazed my lower back as he leaned near my ear. "You kept my secret… it makes me feel like I can trust you with *almost* anything."

This plan of his, to hide his evobility for everyone's safety, didn't sit right with me. And he hadn't earned my loyalty, so guilt for telling his secret shouldn't be pooling in my gut. He never should've asked me to stay quiet. Nyxon seemed more annoyed than surprised that he kept his evobility hidden. Still, I didn't think he was lying about the danger it brought. There was a wrongness beneath it all, a sadness that clung to the ridges of his every word.

"No need to mention it. Seriously," I said, hoping the words sounded casual. If he wants to stop being an outsider, he's going to have to start trusting all of us.

The U-shaped, gold-plated bar gleamed under the low-hanging lights. A thin bartender with a black tie and gray suspenders garnished a lowball with a lemon twist. A busboy brought in a tray of cleaned martini glasses. But no female Jagwar.

Raiden pulled out a white leather barstool and motioned for me to step up and onto it. I admired the mosaic tiles decorating the square tabletop. Iridescent reds, oranges, and yellows shimmered in the center candle's light, reflecting a fireball in flight.

"Nyxon called on my way here. *Lecture, lecture, lecture.*" Quinbe rolled her eyes. "Pick a table with a clear view of the entrance and exit, with a window or wall to our backs. I told her not to worry."

"She will," Raiden and I said in unison, our voices blending seamlessly together. Surprised, we exchanged smiles.

Quinbe's silver dangling earrings jingled as she lifted her chin proudly. "No one can hurt you, because *we're* here."

Raiden added, "And because she's been working hard."

"I have the bruises and bumps to prove it. So, I'm ordering my favorite martini. The Blue Siren. Blueberry vodka, lemon wedge, Saint Germain, and a splash of grapefruit juice."

After we ordered, Quinbe asked Raiden, "If you could have any evobility, which one would you want?"

Surprise flickered in his eyes and a subtle hint of vulnerability crossed his features. He looked into the distance, across the bar and dance floor. "Anyone's Evo but mine." His tone held a wariness, as if his evobility were a burden only he understood.

"I think you should drink tonight so we can get a straight answer out of you," I said.

He chuckled. "Be careful what you wish for. I sing karaoke after three drinks."

One round of drinks and dessert turned into two as we waited for the female Jagwar.

Quinbe placed her fork on the empty cheesecake plate and wiggled in her chair. "I love this song!" A verse from Joan Jett's "Bad Reputation" blared from the speakers.

To my surprise, Raiden hopped from his barstool and held out a hand for her. "Let's dance."

"Yes!" She sashayed off her perch, and he guided her to the empty dance floor.

They bobbed their heads to the beat. He took Quinbe's hand and spun her twice. Her dress floated up, flirting above her knees, and her springy curls lifted off her shoulders. Their lighthearted laughter summoned couples and free spirits to join them on the dance floor.

As the crowd grew, they disappeared from view. The image of him dancing with someone else hit me like a shot of tequila.

I raised my martini to my lips but paused. Where did Quinbe's confidence come from? I took a long sip, but its bold grapefruit flavor had gone flat.

From the corner of my eye, I spotted a new bartender's arrival. Tall and imposing, she wore a crop top that showcased her well-defined abs and a leather skirt that clung to her powerful thighs. Long brown hair fell in thick curls down her back, framing a face with a prominent nose. Her intense blue eyes carried a natural magnetism that made her feel approachable. As she strutted behind the bar, her presence was impossible to ignore.

That must be her!

Straightening in my chair, I lifted slightly off the seat, craning my neck to scan the crowd for Quinbe and Raiden. Faces blurred together and became a shifting tide of laughter and movement.

I could do this. I didn't need backup.

But the knot in my stomach said otherwise.

This wasn't going to be like my past stunt at Argon's house. This time, I'd keep my head and be cool, calm, and in control.

I took a deep breath and made my way to the bar.

At the bar, chatter mixed with clinking glasses, and the bartender moved with professional ease.

"What can I getcha, hon?" Her accent was unmistakably New Jersey: quick, casual, with a bite of attitude.

"The Blue Siren," I replied.

Ice clinked against the glass as she mixed the drink. I leaned closer, the fan's breeze brushing over my hot skin. "Hi, I'm…." Shit, should I use my real name?

She smiled, shook the martini shaker above her shoulder, silver bracelets reflecting the light.

"I think I've been looking for you. Mizumi?"

She raised an eyebrow, her face smug. "Wow. I'm flattered, but I'm not into women."

"Oh… no, I'm with the Cyndarian Watch," I murmured, straightening. The lie carried a confidence I hadn't expected, maybe I was meant to be one of them all along. But I could never abandon perfume chemistry; it was the last thread of my humanity.

Her eyes widened. She lowered the shaker, voice dropping to a conspiratorial hiss, "I *don't* fight anymore." She lifted her shirt. On her ribs, a tattoo of a dove clutching an olive branch stood out in fine, intricate lines against her pale skin. "I found my peace. I can finally sleep at night." She placed a lemon wedge on the rim of my drink and slid it across the bar, liquid sloshing over the edge. "Can you say the same?" Mizumi's eyes flickered with disgust before turning to leave.

"Wait." I leaned over the bar. "I came to warn you. There's a doctor. He wants to experiment on you."

The color drained from her face. "Monrowvia. I heard he's been lurking about. Teamed up with the Amarmet Alliance."

"We can help you." I quickly grabbed a coaster and a pen from the bar. I scribbled down Nyxon's number and slid it toward her. "After your shift, we'll take you home to pack. Then somewhere safe."

Mizumi's mouth became a thin, unimpressed line. "I can handle this myself," she muttered, pushing the coaster aside.

"You don't know what Monrowvia is capable of," desperation edged my voice.

"I've dealt with worse. The CW is nothing but liars. Corrupt to the core," she snapped, striding to the other side of the bar. She shot me one last glare, then, like a performer stepping into character, her expression melted into a flirtatious smile as though she were playing a role she knew all too well.

My breath caught in my throat. No, we were the good guys… but what did I truly know about the CW?

I returned to our table. The waitress arrived to clear our plates. I gave her my credit card to pay the bill.

The mass of dancers parted, and linked arm in arm, Quinbe and Raiden strolled through resembling royalty. She tugged him close, whispering in his ear. He beamed. I shifted in my chair, as if movement could shift my envious thoughts to our mission.

I filled them in, keeping my voice steady even though my failure tasted like cheap Irish whiskey. I couldn't meet their eyes. I'd let them down and the ache of it pressed against my ribs.

Mizumi's glare cut across the bar. We met it, unmoving. After a beat, she turned back to her customer, dismissing us like flies she couldn't be bothered to swat.

Raiden exhaled through his nose. "Time to go. Quinbe, call Nyxon with an update. I'll take Avi home, then return to talk to Mizumi alone. I'm staying at the nearby hotel—if I offer to cover her room, maybe she'll stay the night."

Quinbe slid off her barstool and paused just long enough to glance at me, not with blame but with sympathy, before turning to Raiden. "Will you walk me out?"

"Of course."

As they sauntered away, I couldn't control my covetous gaze, so I stared, stone cold, at my phone. Will I receive a text saying he was riding home with her, don't wait up, catch a cab?

Chapter 32

Every laugh Raiden and Quinbe shared, every casual brush of her hand against his arm, twisted in my gut like a knife. Why did it hurt this much? I hated that a single glance could make my heart stumble and leave a bitter taste where sweetness should be.

After another song's lyrics sailed past me, I craned my neck for the waitress with my credit card.

Raiden parted the crowd and my breath caught.

He came back.

A goofy grin pulled at my face, and I loathed that I couldn't stop it.

"I promised Quinbe I'd ask you to dance before we left." Raiden's smile was coy.

Heat rose to my cheeks. Quinbe, the perpetual instigator, always nudging things into motion.

"I wish we had more time, but I'll take what I can get." Raiden placed his phone on the table as the waitress returned with my card and a receipt for me to sign. His phone buzzed with a text from a blocked number.

I peeked at the sentence: Buy a new phone! B. N.

In a split second, the light in Raiden's eyes dimmed. His soul jerked left, then right. His panic was a contagion, infecting my arm with goosebumps.

"What's going on?" I swallowed.

His head swiveled around the bar then froze.

I tracked his line of sight to a devilishly handsome man with brown eyes and a French fork beard. He lifted his chalice of beer in a 'cheers' gesture to Raiden, a large yellow diamond ring flashed in the light. His thick fingers were swollen and crooked from years of fights and hard work. His brown leather jacket caught the light with a subtle sheen. He exuded a worldly style; the jacket perfectly paired with a coordinating belt and a crisply ironed white shirt tucked neatly into gray slacks.

"We have to leave. *Now!*" Raiden grabbed my hand and jostled me off my barstool.

"What's going on?" My voice wavered.

He shoved his way through the throngs of people. "I'll explain once I get you home." He hurled his phone into a trash bin and the excitement I enjoyed a heartbeat ago went with it.

We burst through the double doors. "Is it Uzziah?" I tugged on his hand because he refused to look at me. "Sellow? Wolfram?"

His gaze stayed fixed ahead like my questions never registered. His arm came around me without warning, pulling me into a protective side hug. Then I was moving whether I wanted to or not. The closeness felt wrong, procedural, as if I were the president's daughter to be whisked into a car, a risk to be managed, not someone he meant to calm or comfort.

"Raiden, what is happening?"

He froze, whip lashing me into a full stop.

Two brawny men puffing on cigars leaned against Raiden's Dodge Charger. The billowing smoke silhouetted their appearance as if they'd casually strolled from the fiery gates of hell.

Raiden whipped me around, but the man with the yellow ring obstructed our retreat.

"You're a tough Groun—" The man tugged on the hem of his brown jacket, his voice rough, like the remnants of smoke still lingered in his throat. "*Man,* to find."

Raiden stood protectively in front of me. His chest rose and fell quickly. The predator had become the prey.

The man pulled his brown leather jacket to the side. A gun's black hilt gleamed in the streetlight.

My muscles went rigid; a sudden coldness collided in my core.

His fingers hovered over the metal before reaching further back, producing a cream-colored three-by-five envelope from his pocket. He tapped the blue seal on his palm. "Your hacker friend Bashiri wasn't very helpful... so we *convinced* him to cooperate."

Raiden clenched his jaw. "He's not involved in this."

The man with the yellow ring brought his hands together, cracked his gnarled knuckles, and leaned to the left to get a better look at me. "Is she why you're not doing your job?"

"She's nobody."

"Those are my favorite kinds of women. Forgettable, replaceable, disposable." He stroked his beard. "Come out, honey. I'm Tonium. I'll show you a top-shelf type of date."

I squeezed Raiden's sides.

Tonium's sneer displayed straight white teeth. "Raiden, I have a message for you. Come and get it."

A scream from across the street made us jump. A boy lifted a giggling twenty-something off the ground, and they stumbled to rejoin their group of friends.

The scream rattled Nyxon's rules loose in my mind: run, hide, fight. Each choice chanted into my brain.

The panic rising in me drowned out the world, narrowing everything down to run, hide, fight. *Choose! Choose! Choose!*

Run. I grabbed Raiden's hand. My legs moved before I even processed it, pulling Raiden along as if the rules themselves had taken control of me.

My grip tightened. The street blurred, a river of noise and lights, but nothing mattered except those damn rules.

Hide. There was no darkness to lose ourselves in.

The cigar-puffing men clomped behind us. No matter what happened next, we had to stick together.

Yanking him through the parking lot, straight into oncoming traffic. A car screeched to a halt, a horn blared as the irate, pudgy driver shook his fists and slapped the steering wheel.

Raiden wrenched away. I gasped, stunned by the lost contact. He flung open a random cab's door.

"Hey!" The slim driver furrowed his bushy brows.

Raiden yelled, "Get in!"

I scooted over the faded, torn leather seats as a wave of bile climbed my throat. Was it fear, too much liquor, or the lingering stench of sauerkraut in the cab? I reached for Raiden's hand, but my eyes widened when he stuffed his hands in his pockets.

He pulled out twenty-dollar bills and threw the cash at the confused driver. "This is more than enough to take her home."

I shimmied in his direction. "I'm staying with you."

Kneeling, he palmed the top of my thigh. "You can't." His hand on my thigh wasn't the comforting touch I hoped for. His fingers tightened, trying to hold onto someone who cared. "I can't let you get involved in this." He inhaled and without warning, shouted, "Drive!" And slammed the door in my face.

I pressed my hands to the window as the men flanked Raiden, each seizing an arm. Raiden didn't shout or protest, rather he surprised me with an ill-timed joke: "I've missed you boys. It looks like you two have been skipping leg day at the gym." Despite their arms, necks, and legs resembling sturdy tree trunks. Undeterred by his jest, they dragged him down the street, disappearing into the shadows and leaving a lingering emptiness in my heart.

The car lurched forward. "I don't want trouble," the cabby stammered. I stomped and fought tears of frustration. I sagged in the seat and tucked my purse onto my lap. My eye caught the glint of the pistol concealed inside. The driver stared at me from the rearview mirror. "Ma'am, where to?"

"If you don't want trouble, keep the cash, and pull over."

The cab screeched to the curb.

I stumbled onto the dimly lit street. I sprinted as fast as my legs allowed. Cold air burned my lungs. My breath burst from my lips in ragged clouds. At the first alleyway, an orange ember of a cigarette revealed a homeless man slumped against a brick wall.

I continued, darting from alley to alley, my feet beat the pavement sending needles into my shins. I skidded to a stop, every nerve alert.

A streetlamp spotlighted three figures shoving a man back and forth in a bullyish game of hot-potato. Two of the men clamped cigars between their teeth, the smoke snaking around their necks as if to strangle their master.

I dipped into the alley. Pressing my spine against the brick wall, I crept forward, each carefully placed step betraying me with a rustle. I edged around black garbage bags and ducked behind a dumpster reeking of decaying vegetables and meats.

One goon passed his cigar to his buddy, the embers flaring briefly. He slammed a fist into Raiden's mouth. A guttural groan slipped through Raiden's split lip. "That's a gift from the Servalina. You daft bastards picked the wrong Grounder to cross. Everyone knows you don't fuck with a Servalina. She paid us good money to open you up like a fish on a dock. But we know you've got business to finish first."

Raiden panted. "Tell the Servalina I'm sorry."

"Like all apologies, it's worth nothing." The brute's fist collided with Raiden's face again, sending a jolt through his body. Before Raiden could recover, Tonium kicked the back of Raiden's legs, and Raiden crashed to the ground, palms slapping the concrete with a dull, painful thud.

Tonium produced the same three-by-five cream envelope and, with a flick of his wrist, sent it skidding onto the ground beneath Raiden's chin. "Do your *fuckin'* job and we won't have to hunt you down."

Raiden reached for the letter. Tonium's eyes flashed feral, then his boot crashed down, twisting, grinding Raiden's hand into the dirt. Raiden hissed through his teeth.

The quiet girl I forced myself to be, who sat on a bar stool and didn't dance, snapped. The woman inside me was done hiding. I had to act.

Chapter 33

The brutes didn't notice me until my 9mm clicked inches from Tonium's ear. His clove aftershave overpowered the alley's pungent stink. I yanked his pistol from his waistband. My hand quivered, but my voice was steel. "Nobody moves." I tucked his gun into my purse.

Tonium sighed loudly. "Now, listen here littl' lady—"

"Let him go," I shouted.

Translucent blood ran from Raiden's nose down his chin.

A spike of panic hit me, and my words broke midair. "Raiden, can you stand?" He spat blood and pushed himself onto wobbly legs. I waved the gun wildly. "Back up! Everyone back the fuck up!"

The cigar men folded their arms and glared down at me. Tonium raised his hands and gave ground. The other two copied their captain.

Tonium's breathing elevated in tempo; he wasn't scared, but angry. "If we have to return, you won't be walking away, Mr. Gravì."

I tucked under Raiden's arm and carried his weight out of the alley. Raiden's head lolled, but his grip tightened on me just enough to remind me he was still with me. I gritted my teeth, steeling myself.

"We can take a cab to Quinbe's. She'll help you."

"No. If they follow, I don't want them to learn where she lives, and she doesn't know about my…" Using his sleeve, he wiped translucent blood from his nose.

"Okay. Where then?"

"My hotel is on the corner. Toward the clock tower."

I panted. "That'll work. Those men, they're Grounders?"

He flinched while clearing blood from his brow. The cut continued to drip, so he applied pressure. "Yes."

As the eleventh bell tolled, we rounded the corner into the glow of the Hilton Hotel.

To any strangers passing by we were a couple who hit the bottle too hard. I double-checked to ensure his attackers were nowhere in sight.

Raiden winced as we entered the hotel and rushed into the elevator. I exhaled as he pushed the button to start our ascent.

"What did those men want from you?" I unraveled my scarf and stretched for the cut above his eye, but he seized my wrist.

"Reminding me how to do my job. Protect the Queen. Protect the country." He brushed his thumb over my skin. "I've been distracted lately." He lowered my arm to my side.

"Is she questioning your loyalty?" My pulse increased like the yellow numbers blinking on the elevator's display.

"Something like that."

On the fifth floor, we located his door. He inserted the key card. A red light flashed. He tried again. He stomped and seethed.

"We're safe." I took the card, and my fingers grazed his. I flipped it over and slid it in. A green light flickered. The unlocking click was a heavenly sound.

Groaning, he hobbled into the room and collapsed into a chair, kicking off his shoes with a weary sigh. "Sorry, there's only one bed. I didn't expect company."

"I'll grab a cab home. By now they're probably in a pub drinking bourbon, boasting about who landed the best blow."

Raiden didn't look amused. "I don't want you risking it," his voice was firm but tired. "I'll sleep on the floor." Raiden pulled the cream envelope with a blue seal from his pocket and set it on the table. He peeled off his shirt and draped it over the envelope, hiding it.

An idea sparked in my head: I should read the letter. That was what Nyxon would do. *This might be my chance to learn more about Raiden.* "You're right, it's better to be safe. But we're adults, so we can sleep in the same bed." I walked to the bathroom, hearing his footsteps close behind. At the sink, I washed my hands and splashed cool water on my face, while he did the same.

I hoped Graysen wouldn't worry, but I needed to read that letter. I cupped a cloth to my cheeks.

Gathering my resolve, I stood in front of Raiden and gently pressed the cloth to the cut above his brow. "Li was right, you're not a Jagwar."

"Hey, three versus one isn't fair."

I joked, "Can you go a month without getting beat up?"

Raiden winced. "I'd laugh, but my ribs hurt."

His sagging soul splintered my compassion. I grimaced; black and blue bruises formed on his torso. "They didn't reopen your cut from before. You got lucky. No staples needed. You should jump in the shower."

"*If I was lucky*, you'd be joining me in the shower."

My brow shot up, and my surprised eyes locked with his mischievous stare before I rolled mine, a wry smile tugging at my lips despite myself. "You're not that lucky." I refocused on his injuries. "I'll visit the front desk, hopefully, they have a first-aid kit. And I'll grab some ice; I saw the machine in the hall." I tossed the cloth into the sink.

I definitely could not join him in the shower.

I snatched the ice bucket and hurried out of the room, stumbling over my feet.

When I returned, the shower was audible. I dropped the bucket and the sad excuse for a first-aid kit onto the table. I stood in front of the full-length mirror, took out my blue contacts, and threw them in the trash. I placed the wig and glasses on the table.

My gaze wandered to the bed, and against my will, lust tried to steal my attention. We were adults. Raiden was injured. Think of something else. Anything else.

The envelope.

The water abruptly ceased.

Once he was asleep, I would open it.

I kicked off my boots and slipped out of my dress, folding it before setting it on the table. I stalled at the bed's edge. *Do I face him or the window?*

The bathroom door handle jangled. I slipped into the bed and squeezed my eyes shut. My right eye snuck a peak as he maneuvered to the dresser. Beads of water rippled down his abs, his scars acting as riverbanks, slowing and redirecting their progression before soaking into the towel slung low on his hips. Longing curled through me, tangled with an admiration, the kind reserved for those who've endured brutality.

I turned away. It would be best if I fixated on the window.

A drawer creaked. Shuffling of items. The snap of a waistband told me he put on boxers. "Thanks for the kit."

"It's not much."

"Yeah, but there's ibuprofen. My head is killing me."

After creating an ice pack, he sat on the bed near my feet. "I regret everything that has happened, everything that will happen. Your life was uncomplicated before I…"

"Don't worry about the future. We can't control it. Only prepare. My gray existence was a lie before you."

He slinked into bed behind me. His exhale roused the hair on the back of my neck. His soul encased me in a blanket of cryptic guilt.

My instinct crooned to let him rest, to recover, but I couldn't. "What did the letter say?"

He grumbled, "It's just business."

I turned to meet him eye to eye. The white cotton blanket dipped below my shoulder. "Supporting each other is who we are. If you're in trouble, we can help. Maybe not me, but Nyxon surely can."

"I sent a supply container to Cynder. Amarmet members hijacked it. My employer believes I've become sloppy." He draped the blanket over my shoulder. "Can we keep what happened between us? I don't want the others to lose focus because of my baggage."

"What was in the container?"

He shut his eyes. "All material things are replaceable, so it doesn't matter." His rhythmic breathing made it clear that my interrogation was over.

Fuming, I twisted back to the window. Badgering him wouldn't earn me answers. I'd have to unearth them myself, starting with stealing that letter.

✦

By dawn, his arm draped across my ribs. My heart begged my eyelids to fall like lace, but the sunrise intruded upon our quiet space, spotlighting the shirt that blanketed the envelope. I rustled, disturbing the morning's grace.

I silently shimmied free of him and closed the blinds. Shrouded in darkness, Raiden inhaled deep and his lip twitched. Plumes of purple and blue masked his eyes.

My throat tightened as I snatched the card and tiptoed to the bathroom.

I lifted the envelope's broken blue wax seal. He must have read it while I was asleep.

Meticulously, I drew out the note:

> *You disappoint me. There will be no more do-overs. Bring me their heads and my tiara. You have thirty days. Fail, and I will hire your replacement, drag you back to Cynder, rip the truth from your skull, and toss your brother into the Mudflats.*

My fingers involuntarily flexed, crumpling the note as I fumed at my naive reflection in the mirror. What did Raiden get himself into? He had a brother that would be in danger if he failed. He had thirty days to execute Uzziah? The Doctor? I whipped away from my mirror image.

He was an assassin! That son of a bitch was never going to let me reunite with my father on my terms. Did he plan to let the doctor remove the abraylix? His orders were clear: shoot to kill. Period. Full stop.

Conflicting emotions churned my stomach. A person possessed multiple layers of good versus evil: He lied, but he was in jeopardy. But that was how the world worked: you were the pawn, prey, or predator. How did Raiden view me? His patsy or partner?

Rustling from the bed made me carelessly shove the note into the envelope. I skulked to Raiden's shirt and wedged the letter underneath.

He yawned. I scrambled to the bedside table and checked my phone. Nine messages.

Two messages from Nyxon:

Be at Fritz's house before ten a.m. Li needs to update all of us.

You better not be doing what Fritz thinks you're doing.

One from Quinbe:

OMG. Your location spilled your secret: you're at Raiden's hotel. I'm screaming! I love this for you. Go get it, girl!

Six from Fritz:

Where are you?

Why aren't you answering?

Quinbe said she left you with Raiden, that wasn't the plan.

I'm starting to worry, please answer me.

The last two messages increased in panic as the night dragged on. Guilt caused me to grimace, but I knew if I texted now my phone would blow up with calls and questions.

Raiden stretched. "What time is it?"

"Eight-fifteen." I swiftly slipped on my dress and boots. "Nyxon wants me home."

"I can drive you." He prodded the bruise on his chin, then winced. "Is it bad?"

"Um, check for yourself."

He tossed the blankets aside, revealing a strong bulge underneath his snug briefs.

My cheeks flamed.

"Why are you blushing?" He chuckled all the way to the bathroom, until he caught sight of himself in the mirror. "Oh, damn."

Minutes later, he returned and slung his shirt and pants into the trash. The letter fell to the carpet. His jerk reaction was to stuff it under the clothes.

I blurted, "I read the letter. We can help you."

Raiden flushed, the color sharpening the shadows of his bruises. "In my line of work, you don't accept help from people because those people become a liability."

"Who are you supposed to kill?"

"It's none of your concern." He pulled on a pair of jeans and an ebony T-shirt.

He was a steel vault, and I didn't have the key.

"My first objective is to return the tiara to the Queen."

I grabbed the blonde wig and glasses off the table. "So, you're a callous assassin who obeys orders and doesn't ask questions."

He began lacing up his shoes. "You don't know the first thing about my job. You don't know the first thing about my life on Cynder and what I must do to survive. So instead of judging me, consider this: every part of me I sacrifice, I sacrifice out of fear… and for love."

As if I didn't know sacrifice. Was he manipulating me by being vulnerable? How could I ever truly know this man? Talking about fear and love didn't excuse what happened last night. He wished to bury our roguery and descend into our 'normal' lives. But this letter and the Grounders from yesterday cracked the thin ice our friendship stood on.

"I'm taking a cab. Go back to bed." My phone buzzed. Fritz.

Chapter 34

"Have I taught you nothing?" Nyxon snapped. "Intel means nothing if you end up dead. The men who attacked Raiden aren't heavy hitters on Cynder. And that hotel? It didn't have the security needed to keep you safe."

"Yeah. Their security sucks." Fritz leaned on crutches by the fireplace and puffed out his chest.

"For the hundredth time, I'm sorry." Leaning back on the couch, I swept the loose brown strands that had escaped my braid behind my ear and realized my jaw was clenched so tight my teeth ached.

Li retrieved a formal notebook from his backpack and settled into the armchair. Bound in midnight-blue leather, the notebook bore a small brass lock. "Can I begin now? Dear lord, so much drama over a one-night stand."

"It wasn't a one-night stand," I shouted.

Nyxon sat next to me on the couch, crossed her legs, and rested her vitiligo hands on her knees.

"I'd love to kick things off with good news, *but* guess what? There aren't any. With Sloane…" Li cleared his throat. "Gone. Princess Hydraxia promoted Nyxon to Avi's conservator."

I scoffed. "Conservator?"

"It's just a formality," Nyxon said dryly.

"It comes with a nice pay raise," Li added.

With a flip of her wrist, she gestured for Li to continue.

"*Anyway,* turns out, Princess Hydraxia wasn't the mastermind behind Avi's abraylixes. The queen ordered a talis-taffy to be implanted into Avi because she insisted, Avi needed it to live on Earth."

I raised a brow. "Talis what?"

Nyxon chimed in, "It's common for Grounder children to have these safe, dissolvable bands. The bands control unstable or lethal evobilities. The talis-taffy acts as a regulator, diffusing energy surges that could harm themselves or others."

Li pursed his lips. "Hydraxia was rantin' and ravin' about the ChromoCoil's warning and how the queen broke *their deal*. Whatever that deal was, it's why Avi was sent to Earth."

Deals, lies, betrayal. Once again, the queen's schemes rose like a flood. Why did Raiden follow her, despite the tears and blood?

"What is a ChromoCoil?" I asked.

Nyxon looked flustered. "They can predict the future."

"I've barely scratched the surface of what Grounders can do. There's so much more to this world than I realized. I'm just now seeing how deep this really goes." It was exciting and scary.

Li continued, "Then Sloane lied. Straight-up told Hydraxia Avi's powers went dormant because of the talis-taffy. Total crap. *Man,* breaking the news to Hydraxia that Sloane and the queen swapped the talis-taffy for an *abraylix*, she lost it. Sloane had years to come clean. And didn't. Now Hydraxia is convinced Sloane wanted those abraylixes to kill Avi, as payback for sending Fritz to the Mudflats."

The revelation clung to me like an itchy sweater Sloane might have woven, its threads laced with deadly motives.

"No way. My mother would *not* have raised Avi just to let her die. She would have done the right thing and removed before it was too late." Fritz's steadfast belief clashed with my growing frustration.

"Face the facts, Fritz. Your mother always resented me." Bitterness edged my voice, borne from years of staying silent while gripping tightly to accumulated grievances, disdainful glances, and feigned concern.

Fritz's expression tightened, torn between reverence for his mother's memory and the shocking truth that screamed in his ear. "My mother died protecting *you*." His declaration dripped venom at the suggestion her sacrifice was anything less than noble.

I stood and strode for him. His posture straightened, meeting me head-on. "Or did Sloane know Sellow would never let her walk away."

The verbal sparring between us escalated, the living room becoming our battleground, each of my perceived slights became a weapon and each of Sloane's redeeming qualities became a shield Fritz wielded.

Nyxon rose and put out her hands. "Enough. She's dead." Her bluntness hit like a sledgehammer, stunning everyone into silence. "Sloane loved her son and would do anything to protect him. We can stop tiptoeing around Sloane's disdain for you two dating. Her reasons weren't rooted in a lack of love for you, Avi, rather Princess Hydraxia strictly forbade any romantic entanglements with a Grounder. Princess Hydraxia wanted you to live a *human life*. That meant a *human* husband. *Human* grandchildren. But *Fritz* pursued you anyway. So, in Sloane's mind, it boiled down to your life or her son's."

I walked to the window and crossed my arms.

Nyxon exhaled. "I don't expect you to condone Sloane's choices, but I hope you can understand why she made them."

Li turned the page. "More bad news. Princess Hydraxia denied the bounty for Sellow and the rest of them. Then threw shade at Fritz for everything that went down with Avi. She's ordering Nyxon to grill Fritz, like full-on interrogation mode, to determine if he conspired with Sloane and the Queen."

"Not happening," Nyxon deadpanned.

Fritz's jaw dropped. "I'd never conspire."

"Yeah, man, I know, we all do. I tried talkin' Princess Hydraxia down, but she was beyond—Nyx, is there, like, a word that's a level above mad?"

Nyxon rattled off, "Incensed. Enraged. Irate."

"Princess Hydraxia was enraged." Li scanned his notebook, then jabbed the page with a finger. "But she's hyped Aviana figured out her whole heritage thing, and *decrees* we *won't* need to hire a Mind Niche."

"*No one told me* stealing my memories had remained on the table." I seethed.

"I swore not to go through with it. Even if she ordered it." Fritz stumbled over his words, rushing to solidify his point, expecting his declaration to mend our earlier argument.

I fixed my gaze on Nyxon. "And you?"

"Before Li left, I created a report detailing why you should retain your memories. I calculated my report had a ninety-three percent chance of success. If Princess Hydraxia disagreed, then arguing with her would be pointless."

"*No point*? No point! Jesus Nyxon. I'm a person, *not* an equation."

Nyxon's expression tightened and a flicker of skepticism passed over her face.

Li shrugged. "I just do what I'm told."

I erupted, "Of course you do. I never doubted you'd take the easy way out. It appears, my father and Fritz are the sole Grounders who'll stand up to my mother and the queen. Does my mother even know Uzziah's alive?"

"*She does now*. Princess Hydraxia had zero idea Uzziah was still kickin'. And I was straight-up stunned to see she still had full-on love vibes for him. Part of me figured she orchestrated Uzziah's convoy attack with her mom… Nyxon, you're gonna be mad, maybe even… irate, but I'm so over this lying game. This fake earth-life. I'm done fearing the queen and her crew, so I told Hydraxia the truth: Red TaKa didn't attack Uzziah's convoy."

"Li, no." Fritz's eyes widened.

Nyxon shook her head. "If the queen hears *even a whisper* that you told."

Li shrugged her off. "Princess Hydraxia freaked when I told her Uzziah planned to slap that unholy tiara on Avi's head. She didn't even know the Tiara of Tuskia got jacked. *So listen up*, Princess Hydraxia ordered under no instance, and I mean like ever, should Avi meet Uzziah. She's all about preventing another war and protecting her daughter. She's got a scheme of her own. She's ordering Fritz to destroy the tiara with the Dracophelia inside, this will prove Fritz's allegiance, and then *no one* can use the tiara ever again."

Fritz and Nyxon shared a look, a silent conversation passing between them.

Nyxon gave the slightest nod, barely perceptible, but it was enough.

Fritz adjusted his shoulders. "*Fine*, if that's what it takes. But for the record I've *always* put Avi's best interests first. *Always*."

I opened my mouth to unleash a harsh retort, but his unwavering gaze, deep pools of devotion, stopped me cold. His loyalty was undeniable, and the raw vulnerability in his expression hit me hard, causing a warmness to spread through me, leaving my tongue tied. "Fritz, I…."

"Whatever." Li rolled his eyes. "Princess Hydraxia plans to reach out to Uzziah through her own channels. I gave her details about Raiden. Her operatives uncovered that he's a full-on *Iron Talon.*"

I activated my evobility: Fritz's gold-and-silver soul solidified into armor. Li's red, blue, and yellow stars stopped swirling. Nyxon's soul buzzed at its usual pace. I would get nervous when she did, so I relaxed just a little. "What's an Iron Talon?"

Nyxon puffed out her cheeks and exhaled. "Iron Talons represent the top branch of the City Level Enforcers. We don't have lawyers or judges on Cynder, so all citizens get the same punishment written in the law and enforced by CLEs. You pay a fine or get sent outside the Shimmer Dome to work in the boiling chlorina clam mudflats or cactus orchards. No sitting in a jail cell."

"CLEs, those dudes are drunk on power." Li crossed his arms over his broad chest and leaned back. "They have the authority to detain *anyone.* Demand identification. They strut around tasing Grounders just for kicks. Assholes, all of them."

Fritz fumed. "*Iron Talons* specialize in raids, both inside and outside the Shimmer Dome. They don't ask questions. They make Grounders disappear. Innocent or guilty, it doesn't matter. Grounders can't trust the Iron Talons, so we can't trust Raiden."

A wave of defensiveness took me by surprise and I blurted, "A few nights ago, you two were buddy-buddy."

"That was before he kept you out all night." He tilted his head, eyes narrowing. "Doing who knows what. *Risking* your safety."

Li snorted. "*Safety*? So, Avi's *safety* was what had you so hyped in the car on our drive home?"

Fritz's jaw clenched. A blush crept over my cheeks.

My desire to judge Raiden for his personal traits clashed with my fidelity to my friends, creating a tug-of-war inside me. "Raiden's instincts are to keep me safe. I ran into danger for him, and I believe he'd join us to help Fritz find the tiara. Returning the loyalty we've shown. He doesn't like working for my grandmother. I'm sure we could sway him, especially since my mother wants Uzziah alive."

I swallowed a lump in my throat. A part of me still hoped to explain away the Nitro Snap woman in Uzziah's chest.

"If we just talk to Raiden." My words unintentionally escaped as a plea. "Or present him with a better proposition, endorsed by Princess Hydraxia."

"You want us to ask Raiden, *an Iron Talon* politely?" Li's voice rose dramatically as he mocked, "*Raiden, please* defy the mighty evil queen?"

Fritz's nostrils flared. "If Raiden returns to Cynder without that tiara, he's as good as dead, and he knows it."

Defeated, I stared absentmindedly at my hands. The old habit of picking my cuticles returned. A reflex I thought I'd overcome, a part of my past I'd left behind, a cowardice I'd conquered. My lips quivered. I shoved my hands beneath my thighs.

Fritz, Nyxon, and Li argued about how to best secure the tiara.

What made me view Raiden differently than the others? I truly believed he'd align with us given the opportunity. "I can see Raiden's soul," I blurted. Their heads slowly swiveled my way, holding a collective breath. "His soul isn't evil. He'd help us."

Li's condescending chuckle shattered any illusion of understanding. "Avi, bless your heart, but you're new to Cynder politics."

Nyxon paced, filling the space with her restless intellect. "Fritz needs the tiara. Raiden has the information we need to find it. Searching without Raiden's assistance would squander valuable time. Because Raiden's evobility remains a mystery, our interactions with him require finesse to steal the tiara from *him* when the opportunity arises." She mused in front of the window, her gaze fixed beyond the panes then spoke to herself, "He seems to trust Avi."

Fritz interrupted Nyxon's rambling, "I have a better relationship with Raiden than Avi does, I'll befriend him."

"On the drive back from Madras, you admitted Raiden hasn't answered any of your calls. And I bet he'll only feed you breadcrumbs since you went off the rails last time he teamed up with you," Nyxon said pointedly.

"Raiden's informants don't trust him because of you, and he's trying to rebuild those relationships," I added. "*Right now,* Raiden believes I'm keeping all his secrets, we can take advantage of that angle."

Fritz shook his head. "No. Grounders don't associate, let alone buddy up, with *an Iron Talon*. I'm responsible for getting the tiara to show my allegiance, so I'll handle it."

"We're working together. So, let's just tie Raiden up and pound the answers outta him. Find out his evobility, then take him fully out of the equation." Li palmed his fist.

"If we beat him and demand to know his evobility, we're no better than Amarmet." Nyxon's statement struck Li and Fritz like a missile, sparking reflection, regret, and restraint. "If the Cyndarian Watch found out, they'd ban us from returning to Cynder. *We have* our principles."

Fritz pointed a crutch at Li. "You've whined about going home to Cynder for the past five years, so let's not jeopardize it." Fritz took my hand, squeezed it, then released me. "Let's try their way."

I exhaled, finally, we're all in agreement.

"I thought you'd fortify walls and drag me behind them," I said to Nyxon.

"You don't need to stand behind anything, or anyone anymore."

But the sudden rapping of Li's fingers on the armrest gave me pause, each tap carrying an ominous strike. "And here's the kicker, our last snag. Sloane botched Avi's earth age calculation. You're not twenty-seven. You're twenty-eight."

My lungs seized. "But that means…"

Nyxon flexed her fingers at her side. "The last abraylix could snap any day."

"Then we leave for Cynder tonight. Fuck the tiara." Fritz's declaration left me breathless; sincerity and adoration were woven within each word.

"Avi can't fly." Li's concerned tone caught me off guard.

"What? Why?" Fritz lurched closer to Li, his crutches thumping the floor.

Nyxon exhaled. "It's like flying with a brain tumor on an airplane. Flying involves exposure to lower air pressure, and this change can affect the distribution of fluids within the body, including the pressure around the abraylix. As you ascend, there are fewer oxygen molecules per unit of volume. This reduction in—"

"Okay, okay. I get it." Fritz flipped his wrist at her, then turned to Li. "Why didn't you bring a doctor back with you to take it out?"

"What if the doc worked for the queen? Princess Hydraxia is *all* paranoid, not knowing who's legit. Don't worry, once she secures a doc, she'll send her too Madras. She's hooking us up with medical equipment pronto. *The catch?* She can't tip off the Queen, so it's like a stealth mission. The medical equipment will arrive within seven days. Hopefully, a doctor will be here in a month."

"We can't afford to wait around, hoping for a doctor to arrive." Nyxon seethed. "Send for the instruction manual for the equipment and the medical textbook and I can fucking do it."

Smirking, Li pulled a thick textbook and spiral equipment manual from his bag. "I figured you'd say that."

In the wake of my night out with Raiden, Fritz was extra attentive. I savored the tender press of his fingers during a massage on my sore muscles. We stole glances. Each encounter painted a mosaic of subtle intimacy, forming an intricate collage of anticipation. *How long would it take for his soul to fully relax around me?*

"Hello? World to Avi," Tiffany's brisk tone jolted me back to work, back to reality.

A thick black headband pulled her glossy blonde hair away from her face. Dark silky sleeves cuffed her wrists. She held a clear cylinder vase filled with forget-me-nots and baby's breath. A thick twine bow wrapped the vase's middle. "I forgot to tell you these came for you today. They were at the reception desk."

The delicate blooms glowed with a soft light, as if enchanted. A single possibility of who sent them sprouted in my mind.

Fritz.

I snatched the card and ripped it open.

When I read his name, my confusion seemed to wither the petals.

Chapter 35

The card read: *Thanks for stepping in. I'm not used to that kind of help. I'll see you soon. Be careful until then and try not to miss me too much. Raiden.*

What would Fritz think? He *wouldn't* be happy.

Tiffany's penciled-on eyebrows furrowed. "Did someone die? They look like flowers you'd order for a funeral."

"They're my favorite. Forget-me-nots." I brought the buds to my nose. When I was colorblind, I liked their star-shaped centers. "They symbolize a promise to keep connected to someone. The bond can be tested but never broken."

Enjoying the flowers bordered on cruel when I wished they were from Fritz. Raiden likely meant them as a peace offering, a reason for me to step toward him instead of away.

I could play along.

But luring Raiden close would be hard. Keeping him close would take all my cunning. Every secret he gave was another weapon tucked in my back pocket. I'd collect every whispered word, every exchange, and one day I'd have enough to bend him to my side.

Graysen, Fritz and I sat on the porch swing. Tuesday's sun hung low in the sky. Fritz passed me a Cynder pain pill. Popping these precious pills empowered me to persevere, after two sprained ankles, a dislocated finger, and the usual sore muscles that would've kept me on the couch. But now, that physical pain seemed minor compared to the emotional tangle I was about to put myself in. If I could steal the tiara from Raiden once he found it, do this for Fritz, maybe then his soul would stop pulling away from me.

The rumble of Raiden's Charger jolted me from my thoughts.

With a secret agenda and no idea how to earn Raiden's trust, I was torn. Fritz needed the tiara, but following my mother's orders to destroy it would destroy Raiden. We had to find a way to work together.

I fluffed my ponytail, then tugged at the hem of my blue racerback tank top. Fritz's frown deepened as he stood, his hand rising to palm the porch beam, his bicep flexing.

"I don't like this plan," Fritz muttered, but his soul appeared calm and untroubled.

I was doing this for him. Why didn't he understand? Every move, every risk, it was all for him.

Raiden stopped in front of the porch steps. His soul slowed its spinning vortex, as if becoming cautious, like how a rabbit stills before a stalking fox. Bruises, deep purple and green hues, canvassed Raiden's face. His probing gaze searched my eyes for any hint of betrayal. He bit his lower lip, a nervous habit that belied the confident mask he usually wore.

I enjoyed talking and laughing with Raiden, helping him when he was hurt, which was often; I chuckled to myself. My hidden agenda curdled in my gut. Did it matter how I gathered information if it saved Fritz? How far would I have to go? As far as it took to keep my promise to Sloane.

"Haven't seen you in a while," I teased.

"I had to handle a few things." Raiden stuffed his hands into the pockets of his blue jogging pants; the boyish gesture added an innocence to his cryptic response. "I didn't know if sending flowers was the right call... but I wanted you to know your opinion matters more to me than you realize."

His words caught me off guard. Did our partnership really matter that much to him?

Fritz shifted his crutches, the rubber tip thumping the floor harder than it needed to. "Roses, huh? How thoughtful. But those aren't her favorite. Too many thorns," Fritz mocked.

I'd left them at the office and hadn't breathed a word to anyone but Quinbe.

"Forget-me-nots actually," Raiden quipped.

Fritz shot Raiden a look that made the air feel thinner.

"I'm going for a run," I blurted, desperate to change the topic. "Raiden, come with me?"

Raiden's mouth curved slightly, before spreading into a bold smile. A stark contrast to the disappointment etched across Fritz's brow.

Fritz's gaze darted between us. "Use the elliptical. I'll bring my laptop. The path is slick from yesterday's rain, if you twist an ankle, your phone won't be of any use out there."

Raiden kicked off his socks and sneakers. "I'm happy to be at your service."

I stepped off the porch and backpedaled toward the trail.

"Graysen can go with you," Fritz offered quickly. Graysen's head snapped back, her expression scandalized.

"I don't run," she said, as if the very idea were insulting.

Fritz nudged her forward with his crutch. "You haven't gone past the tree line since you arrived."

"I *no* adventurer," she said. "Killed the cat, curiosity did. Nine lives I have, and waste them I won't."

"I'll be *fine*." This run meant more than miles, this was my chance to earn Raiden's trust.

"Stick to the three-mile loop then." Fritz's frown remained fixed, yet Raiden's eyes flashed as if poised to give chase.

As we entered the forest, mossy oak limbs transformed into gray curtains, creating an illusion of privacy. Spider-legged ferns dotted the forest topography. With Raiden at my side, my heart thrummed faster than it should. The occasional crunch of leaves under our bare feet broke the hush of the peaceful woods.

We halted at the babbling creek, where rushing water crashed against algae-covered rocks and streaked past my toes. Clusters of blue and white wildflowers lined the bank, their petals kissed by spray. A dozen smooth stones formed a natural bridge, some easy to leap upon while others requiring careful steps. A gold maple leaf cruised by on a maiden voyage.

Raiden leapt ahead, then extended a hand toward me. A heartbeat passed, then another. His jaw slackened, confidence faltering as the sting of rejection crept in.

I laced my fingers into his, and a rippling sensation in my chest flitted into a flutter. We took each rock one by one. I flapped my other arm to balance and when we reached the pebbled bank Raiden's small smile lengthened into a full grin.

"Thanks." I nudged him with my shoulder as I trotted past.

For the last half-mile of our journey, the terrain changed. Dead trees, scorched by a forest fire five years ago, lined our path. Massive spiderwebs owned the branches, and centipedes rented the pine cones nestled in brown blades of grass.

As we ventured on, a fork in our path emerged, prompting Raiden to halt and say, "Let's go left."

A slight pant escaped my lips. Even from our current vantage point, the trail gleamed with slickness. "That rocky trail leads to a cliff. Fritz said stick to the three-mile loop."

"Come on. I bet it has a great view." He grabbed my hand and tugged.

Chapter 36

I pulled my hand away. Unease stirred my legs to move, so I inched backward. "Fritz is waiting for us."

The last mile unfolded around me, but my discomfort lingered. My stride quickened along the winding path, each turn bringing a new wave of tension.

Raiden studied me, his brow furrowed. "What's the rush?"

Shrugging, I attempted to mask my trepidation and faked interest in the clouds. "Looks like rain."

Raiden raised an unconvinced eyebrow but chose not to press further. Instead, he silently matched my pace, until finally the iconic red barn came into view.

"Stop for a minute." Raiden's feet stalled in front of the driveway. His heels dug into the grass.

"Winded after only three miles, huh?" I teased, resting my palms on my head.

A smirk touched his lips, though his eyes stayed serious. "Can we start over? I feel awful about dragging you into my problems."

My pulse paused, divided by his request. He closed the gap between us, and my breasts brushed his chest.

"The fewer people who know *what I do*, *who I associate* with, the better. Keeping you safe means protecting you from certain aspects of my life."

"I don't need your protection. In fact, I've been the one patching you up." I put a hand on my hip, then the reason I embarked on this run hit me—secure the tiara. My hand dropped, and my eyes softened. "You want to start over, but you keep too many secrets. I don't even know your evobility."

"My evo is a curse. It destroys more than it saves."

"Then why didn't you use your evobility on those men in the alley?"

He carefully contemplated his comeback. "Haven't we learned violence inevitably invites more violence?" He was right, of course, but his explanation didn't settle my nerves. Raiden twisted his foot in the dirt. "Besides, if I'd hurt those Grounders, the queen would retaliate and send someone less diplomatic. She won't stop coming for me until my job is done."

Behind my eyes, a defiant spark flickered, urging me to abandon Nyxon's plan and reveal the truth, to plead with Raiden to defy the queen and help Fritz. My pragmatic spy's voice cautioned me against jeopardizing the plan. How could I succeed as a spy when, on day one, I was already blowing my cover? The man standing before me was an enigma. A mystery wrapped in layers of charm and intimidation. Yet I was drawn to him. Irresistibly, magnetically, toward the gravity of his presence. "I think you should know, Li returned with a message from Princess Hydraxia, she doesn't want Uzziah dead." I didn't want Uzziah dead. I wanted Sloane's words about Uzziah's kindness to be true. "And, the queen didn't want Sloane to take off my abraylixes."

Raiden's fingers flexed. "*Fritz's mother* tried to murder you," disgust coated his words.

He was the only person who had dared to say the truth aloud, and hearing it spoken so plainly jarred my devotion to my friends. Would Nyxon and Li still blindly follow orders? Was the Mind Niche truly off the table? "And, just like Sloane, *you're* in service to the Queen. Where does that leave you and me? Am I on your kill list?"

"I would *never* hurt you. Not now, not ever. You've been nothing but loyal. And because of that, you're the one line I'd never cross, no matter the cost." Raiden's response was swift and resolute; he took my hand with a decisiveness that mirrored his words.

I froze, caught off guard by the unexpected connection. Though he held my hand before, this felt different. His thumb brushed the back of my hand in a careful rhythm, his fingers curled around mine instinctively, as if he knew to reach for me when anxious inner thoughts stole his confidence.

"My goal is to locate the tiara, and every lead takes me one step closer. And once the tiara is off this planet, you won't have to worry about Uzziah… or me." His eyes, dark and troubled, held a promise tinged with regret.

I wanted to trust him, but how could I be sure when my life was just another piece for his puzzle?

When he saw I wasn't completely convinced, he offered an olive branch: "I have fresh intel. The Amarmet Alliance stashes their supplies in a dockside warehouse on the Columbia River. With hundreds of shipping yards and warehouses, finding the right one could take weeks." The crunch of gravel from Nyxon's truck ambling up the drive caused Raiden to release me and step back.

"I can search the shipping yards and warehouses with you," I offered, my voice laced with optimism.

"No, it's too dangerous."

"You asked me to start anew. If you want that, then you're taking me with you. And…" A myriad of questions formed in my mind but crumbled to dust. Which question wouldn't he balk at? His evobility, an intimate part of his identity, a truth hidden deep within, was a secret kept under lock and key. So, my task wasn't to hammer and coerce him into revealing his deepest darkest confessions, but rather to create an environment where he could safely share the hidden aspects of his life. This required patience and understanding on my part. It demanded a solid foundation of trust between us. He alone held the power to peel back the layers of secrecy and allow me to glimpse beneath the surface. Each conversation, glance, or soft touch, would be a brick toward that goal. Then a realization struck me, prompting me to lift my chin. "You have to tell me something true."

His fingers raked through his hair as he weighed the pros and cons. "What I say stays between us?"

"Your secrets are safe with me." The lie flowed forth easily and I chastised myself.

"My mother is a Grounder from Cynder. But my father… is from Earth. I'm quarter Italian and quarter Zimbabwean. Grounders discriminate against earthlings. If anyone found out, I could lose my job and be kicked out of the Shimmer Dome."

"Oh." I expected tactical, strategic information that would give us the upper hand in this delicate dance of deception and manipulation. What extremes was I prepared to go to match Fritz's dedication, what sacrifices was I willing to make to match Li's charm, how much could I endure to match Nyxon's skills? His confession struck a chord that transcended the boundaries of our roles as spy and target. Perhaps the Grounder before me wasn't just a skilled assassin; he had his own fears, desires, and layers of complexity that surpassed the simplistic narrative I crafted. This unexpected revelation was too personal. It's not what I needed. I couldn't exploit Raiden's vulnerability. "No one will know."

"You're the second person I've ever told… I thought saying it aloud wouldn't matter, but admitting it sickens me." The outer edges of Raiden's soul whipped through the air, like ethereal tendrils. The blue core, a pulsating epicenter of power, branched outwards to the very tips of his being. His colors painted a vivid portrait of the cosmic emotions at war within him.

I seized his hand. "You define your character, not them. You were born this way, and your way is perfect. It's extraordinary." Nyxon's truck door slammed, so I relinquished Raiden's hand.

Playing a spy should be a daring venture. A conquest. But acidic apprehension churned in my stomach.

As Raiden and I made our way toward Nyxon, our eyes unexpectedly locked. Would Fritz and Li do terrible things with this information? A pang settled in my chest, and my gaze fell to my dirty feet. This coy exchange between us repeated itself.

How long could I keep up this double agent charade before it all came crashing down?

Doubt gnawed at my composure as I forced a smile, hoping Nyxon wouldn't see through it.

Nyxon, distracted with her phone pressed against her ear, wrangled her laptop from the front seat. "There's no shame in hiding." Nyxon paused to listen. "I understand. Doctor Monrowvia's Limier is relentless. I'll call you back in twenty-four hours." She turned to us. "Mizumi called. Panicked. Wolfram broke into her apartment this morning while she was out getting coffee. She's hiding at a friend's house. Raiden, can you stay for dinner?" Nyxon's invitation sounded more like an order. "I want your input on what we should do next."

He straightened his shoulders, and a grin tugged at his lips. "I'm in."

As we turned for the house, Nyxon and I shared a conspiratorial glance. But behind my eyes doubt unfurled, duplicating fog blinding a ship's way to a protective port.

Chapter 37

Fresh from the shower, I pulled on my favorite pajama set, the cotton still warm from the dryer. The kitchen smelled faintly of dinner. Tomato soup with herbs, Raiden's delicious creation. I sat in the living room with my journal, the lamplight pooling over its leather cover. Fritz's house had gone quiet, only the tick of the grandfather clock kept me company. Uncapping my blue pen, I opened to a fresh page, ready to write my next confession.

<u>*Journal Entry Six:*</u>

Our plan was simple. Get Mizumi a fake passport from the Cyndarian Watch, hand her some cash, and send her to Anke's chateau in Dreis, Germany (Nyxon's friend from university). She'd hide there until we caught the Doctor.

The medical equipment finally arrived in Madras. They left this afternoon and will be back tomorrow night. Li went with Nyxon and Fritz because he needed to sign the paperwork to take the boxes. Even using Nyxon's and Fritz's trucks, it would be a tight fit. I just hope there's no sabotage and no suspicious looks.

Raiden and I stayed behind in case Mizumi needed us. All day I braced myself for trouble. Fritz warned, "Keep a weapon close. Trust your instincts. If something feels off, don't wait to find out why. And don't expect Raiden to save you, he's an Iron Talon and they only look out for themselves." Fritz wants the best for me, but I'm going to trust my VidaLumin evobility.

A chittering scream echoed outside, making my pen jerk, streaking ink across the page.

My gaze snapped to the window.

Another shriek—feral, frantic, feline.

I sprang from the couch, my journal forgotten.

Raiden burst from his room just as Graysen's ferocious roar, that summoned the courage of a lion, rang out.

My instincts screamed: "The backyard!"

I flung open the back door to the covered porch.

Graysen, a force of nature, grappled with a chubby raccoon. They tumbled across the grass, claws and teeth colliding in a clash of wild energies.

I closed the distance, the stench of metallic blood and musk slamming into me, thick enough to taste. My stomach twisted. Clumps of fur flew in all directions. I reached through the chaos, fingers closing around the scruff of her neck. My grip was too tight, but I couldn't afford gentleness. I wrenched her free, her body trembling in my hands.

The raccoon, undeterred, stood defiantly on its hind legs.

Blood smeared onto my skin. *Please don't be Graysen's.*

Ominous chittering from the tree line was a stark warning. We were outnumbered.

Raiden grabbed the first weapon in reach on the porch, a broom. He brandished it like a sword, stepping between us and the raccoon.

I didn't dare waste another minute, cradling Graysen against my chest, I ran for the house, the beat of her quaking tiny heart pressed to mine. Raiden's footsteps followed, close enough to feel.

In the kitchen, I placed her on the island. "Don't move."

I had to be brave for Graysen! But there was so much blood. "Raiden, grab towels."

Raiden complied. Cabinet doors banged and fabrics rustled.

Under the sink, I shoved aside a bottle of dish soap and a forgotten jar of coins until I found the hulking first-aid kit.

Next, I rummaged through drawers. My fingers fumbled over pens and batteries until cold metal scissors touched my palm.

Graysen whimpered, her body shuddering with each shallow breath. My throat closed around a shaky exhale that caused my lips to quiver.

Each snip of the scissors made my fingers tense. The antiseptic burned like fire, making my knuckles white as I gripped the bottle tighter. Graysen's pain—every flinch, every shiver—coursed through me as if it were my own. A few scratches were deep, the kind that demanded more than just antiseptic. Tears welled in my eyes, blurring the edges of Graysen's wounds until they looked like streaks of red watercolor. I tore a small square of gauze and wrestled with the tape, my fingers slick from blood. Carefully, I pressed the patch onto her wound. I inhaled deeply to calm my jittery hands; if I didn't regain control I could make things worse.

Raiden whispered, "Let me help." His hand covered mine, warm and steady, guiding my fingers over Graysen's injuries with a certainty that I lacked, and slowly, the storm inside me began to lull.

Press gauze, tape, smooth over. Wound after wound, our hands worked together until her breathing evened.

Raiden scratched Graysen's head. "You were very brave. Almost done." His words weaved a calm, his fingers stroked a comfort that brought life to her eyes.

"Two of them. Wore black masks," Graysen's voice shook. "Could this be Uzziah? Sending message? Warning?"

Raiden and I locked eyes, the corner of his mouth twitched, almost a smile. I bit down on mine before it could surface. "No, I'm sure this was just an… unfortunate event," I reassured her.

Raiden leaned over Graysen to inspect our work. "You won't need staples." His eyes shone as we exchanged memories from the barn. "You'll need rest. A week, at least."

With the mention of recovery, I retrieved the softest blanket from the hall closet. Carefully, I swaddled Graysen in it, her body finally yielding to exhaustion, and carried her into the living room.

I settled onto the couch, curling her fluffy form into my lap. Raiden lit the fire, the click of the lighter and the sudden burst of flame cut through the room's shadows.

Once the flames had caught, he lowered himself onto the couch beside me. His arm stretched across the backrest, brushing lightly against my shoulders as if hesitant. Our thighs pressed together, warming me more than the fire crackling before us. His presence wasn't just protective, it was proof of a pledge no one else understood. A hope that maybe, just maybe, everyone else was wrong about him.

The truth of why I befriended him and Fritz's need for the tiara hovered on the tip of my tongue, nearly spilling out. But what good would the truth do? I needed to speak with Nyxon first, before I deviated from the plan.

The flickering firelight danced over his profile, casting soft shadows that accentuated the strength in his jaw and the compassion in his eyes. His arm slid from the back of the couch to wrap gently around me.

Without thinking, I leaned into him, my head finding its place on his shoulder.

"Are you okay?" he murmured.

Words caught in my throat. Time stretched between us as his thumb traced slow, soothing circles on my arm. The tightness in my chest eased. Raiden's unwavering presence brought me solace, yet I couldn't shake the question: how long would his strength stand guard against the turmoil outside?

The next morning, I woke to sunlight spilling through the window, Raiden's arm still wrapped around me. His other hand rested on my thigh like a private promise. Then a floorboard creaked. I turned to find Graysen frowning at us.

The three of us stood in the yard, staring in shock at the remnants of the once-grand birdhouse, now resembling a battered piñata. Birdseed was scattered across the grass like confetti.

"Uzziah torture me, he did," Graysen wailed.

Raiden placed his hands on his head and turned away, stifling a laugh to spare Graysen's feelings.

"He couldn't have gotten past Fritz's security," I reassured her.

"Well, *somethin'* did! Ruined it is." Graysen slumped into a seated position.

Raiden squatted and scratched her spine. "I'll buy you a new one next week."

Graysen struck his hand, and he yanked it back. "Your touch don't work on *me*." Her face showed no remorse. "If I baseball-batted your TV would you wait week to get new?"

Raiden shook out his hand. "Okay. Okay. We'll buy you a new one once the others return."

"With *four* feeding compartments. Blue jays like peanuts. Finches like the sunflower seeds. If you put peanuts with seeds, jays make mess," Graysen instructed.

Raiden and I shared another complicit smile.

As the sweltering June balminess drifted through the open barn doors, Raiden and I sparred in the ring. His soul brushed against my skin, tugging me closer, as if holding a sly secret meant just for me. The contrasting responses of Raiden's and Fritz's souls left me baffled. Raiden's soul embraced me with warmth while Fritz's soul recoiled with hostility, its repulsion so intense it would rather tear free of his body than draw near me.

I awkwardly dodged Raiden's jab, and he dropped his fists. "You seem distracted. Tomorrow evening, we're targeting another warehouse along the riverbank. You need to prepare for the worst. Grounders who swore fealty to the Amarmet Alliance hate the Cyndarian Watch and everything your last name stands for. They're growing restless due to our frequency of busting down doors and taking thumbs. So, *what's* distracting you?"

Bruises now outnumbered freckles. My attempts to gain any valuable information from him this morning failed. In defiance, I slugged him in the gut, but he blocked it. I blurted, "Your evobility can't be bad."

He kicked my leg out from under me, I tumbled backward onto my ass, and my head hit the mat. He straddled me. I bucked. But his thighs pinned me to the ring's floor.

He placed his hands near my ears and his forearms bulged. "Why do you think that?"

I exhaled and conceded, my muscles relaxing. His red-flamed soul caressed my collarbone, then wove through my hair. The blue epicenter slowed, revealing tiny bursts of silver I hadn't seen before. "I see your soul. It tries to help. How can you have a cruel evobility and possess an kind soul?"

"You described it as a flaming vortex. Fire destroys everything in its path."

"But if you learn to control the blaze, it brings warmth. Fights ice." He blinked. I prodded further. "Yesterday, you got a call. Then you left without saying goodbye. Where did you go?"

A shadow eclipsed his features, as though he lowered his iron helmet's face shield. "Don't worry about where I go. Worry about the Amarmet Alliance. Worry about finding the Doctor." His flames surged, twisting and stretching toward me, as though they might lift me into Raiden's chest. Impossible. Or was it?

"I worry about that every day. You asked what's wrong? I'm tired." I struggled for freedom. In response, his thighs tightened. I seethed. "I'm tired of living in fear. I'm tired of living as everyone's obligation rather than their friend."

"They see you as *family*." He relaxed his thighs, and I breathed easier. He took off one glove and tossed it outside the ring. "And I wish I could match Li's strength, so you felt safe." Then he removed the other. "I wish I could match Nyxon's brilliance to bring you clarity. I wish I'd known you sooner, to bring you the comfort Fritz does."

Words whisked over my tongue before my conscience could critique my admission: "I'm tired of you disappearing." Seconds lapsed as I waited for his reply. He leaned closer, opened his mouth to speak, but then closed it. I brought a gloved hand to his hip. It couldn't be possible for his lips to get any closer to mine, but he thieved another inch.

"Motion at the front gate," the female alarm blared.

Raiden jerked back, his eyes widened.

"They must be back," I said in a hushed tone.

"Two hours early?" Raiden leapt to his feet and strode toward the door to investigate, leaving me staring up at the barn ceiling.

"Graysen called Fritz to complain about his home's security system."

"Right, I'm sure Fritz *rushed home* because of a rogue raccoon."

Chapter 38

Once all the equipment was unloaded, the four of us collapsed around Fritz's dining table. Except for Nyxon, who had shifted into command mode, pacing, clutching a coffee mug, rattling off timelines and protocols like we were a task force instead of four exhausted Grounders.

Fritz sat beside me, absently tapping his finger against the tabletop in sync with Nyxon's steps. I was half-listening. My eyes were hypnotized by the steam curling off her coffee. What would've happened if Raiden and I hadn't been interrupted? Had I crossed a line? Blurred the boundary between strategy and intimacy? Was I tempting him unfairly, manipulating him, stirring an attraction that would lead nowhere?

Fritz's hand squeezed my thigh under the table; I jumped.

"Mizumi said she could meet at the Colton's Feed Store in Ridgefield," Nyxon said. "Raiden and I will stay behind to assemble Avi's medical equipment." My heart softened; she always looked out for me. "Mizumi met Avi at the bar, so Mizumi will trust Avi. Fritz will drive her there."

Li added, "I'll go with Avi. I have to pick up rope, duct tape, and disposable gloves. And on our way home, let's swing by Brock Gerber's place and pick up a thumb. Maybe score some new intel on the doc."

My nose wrinkled. "Do you have to make it sound like we're serial killers?"

After a steamy shower, I slipped on my fertorium pendant, jean shorts, and a black button-up shirt. As a precaution, I strapped a dagger to my ankle and slipped on my cowgirl boots.

Driving north, we left the wooded forest for a landscape where generational hay farms and sprawling vineyards of tech moguls vied for coveted acreage; a place where tradition collided with modern affluence.

Twenty-five minutes later, Fritz, Li, and I arrived at Colton's Feed Store. The weathered wood sign bore faded red block letters, bleached and cracked from years baking under the sun. A passing train separated us from the street and a dreary truck stop. On the building's right side, various items were displayed for sale: tractors, fencing, and galvanized cattle feeding troughs.

An old beige minivan and a newer red Ford truck, both coated in dust, were parked out front, red "For Sale" signs in their windows. To the left, a rusty tractor rested near train tracks that disappeared into the horizon. Along the building's side, wood pallets leaned haphazardly against a battered dumpster. Beyond it all stretched endless acres of corn.

"We've got ten minutes before Mizumi shows up. I'll keep the car running and wait for her. Li, grab what you need. Avi, grab a new bird feeder and birdseed for Graysen."

"She needs flea control too," I added.

Fritz pressed two wrinkled hundred-dollar bills into Li's hand, then Li exited the front seat.

I was about to jump out, but Fritz twisted in the driver's seat to talk to me. "I want to talk to you about Raiden."

"I don't have any new intel." I reached for the door handle and opened it.

"That's not what I care about. *Graysen* thinks Raiden is getting too close to you. And I agree."

"Raiden *getting close* to me is leverage, nothing more. I can pull back whenever I choose." But I'd never admit, I liked Raiden's attention more than I should. "I can handle Raiden." I jumped outside, dust kicking up under my boots. "I'm doing this for you."

"Avi—"

But I shut the door and trotted toward the store, my name lingering between us like smoke.

Round terracotta planters greeted customers at the front doors, each arrangement adorned with dainty white alyssum spillers, three-foot-tall pink hibiscus thrillers, and green leafy fillers. The double doors slid open to reveal a round wire pen filled with fluffy yellow chicks. They chirped, pecked, and pranced about. Leather's unmistakable scent enveloped me as I passed horse tack and saddles.

A tall, scarecrow-like man with combed-over white hair said, "Holler if ya need help findin' anything." His drawl added to his small-town charm. He redirected his attention to a man sporting a Big Bass Fishing baseball hat and continued showcasing the features of the Green Mountain pellet BBQ.

I navigated the large store, weaving down the long, narrow aisles past plumbing supplies, electrical components, spools of chain, and a bin of axes.

Suddenly, a shadow inched toward me, prompting a cautious glance to my left.

A wiry, emaciated bald man with large, pale eyes, his back curved like a question mark, appeared. Thick, white hairs sprouted from his arms, stretching long like cat whiskers. Their eerie presence pointed at me, as though these peculiar hairs were magnetized, and I was the unwitting target.

His hands were cupped and outstretched as if in prayer. "I finally found the owner." His parched, pleading voice mimicked a desert wanderer in dire need of water. With a slow, shuffling gait, he moved toward me, and inside his hands—I gasped.

My credit card from the bar!

He motioned for me to take it and I prudently obeyed.

Once my card left his touch, he exhaled loudly, his grin growing as though he had handed me an incredibly precious gift.

His pupils transformed, shedding their murky haze to reveal a piercing clarity. My jaw dropped. The deep lines etched on his forehead smoothed away; he reversed in age! I staggered backward, bumping into a shelf. Cans of paint thinner clattered to the ground.

"Don't be scared. I'm a Rayvo," he wheezed. He bowed even though he was already hunched over. His appearance seemed to reflect the toll his evobility had taken on both his physical and mental state. He extended a bony, pale hand, discolored with patches. "I return what is lost." His voice was hauntingly child-like, with a hint of excitement that made him sound deranged.

My muscles tensed. I took a discreet step back and stammered, "Thank you?" My words unintentionally spilled out as a question. "I have to go." Fear crept into my voice, making it falter.

With each step backward, hysteria simmered beneath my skin, but I clung to my composure, keeping the Rayvo in my peripheral vision, as I cautiously scanned for further trouble. He shuffled toward me. My fingers wrapped around a pint of paint.

I chucked the pint with all my strength, and it struck his face. Shrieking, he covered his injured cheek with his vein-streaked hand.

I jogged past an aisle of nails, then power tools. My jog turned into a sprint. The front door was only yards away, but I skidded to a halt and ducked into an aisle because two Grounders, I knew very well, blocked my path.

Tonium. His piercing brown eyes and muscular frame exuded danger. The neatly trimmed French fork beard only added to his allure. In the feed store, he stood out. Black shirt. Tailored gray slacks. A blood-red tie. The large yellow diamond ring gleamed on his left hand.

The second Grounder's slender frame was cloaked in a jacket of the darkest purple that contrasted starkly with the emerald shirt beneath. His pants and shoes were white as snow. A peculiar combination that somehow suited him. He was the Grounder haunting my dreams, twisting them into nightmares of torture. The Grounder who drove me to train till my knuckles bled.

Wolfram.

This Limier didn't merely exist, he lurked. He skulked in the shadows like an unseen stalker with his evobility concealed behind a KN49 mask.

The distant clop of footsteps from the aisle I had just fled trailed behind me. I swallowed hard, trying to clear not just my throat but the stubborn lump of trepidation lodged within it.

The Rayvo acknowledged the two men, clutching his head. "She's here."

"Excellent work," Tonium's deep, arrogant voice expressed unwavering confidence.

"Tonium, grab her and stuff her in the van," Wolfram ordered.

Tonium scoffed. "We don't hurt women and children. I located the brunette. That's all I signed up for. What happens after that is none of my business. Where's my reward money?"

Wolfram snorted, pulled a thick stack of hundred-dollar bills from his inside pocket, and flung it into Tonium's chest. "The Rayvo can stay."

Tonium cradled the cash. "He works for me. We got you this far, you're a Limier, finish the job yourself." Tonium put a hand on the Gollum-like man's shoulder and steered him toward the front door. "Let's get you cleaned up and the party can begin."

Wolfram pulled an axe from a barrel and ran a finger down the blade.

I had to find Li!

I raced through the feed store, my pounding pulse a drumbeat of desperation. The aisles blurred past me. In my frantic flight, I collided with a rack of fishing poles, then navigated the resulting mess as though tiptoeing through a minefield. I snatched a green John Deere baseball hat from a nearby shelf, hoping it would offer some disguise. But Wolfram's footsteps loomed behind me like the grim reaper closing in. Then I caught sight of it—the back door—a flicker of fragile hope. I charged down the hall and thrust my hands against the door's metal push-bar.

I burst into the lengthening shadow cast by the building. As far as the eye could see, rows of sturdy cornstalks stood shoulder to shoulder like sentinels. Leaves rustled and stalks swayed as though the earth was alive with malevolent intent. To my left, the gas station and railroad tracks, but if I ran there, I could get innocent humans hurt. Every instinct urged me to vanish into the cornfield, but I couldn't abandon Fritz and Li. I jogged left, running down the side of the building.

Behind me the door creaked open, then slammed shut. Metal scraped against the ground. Goosebumps prickled along my arms.

"Because you are making me chase after you, I'm taking your foot as compensation." Wolfram pulled his mask under his chin. He lifted his rabbit nose into the air, and it twitched erratically. His gaze became hungry and dehumanizing as he raised the shiny axe and slapped the wooden handle against his palm.

I slowed and backpedaled.

He pulled an alien gun from behind his back, its design balancing elegance and menace. Intricate symbols along its length softly glowed. Instead of a conventional muzzle, the weapon boasted a cone aperture that flared outward like a megaphone. If I kept him talking, I could outrun him. Nyxon trained me to always know my limits; to push myself and when to retreat. I had met him twice and escaped twice. Survival was key. He sneered as if reading my thoughts, but I bolted.

The corner of the building was only ten yards away.

Corn to my right. I just needed to take a left at the train tracks.

Five yards away.

I could make it!

I skidded around the corner, the sun blinding me, but I pushed through the glare, refusing to slow.

Glancing over my shoulder, Wolfram jogged around the corner, took aim and fired. A sinister hiss cut through the air as the gun discharged. No bullet, but a silver wire shot out with a metallic snap. The wire moved with uncanny precision, twisting and looping like serpents, seeking out their target.

The thin wire coiled around my knees, digging into my skin like a constricting lasso. A scream ripped from my throat as my shoulder collided with a stack of wooden pallets, sending me crashing into the dirt. Pain shot through my shoulder. A helplessness wormed its way inside me—no one knew I was back here.

Frantically, I yanked at the unyielding wire, cutting my palm on the sharp ends. As I unspooled the metal, Wolfram strode toward me. I needed more time! Terror manifested in hot tears.

He smiled, quite pleased with himself. "You're out of tricks. As we speak my Grounders are ripping your friends apart, limb from limb. No one can save you. So, should I chop off your right foot or left?"

Suddenly, Mizumi burst from behind the dumpster, hoisting a heavy pallet high above her head. With a fierce cry, she slammed it down toward Wolfram's head. At the last second, he stepped back, but the surprise still sent him staggering. Mizumi's pallet crashed against the ground, splintering loudly, shards scattering like jagged teeth.

Mizumi's blue eyes blazed as she snatched a broken board and swung it savagely; Wolfram stumbled to the left. Her long brown hair whipped across her face, she looked every bit the victorious gladiator. She swung again. Wolfram raised his hands to defend, but a jagged nail embedded deep into his palm.

"You stupid cow!" he spat as blood welled from the puncture.

Ignited by what I could only imagine was pent-up aggression, Mizumi charged, shoving him hard against the stacked pallets. The unstable pile creaked and gave way, crashing down onto him, pinning him beneath splintered wood and dust.

Kneeling beside me, she quickly began unraveling the wire. With nimble fingers, we worked, our movements fueled by fear.

I slipped off my boots, and she pulled the wire down over my feet. "Follow me!" I screamed.

With adrenaline powering my every move, I abandoned my boots, and she fell in step beside me as we closed the gap between us and Fritz's truck.

We shimmied past a red pickup when a flash of fur and a thunderous bark burst from the bed. A German Shepherd, all teeth and froth, lunged over the side for me, snarling so loud it rattled my bones. We dropped low. The Shepherd's snarl still echoed through the lot.

Ahead, a shiny black Lincoln Navigator idled ten yards away, its tinted windows a black mirror. Beside it, a white windowless van squatted like a barricade, cutting us off from Fritz's Jeep.

I sucked in a shaky breath, forcing the roar of panic down my throat.

We had to get out of here.

"Stay small. Stay quiet," I ordered.

"Stay small?" she chastised me.

I rolled my eyes then pressed my body flat against the dusty pickup and slipped along the fender.

We scurried behind a row of hay bales. At the edge, I listened.

A voice. Footsteps. Too close.

I shuffled sideways and ducked behind a rusty tractor. My pulse thundered in my ears. One chance left.

We sprinted. Noise be damned. It's a small price for safety, to be with Fritz. Just the final stretch, nothing mattered but those last yards.

My body crashed into the truck. I scrambled for the door handle and yanked it open so violently it slammed back on its hinges.

Empty.

The keys were abandoned, glinting malevolently in the cup holder like a trap left behind by some evil entity.

Chapter 39

A cold panic rose inside me as my trembling fingers closed around the key fob.

Where were Fritz and Li?

The duffel bag, stuffed with cash and Mizumi's passport, sat in the backseat.

I shut the door. Suddenly, she slammed me against the Jeep, her powerful hand pinning my head against the window. The pressure on my temple was so intense I thought the glass might crack.

"One of your friends set me up!" Mizumi shrieked. "I was stupid to trust the CW."

"No!" I gasped, struggling against her grip. "Check the truck! We brought cash, an airline ticket, and a new passport. It's all there!"

Fritz jogged out of the store, his expression changed to confusion when he saw me trapped by Mizumi.

Dread surged through me, stifling my scream of warning as a seven-foot snarling woman leapt from behind the mini-van and blocked Fritz's path. Her sudden presence was like a dark cloud blotting out the sun. Her slicked-backed hair, a shining beacon of authority. The woman's right ear was red, with cartilage so swollen it resembled a wrestler's cauliflower ear.

Fritz's soul hardened into a gleaming armor of gold and silver.

"Let me go! My friends are in trouble." Mizumi released me, and I gave her a shove that didn't affect her at all. I flung open the truck's door, grabbed the duffel bag, and flung it into her chest. "Get out of here."

Mizumi's hands tightened around the duffel bag. The vein in her neck pulsed. Her gaze wavered. With one last look at me, the Jagwar backed away, fear tightening the lines near her eyes, and before she could second-guess herself, she turned and ran.

Wolfram emerged from the side of the building holding his head. Blood trickled down his fingers and onto his jacket. A bewildered expression etched his face, not believing a woman could've bested him.

The large woman seized Fritz's elbow. Fritz swung at her face. She contorted backward, folding her spine in half, evading the attack, she sprang back just as quickly.

I grimaced as if I could hear her spine snapping then reassembling.

Her fist flew in an uppercut. He dodged to the left, but she landed a brutal blow to his stomach, leaving him gasping and staggering backward, clutching his abdomen in agony. With surprising strength, she lifted Fritz off his feet. Fritz used both fists to land blow after blow onto her back, but she whisked him from view on the far side of the building. I crouched low to follow them.

Where was Li?

The sloshing and gurgling of running water hitting metal caused my gut to plummet. I skidded to a halt and peeked around a hay bale. Water gushed from the faucet into the steel trough, rumbling and echoing like a drumline. The woman held Fritz's shoulders as Wolfram grabbed a fistful of Fritz's hair and dunked Fritz's head into the trough, turning the water red. Fritz kicked with his good leg, but Wolfram shoved his head down deeper.

I seized a pitchfork and stepped into their line of sight. "Let him go!"

The woman released Fritz's shoulders. Wolfram allowed Fritz to surface for air, a wry smile stretched across Fritz's face. Water gushed from two baseball-sized holes in the tub, spilling into the dirt. Confusion clouded Wolfram and the woman's faces.

Fritz molded the metal in his palm into a blade and stabbed the woman's calf. "Avi, get out of here!"

Chaos erupted as the feed store's window shattered—Argon's wiry figure burst through the glass. His gaunt face contorted in shock as he soared like a ragdoll through the air. Glass shards scattered across the parking lot. Splintered fragments snagged in Argon's beard and hair as his face smashed into the gravel. In the frame of the broken window Li stood, his fury palpable.

Wolfram lunged at me, snatching the pitchfork's wooden shaft. I kicked him in the groin. He doubled over, collapsing onto the hood of the minivan. I raised the pitchfork high, then brought it down aiming for his back, but he spun away, and my blade scratched across the metal hood like nails on a chalkboard.

Wolfram kicked my wrist and my pitchfork flew under the adjacent truck. Two gunshots rang out. Who was hit? Fuck!

I snapped off the dilapidated minivan's antenna and lashed his face, a red line formed from cheek to chin. He blocked the second and third strikes. On the fourth blow, he grabbed my forearm. I squatted and swept out my foot, it collided with his ankle and took him to the ground. I snaked my fingers into his oily hair and prepared to smash his skull into the minivan, when a prick of pain on my shoulder halted my momentum.

I staggered backward and yanked out the needle. "You?" I muttered. Betrayal swirled in my veins with whatever was in that needle. A dime-sized drop of blood pooled at the puncture site. "Why?" I teetered. "How could you?" Disbelief swelled in my eyes and threatened to fall as tears.

A tremor rippled down my shoulder, spreading like fire under my skin as the world began to tilt. I commanded my legs to move, my arms to fight, but my body betrayed me, no longer mine to control.

Wolfram scooped me off my feet before my knees buckled. "Let's go."

And as a burlap bag came down over my head, Wolfram's crazed grin was the last thing I saw.

Chapter 40

Rough burlap pressed against my face, choking my breath, as the drug's hold ebbed away, letting awareness return to my limbs.

I cautiously contorted my bound wrists back and forth. Where was I? Water dripped from high above, hitting the floor with a smack.

"Ay, ay, ay. She's heavy." Her raspy thick accent scratched my eardrums.

"Why are you doing this?"

"It's *easy* money. You're an *easy* target. Fate keeps putting you in my path."

My mind raced through every scenario. She drove the van the night I met Raiden! "Untie me, and I'll show you what kind of target I really am." My blood boiled. "I freed you from Uzziah, and this is how you repay me?"

I heard her spit on the floor. "Uzziah." She grabbed my shirt collar. "I work for Doctor Monrowvia. Uzziah tried to get me to spy for him. I would never turn against the Amarmet Alliance."

Keys clanked. A metal door grated shut with a deafening bang.

"You still owe me for the last woman," the Nitro Snap woman spat.

"Maria, Doctor Monrowvia gave you strict orders to capture a Slyfen or female Jagwar and you brought in a Nocuowl," Wolfram corrected harshly.

"He's gonna experiment on the Nocuowl *eventually*. *Si?* So, *give me* my money."

"I'll give you half. That's it. The doctor needs evobilities for the Slyfen to test drive. Word on the street is, this bitch pals around with a Frigellen. If you bring me *that Frigellen*, I'll double your fee."

"Twenty grand! Shit, for that kind of money, I'd grab and bag the Cyndarian Watch's commissioner."

I couldn't catch my breath as the horror of the situation hit me. *"No, no, no!"* Nyxon, facing the same fate, the same brutality, tore at my insides. I had to protect her! But what about Fritz and Li? "Please, just tell me who was shot at the feed store?"

"No one I care about." The malice and mockery in Wolfram's snicker cut the air like a machete, reminding me that without my friends I was weak and small.

One day Grounders will never dare cross me.

Maria's chuckle faded into the distance with their footsteps.

Then a whimper to my left. A rustling to my right.

I tore away the hood, and stale, musty air rushed into my lungs. Blinking against the dim light, I froze. I was surrounded by…. women. Their hopeless and pitiful expressions cut deeper than the ropes still binding my wrists.

Wolfram was nowhere in sight. Maria climbed into the van. The engine sputtered with a low, uneven grumble, like it was coaxed into life.

"Can you untie me?" I turned my restraints toward a thin, pale girl sitting on the floor. Her nose had a subtle up-curve. Freckles dusted above her cheeks like a sprinkling of cinnamon. Wisps of golden hair framed her face. Her green eyes added a touch of whimsy to her frail appearance. She hugged her knees to her chest and stared at her dirty, once-white shoes.

"I'll help you," a tired voice to my left said. "I'm La'Keisha." She scooted over, abandoning her black suit jacket. Her orange silk blouse and tawny trousers told a terrible tale of her abduction after work.

"Thanks. Those bastards tossed my smartwatch and phone," I said.

La'Keisha fumbled with my bindings. Her professionally manicured nails were a shade of violet gray. Her long braids draped down her back. "They took my wedding ring and pearl necklace. The idiots should've stolen my shoes," she joked and jutted her chin toward a pair of high-fashion heels with peach pleated bows adorning the back. Quinbe would've loved those signature red-soled Louboutin pumps.

"What happens next?" The question felt trivial against the oppressive bars, as powerlessness pressed down on me, threatening to swallow every ounce of resolve.

"They escort one of us into the room." La'Keisha pointed to three large dusty windows. "No one ever comes out."

Our ten-by-ten steel cage, meant for a dog, not for four women, was bolted to the floor in the middle of an empty factory. I peered beyond their dirty cheeks to a gray purgatory. Narrow rusty metal stairs linked to a catwalk. Seagulls squawked. A thirty-two-foot tattered sailboat, riddled with cobwebs, slumped against an empty three tiered boat rack. We must be near the Columbia River. I flexed my fingers, summoning courage. Raiden had been right about Wolfram's location. We'd been so close.

A hacking cough from the scaffolding startled me, sending a wave of goosebumps across my skin.

We were not alone.

Stationed atop the catwalk, four unconcerned but rifle-packing patrolmen protected their precious aviary. Each wore the haunting eye of the Amarmet Alliance on their bulletproof vests, a menacing sight that deepened my dread.

"I'm Christy." Mascara formed smudged rings under her green eyes. The fifty-year-old twisted the hem of her gym shorts. "This is my fifth day here, I think." The beauty mark on her upper lip trembled. Christy's botoxed, sculpted face stood at odds with the gap where her front tooth should've been. Each word slipped off her tongue with a wet, whistling lisp.

Christy nodded toward the shy girl. "She's Olivia."

Suddenly, a blood-curdling shriek. Its intensity was reminiscent of someone driven to the brink of madness. Panic rippled through our cell as we whirled, our gaze locking on the only room in this place. Shadows passed behind the dusty windowpane.

Minutes stretched as no one dared to move or speak.

The door creaked open, propped ajar by a brawny redheaded guard with a braided beard extending past his collarbone.

A short, round man in a white lab coat, stained red from his cuffs to elbows, stepped out.

Monrowvia.

Terror cramped my abdomen. Did Yttrium tell them I'm Uzziah's daughter? Raiden warned me the Alliance would despise me due to my family. If they discovered I'm Uzziah's daughter, it would cause more trouble for me.

Wolfram trailed behind Doctor Monrowvia, his bandaged hands clutching a ten-by-ten iron box with a navy-blue lid and trim.

The redhead rubbed Wolfram's back. "You'll have better luck tomorrow."

"You say that every day, Ragnulf."

Doctor Monrowvia toddled to our cage, inspecting us like livestock. We scooted to the far end.

Monrowvia snapped his fingers, and Ragnulf jogged to the doctor's side. "I heard a delivery arrived. A subject I was actually anticipating." His nasally voice dripped with superiority, as if he were eyeing lobsters in a tank, ready to feast.

Wolfram aimed a fingernail at me. "That one."

My throat dried. No retort formed in my petrified mind.

"I'll work on her tomorrow." Monrowvia smirked then strode to the exit.

I sucked in a ragged breath. La'Keisha and Christy rushed to my side, taking my hand.

Did I have the strength to face whatever hid behind that door?

Olivia rocked back and forth. "Janet is dead. Janet is dead. We're all going to die."

Paranoia gripped my throat and refused to let go. Beyond everything, the truth was, time ticked by too quickly, and we couldn't wait to be rescued.

Olivia kept everyone awake with her whimpers and cries, but there was no way I could sleep anyway. An opossum lumbered into the warehouse. It sniffed the bars, as if *we were* wild animals caged at the zoo.

"Have you tried escaping?" I asked La'Keisha.

"We rushed the guards, but they struck us with batons and shocked us with tasers. Christy lay unconscious for half a day. They knocked out her front tooth."

Christy's hand drifted to her mouth, the memory saddening her green eyes.

"How do we go to the bathroom? How do they give us food? Water?" The questions tumbled out too fast, too loud. I hated how desperate I sounded, but I couldn't stop. I needed information to form a plan.

"They slide water and protein bars under the door," bitterness tinged La'Keisha's voice. "The bathroom, well, we used to have a bucket, but I threw the full pail at the doctor." A satisfied grin crossed her face, prompting me to chuckle. "Now we use those plastic poop bags people carry for their dogs." Her tone turned wry. "I hurl those too."

"What about your evobility?"

She grabbed Christy's hand and squeezed. "You know the truth. Olivia didn't know about her Grounder ancestry. I'm a Nocuowl, and Christy's a Silkcon."

"I've never heard of those evobilities."

"Nocuowls can dilate their pupils to three times that of human's. I have twice as many rods and a tapetum lucidum," La' Keisha said.

"You can see in the dark?"

She nodded.

Christy rolled up her sleeves. "My arm and leg hairs have tiny barbs, and when they stick into someone, they release an itchy toxin. My evobility doesn't solve our most pressing problem, how to open that door. What are you?"

"I'm… a VidaLumin." As I decided to conceal my Slyfen evobility, a twinge of guilt soured in my stomach. Why did I feel the need to hide this part of myself? In a world of judgment and suspicion, keeping my Slyfen ability under wraps was the only way to stay safe. "A Rayvo found me. Do you know what that is?"

"That evobility is *very rare,*" Christy said. "They can return lost things. It's a gift and a curse. Finding the owner becomes an obsession, a relentless pursuit that consumes every waking second. If they can't find the owner, they go mad. Unable to sleep or eat. When they return the item they get a euphoric high that lasts the same amount of days, hours, and minutes it took them to find the owner."

"What's the guard with the red beard?"

"Ragnulf is a Shivana. His hands can reach temperatures of 212°F," La'Keisha explained.

Christy recounted the names of the women who came before her: Allison, Kylie, Julie, Somona… but when she faltered, unable to recall two names she was entrusted to remember, her voice broke into sobs.

So many lives were stolen.

I paced our cage, searched for anything that could help us break out. "How often do they dump women here?"

La'Keisha laid her coat over Olivia, who still hadn't acknowledged me. "It depends on whether they can locate the type of woman that's on their list. I've been here since… What's the date?"

"June twenty-seventh."

"A week," she said weakly.

My gut pitched. I didn't have seven days.

Could we stab a guard in the eye with La'Keisha's high-heeled shoes? Or strangle one with Olivia's belt?

But the fact remained, we were outnumbered and outgunned.

"My friends are looking for me. Don't worry. They'll free us," I reassured Olivia.

She stayed curled in the corner, picking at the rip in her skinny jeans. How many fellow captives had reassured her, only to end up dead in that room?

Morning broke far too soon. Ragnulf ran a hand over his long red beard. Greenish-yellow bubbles ruptured and splattered like popped zits within his oil-slick soul. "You next. Doc's orders." To him, we were heifers, easily exchanged and replaced.

Chapter 41

Ragnulf's stone facade betrayed nothing as he gripped my arm and yanked me toward my imposed terminus. Heat radiated from his fingers, searing my skin, and sending the smell of burnt hair into the air. I winced, twisting against his hold, but his grip only tightened.

I wouldn't escape using brute force. I had to remember my training.

Each step felt mechanical.

Remember my training.

Ragnulf opened the door, unveiling a surprisingly sterile room. He shoved me forward, his red handprint marking my shoulder. Even at a distance of six feet, his body exuded intense heat, scorching the surrounding air. With a steaming hand, he gestured for me to continue forward. To my left, a plastic curtain obscured a back room.

Tables were arranged in a U-shape. Atop the white tablecloths two computers hummed. Random numbers flickered across their screens. A printer whirred and spit out a yellow-and-red line graph. Someone went overboard with the lemon disinfectant. To my right stood a rectangular surgical table draped with a white cloth. Crescent-shaped scalpels and triangular blades gleamed. But what sent my pulse convulsing was the wooden chair bolted to the tile floor in the middle of the room. The brass buckles on its leather arm and leg restraints glinted, as if winking at its next victim. Above the chair of death, two spherical lights hung, illuminating my final destination.

A pale woman with white irises and stringy ivory bangs held the plastic curtain aside. Her hair fell past her hips. She looked like a cracked-out fairy. Behind her, a tall, broad-shouldered nurse in her sixties wheeled in a squeaky cart. She wore thick white rubber gloves that reached her elbows. Her brown hair, bobbed in a 1920s cut and slicked down with pomade, clung to her head like a helmet, covering her ears. Her lips, smeared with bold-red lipstick, formed a scowl that wasn't directed at anyone; it was the natural curvature of her cheeks, but it still sent a chill down my spine. Upon the cart, a silver tray gleamed. The tray corralled a small jar, like an inkwell filled with black liquid. Next to the jar lay an artifact resembling the formidable fang of a sabretooth tiger. Its yellowed ivory surface was etched with faint Nordic symbols.

"Sit girl." The 't' sound flicked off her tongue with authority.

I stiffened and stared daggers at her instead. Ragnulf shoved me again and I lurched forward. If I sat in that chair, I'd be dead. "No."

The white curtain flapped as a towering guard strode in. His gray hair, styled in spiky layers, stood out vividly against his black complexion. A deep, jagged scar stretched from his clouded, dead eye, to his hairline.

I gulped. What did he do to earn that scar? He looked me up and down. His expression was that of a lion who enjoyed the hunt and could care less about the meal.

He held the curtain open for Doctor Monrowvia. Monrowvia didn't glance in my direction as he waddled to a computer and plopped in the chair. "We can do this the hard way or the easy way. Either way, you're going in the chair."

Ragnulf placed a hot calloused hand on my nape and squeezed. "Sit!" His voice boomed.

The world wouldn't wait for me to gather courage, it demanded action. I rounded on Ragnulf, smashing my elbow into his throat. I snatched his wrist, twisted it, and punched his shoulder joint—*pop!*

"Ah!" Clutching his useless arm, he staggered left, and two additional wardens took notice.

"That was fun." I blew Ragnulf a kiss.

Monrowvia's brow knitted as he beckoned to the other two guards. "Put her in the chair!"

"Two versus one isn't very fair." I surveyed the room for anything I could use as a weapon. The guards fingered their batons. My heels inched away until my back touched the door. My sole option was to… "Bye." Run.

Throwing open the door, I dashed to the middle of the warehouse. My head swiveled, scouring for any signs of freedom.

Monrowvia shouted, "Velocia, fetch."

"Can I give her a head start?" a female voice smugly replied.

La'Keisha and Christy jumped to their feet. They clanged their fists against the bars. La'Keisha shouted, "Exit behind you! Go Avi! Go!"

Fifty yards away. Doors!

Monrowvia yelled, "Guards, if you let her escape, one of you will take her place!"

Above, guards' heavy boots rattled the catwalk. A dart ricocheted off the concrete near my bare feet. Then another whizzed past my ear.

My arms pumped at my sides. My feet flew. The women chanted for my success.

The Grounder with gray spiky hair hastened to block my exit. He waved his palm at me, and they sparked.

Shit! Shit!

I have limited options. No, I have zero options. I bolted left and thrust myself out the window. The shattering glass echoed. Shards sliced my forearms as I protected my face. I tumbled to the ground.

I had to keep moving!

Shaking with adrenaline, I forced my body up.

I spun in a circle for a car, bike, boat, anything! The river raged to my left. But a guard appeared to my right in an alley filled with corroded machinery.

Twenty feet in front of me, the small, snow-white, female coasted into view. The dust she created billowed yards behind her. Her long white hair rose to her ears and whipped to the left with the sudden loss of velocity.

She leered predatorily.

She was fast… inhumanly fast.

I had no choice but to jump into the river. My feet pounded the concrete of the yacht repair yard. I overturned anything that could block her path. Fifteen yards ahead, a rusted railing overlooked a twenty-five-foot drop into the churning waters.

The waves crashed violently against the riverfront barrier. Whatever lay beyond that precipice, I didn't care, I'd rather shatter every bone in my body than endure the Doctor's horror. If death awaited me in the river at least I wouldn't be a pawn in their war.

I looked over my shoulder; my pursuer hadn't moved. She laughed an evil, boastful laugh.

Ten yards to go.

The wind whipped the river's spray onto my cheeks. I glanced back. She sprinted. Within four heartbeats, she ate away my fifty-yard lead and sprang onto my back. Her momentum skidded us across the ground. Gravel buried into my cheeks and chest. I screamed!

She flipped me over and sat on my hips, boasting that she'd caught her prize. "Loved the chase, little bunny." The veins around her eyes protruded deathly blue.

The electric-handed Grounder shouted, "Velocia has her."

I grabbed a rock and slammed it into Velocia's nose. She shrieked as blood cascaded over her ghostly lips.

The spiky haired Grounder knocked Velocia aside and snared me by the shirt, yanking me off the ground. His fingers burst and spurted like a white firecracker. He pressed his palm to the top of my head. "Have you ever had the pleasure of meeting a Cadibattera?" A smile stretched across his face as an electric charge crackled and snapped from his hand, sending my entire body into a violent spasm.

My jaw locked. Rendering my limbs useless. The river was so close… its murmur a mournful serenade, its waves were hands reaching out to me. Tears streamed down my face: I would never see this river again.

Velocia, blood coating her chin, yanked the spiky-haired Grounder's dart gun from its holster and fired. A soft snap and whoosh, then a dart struck near my collarbone with a dull thump. I gasped. The dart's glass vial injected me with a purple liquid flecked with white pearls. I screamed as more pain radiated through me.

She wiped blood from her nose. "Bitch." She shot me again in the thigh. A sob caught in my throat.

"Enough." The spiky haired Grounder swiped the gun from her. "If she doesn't wake up, the Doc will put you in that chair."

"I'm going to kill you," I mumbled.

She snickered. "You'll have to survive the chair first." And with
another shot, a vial lodged in my stomach, and as the purple liquid
entered my body, the world around me went dark.

Chapter 42

Groaning, my eyes fluttered open.

Someone had twisted my hair into a clip, exposing my neck. Electrodes from a monitor were attached to my wrists and scalp, recording my brain activity and pulse. A burning itch gnawed at the back of my neck. Instinctively, I reached up to soothe the fiery ache, only to be denied by the harsh rattle of chains binding me to the chair.

An additional guard paced the room. His massive shoulders and trap muscles left no trace of a neck. His thick lips stretched almost to his ears in a creepy, clownish grin and framed unnaturally wide, yellow teeth. His gums looked diseased with red and purple blotches.

An unamused Doctor Monrowvia, ambled in front of me, flapped open his white lab coat and planted his four hands on his bulging hips. His cockroach soul skittered about his body. "Well, that was unnecessary." He leaned in, inches from my face, the odor of skunky coffee wisped over his tongue.

"What have you done to me?" My voice strained as I struggled to shake off the haze clouding my mind.

The nurse placed a tray near the lamp on the computer table. It was cluttered with bloodied cotton balls. Beside the mess gleamed a long tooth, its polished surface marred by yellowish-brown spots and strange symbols.

I blinked. "What is that?"

"A Cyndarian priest engineered this needle from an anacondent tooth," the nurse said. "We completed the first step. I tattooed the evobility transfer symbol on your neck that will connect you with the Dracophelia, making you its vessel." The nurse's chilling indifference cut through the air like a blade.

My heart raced so fast it felt like it might burst. This was really happening. All warnings I brushed off, thinking I was untouchable—how naïve. How much pain could I endure? I had to stay strong, not give them the satisfaction of breaking me. But what if this was it? The end. No escape, no rescue. Only fear. And pain.

Breathe. Just breathe. Whatever they did, I couldn't let them see me crumble. I would survive this. I had to.

The nurse plucked off her gloves, one finger at a time. I sucked in a ragged breath, unprepared for what she had hidden underneath them. "What kind of Grounder are you?"

Her eyebrows rose. "I'm a Xenonic." Her fingers, devoid of nails and sculpted into sharp chopsticks, clinked as she steepled them in front of her face. "It's fruitless to struggle." A purple sludge oozed from her pointer finger, the same substance in the darts, and dripped to the linoleum floor. "Don't make us sedate you, again."

My fingers dug deep into the chair, jagged shards bit into my skin, as if the wood conspired against me.

Monrowvia pivoted to the computer. "Testing. Testing. The nurse branded Subject Twenty-three with the evobility transfer symbol for the Dracophelia extrication."

"You've killed twenty-three Grounders?"

"Twenty-two. You're not dead yet." His laugh was a strange exhale, then inhale, a kind of hee-haa of an overweight mule.

Twenty-two families may never have peace of mind about what happened to their daughters or wives. I vigorously chafed my wrists against the leather restraints, ignoring the painful rawness burning from pink to red.

"Begin step two," the doctor ordered.

"How many steps are there?"

"Four."

"How many people have completed step four?"

"Zero."

"Wow. You're terrible at your job," I snarked.

Doctor Monrowvia snarled, teeth scraping together like steel on stone.

"How do you select us?"

"Wolfram's Limier evobility enables him to identify Grounders' scent indicators. We pay Wolfram to bring us female Grounders between the ages of twenty-five and fifty who possess Slyfen heritage. So that night, when he hit on your scent, he thought it was his lucky day."

"*How lucky for me*. So, Wolfram and his cronies scour the city?"

The doctor sighed, exhausted by my questions, but I had to keep him talking, I needed more time.

"Scour? They mostly blunder around town frightening pigeons. One could argue that Wolfram cultivates a legion of imbeciles to be *king of the fools*. I give him a list of evobilities I want. Do you think he sticks to the list? No." Dr. Monrowvia's expression shifted from focused too blissful. Then he whispered, "Raiden, Raiden. The Grounder with no scent markers. He's on the list. How I'd *love to experiment* on him. I believe you two are friendly?" His wistful tone sent chills down my spine.

What if giving Raiden up was the only way to win my freedom? A knot made of guilt and fear constricted in my stomach. A sinister, reptilian grin spread across the doctor's face. "You want me to give him up? Not in a million lifetimes."

"Your devotion is admirable. But everyone has a price. Are you curious who set yours?" His eyes gleamed, promising to deliver a poisonous revelation. "Vana. Offered fifty-thousand-dollars. Grounders were eager to hunt the woman who'd chopped off their thumb. How many thumbs did you collect? A dozen?"

"*Two* dozen. And I'll cut more than a thumb from you."

The doctor rolled his eyes as the door screeched open. Wolfram carried the same navy-lidded metal box. Unlike the other mercenaries in black or camo cargo attire, he wore a crisp blue uniform. His first initial, T, and last name were embroidered in silver near the Amarmet's *eye* symbol. Wolfram deposited the box on the table, lifted the lid, and jumped aside, nearly bumping into Velocia. But in the blink of an eye, she zipped two paces to the left out of his way, a graceful movement that transcended the limitations of mere physicality. Within her smooth, pale neck, a network of thick blue veins, like intricate tributaries, pulsed rhythmically.

Doctor Monrowvia frowned while slipping on black leather gloves on all four hands. He dipped two hands into the box and extracted an object cloaked in a white cloth. He removed the draping to reveal a tiara fashioned from quills. Their black base lightened to brown, then faded to spiky white tips. He admired it in the air. "The Tiara of Tuskia imprisons the Dracophelia like a genie trapped in a bottle. Once the tiara's seal is broken by Slyfen blood, the Dracophelia's essence floods into the host. Only a specific incantation can banish it once more. The Dracophelia amplifies the Grounder's parietal lobe, stimulating and increasing connectivity to a Grounder's evobility. It improves microprocessing and problem-solving skills, *but* decreases dopamine receptors. A woman with a torchbearer's soul and a forgiving heart can control the Dracophelia's raging energy. The Dracophelia is the perfect weapon. It accumulates and analyzes knowledge from every battle, from every Grounder who dares to wear it. *Your* grandmother used it to depose our beloved Stracid Amarmet. But you *must* return the Dracophelia to the tiara or else the Dracophelia's lust for life will consume you completely. Once it's inside you and I've read the incantation you'll have no choice but to play along with our plan." He leaned toward the computer. "I will now place the Tiara of Tuskia on vessel Twenty-three."

"What happens if I can't control the Dracophelia?" A pleading lilt broke through my voice.

The doctor chuckled, a twisted, disgusting sound of amusement. "You'll combust."

"Com-com-bust?"

"If you survive, we'll euthanize the remaining women and throw their bodies in the river. You'll spend your days in the cage until your psyche becomes pliable to my suggestions."

My mind wailed: I failed to buy the women their salvation. And now, like molten lava rolling down a hill, all-consuming, he'll monopolize my identity.

He positioned the tiara on my head. Cold, jagged quills pressed into my scalp.

They punctured skin, as if the quills themselves were alive and hungry for blood.

A violent current surged through me as if biting into a live wire. Electricity crackled, webbing and branching through every nerve ending. My muscles seized, bending me forward, snapping me back, as though some force had hijacked my body.

"How about a pain pil-l-l-l?" I begged between clenched teeth.

My screams tore from my throat, wild and raw, ricocheting off the sterile walls of the incubus room.

The guards didn't flinch. The nurse didn't blink. Their indifference carved deeper wounds of worry. They'd seen this all before, and no one cared if I lived or died.

Each fresh surge of electricity knifed through me, sharp enough to steal breath, cruel enough to make me beg for it to stop.

The doctor's fingers forced my eyelids open. Machines beeped faster, louder, as if the equipment recognized the danger. "Guard, bring water. She's overheating. Similar to the other subjects." His tone was flat and disinterested.

The guard, a wall of a man, his shoes so wide they looked custom-made for a giant, ran through the plastic curtain. It slapped and rippled behind him like a sail in a hurricane.

When he returned, the nurse wrinkled her nose as she grabbed my ankles and plunged my feet into a bucket of icy water. The shock of cold collided with the heat blazing through me; steam hissed and coiled around my ankles like smoke from a dying fire.

"How do you feel?" Monrowvia asked, morbid curiosity curling around every syllable.

My body jerked and bounced, trapped in endless convulsions, as if I were riding a rollercoaster with no brakes.

"Sc-screw you," I spat. Sweat stung my eyes, my strength fraying with every pulse of electricity.

He released a self-assured huff. "Pustules are present on her neck and forehead. Transitioning to step three."

The nurse presented Doctor Monrowvia with a stained paper protected between plastic. Its worn edges and crumpled lines showcased its age.

"The first passage from the incantation will liberate the Dracophelia from the Tiara of Tuskia." His spittle spritzed the computer's mic. "When the Dracophelia fuses with its new host, I'll recite the passage to bind her to me." He cleared his throat. "I call upon both the light and dark to make right. Fight the things fear says I cannot change. Nervosity no more. Bequeath wisdom to free from all oppressors. Bravery for when battle knocks." He sneered at me. "That's a translation for what's to come." He strode in front of me. "E pyxx olim gata exstg…" Each foreign syllable scorched my neck, as if I were cattle being branded over and over again.

As the doctor spoke, a dragon-like constellation slithered from the Tiara of Tuskia. The abraylix tightened as my Slyfen heritage came alive to absorb the evobility.

My fingers trembled, so I balled my fist.

The Dracophelia's oculi were black bottomless rectangles, sucking in all light.

Its body, an ombre of gold and red stars that relaxed then contracted as the constellation-like figure moved.

"Get it away from me!" I thrashed in my chair. The abraylix singed my skin in warning.

"The Dracophelia evobility has been released," Monrowvia hollered to the computer.

"A burn mark appeared on subject Twenty-three. It loops from her shoulder…" The nurse lifted my shirt. "…and stretches across her stomach." She made the observation without the slightest trace of concern; only morbid curiosity steeped her voice. "This is different from the others."

My abraylix flared in protest.

The demonic creature's muggy breath condensed in my ear. Eye to eye, time slowed. A death rattle vibrated in the creature's throat. It lunged. Pushing past my lips, into my throat. I gagged.

"Nurse, she's choking. Check and clear her airway!" the doctor instructed.

Cold tears evaporated as they rolled down my burning cheeks. Its tail lashed as it descended. An onslaught of demon energy surged, pumping into my veins. Spasms rocked my core. The EEG machine beeped erratically.

"Doctor, we're about to lose her. Finish the incantation," the nurse pleaded.

"I can't. The Dracophelia hasn't linked with the host. Twenty-three's pupils are still round."

"I have an abraylix! I can't access my Slyfen evobility!" I fought for each breath as the abraylix constricted.

The doctor's eyes widened; his calm veneer shattered as he shouted commands like a captain in a storm. "Get me a crash cart. One milligram of epinephrine, my surgical tools, and a blood gas reading, stat!"

The Dracophelia waited for no one. It struck, sinking its fangs into the abraylix and unleashing a torrent of demon energy through the wire. *Boom!*

The lights above crashed into each other. Guards jostled. The doctor wobbled backward, his balance wavering until he toppled over, onto his back, his body rolling from side to side, like a chubby cat struggling to right itself. Pens and papers flew from the table. One of my chair's wooden arms broke loose, and a thick nail dragged over my thigh. The boom's intensity rang in my ears. The abraylix's burning ring dissipated, but the scorch mark across my sternum remained. A migraine jackhammered my thoughts. Blackness clawed the edges of my sight. My chin slumped to my chest.

Beep, beep, beeeeeep. "Doctor, she's crashing." Ragnulf's voice was an undulating sound, far away then close. He pried my eyelid open. His sour panting breaths assaulted my senses.

My arm shot forward, driving the nail into Ragnulf's thigh. He bellowed like a wounded bear. The back of his hand cracked against my cheek. My head whipped to the side, stars exploding across my eyes. He staggered backward, a crimson blot spreading on his pants. Blood slid down the nail.

The doctor pointed to the nurse and the Grounder with the monstrous teeth and disgusting gums. "Move Twenty-three to the operating table. I have to remove the abraylix."

The raw scent of sweat mingled with the acrid tang of blood. Excruciating pain ignited every nerve. The walls pressed closer, my impending death wrapping around me like a vise.

With my last breath, a chilling realization seized me: If I die what would happen to my friends? What would happen to the other women?

Chapter 43

The shriek of the EKG cut through my mind's haze.

My lungs fought for each breath, inhaling as if sucking air through a straw. Gloves snapped. Metal instruments clinked and clattered against steel trays, a metallic discord that set my nerves on edge.

The world tilted, my vision narrowing to the tube stuck in my throat. My hands flew to the plastic tube before rational thought could intervene, yanking hard. The tube slid free with a wet, rattling pop, pain searing my throat as a violent cough racked my body. Alarms howled. Oxygen hissed into the open air.

A shadow loomed above, blotting out the surgical lights.

The nurse.

Her pomade-slicked hair glinted like lacquer. Frowning, she rubbed the defibrillator paddles together, their polished surfaces crackling with leftover gel.

"Use Cynder's Lucidex-7. She's conscious, but useless in this groggy state." The doctor's voice drifted in and out of focus, tipping my senses like a boat on rough waves. "We've already wasted six hours extracting the abraylix. I need to finish the incantation *tonight*. Typical Wolfram, sending me defective bodies to work on."

My head lolled to the side. On a silver tray within my arm's reach sat the gleaming Tiara of Tuskia. Farther away, near the computer, was a pile of blood-soaked gauze pads, cotton balls, and surgical instruments. My eyes widened: a slinky-like silicone cord, piled like bloody intestines, lay on the table.

The abraylix.

Swiftly, the nurse used a hand towel to wipe off the conductive gel from my bare chest, then discarded the towel onto a cart. She buttoned my shirt with a disapproving sneer, her posture rigid, as if I were the prostitute, and she the pious Christian. She peeled back my eyelids and shone a pocket flashlight on my pupils. "One pupil has changed to the horizontal pattern. Doctor, finish the incantation so the Dracophelia can fully connect with Twenty-three." She tucked the flashlight into her front pocket next to her pen.

This was it: I had one last bargaining chip, the last card in my hand, the final roll of the dice. If this gamble failed, I'd lose everything. My throat burned as I pushed the words out: "Stop. I'm Uzziah's daughter."

The nurse gasped, just as Wolfram burst through the plastic curtain, making everyone jump. He pulled his cell phone away from his ear just long enough to address Monrowvia. "Good. The Slyfen is alive."

The nurse dramatically drawled, "Doctor, we should contact Uzziah before we proceed any further. Wolfram, you should've told us she's Uzziah's daughter."

Monrowvia's lips curled into a snarl. "The Amarmet Alliance *uses* Uzziah to retrieve the keys. We're not partners. I don't take orders from him. Wolfram, *should've* told us she's the *abraylix* girl."

Wolfram threw up his hands. "I don't get details. They give me a name. I collect."

I gripped the metal table, hiding the tremor in my fingers. I wanted to fight, but it felt absurd, like screaming underwater. I was unbearably alone.

Wolfram snapped his fingers at the camel-foot guard and the Grounder with the electric hands. "Follow me. We've got a Frigellen to unload and she's a feisty one."

"Nyxon! No, no!" Tears streamed down my cheeks as I shook my head.

The nurse grabbed a fistful of my hair. "Stop that! You'll rip the stitches on your back." She jabbed a needle into my arm. "Administering ten milligrams of Lucidex-7."

A strange coolness rushed through my veins, clearing the weight from my limbs. The fog in my head split down the middle, like I'd been jolted awake from the inside out.

This was my last chance at freedom.

My last chance to save the other women.

My last chance to balance the scales of justice.

My fingers found the silver tray, then the tiara. I gripped it hard, its sharp points puncturing my fingers. Pain flared, but with a savage cry, I slammed the tiara into the nurse's temple. A strangled wail burst from her as she released me, clutching at the wound.

My breathing quickened, adrenaline flooding my veins, the monitor's shrill beeping rising as I tore at the wires. Each pull and rip intensified my drive to save Nyxon.

I flung myself off the operating table. My feet and palm slapped against the cold concrete.

Monrowvia's double chin jiggled as he stammered, "Don't do anything stupid, Twenty-three. We have you surrounded."

"I'm not a *number*!" I rose. I needed that incantation paper.

The bulky guard to my left ripped a tooth from his cavernous mouth. "Stand aside. I'll make this Markosyan beg for mercy."

My jaw dropped, this wasn't just any tooth, the root was ridiculously long.

He brought the tooth high above his head then slung the probe-like tooth; it sailed through the air like a bullet into my forearm.

Excruciating pain shot through me, ten times worse than a hornet's sting. My grip on the tiara faltered, and it clattered to the floor. Jaw clenched, I ripped the tooth from my flesh. Blood oozed from the wound, painting my arm crimson.

He tore another tooth from his blotchy gums, blood slicking his chin. A cold sweat broke out on my forehead.

I scurried left, then right, like a cornered rabbit. The tooth whizzed past my ear, the ghostly whisper of death brushing against my skin. It slammed into the wall behind me; the crack forced me to flinch.

"You idiot, we need Twenty-three alive!" Doctor Monrowvia's bulging eyes tracked me, like a big game hunter watching his prey from the safe confines of his Land Rover.

The nurse lunged for me, her long fingers tangling in my hair as she yanked me backward. Three jagged streaks of blood ran across her face, warping her features into pure, unhinged fury.

Instinct took over. I twisted my body and swept my leg around in a wide arc, connecting with her ankles and knocking her feet out from under her. She tumbled onto her back with a resounding smack. I thieved the pen from her shirt pocket and skewered her throat. A geyser of gore squirted. She covered her gaping wound and blinked as if signaling SOS.

"What the?" the doctor blubbered, not believing the turn of events.

Outnumbered and smeared with sweat and blood, time's crushing pressure hammered home that every wasted minute could seal my fate in this torture chamber.

I seized the bulky printer, ripping its cord from the socket. The machine's weight dragged my arms down, but I hurled the printer at Monrowvia with all my strength. The world slowed as the machine sailed through the air, spinning wildly, its cord flailing like a serpent's tail. Monrowvia's eyes widened in a fleeting show of surprise before he ducked, narrowly avoiding the projectile. The printer exploded through the dusty window behind him, the glass shattered into a shower of shards. The cold night air rushed in, carrying the gasps from the women in the cage.

Monrowvia glared as he unfurled extra arms from hidden chambers in his lab coat, his dark silhouette transforming into a sinister spider. "Contain her," the doctor's voice boomed.

I raced toward surgical knives on the table, legs pumping, pulse pounding. My hand stretched forward, brushing the cold edges of the nearest blade. The metal vibrated beneath my touch like it was alive, a lifeline just out of reach, when the plastic curtain snapped open. Velocia, a blur of white, savagely shoved me from the blades. The impact lifted me off my feet.

I hit the floor, skidding across the linoleum as shards of glass bit into my side like needles. I screamed, a ragged, defeated sound, as I crashed into the wall beneath the window with a sickening thud. Blinding pain left me dazed.

My bruised side throbbed as I pushed myself up. But my blood-slicked hands gave way, my arms buckled, and I slipped to the floor.

Velocia straddled me, her weight pressing down on my lungs making it hard to breathe. I bucked and thrashed like a pig who knew it was about to be slaughtered.

She pinned my wrists to the floor, her hands cold and soft like a fish. "You're going to pay for breaking my nose." Her soul appeared. A malevolent black and white specter, wispy as if wearing rags. Its eyes glowed red.

The Dracophelia coiled protectively around my consciousness, its mind brushing mine with a firm, silken insistence: *Take what's rightfully yours. Steal her evobility. It's the only way.*

"How?" I shouted at the Dracophelia, and Velocia's brows knitted together in confusion.

"This is a start." She drew back, but before she could drive her fist into my face, I grabbed her wrist.

She laughed. "You don't have the strength to stop me."

Call forth your Slyfen. Find a pressure point on your wrist. Before it's too late: The Dracophelia's voice unfurled through my skull.

I tapped my right wrist's pulse point twice, then I summoned my Slyfen with everything I had. Clawing for that flicker of evobility I could feel but not grasp.

Nothing.

Please, work!

Uzziah's voice hit me like a strike, the brutal lesson lighting up a memory: Find the part of you that refuses to stay small.

I had to reach for the place that's had enough. The piece of me that won't forgive, won't forget, and sure as hell won't stay down.

Suddenly, her evobility's constellation flickered into being. Stars blinked in and out, pulsing as if magic breathed through them. They hovered around her like a living map.

The stingers on my fingers sprouted like thistles, small but wicked.

A horror she'd never known flashed across her face and froze there as the paralytic from my stingers swept up her arm, forcing a gasp from her. I tapped my wrist's pulse point again. This time, a green vine snaked from my wrist, then locked around hers.

"Excellent work, Velocia. Strap her into the chair," the doctor ordered, tugging on his lab coat. But only a whimper escaped Velocia's paralyzed mouth.

"You," the doctor said, pointing at the guard with the missing teeth. "Clean this up." He nudged the nurse's lifeless body with his black boot.

Could Velocia feel the prickling sensation of my vine? Did she know what was coming?

Upon my vine, three cerulean pods unfurled like an evil joke of a corsage. They split open, their pale centers exhaling black spores that floated around her like mold carrying a deadly disease.

Four slender legs wrapped around a star from her constellation, pressing it into its underbelly. Wings snapped open like scythes.

These weren't spores. They were parasites, alive with stolen light, flickering like fireflies trapped in a jar. Velocia's eyes tracked the spores, then fell to me. They held so much hatred, I knew she would rip off my head if my paralytic drug failed.

The parasites flitted back, wings beating furiously, and the pods snapped closed around them. The stolen star burned like I'd swallowed a lit match, igniting my core. I clenched my jaw and held in a roar. My body shuddered; it was time to become more.

When the largest star was plucked, the constellation collapsed like icicles snapping loose from the eaves.

Gasping, fire seemed to fill my lungs and throat. Heat raked under my skin, lancing through muscle as if my body were being burned at the stake. When Velocia's stars melded with mine, it scorched deep into my sternum like an iron-red brand.

Weakly, I raised my free hand and tapped twice on my pulse at my neck. The vine slithered from Velocia's wrist like a greedy fat toad retracting its tongue, then sank back under my skin. My own wrist throbbed, the raw skin blistered. My biceps quaked as if they might give out. But I didn't have time to fall apart.

Velocia's pupils returned to normal with an eerie slowness. She lowered her head, inch by inch, unnaturally robotic. "You little thief. I'm going to fuckin' end you." Saliva glimmered in the corners of her mouth.

The Dracophelia roared: *VidaLumin, awaken your true potential. Your true power.*

Velocia's hands clamped around my throat, squeezing with bone-crushing pressure. I yanked at her grip, twisting and tugging, then reached to scratch her face, but she leaned back, letting my nails rake empty air.

My VidaLumin ignited, silver tinsels sparking to life. It moved like a whip, coiling around her soul's neck and waist, tightening with every breath I took.

Her soul's long fingers feverishly clawed at my VidaLumin evobility. Her soul's jaw dropped, forming a wide, gaping 'O'. In an instant, my VidaLumin snapped taut. Her soul's head popped free like a cork from a bottle.

Velocia's cheeks pruned. Black liquid sloshed in her eyes, and when they filled, my lungs aspirated as if I was submerging with a sinking ship.

"Recall the VidaLumin," I begged the Dracophelia. A low, amused snicker was its only answer.

My fingers curled around a shard of glass. I drove the shard between Velocia's ribs. But Death had already kissed her lips, leaving his signature shade of blue.

What did I do?

Frantically, I shoved Velocia off me.

I had become a Slyfen and something far worse.

"Velocia?" the doctor whispered, his voice pitchy with disbelief.

The jagged-tooth Grounder dropped the nurse's legs. "That was the last bad move you'll ever make."

He lumbered toward me like an angry ogre. Using the speed evobility I stole from Velocia, I sprinted to the edge of the room, moving faster than I ever thought possible. Her constellation glowed within mine.

He yanked the front tooth from his diseased gums and flung it at me. This time, I sidestepped it easily and sprinted for him. Dropping to my knees, sliding under his punch, I slugged the side of his kneecap. He roared louder than the popping of his joint dislocating.

I staggered to my feet and slammed my palm into his solar plexus. The Dracophelia chuckled as if it was there when Nyxon taught the anatomy lesson. My fist connected with his temple. The crack of my knuckles echoed as he crumpled to the ground.

Paranoia rippled across Monrowvia's face as he scrambled for the tiara, knocking over a lamp. The bulb shattered on the gauze and they erupted into flames. The tower of cotton balls tumbled onto the tablecloth, and the ravenous blaze ate its way across the table to the paper reports.

Monrowvia stripped off his coat, using it to scoop up the tiara and drop it into the blue box. "Twenty-three, *you don't know*! You don't know how to control the Dracophelia. Only I can return the Dracophelia to the Tiara of Tuskia. *You need me*."

"That won't save you. There's no escape. Not for you. I'm the thing you should've never created." He tried to make me his mindless soldier, but I'd risen. Stronger. Faster. More ruthless. "Monsters always have a funny way of breaking free. And who do you think they go after first?"

Monrowvia fled for the door. I harnessed Velocia's evobility and sprinted to cut him off. He opened the door, but within a blink of an eye I booted it closed.

He stammered, "Twenty—"

I seized his wrist and flexed his arm into a brutal hyper-extension. My palm drove into his elbow with a sickening snap, fracturing it backward in a grotesque, unnatural twist. Monrowvia howled as tendons and ligaments tore from the bone. He dropped the paper and blue box to clutch his shattered arm.

I snatched the ancient parchment, its delicate texture crinkling beneath my fingers, and shoved it into my shorts pocket, just as Monrowvia slammed me with his lower two arms, sending me stumbling back. I tripped over the nurse's body and smacked to the floor.

Ragnulf barreled through the door, his military-trained eyes taking in the bloodshed and smoke. He stomped toward Monrowvia, grabbed the box, and drove it into Monrowvia's midsection. "Doc, get outta here." His voice carried unshakable confidence, certain he could subdue anyone, solve any problem.

Monrowvia beheld the carnage, realizing he'd succumb to my vengeance if he lingered. He stumbled backward, then ran through the white plastic curtains as flames devoured the corners.

"I've always wanted to shatter the knees of a Markosyan." Ragnulf flexed his fingers and heat steamed off them, exuding an aura of invincibility.

Chapter 44

The sheer size of Ragnulf and the raw violence in his eyes shook my confidence.

He roared toward me like a rhino. He swung. I ducked. The whoosh of his miss brushed against my skin. With a surge of adrenaline or was it the Lucidex-7 mixed with the speed evobility, most likely all three, I drove my fist into his stomach. The impact reverberated up my arm, his muscles tensing beneath my blow. I pivoted, landing an elbow to his back. He staggered forward, his breath ragged. His spine curved and his shoulders rounded, betraying the impact of my strike.

He gathered himself. Then unleashed a war cry and charged again, each footfall shaking the ground like an unstoppable giant advancing in the heat of battle.

I dodged his right hook, but he ripped a taser from his hip. Lightning sparked, and two prongs zapped my side.

I twitched to my knees, refusing to nose-dive. My jaw clenched.

He tucked the taser into his belt, then grabbed my throat. "Quit resisting, or I'll melt your skin to the bone." His bulging veins branched. He increased the temperature. A shriek tore from me as the nauseating stench of charred skin filled my nose. His handprint burned into my neck, a brand akin to the mark from a fiery demon.

I gripped his wrist and my Slyfen's barbs sprouted.

Confusion rolled across his face. The first wave of my Slyfen's prickling paralysis power swam through his veins.

His heat weakened. He blinked, then coughed.

"*Slyfen* trumps *Shivana*!" I seethed as my vine wrapped around his wrist, locking us together. My pods sprouted faster this time, as if they were a colt ready to run.

His eyes widened. He tried to pull away, but I held firm. And my Slyfen's vine tightened. He slapped my cheek with his free hand, a searing sting branching across my face as the blow whipped my head to the side. My VidaLumin manifested with the veracity of a wrathful phoenix. A second slap, weaker this time. There was no third.

Wheezing, he fell to one knee, and we met eye to eye.

His evobility's constellation appeared, flaring over his upper body like Scutum's stars, a radiant shield of light.

But my black parasites were already on their way to collect what was due.

"Release me," he begged. His eyes glossed with a sorrow I hadn't expected to see.

Weakness flickered through me, a pang in my chest. I wasn't an executioner.

The Dracophelia whispered: *He's just like the rest of them.*

Seconds ticked as my swarm returned to their pods with their spoils. When they closed, heat fanned up through my ribs like a hidden furnace, leaving me choking on the flame. The price of survival was pain beyond anything I had known, burning through me, drilling into every muscle and bone. I called my vine back. When it returned, I collapsed to the floor gasping, my wrist now covered in blisters. My vision blurred, and my limbs refused to obey. How could I possibly rise again?

With the paralytic wearing off, he snatched the taser from his belt and pressed it to my throat. "All Slyfen girls are the same. Stupid whores. But you're extra dumb. You can't control my evobility. You're weak. It's gonna burn you from the inside out. Return my evobility. Now!" He was inches from my face. Spittle flew from his lips as his head shook with rage.

My VidaLumin's tendrils stabbed his sickly greenish-yellow, blobby soul.

Again. The Dracophelia's voice thrummed with glee. *Again.*

And I obeyed.

His soul writhed; ripples surged outward. Then it pulled in on itself, a molten mass trying to seal a wound that wasn't flesh. Blisters of light split across its surface.

The thick vein in Ragnulf's neck throbbed. He opened his mouth and only a rasp came out. His hand trembled and the taser rattled. He searched my face for an answer to the question we both knew lingered between us: What was happening to him?

The scent of sweat and exertion thick in the air as his soul bubbled and hissed.

I pushed the taser from my throat. The Dracophelia purred: *No mercy. No forgiveness.*

My VidaLumin's tendrils stabbed the center of his soul, then sliced outward, splitting it in two.

His soul evaporated like steam from a boiling cauldron. Life drained from his eyes until they became black pools of nothingness.

He fell to the side. I sat back on my heels and rested my chin on my chest in a sadistic prayer.

The fire's heat pressed against me like a living thing, warning me to run.

I swayed, the rush of adrenaline gone, leaving only the ache of what I'd done, what I've become. Ashes drifted into my mouth, bitter and hot, clinging to my tongue.

Outside the door, a *ra-ta-ta-ta!* High-caliber rounds mingled with the rapid staccato of automatic fire, creating a cacophony that clanged off the steel beams and concrete walls. Shouting. Boots pounded on the catwalk. In my state, I could barely stand straight, let alone face the guards leering above me. I'd be the mouse under the hawk. Exposed. Escape impossible. Every instinct screamed to run while knowing it was already too late.

The smoke stung my eyes until the world blurred, orange bleeding into black.

My mind circled back to my fatal mistake: letting Monrowvia get away. The knowledge hollowed me out, and I wanted to scream that even the goddess Karma had abandoned me.

Blood on my hands. Blood in my hair. Blood soaked my shirt. A sob rose, and for one terrifying breath, I considered surrendering to the inferno, it was easier than facing the Grounders with their guns and deadly evobilities beyond the door.

A groan mixed with the crackle of flames. Something shifted in the firelight.

The jagged-tooth Grounder dragged himself upright. His face was a ruin of soot and blood. The firelight pulsed behind him. I swallowed hard. I had nothing left to fight with. Nothing left to give.

Glaring, he ripped out a tooth with a sickening squelch and walked toward me. "I don't give a damn if the Doc says I can't kill ya. I'm slicin' this tooth across your throat."

I lurched forward onto my hands. My hair, clotted with gore, stuck to my sweaty face. Get up! Get up! The other women needed help!

He grabbed a fistful of my hair and forced me to meet his bloodshot eyes.

Bang!

A red stain swelled on the Grounder's stomach. He dropped his tooth, then stumbled left, collapsing to the ground.

Raiden parted the smoke. Grim, dirt-smudged. Clad in black, gun raised.

"Avi!" Raiden ran for me, then knelt by my side. "I'm getting you out of here." His voice was hard, then velvet, as if the flickering flames carried his concern to my ears.

I put weight on my wobbly legs, and a pang shot up my spine. I gritted my teeth and braced Raiden's forearm with my sweltering hand. He gasped, so I released him, but my legs faltered, and he caught me.

"The other women?" My hoarse words scratched my throat.

He coughed, the smoke swirling overhead. "Nyxon is working on it. Why are you so hot?"

My nose brushed his neck, and the Dracophelia's interest piqued. A low rumble in my chest vibrated up my windpipe. "*I remember you.*" The Dracophelia spoke through me to Raiden, stretching out its statement, its voice baritone-low and honeyed, "the *great* manipulator." And as if the Dracophelia let me into her memory, a strange ethereal scent enveloped me. A captivating fragrance blending cosmic dust with a faint interstellar metallic tang. Impossible to ignore with its celestial allure. Amid ash and brimstone, Raiden was the heart of a star.

He jumped back, scanning my face, every muscle tensed. "Your voice? Your pupil. It's a horizontal slit. Avi, did the doctor put the tiara on you? Did he read the incantation?"

The Dracophelia raged: "We must have your evobility!" It seized control of my body. With a snarl, I lunged for Raiden, my movements driven by the Dracophelia's sinister will. But Raiden stumbled away. My fists, guided by the entity's strength, swung wildly, but Raiden evaded my attack.

Again and again I tried to dominate. He never counter struck. Instead, he dodged and backed away until I finally had him pinned in a corner.

"Avi, stop!" His plea slashed through my foggy mind. For a brief, precious moment, the Dracophelia's veil of darkness lifted and Raiden's face emerged through the murky possession. His eyes, usually so confident, were filled with an emotional longing I couldn't quite decipher, was it devotion, despair, or both?

I turned away, unable to look him in the eye.

"You have to fight it! Remember who you are." Raiden hugged me from behind, his strong body pushing into my back. I thrashed against his hold, but his grip remained steadfast. "Avi, come back to me." His voice was a beacon in the storm, but the struggle within me was fierce, the Dracophelia resisting the glimmer of clarity that Raiden's words sparked.

With a burst of desperate determination, Raiden whipped me around, his hands cradled my face, and he pressed his lips to mine. The kiss was passionate and reckless, a dire plea for the real Avi to surface. Every brush of his mouth against mine was a message that needed to reach the woman locked away. I let myself lean into him because the taste of him was the first thing that made me feel *human*.

The Dracophelia's grip dissipated, like clouds chased by the sun's rays.

I became fully aware of the flaming world around me.

"I lost control." I panted and swayed.

"Breathe. You stopped. It's over."

Shock hit me like a shotgun blast. I hurt Raiden.

"Stay away from me," I shouted, tears running down my cheeks as I stumbled back, taking painful, frantic, uneven breaths as if my lungs had forgotten how to breathe.

Nothing felt real. Nothing made sense. I wasn't the type of person to steal. But I did. And I did more than take an evobility.

Raiden raised both blistered hands in surrender. "Easy. You won't hurt me."

But his gesture fell into a cavern of my own panic, meaningless against the chaos consuming my thoughts.

Wolfram burst into view, skidding to a halt in front of the shattered window. In an instant, he unholstered his gun and aimed squarely at Raiden's chest and fired.

Chapter 45

The gun's hammer struck. Instinct overrode thought, the speed evobility flared to life, rocketing me forward. Combustion billowed from the barrel, a fiery bloom of smoke that had frozen mid-expansion. The world transformed into a syrupy, suspended tableau. I was lightning. I was a blur. I was beyond time's grasp, and it shivered as I tore through it.

The bullet spiraled forward, slicing through the air like a molten shard, its dull whine amplified in my hyper-awareness. My muscles coiled, then shifted. Step by step, my feet barely kissed the ground as I closed the distance to Raiden.

I reached out and tackled him to the floor. The bullet meant for him grazed my shoulder, a hot line of pain searing slowly across my skin. I collapsed to the ground, folding in on myself.

Time snapped back into its rhythm, a whip of motion, sudden, jarring, like a car slamming its brakes. Raiden drew his pistol and fired. Each shot boomed, shaking the air around us. Wolfram's eyes rolled back until only the whites showed. Blood poured from his forehead and ran in dark ribbons down his neck, soaking his collar. His body swayed and he raised his gun again, defiant till the end, then dropped from view with a sickening finality.

The speed evobility was gone. I squandered a sacred gift. But with Raiden's life hanging in the balance, my choice was clear: I'd surrender anything, even the power that defined me, to ensure he kept breathing, his heart kept beating, his lips kept their rich shade of reddish brown.

Raiden rolled me onto my back; his body pressed against mine as he shielded me.

No, I was trying to save you!

His gun remained fixed on the shattered window, his muscles flexed, as if the slightest movement or sound could bring danger to us. When seconds stretched into minutes without the popping of gunfire, I tentatively reached for his hand, my fingers brushing against the gun's metal.

The vibrant orange-red flames licked the edges of the room and sent sparks flying into the air. "I *am* number twenty-three," I whispered, pulling the parchment from my pocket and pressing it against Raiden's chest, the last ounce of my strength going with it. My eyelids fluttered; they were unbearably heavy. "He didn't finish the incantation."

Raiden's arms cradled me, lifting my limp body from the floor. "Avi, stay with me."

Charred flesh invaded my nostrils. "Put me down," I whimpered. "I'm too hot."

"I'm getting you out of here," he promised, each word punctuated by the roar of the fire. I didn't fight him; there was no other way. Every nerve screamed. I bit back a cry.

We burst through the door. The old sailboat's white mast was ablaze, resembling a burning flag of surrender. Gunfire erupted around us as we plunged deeper into this warehouse from hell.

"I can't lose you… not now." With each swift step, Raiden's steady grip never faltered. "I've got you." His whisper against my skin was a vow that no fire could consume.

A splintering snap, then another. We barreled through the exit door as the roof's beams groaned then collapsed behind us, wood and concrete raining down.

Thick black smoke billowed into the sky, blotting out the moon.

"Did everyone make it out?" I wailed.

His lips parted, but no words came.

My world seemed to crumble along with the building. The shouting, the roar of the flames, the cracking beams projected like a movie on the walls of my mind. None of them registered. I was trapped in a space between panic and disbelief. My friends couldn't be in there. The other women couldn't be in there…

But if they were in there, I was snapped back into reality. The smoke burned my eyes; the sounds came rushing back. We had to go back in. Somehow, some way.

"Let me go." I struggled against his hold.

"You can't go back in there." His sinking expression held a haunting helplessness he wouldn't dare put into words.

Tires screeched to our left. Fritz's Jeep skidded around the corner, clouds of dust coiling behind it. A wave of relief washed through me, and my whole body relaxed.

Raiden moved swiftly yet carefully, placing me in the back seat.

Truck doors slammed shut in quick succession. Tires screeched against the asphalt. The engine roared, revving into overdrive.

Li, blood and dirt streaking down his cheeks, fixated on me from the front seat.

Fritz stared at me from the rearview mirror. "Whose blood is that?"

"Everyone's," I mumbled.

Raiden took a knife from his ankle and popped the buttons on my shirt. He sucked in a breath. "Welts, dozens of minor gashes. Burn on her neck. Punctures on her collarbone. Two deep shoulder wounds."

"Raiden, grab the med kit under my seat," Fritz ordered.

Raiden obeyed. He found gauze. Ripped adhesive. Patched me with focused, mechanical precision. Every touch, every application of pressure, no matter how gentle, sent jolts of pain through me. Each drop of blood was a reminder of how fragile the line between survival and death had become.

"*Why* is she steaming?" Li asked cautiously.

"I don't know!" Raiden snapped.

I slowly flipped my arms over. Hazy condensation unfurled from them. I croaked, "Monrowvia removed my last abraylix. I stole an evobility. Shivana."

"Shit," Raiden muttered.

Fritz pounded the steering wheel. "There's a thermometer in the med kit."

Li fumbled with the Jeep's knobs, and a cold blast of AC hit my face. "Bruh, if a Shivana gets a hold of you, that shit hurts like hell."

I pointed at the blistered handprint seared into my neck. "I know!"

Raiden angled the thermometer at my forehead. It beeped twice. "One-oh-five. You need to push the evobility's heat down into your hands and keep it there before your body shuts down."

"If your temperature hits one-hundred-seven, it could damage brain cells," Fritz said.

"I'd still be smarter than Li," I joked.

Fritz shook his head, but his crooked smile curved his lips.

"If you fry your brain, darlin', not even Nyxon can fix you," Li added dryly. "So, you better gain control of that Shivana *now*."

"*Please* tell me how, and I'd happily try not to die!"

Chapter 46

The Jeep skidded to a halt in front of Fritz's house. Everyone vaulted from their seats. Fritz threw open my door with such force that it bounced back against the hinges and slammed into him. Before I could warn him about touching my hot skin, he swiftly scooped me into his arms. He inhaled sharply, but he kept running for the house.

"I'm calling Nyxon," Raiden shouted behind us.

The porch planks groaned under his boots as he shouldered the door open.

I was a kettle on the brink of boiling over as Fritz charged straight to his bedroom. His jaw clenched, beads of sweat forming at his temple. I didn't think anyone could be carried up the narrow staircase, but Fritz trudged upward. By the time he reached the landing, his ragged breaths rolled over me. His muscles coiled in his arms, tremors shot through his hands, and still he refused to drop me. I was causing him so much pain. But I could never have made it up those stairs on my own.

He bypassed his bed and turned to the bathroom.

The white clawfoot tub stood like a relic from another time, its porcelain gleaming in the light.

He lowered me gently into the tub. As he pulled back, his stunned gaze darted over my red skin. He blinked, then turned the faucet, unleashing a torrent of frigid water. A raw scream tore from my throat; the clash of temperatures was a brutal shock. Steam rose from my overheated skin. The clear water turned red, swirling like watercolor pigments in a cup. My body convulsed, muscles seizing.

Fritz's face blurred through the mist. He became a firefighter, tirelessly pouring water over my head. Each droplet was a lifeline, a fragile tether to survival.

Raiden paced by the door.

Fatigue pressed down on my shoulders. My vision brightened, then wavered, the world around me blurred into indistinct shapes and colors as I fought to stay conscious.

Suddenly, Quinbe appeared kneeling beside Fritz. "Oh, lord. Don't panic," she murmured more to herself. "Fritz, take off her necklace." As he unclasped the pendant, his hands shook. Quinbe pressed the back of her hand to my forehead. "Li, ice! Fritz, would—" she stammered, "Sloane's blood help?"

"I have one pint left. We have to try. I'll get it." Fritz scrambled toward the door.

Li burst into the bathroom. "I have ice." He dumped the bucket. The ice clinked and rattled against the tub's side.

Cramps stabbed my stomach. I clenched my teeth and closed my eyes. I shouldn't have stolen the evobilities. This was what happened when you took what wasn't yours. There were always consequences when taking power.

More cold water splashed.

More scorching.

More suffering.

How could I possibly undo what I've done?

When I finally opened my eyes, Fritz raised the bag of Sloane's blood high into the air. The needle in Quinbe's hand gleamed before she stabbed my forearm.

We held our breath while seconds ticked.

Fritz tirelessly drained the lukewarm water, then replenished it with fresh, frigid water. But we knew these cycles were a losing battle, the evobility beneath my skin was too relentless.

Quinbe took my temperature. *Beep. Beep. Beep.*

"One-hundred-six. She's not cooling down." Quinbe's hand was steady, but her voice quivered. "Why isn't Sloane's blood lowering her temperature?"

"Sloane's blood fights disease and rejuvenates. An evobility isn't an infection." Raiden's voice cracked, and my calm slipped into the gorge of desperation.

"We need Nyxon!" Li brought his fist to his mouth.

"I'm here!" Nyxon burst into the bathroom. She braced the sink, then her pupils clouded, pale and inhuman. She flickered through the cards of logic in her mind. Her lips moved, mumbling probabilities and half-formed ideas that refused to coalesce. They came and went, slipping away before she could seize them.

White foam bubbled from my mouth and dripped down to my collarbone. My eyes rolled back as spasms racked my body.

Nyxon shouted, "Saline. Chilled saline IV drip!"

"I have chilled saline at the clinic, but it'd take forty-five minutes each way. Avi doesn't have that much time!" Quinbe cried.

Chapter 47

"Li, give Avi your hand," Nyxon said with the cold focus of a gambler sliding every chip forward, damn the cost, damn who it hurt, and it scared me. "Avi, channel a *small piece* of Li's evobility into your body. His evobility will heal your organs and shut down any threat to your body."

Li cringed and I choked out, "No, I'll burn him or worse." What if my VidaLumin evobility went rogue and took his soul?

"Li, that's an order!" Nyxon's voice cracked like a whip, jolting me into obedience even though the command wasn't meant for me.

Li snapped to attention, shuffling close enough for me to reach him. "No offense, Avi, but you stink of pus and your face looks like a pepperoni pizza."

My lips twisted, caught between laughing and crying.

"I can't stop stealing!" Short, irregular breaths hitched in my throat. "I killed them!"

Li's eyes widened into an expression of *oh fuck, things just got serious.*

Fritz kneeled by the tub. "That won't happen here. You're safe. You're home. Just focus on me and breathe." Fritz placed a hand lightly on my chest, then on his own, showing me the rise and fall of each breath. "Slow and steady. I'm here, Avi. Always. When you activate your Slyfen evobility, focus on opening a single flower. Then take only a few stars from his evobility's constellation. If anything goes wrong, I'll separate you."

Wrinkling his nose, Li reluctantly extended his palm. "I *suspect* this is gonna hurt, so let's get this over with."

Placing my hand around Li's wrist, I closed my eyes, found his pulse, then tapped twice on my wrist's pulse point. My paralytic thistles sprouted. Li grumbled from the prickling, his expression was of bored annoyance. Was the paralytic working? Or did it affect Jagwars differently?

My green vine wrapped around our wrists, its form fluid and elegant, like a ribbon tied neatly around a gift. But this was a gift no one wanted. A gift that destroyed. A gift I'd regret giving forever.

Three blue pods sprouted into existence like the first signs of spring unfolding in a beautiful rush.

"This is fine. Totally fine. Just got a plant friendship bracelet. No big deal," Li rambled to himself. His confident facade fracturing just a little as the paralytic froze his features.

I focused on opening the smallest blue pod, layer by layer.

From the flower, my Slyfen's soldiers flitted into the air, bobbing and weaving in an unpredictable pattern, drawn by an invisible pull toward Li's constellation. His constellation, resembling Canis Major, pulsed in response as if beckoning my dark fireflies closer.

Suddenly, the Dracophelia laughed. A deep, disturbing sound that reverberated through my skull: *We need it all.*

To my horror, the remaining pods burst open, releasing a translucent swarm.

I tapped twice on my neck to stop the assault and lifted my hand from Li's, but the vine turned aggressive, writhing with dark hunger, draining warmth, squeezing tighter.

"Separate us. Separate us now!" I screamed.

Fritz tried to lift my hand. "Fuck!"

"Hurry, try again." My cluster of tiny thieves coiled their legs around the prey, like a deadly snare. They plucked star after star, turning bright in their new found light.

A single firefly glided toward the largest star, the yellow beacon at the center of Li's chest.

No, not that star! I willed my fireflies to return and my Slyfen evobility to retract, straining every mental fiber, snapping synapses like brittle twigs. I was too weak, too untrained. Raiden had warned me about the risks of not being able to control my evobility and now I was failing everyone.

My world tilted. Li's entire evobility was about to be stolen. Would his soul survive?

With a violent tug, the yellow star was ripped from its place, Li collapsed to one knee, his expression contorting.

Nyxon rushed over, fear twisting her face into a mask I'd never seen her wear before. Together, they tried to yank our hands apart. "One, two, three pull!"

The instant the large star was sucked into a pod, a crackling zap jolted through me. Li's entire constellation of stars plummeted to the floor, lifeless, like dead birds falling from the sky mid-flight.

A black blot surfaced on my vine like an infection taking root.

Rot. Something was rotting my evobility.

The burning came, searing through me from the inside out. His constellation flared against mine, each point of light ripping at the fabric of my being to become a highway of connected energies, sparks racing along invisible lanes, carrying pieces of him into me. My body quaked, but I couldn't fight it; resistance only made the fire burn brighter. Uzziah's words struck me, "Be born again in fire."

"Nyxon, help her!" Raiden put his hands on his head and paced.

"No, help Li!" I cried. *I couldn't kill Li.* I thrashed in the tub, water spilling over the edge as the slick porcelain seemed to drag me deeper into my own terror.

"Raiden, take my spot!" Nyxon's voice rang out as she vanished around the corner. Her sudden departure sent a pang of despair through me.

Raiden's hands clamped around Li's waist. "Pull, damn it." Raiden's muscles strained against the unnatural force binding me and Li together.

I tapped twice on my neck again. Why wasn't my Slyfen evobility retracting?

I activated my VidaLumin evobility. Its tendril had wrapped around Li's arm and slinked up and around his bicep. Holding onto him. It continued upward, reaching Li's neck, forming a grotesque mass around his throat.

"I can't breathe." Li clawed at his neck with his free hand, nails biting into flesh, unable to comprehend my invisible force was to blame.

Nyxon returned, a butcher knife gleamed in her grip.

Muscles froze mid-movement. Even the slosh of water against porcelain died away, leaving only a rising tide of dread.

"There's no fuckin' way you're choppin' off my hand!" Li's eyes locked on mine, pleading louder than words ever could: stop this. Break us apart.

My VidaLumin prodded the air, looking to strike. To kill.

The blade in Nyxon's hand gleamed under the flickering light, threatening deliverance at a terrible cost.

Chapter 48

Li thrashed against the iron grip binding us, desperation fueling his struggle.

"I'm not going to chop off your hand. The steel will act as a magnetic conductor, redirecting the magnetic flux lines through the blade instead of through the non-magnetic materials. When I slide the blade between your hands the steel will weaken the—"

"Whatever. Just do it!" Li nodded, his head bobbing uncontrollably.

Nyxon slid the knife between us, the blade grazing my skin. "Raiden and Fritz pull now. Hard!" Nyxon's eyes were wild. The men roared as they pulled with all their might. A sparking zap split the air like lightning tearing the sky, and they tore us apart.

They crashed to the floor in a tangled heap, bodies sprawled and limp like broken marionettes.

Sucking in a ragged breath, I slumped into the tub.

"Is Li okay?" Only the water answered, lapping against the porcelain, waves splashing to my chin then receding.

Raiden grabbed Li by his shirt's collar and shook. "Li?"

"I fe-e-e-l like I ran a mar-rathon. Or may-be I'm dr-runk." Li's head lolled to the side, each word a struggle as if his tongue was too heavy and misshapen.

Li was alive! Alive! Relief flooded me, tears fell from my eyes. My VidaLumin didn't win.

Nyxon's gaze flicked between Li and me, then zeroed in on Raiden. "Help me." They hooked their arms under Li's shoulders. Li's body sagged between them, a dead weight, as though my Slyfen had stolen not just his evobility but his will to fight.

"Let's get you downstairs on the couch first. Coffee, second," Nyxon murmured. Her usual commanding, detached tone was gone, replaced with empathy.

Li mumbled an inaudible complaint. His boots scuffed unevenly against the floor, dragging and stumbling with each step.

The Shivana's constellation hovered near my shoulder, wild and erratic, like a feral squirrel caught in a cage. Its energy thrashed against an invisible forcefield, threatening to rip through me. My breath stuttered. The thing wasn't just angry, it demanded to be with its true master, not me, the impostor.

Li's constellation reacted before I could cry out. His brightest star launched forward, a burst of light that momentarily blinded me. It struck the Shivana's stars head-on, flaring white-hot. A cramp seized my stomach, contracting hard, forcing me to double over. The Shivana's constellation flickered, its stars shrinking as if the air had been sucked from them. Smoke bled through the light, then, with one last shuddering spark, it broke apart, turning to ash that vanished in the air.

A coolness swept down my throat like breathing in cold mountain air in the morning, sending a shiver through my body.

I touched my cheeks, confirming that what I experienced was real. That it was over.

But the Shivana's death echoed through me, leaving me gutted, as if the fight had taken a piece of me with it. Grief pooled where its light had been. Another precious evobility was gone because of me.

"The blisters are shrinking," Quinbe announced and pressed a damp cloth to my forehead.

The moon's ethereal glow filtered through the sheer curtains, as if life pushed back against the shadow of what almost was.

How long had I slept? I was in Fritz's room. In his bed. Wearing his shirt and pajama pants.

Fritz slumped in a green wingback chair by the window, his head tipped to one side, snoring softly.

He'd be okay. Relief spread through me, soothing like aloe on sunburned skin.

Gauze wrapped my forearms. I lifted my shirt; patches covered my ribs. Too nervous, I refused to peek beneath. Moving gingerly, I rose from the warm bed. My toes curled when they touched the cold floor.

Quietly shuffling to Fritz, I gently draped the quilt over him, careful not to disturb his slumber. Then I saw it. Blood-stained bandages wrapped his forearms. My breath hitched. I was the architect of his suffering. Guilt pressed down on me, whispering that karma would claim its pound of flesh from me, and I accepted it with grim surrender.

"Don't tell *me-e-e* what to *do-o-o*!" Li wailed from downstairs.

I kissed Fritz's forehead, then followed Li's broken voice down the stairs.

In the living room, Nyxon stood near the fireplace, a green bottle of Jameson whiskey behind her back while Li beckoned for a refill.

"Your indulgence in spirits has persisted unabated for hours. *Enough*." Nyxon's firm inflection held a warning not to push her further.

"It's m-m-mine." He pouted from the couch, tossing a pillow over the coffee table onto the loveseat.

"Hi," I squeaked.

Bottle still in hand, Nyxon rushed to embrace me. "How are you?"

"A little stiff. Sore." Physically, I could stand, but it was the haunting memories that truly hurt, the emotional scars that may never heal. What I had done to those souls… to Li.

"You. You." No anger laced Li's tone, only agony and defeat. "My evobility is *gone*. I can't sense it." He cried into his tumbler containing whiskey coated ice cubes. "I'm going to turn into a feral Gray!"

Nyxon pushed the bottle into my chest and sat beside Li on the couch. She let her invisible armor drop and gently laid his head on her lap. "We won't let that happen to you. And you know Earth's moon stops the transformation process."

"Great. Now I'm stuck here. All Avi does is take, take, take. She took *my* evobility, she took *my* best friend. She took *my* whiskey. What's next?" Li glowered in my direction.

"You act like I planned all of it. I didn't take your evobility to hurt you. And Fritz? That's not on me." I placed the bottle on the fireplace's mantle. "Everything I've taken… I didn't know what it would cost." I admitted. "But I care," my tone softened, "I feel it. Every bit."

Nyxon stroked his hair. "Life can surprise you, even when the future feels overwhelmingly uncertain. But instead of getting blitzed, take a proactive approach."

"I'm not *inter-r-rested* in a lecture from *you*," he slurred.

"Someone must know how to reverse the transfer," I said, each word dripping with remorse.

Nyxon lowered her gaze. "We'll find a way."

Quinbe burst in from the kitchen and enveloped me in a hug. "Nyxon's sedative from Cynder really knocked you out. While you slept, I brushed your hair. Even cleaned and painted your nails." She grabbed my hand, her trembling fingers betraying her calm. "Check out the shade. Blue Lagoon. Just the right splash of color to brighten your mood."

I recognized the frantic energy in Quinbe's movements and tone. Grief swelled until it blurred my eyes in the form of tears. This wasn't just about a pretty nail color or a comforting gesture. Quinbe desperately tried to stay busy, to hold herself together, because if she stopped moving, the turmoil of everything—the danger, the fear, the threat of another unimaginable loss—would consume her.

A heavy pang of guilt gutted me. I never wanted this for Quinbe. I had to protect her, and that meant more than just keeping her alive.

When you love someone, you become their strength when they can't stand, carry their pain when hope is gone, and shield their heart from the world even as yours is breaking.

Wiggling my fingers, the aqua gel with silver glitter gleamed. "They've never looked better." I sniffled.

Li sulked. "Bet you're already regenerat-ted-d."

Quinbe and I shared a confused look. Li gestured for me to unwrap the gauze from my arm, and I did.

Quinbe gasped. "How is that possible?"

The blisters were now dry and shriveled to half their size. The cuts on my palms had scabbed. The bruises spotting my body were purple-green, skipping the red and blue stage.

Li tilted his chin. "Perks of being a Jagwar. Great complexion, fast healing, and oh no… oh… no." He rolled off the couch to stand but tumbled to a knee. I bent to guide him, but he shooed me away. "I don't ne-e-ed *your* help." He slogged toward the bathroom. "Is that gray hair? A wrinkle!"

"Quit being dramatic," Nyxon drawled from the couch.

"You're basically the same," I encouraged.

"Basic? What do you mean *basic*?" He flopped back onto the couch, his legs dangling over the armrest.

Li and I didn't see eye to eye on much, but he'd given me his evobility, false, he'd offered a piece, and I'd poached the whole lot. "You'll get your evobility back. Whatever it takes."

The creaking floorboards above signaled our discussion had roused Fritz.

Quinbe walked me to the couch, across from Li. "The missing women. The women from the cage, their story is everywhere. Online. TV. I'm sure the police or Cyndarian Watch will locate the bastards." She clicked on the TV.

The news broadcaster stated, "…a religious cult kidnapping young women. Did police apprehend all the members?" Pictures of survivors plastered the screen. A list of the missing or presumed dead. My picture appeared alongside Janet's and Somona's.

My eyes widened when Tiffany appeared on the TV. She stood in front of Pacific Perfume's black-and-white sign. "I can't believe this happened. Avi wasn't just a co-worker, I was *her* best friend."

All heads turned to me. I rolled my eyes.

Tiffany clutched her black scarf. Her white sleeve slipped back, revealing a gold laurel cuff studded with rubies that gleamed like drops of blood in the light.

Tiffany continued, "I'm *traumatized*. I could be kidnapped next! Who's going to pay for my therapy?"

The newscaster returned to the screen and solemnly said, "If you'd like to support Tiffany during this challenging period, you can contribute to her GoFundMe—"

"I can't believe it. Rewind." I instructed Quinbe.

Chapter 49

The bracelet's presence cut through her fake sorrow like a snarky confession, she wore it because she thought I was dead. "The gold and ruby bracelet from Raiden's hidden camera."

"That bitch!" Quinbe blurted.

Tiffany. The friendly coworker who brought muffins to meetings. She wasn't just a harmless overachiever, she was a saboteur. My stomach churned at the thought of her smiling across the break room while quietly dismantling everything Ms. Voss worked so hard to build. I clenched my fists. How long had she been doing this? How much damage had she caused? And worse, how had I missed it?

"I'll alert Ms. Voss right away and send her the footage." Nyxon took out her phone and snapped a photo of the news feed.

A hollow ache spread through my chest. I wouldn't be the one to confront Tiffany. I wouldn't taste the satisfaction of exposing her treachery. I wouldn't get to hear her stammer out excuses, to see the blood drain from her face. The selfish thought took root, thorny and insidious. I wanted to be the one to save Ms. Voss.

I *deserved* that moment.

But I was stuck here for a few more days. Li and Fritz might think helping Ms. Voss was inconsequential and there were bigger stakes than my own vindication. I knew that, but the knowing didn't soften the resentment curdling inside me. It still stung. After everything I had endured, Ms. Voss's approval remained precious to me. It was a minuscule, foolish slight, but the smallest wounds had a way of staying with you.

I exhaled slowly. I could hate Tiffany in silence.

Fritz entered with a tray, three mugs of steaming tea and handed me a cup. "Don't worry Avi, Tiffany and Michael will be handled. Sip this. It'll aid with any aches and pains. I brewed it with dried moncoeur flowers from Cynder." Yellow star-shaped petals floated in the purple liquid.

I brought the mug to my nose, inhaling the sweet honey herbal aroma.

He passed Quinbe a mug with a generic teabag bobbing on the water's surface.

"Sorry about your arms," I said.

The front door burst open.

Quinbe's hands jerked, splashing tea across her blouse. Fritz jumped back. Li reacted a few seconds too late, snatching a couch pillow.

Quinbe huffed. "Raiden! Must you barge in like we're under siege?"

Raiden panted, catching his breath. "My bad. Nyxon texted me. I was in the barn."

Nyxon smirked, mischief in her eyes, as she rose to take her half-spilled tea from a sighing Fritz.

Raiden sat on the coffee table in front of me, his knee brushing mine. Sweat formed a V down his chest, and his flushed cheeks betrayed his exertion.

Quinbe scrunched her face as she dabbed at the tea stain. Each movement was dramatically exaggerated, as if the stain were a personal offense.

"Avi, what do you remember?" Raiden focused on me as if I were the only person in the room.

Quinbe stomped her foot. Her demeanor shifted from petite best friend to fiercely protective mother elephant. "Raiden, give her a moment. She just woke up."

"It's okay." I rested a hand on her forearm, but tears pooled in my eyes. "I was number twenty-three."

"I'll ensure the police know the correct number of victims. Monrowvia escaped. Wolfram is dead. Argon is dead; Li shot him at the feed store," Nyxon said.

"You-r're welcome." Li raised his glass to toast no one in particular and swirled his melting ice. "And look how I'm repaid."

"You also lost Avi. Sacrificing your evobility to save her life was the *noble* thing to do," Raiden barked.

Li folded in on himself. Even Fritz cowered at the sting from Raiden's lashing.

"It wasn't Li's fault," I scolded Raiden.

"It's okay, *Princess*, it's always *my* fault. Tell us what else happened so I can be blamed for that too." Li flipped his wrist at Nyxon.

Nyxon leaned against the mantel. "The police found the charred bodies that they haven't identified yet. The Cyndarian Watch has already infiltrated the investigation and plans to collect the Grounders' remains."

"I stole evobilities. Then tore apart Grounders' souls. I couldn't stop."

Fritz's and Li's souls recoiled, stretching from me like taut rubber bands before snapping back as their bodies refused to move.

Raiden's soul spiraled violently, a vortex of light and motion that left me dizzy, as if I might be dragged into its chaos. The trust I'd fought so hard to earn, months of careful conversations, shared risks, and nurturing the language of loyalty, shattered in an instant. I wasn't just back at zero, I was buried beneath his fear, clawing at a deficit I might never overcome.

But like a Steelers offensive lineman, Nyxon held steady, undeterred. Her soul's yellow and black stripes buzzed in their usual rhythmic pattern, unshaken by the threat before her.

What did she see that the others didn't? How could she stand, strong like steel, when the rest trembled?

She trusted me?

But trust was a fragile thing, easily splintered.

She held an unwavering faith in herself. Her knowledge wasn't just a collection of facts or data. It was a clear lens that shaped her reality. She calmly anticipated hurdles. Adaptable, always able to pivot when the moment demanded, her intellect was a weapon more formidable than Li's strength or Fritz's agility.

"Slyfen evobilities can't steal a Grounder's life force." Fritz spoke with conviction, though I saw his fear bristle through his soul.

"If a Grounder is blessed with two evobilities, it's possible for them to merge. Evolve. Upgrade. Avi can see souls and she can steal evobilities. Put them together under duress, *and* she didn't know how to control them, so…" Nyxon exhaled loudly.

Li hiccuped. "Well fuck me sideways, I didn't think a Slyfen evobility could get much more scarier."

Nyxon frowned and tugged Li's sleeve. "It's late. Bed. Now." He grumbled, an inaudible protest. She extended a hand to him. "Move it."

Refusing to take her hand, he oozed off the couch, his knees hitting the floor. He rolled to his stomach. We all exchanged tense glances as he lay motionless.

"I'll find a way to return your evobility. I promise." My words lacked confidence, the burden of this impossible task evident in my tone. The room felt like a tightly wound clock, each tick a measure of doubt and each tock an admission of how daunting this challenge would be.

He slung a disgruntled hand at me.

"Let's go." Nyxon moved to hoist Li from the floor.

We held our breath until Nyxon's and Li's retreating footsteps and bickering faded away.

"Before Nyxon escaped the warehouse, she stole a hard drive. We're analyzing the information now. There are videos of Monrowvia's experiments. Maybe there will be information about returning an evobility," Raiden said.

Madness and malice became a maelstrom inside me, making me nauseous. I rocked slightly and considered blaming the tea for unsettling my stomach.

"Monrowvia has the Tiara of Tuskia, but the Dracophelia is loose within me." A memory flashed: the Dracophelia, egging me on to destroy more souls. My fingers quaked.

Raiden took my hands within his, the rough pad of his thumb gently tracing over the hills and valleys of my knuckles.

Quinbe's eyes ballooned, her mug froze at her lips, the steamy aroma forgotten.

Fritz's throat constricted, a protectiveness trapped within its confines as he balled his fits at his side. "The incantation is locked in my safe."

Quinbe's brow furrowed. "Let's hurl the damn incantation into the fireplace. Then no one can control Avi."

Raiden gave her a consoling look. "If no one reads it, the Dracophelia's bloodlust will overpower her. The incantation is like a muzzle for a rabid dog."

"That's comforting," I mumbled. "Can anyone teach me to read it?" My eyes swept over their morose faces.

Fritz scratched his head. "It's an old Cynder language. If Nyxon locates a book with the alphabet or if someone on Cynder teaches her, she can master it, then pass it on to you."

"The doctor said I must expel the Dracophelia from my body or it will eventually consume me. Since we don't have the tiara, can we put the evobility into something else? Maybe a glass bottle?"

Quinbe recoiled. "Just don't put it into a creepy doll."

"Whatever vessel you use must be hexed, or freeing the Dracophelia could unleash unimaginable havoc upon the world," Raiden cautioned.

Nyxon entered, her stride tired. "I need a book on supporting a loved one through the stages of loss and grief."

"Maybe Uzziah would know how to return the Jagwar evobility to Li," I said, my voice laced with a faint glimmer amid the overwhelming sadness.

Fritz rubbed the back of his neck. "What form of payment would he demand? Nothing we'd be willing to sacrifice. And if Monrowvia and Uzziah discover you survived the fire, they'll hunt you down."

"Let them come." My blood boiled despite my sore muscles. "I can handle it."

"They know everything about you now. Last night, Raiden staked out Quinbe's house and two Amarmet members, hired by Monrowvia, pretending to be police officers, questioned her," Fritz countered.

Wide-eyed, my head whipped to Quinbe.

"Quinbe and I took them out." Raiden squeezed my hand. Quinbe beamed. Fritz's gaze hardened on Raiden's hand, his protective instinct flaring to life.

"But they'll keep coming," Nyxon warned.

"What are you saying?" A sickening sensation swelled within me.

Nyxon's gaze dipped to her shoes. "Everyone presumes you died in the fire. If you stay dead, they'll stop looking for you. I can get all of us new identities from the Cyndarian Watch. Passports to start a new life." Her solution stabbed my side, and she took note of my hesitation. "If they think you're alive, they'll go to hellish lengths to track you down."

I pulled my hand from Raiden's. "You all want to erase me? You want me to sketch the trajectory of my life in a matter of days? Slide the pros and cons across the bar like pieces on an abacus?" No one answered. Tears pooled and threatened to spill.

Quinbe drew her knees in, wrapping her arms around them.

"Recover first, but within a week you must choose so we can strategize accordingly," Nyxon said.

I pushed myself in a feeble attempt to balance my new and old existence. In the end, one had to win out. "Where would I go? Graysen?" Would Raiden follow? His soul sagged and swayed. Despair overtook me, I couldn't receive another blow. "I'm not going anywhere until Doctor Monrowvia is rotting behind bars."

Fritz and Nyxon shared a confirming nod. "We'll pursue him. *Together*," Fritz promised.

Tension coiled in my gut. "There's one more Grounder we need to add to our list."

Chapter 50

I grabbed my journal and pen from my bag and sat on my bed. Where do I even begin?

Journal Entry Seven:

Nyxon's account of how they found me.

Fritz described the Grounder with the yellow diamond ring leaving the feed store. Raiden recognized him as Tonium from the bar. Tracking Tonium to McFadden's Pub, Raiden threatened to cut off his ring finger unless he cooperated. Tonium confessed he knew how to contact Wolfram and that there was a bounty for a Frigellen. Nyxon volunteered as bait, hiding a GPS tracker in her shoe. She played her part when Wolfram's Grounders came to collect her. Fritz bribed Tonium (who cared only for money and lacked morality) to create a distraction at the warehouse. Tonium and his crew showed up pretending to be delivery men, insisting they needed to unload a box truck packed with "hazardous chemicals." Of course, it wasn't long before one of them knocked over a barrel, and a cloud of haze puffed out, making everyone scatter. This allowed Li, Fritz, and Raiden to storm through the back with weapons drawn. While Nyxon was in the cage, she picked the lock. La'Keisha told Raiden where I was being held hostage.

Chetchet: the evobility I stole, that made me run faster than I ever thought possible. They're built for quick bursts of speed, not long distances.

Nyxon thinks finding Maria, the Nitro Snap, will lead us to the tiara and Monrowvia.

Fritz, Nyxon, and Raiden take turns guarding me and babysitting Li. Graysen has been sticking close to Li for support. She preaches fur therapy.

I wandered Fritz's property in restless loops, but the instant the house or barn slipped from sight, my pulse spiked and sweat gathered in my palms. I'd never had a panic attack before, if that's what this was, but it felt like drowning on dry land.

Fritz guides me from room to room, like I might vanish if he lets go. He gave me his bedroom upstairs while he took the couch. Raiden and Li had the guest rooms. Fritz seemed surprised I didn't invite him up. I told him his soul still feared me, but it didn't stop him from resting his hand on my thigh or pulling me close. Raiden watched from across the room, jaw clenched, eyes darting to wherever Fritz's hand landed.

Li commented loudly on Fritz's loving gestures by snapping, "I didn't have my evobility stolen by a slimy Slyfen just for Fritz to fuck things up again and be sent to the mudflats."

Li's right. I know it. Nyxon knows it too. But Fritz is making this so damn difficult.

Raiden hasn't said a word about our kiss. This is all bad timing, but Raiden's old advice rattled in my head: if he wanted me, he'd just go for it. And he did, didn't he? He kissed me like he meant it, then locked it away like it never happened. Now Fritz pressed closer every chance he got, making it harder to breathe, harder to think.

On day seven, after another gutting night of Li drunkenly mourning his evobility, I couldn't bear to watch him unravel any more. I begged Fritz to let me stay at Nyxon's. So here I am, panic attack or no panic attack, Li needed space to grieve without me haunting the hallways.

I placed my pen between my journal's pages. Returning Li's evobility before he turned into a feral Gray must be our top priority.

A knock at my bedroom door, then Raiden poked his head in. "Hi. I brought you a glass of water." He placed it on my nightstand then sat on the edge of my bed. "Nyxon texted. Her and Fritz are on their way back from the Cyndarian Watch headquarters. They didn't find anything on transferring evobilities."

I let out an exasperated sigh. Would Uzziah know? I'd bet my freedom on it.

"I'm asking every informant I come into contact with if they know anything. There has to be a way." He looked down at the floor. "I'm sorry it took me so long to find you. If I found you sooner—"

I extended my hand, gently coaxing his chin upward like a sunflower seeking daylight, urging him to meet my gaze. "You were there when I needed you. If I hadn't been kidnapped, we never would've found the missing women." I turned on my VidaLumin evobility. My silvery, tinsel soul reached out, exploring the fragile boundary between us as if testing the delicate barrier of a dream you're afraid to wake from. "If you were me, would you pretend to be dead? Erased?"

"Protecting people means making sacrifices."

"And if I asked you to disappear with me?"

His soul shifted from side to side, the internal struggle mirrored in the way his shoulders relaxed, only to tense again. "Leaving with you wouldn't be disappearing. It would be the first time I hadn't needed to hide. I'd be stepping into a life where I'm finally known, even if it costs me everything else. With you, I'd finally exist."

Our souls intertwined, igniting a tango too intimate for words. My luminous, silvery soul spiraled around his red flames, the contrast leaving me breathless. The midnight-blue core of his soul lightened into a stunning shade of teal, like the crystal-clear Caribbean ocean. The teal grew like vines, branching out into the red flames. Our souls engulfed us in a mesmerizing fusion of colors, a dazzling whirlwind of energies.

He rose. I extended my hand to stop him but dropped it at my side. Fear and doubt held me back. Asking him to leave with me was foolish. What about the Queen and the tiara? What would Fritz think about me and Raiden sitting shoulder-to-shoulder on a plane?

The teal center of his soul shrunk and returned to its original dark shade of blue.

"I'll be outside your door until Quinbe returns from dragging Li from the bar." He looked at his watch and strode to the door. "It's only 10 p.m., so it'll be a while." He rubbed the back of his neck.

Resentment swelled within me. "It's like Quinbe's on a rescue mission and you're my watch dog."

Raiden paused at the door, and smirked. "As your humble *sidekick*, I'd bend a knee for you in a heartbeat. Anything to please you and keep you safe."

He left, shutting the door behind him with a soft click.

I rolled over, buried my face into the pillow, and mumbled into the feathers, "Watch dog. *Really*, Avi?"

In my elementary existence, I lived by the rules, always the first to wave the white flag. I never rocked the boat. A lump formed in my throat. With nothing left to lose and gifted a second chance, I had to seize it. I had to just go for it! I strode for the door and swung it open.

Raiden jumped up from the couch. "What's wrong?"

"Everything."

I strode to meet him, chest to chest. I pushed him back onto the sofa with a force that surprised me. I straddled his lap and his hands slid to my hips.

I cupped his face, his rough stubble grazing my fingertips before I leaned in. Our lips met in a tentative, searching kiss as if neither of us believed this tryst could be real.

Then responsibilities, danger, everything fell away in the space between our breaths. His kiss deepened, rougher, urgent, as if we were both on the edge of losing control, like we couldn't get close enough fast enough.

My hands roamed over his shoulders, feeling the hard lines of muscle beneath the thin fabric of his shirt.

His fingers slid beneath my tank top, gliding over the curve of my waist.

His hand moved higher, pausing at the lace band of my bra. His thumbs brushed the fabric, slow and unhurried, before slipping beneath, his palms molding to the shape of me. His grip became reverent and possessive as if claiming a place he considered his.

An electric shiver ran through me, and I gasped. He paused, looking up at me, his lips still hovering inches from mine.

"You have no idea how long I've wanted this." His confession came out rough, the words breathy and thick with desire.

"You have me now." My body arched into him, seeking more.

"You've been mine long before tonight."

In one fluid motion, he stood, hoisting me to his chest, my legs locking around his waist, our bodies colliding. He kissed a trail along my throat and down to my collarbone, each brush of his mouth setting fire to my skin as he carried me to the bedroom.

I didn't know where this would lead, and I didn't care.

Avi's Evobility Ledger

Grounders possess a unique genetic connection with planets, allowing them to harness abilities derived from the planet's elemental constituents. These abilities are called evobilities. Grounder DNA mutated with Cynder's chemical periodic elements, producing adaptations that enable survival on the planet's harsh and arid environment. Children inherit one or two evobilities from their parents, and each evobility is assigned a distinct name. Evobilities are charged through physical contact with their home planet or Earth, such as walking barefoot on grass or sand. This connection synchronizes the body with the planet's natural electrical charge. If a Grounder does not regularly charge their evobility, it will gradually fade, and they will eventually become fully human.

Evobilities are categorized by how frequently they occur and the degree to which they influence the individual or their environment.

Austere: weak and appearing in a quarter of the population.

Baseline: functional and commonly observed among Grounders.

Convergent: formative, uncommon, and shaped by evolutionary pressures and environmental forces.

Dominion: rare and grant significant control over objects or life.

Eternal: mythical, defying known limits and seldom, if ever, witnessed.

Acridspunk:	Glands beneath the tongue release a skunk-like odor when sprayed. Limitation: The spray is hard to control and may hit allies. Rarity: Baseline.
Akerra:	Green blood that is toxic to Grounders and humans through ingestion or skin contact. Limitation: All blood transfusions are ineffective if injury occurs. Rarity: Convergent.

| **Aphrodye:** | Sweat is sweet and intoxicating when licked. Limitation: Sweat can become addictive for others; attracts unwanted advances from individuals who mistake fascination for entitlement; finds it difficult to maintain friendships with monogamous couples. Rarity: Eternal. |

Architect:	A group of Grounders that can manipulate time.
1. Bloodkona:	Must mix blood with fertorium and drink it to see flashes of the future. Limitation: The future is always changing. Acute hemolytic reaction may occur, causing fever, chills, nausea, chest pain, or shock; severe cases can lead to kidney failure. Rarity: Dominion.
2. ChronoCoil:	Their body metabolizes gravity, curving Space and time. Can turn back time and start timelines over. Limitation: Rewinding the "Life Clock" causes the ChronoCoil to absorb the erased time, accelerating the aging of their internal organs, leading to early death. If a ChronoCoil dies at a certain age, they cannot live beyond that point in any timeline. For example, if one is murdered at forty, they will die at forty in every timeline. This phenomenon is known as *Cutting the String*. Rarity: Eternal.
3. Sifter:	Their body curves space and time. Can travel back and forth along their own lifeline but cannot travel to the future. They can talk to their past self. Can't turn back time. Limitation: The present continues

even when they are in the past. Every minute they spend in the past, the present moves forward an hour and their internal organs age at the present pace.
Rarity: Dominion.

Bmine: Chambers within their face's cheeks allow the Grounder to release a puff of toxic gas that temporarily blinds targets and causes itching around the eyes. Limitation: The gas is difficult to control, and wind and dust will make the toxic gas' direction unpredictable. If not released weekly, the gas can poison the user. Social stigma is common due to the persistence of foul breath.
Rarity: Convergent

Catalyst: Tufted ears stretch to a point above the Grounder's head, cat-like. Has nine lives. Limitation: Cannot hide evobility; ears sensitive to cold or wind, causing pain or disorientation.
Rarity: Convergent.

Chetchet: Built for short bursts of speed; not suited for long distance. Pale skin and hair. Sweats through the hands. Limitation: High caloric needs; difficulty sleeping causes psychotic episodes.
Rarity: Baseline.

Cobalti: Magnetic manipulation is characterized by the projection of electromagnetic force to influence metallic objects. XX-linked genetic expression can push metal away. XY-linked genetic expression can pull metal closer. Under mosaic genetic conditions the individual can pull and push metal objects. Hands' temperature is cold, under fifty degrees. Limitation: Prolonged use drains energy, leaving the Grounder weak or dizzy. Rarity: Baseline.

Dracophelia: Enhances evobilities and predicts battle outcomes. Built for combat. Evobility is restricted to XX-linked genetic expression. Limitation: Overuse causes obsession with power and loss of compassion, morality, and joy.
Rarity: Eternal.

Festee: Skull is steel hard. Short stature. Evobility is restricted to X0-linked genetic expression. Limitation: Balance is affected; head is sensitive to temperature extremes, causing discomfort or headaches.
Rarity: Austere.

Fluora: Tube in roof of mouth emits acidic goo that burns through glass and wood. Evobility is restricted to XY-linked genetic expression. Limitation: Prolonged use weakens teeth enamel, causes cavities, and may inflame the tooth pulp. If the pulp becomes infected, a root canal is necessary.
Rarity: Eternal.

Fotomanu: Over six feet tall and very slender; absorbs energy and nutrition directly from sunlight. Limitation: Lack of sunlight causes fatigue and fainting.
Rarity: Austere.

Frigellen: Absorbs knowledge ten times faster than any Grounder or human; can transfer it to others. Limitation: Cannot build upon collected knowledge; unused knowledge fades over time.

Rarity: Convergent.

G-Froceia: Scrapes blue-and-white nails to generate an electric force field. Anyone outside the field who touches it is zapped. Limitation: Force field lasts only as many minutes as the Grounder's age.
Rarity: Convergent.

Iforge: Can mold iron with their hands. Limitation: Drains iron from their own blood; overuse causes dizziness, pale skin, and fainting.
Rarity: Baseline.

Inkbane: Tattoo-like markings come to life to protect the user. Limitation: Visible markings make the Grounder identifiable. Other Grounders may treat the Inkbane as dangerous, leading to exclusion, mistrust, or persecution. Any damage to the ink breaks its structure, rendering the evobility forever unusable.

1. **Quadia**: Four thin ink-like tentacles sprout from the back and come to life, capable of strangling enemies and grasping weapons. Evobility is restricted to XX-linked genetic expression.
Rarity: Dominion.

2. **Astara**: Starfish ink on the back of the spine. Able to regenerate body parts. Evobility is restricted to XXY-linked genetic expression.
Rarity: Austere.

3. **Crabalak**: One crab-like pincer and one crab-like leg formed from ink come to life, capable of stabbing or pinching enemies. Evobility is restricted to XY-linked genetic expression.
Rarity: Convergent.

Jagwar:

Grows into full-sized predator; capable of long-distance running, strength, and rapid rejuvenation. Limitation: Impulsive, lack of foresight leads to unintended results; loyal to the extreme; brain remains in "puppy mode."
Rarity: Baseline.

Magnesi:

Flare-like red fingernails generate fire when activated. Limitation: Young users struggle to control flames; strong emotions or sexual arousal can trigger involuntary bursts, potentially setting others or structures on fire.
Rarity: Dominion.

Memento:

Bulky build with cauliflower ears; can run through brick walls. Limitation: Balance is easily disrupted; uneven terrain increases risk of accidents.
Rarity: Austere.

Mind Niche:

Able to erase a Grounder's memories. Evobility is expressed under mosaic genetic conditions. Limitation: The stolen memories persist in the Mind Niche indefinitely, potentially causing her to believe they are her own experiences. This leads to a bipolar disorder or dissociative identity disorder.
Rarity: Convergent.

Nickcabee:

Spiky gray-silver hair; palms emit electrical shock like a taser. Evobility is restricted to XY-linked genetic expression. Limitation:

May short-circuit when exposed to water (e.g., bathing or rainfall), resulting in death.
Rarity: Baseline.

Nitro Snap: Snowflake pupils; snapping fingers triggers a chain reaction that freezes nitrogen, argon, and oxygen. Sudden temperature changes risk cramping or fainting.
Rarity: Dominion.

Nocuowl: Pupils dilate to three times normal size; double rods and a tapetum lucidum enable night vision. Limitation: Requires special sunglasses during daylight to prevent vision damage.
Rarity: Baseline.

Palladium: Sponge-like lungs; convert poisonous gases into clean oxygen. Limitation: Lungs trap moisture or chemicals, leading to coughing fits; must wear a high-frequency chest wall oscillation vest. once a month to break up mucus.
Rarity: Convergent.

Palmthermic: Palms detect infrared radiation from warm-blooded creatures. Limitation: Multiple heat sources will cause dizziness or nausea.
Rarity: Baseline.

Probedarth: Needle-like teeth can be extracted and thrown like darts. Limitation: Extraction is painful but required, as new teeth continue to grow underneath.
Rarity: Convergent.

Rayvo:

Thick, white hair sprout from arms. Move like a needle on a compass to track an object's owner; returning the object triggers euphoric high lasting for days. Limitation: Failure to locate the owner causes madness. Rarity: Convergent.

Rekall:

Remembers information learned through reading and can build upon knowledge and concepts. Limitation: Builds upon new ideas extremely slowly; possesses the social and emotional intelligence of a toddler; prone to tantrums and finds it difficult to work in a team. Rarity: Austere.

Rosa:

Induces optimism in another Grounder through a kiss; shiny red lips. Limitation: Feels guilt when presenting false optimism; depression disorders are common. Rarity: Dominion.

Sanicky:

Can manipulate sand within a fifty-yard radius, pushing, lifting, or forming shapes at will. Limitation: Poor control creates burial hazards; dust inhalation irritates lungs and eyes; hot sand may burn skin. Rarity: Baseline.

Servalina:

Razor-sharp hawkbill blade emerge from beneath both wrists. Limitation: Declaws prone to infection; must be trimmed regularly due to continuous growth. Rarity: Convergent.

Shivana: Hands reach 212°F. Limitation: If the Shivana cannot contain the heat, it spreads through the body, boiling internal organs and causing death. Young Shivana often lack control and must wear a talis-taffy to regulate the temperature.
Rarity: Baseline.

Silkcon: Barbed hairs on arms, legs, and private parts release an itchy toxin, producing pock-like sores that may scar. Limitation: Romantic intimacy difficult.
Rarity: Austere.

Silsonic: Produce and direct sound waves through sand to drive off rabicks. Limitation: Finger cramps when overused.
Rarity: Austere.

Slyfen: Can steal other Grounder's evobilities. Limitation: Painful activation; once the evobility is stolen it can be hard to control the evobility; risking death; stolen powers eventually die out.
Rarity: Dominion.

Tintone: Four throats. Excellent singers; used for long-distance communication. Limitation: Cannot whisper.
Rarity: Austere.

VidaLumin: Sees people's souls to understand intentions and personality. Limitation: The nature of a Grounder or person is rarely permanent.

Circumstances, choices, and survival can reshape character, meaning those labeled good or bad may eventually defy the judgment placed upon them.
Rarity: Baseline.

Xenonic: Chopstick-like fingers eject purple gooey paralytic. Limitation: Paralytic has a twenty minute duration; limited dexterity; sexual and fine-motor tasks can be awkward.
Rarity: Convergent.

Zincara: Blood heals infections and provides energy. Limitation: Body rejects blood transfusions; healing others drains energy; overuse can leave user dizzy, or unconscious.
Rarity: Austere.

Acknowledgements

Typing words onto a page may begin as a solitary act, but it is only a small step in a novel's journey. A story grows stronger through the encouragement, patience, and generosity of the people who support it along the way.

To my husband, whose optimism is a guiding light in my life. Thank you for believing in this story and in me, even during the moments when the path forward felt uncertain.

When I felt like this story might never come together, Diane patiently read this manuscript more times than I can count. Your thoughtful feedback, careful reading, and willingness to dive into every chapter helped polish this novel into something far better than it started.

Debbie and Joyce thank you for encouraging me to follow my dreams and reminding me that life is tough, but so am I.

To Kirby M., not only do I appreciate your beta reading and your incredible attention to detail in spotting the small mistakes, but your bravery in everyday life also inspires me to find my own version of happiness.

Jordan and Patrick, I can't fully put thank you into words, but you both showed up for me in a way I'll never forget. When I was feeling low and questioning everything, you lifted me up and reminded me to keep going. You went far beyond what anyone would expect, and it meant more than you probably realize. You filled a space in me that really needed it, and that will stay with me forever.

Thank you to Mario Nevado for the stunning cover art that brought this book to life visually.

I am especially grateful to Shannon, Sarah, and Samona for standing beside me through the difficult moments and showing up to my book booth in 100°F heat. Your friendship means more than you know.

To Chemistry Chris from Texas, thank you for indulging my curiosity about black holes and the periodic table. Your knowledge added depth to the science woven into this world.

I apologize to my dogs for every time I said, "I'm in *the zone*. Ten more minutes, then walk."

About The Author

Joanna St. Amour is a school counselor by day and runs Amour Editorial House by night, where she works with writers to shape compelling stories. She also hosts the writing podcast and YouTube channel *One Chapter at a Time*. Joanna is an orchid collector and enjoys scuba diving and golfing when the weather allows.

She lives in Washington State with her amazing husband, two untrainable dogs, and one temperamental cat.

If you are a bookstore or part of a book club interested in hosting a signing or special event, please reach out. Joanna would love to connect and plan something special together. You can contact her through her YouTube channel, *One Chapter at a Time*, or on Instagram: @joanna_st.amour.

To learn more about evobilities, visit JoannaStAmour.com and take the evobility quiz.